ASHES TO FIRE

Also by Emily B. Martin

Woodwalker

ASHES TO FIRE

EMILY B. MARTIN

HARPER
VOYAGER
IMPULSE

An Imprint of HarperCollinsPublishers

HarperCollins
PUBLISHERS
Since 1817

Cover art and map by Emily B. Martin.

ASHES TO FIRE. Copyright © 2017 by Emily B. Martin. All rights
reserved. Printed in the United States of America. No part of this
book may be used or reproduced in any manner whatsoever without written permission except in the case of brief quotations em-
bodied in critical articles and reviews. For information, address
HarperCollins Publishers, 195 Broadway, New York, NY 10007.

Digital Edition JANUARY 2017 ISBN: 978-0-06-247372-1
Print Edition ISBN: 978-0-06-247373-8

Harper Voyager, the Harper Voyager logo, and Harper Voyager
Impulse are trademarks of HarperCollins Publishers.
HarperCollins is a registered trademark of HarperCollins Pub-
lishers in the United States of America and other countries.

FIRST EDITION

17 18 19 20 21 OPM 10 9 8 7 6 5 4 3 2 1

To Will

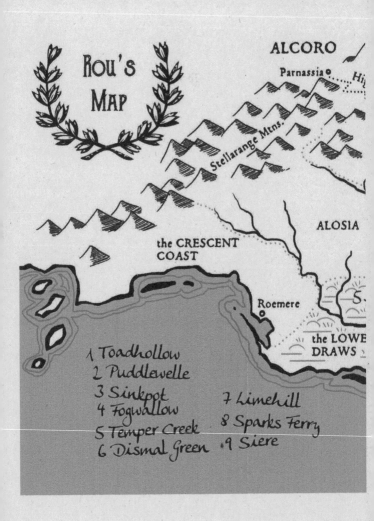

ROU'S MAP

ALCORO

Parnassia

Hi

Stellarange Mtns.

ALOSIA

the CRESCENT
COAST

Roemere

the LOWE
DRAWS

1 Toadhollow
2 Puddlevelle
3 Sinkpot
4 Fogwallow   7 Limehill
5 Temper Creek   8 Sparks Ferry
6 Dismal Green   9 Siere

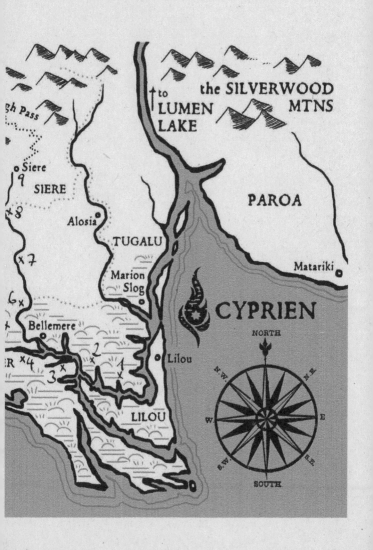

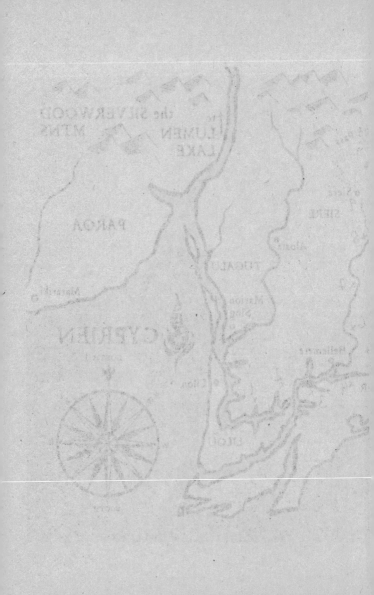

PROLOGUE

The Alcoran messenger mopped the sweat off his forehead. Great Light, it was hot, even now, on the threshold of autumn. Perhaps no hotter than home in the canyons, but the swamps of Cyprien seemed to cling to every shred of heat and magnify it with humidity. It made him sluggish and short-tempered, and he longed for the fresh, dry breezes that swept off the canyon rim.

If the Cypri folk noticed the heat, they didn't seem to care about it. They went about their usual tasks in the dockside marketplace, hauling catches of crawfish and catfish and other river goods. Down from the quays, the steel mill of Lilou spewed smoke into the air, the groaning of the waterwheel present behind all the other sounds of activity. Lolling on posts every few yards were russet Alcoran flags bearing a prism and seven turquoise stars—as was expected. Cyprien, after all, had been occupied by Alcoro for over fifty years. He couldn't even recall what the antiquated flag of the country had been before his folk had "adopted" their eastern neighbor.

The messenger paused to let a cart pass by and blotted the sweat from his brow again. As he stopped, something caught the corner of his eye. He turned his head. It was one of the Cypri, a young riverman with brown skin and dark hair that curled in tight corkscrews. He would have been no extraordinary sight except he was watching the messenger, leaning against a market stall full of okra, his hands in his pockets. When the messenger noticed him, he smiled slightly, raising his eyebrows. The messenger pocketed his handkerchief and hurried on. The message in his bag was of utmost importance, and he didn't want to loiter on the docks any longer than necessary. And he certainly didn't want to draw impertinent stares.

He wound his way among the marketplace stalls bustling with color and late-summer produce. Though the River-folk's annual festival was still several weeks away, many stalls sold items in preparation—golden masks, golden ribbons, and fire implements of all kinds: torches, braziers, lanterns, and many other devices the Alcoran couldn't name. What kind of fiery display could one put on with a metal fan? He had no idea, and what's more, he didn't want to know. Like most Alcorans, fire made him wary. The River-folk seemed to have a borderline-reckless regard for it, but then, they probably didn't have wildfires raze entire villages every summer. The benefits, he supposed, of living half-drowned in the bayou, rather than out in the sun-crisped canyons.

He pulled up short. He'd made a wrong turn somewhere, finding himself at the end of an aisle blocked by a stall of honking geese. He cursed vaguely and turned around, retracing his steps. To his irritation, he saw the same wry-smiled riverman from the okra stand, now loitering near a pastry vendor. The Alcoran quickened his pace. His king should have chosen a messenger more familiar with the city to deliver this message to the governor, but the council hadn't wanted the letter changing hands multiple times. He could worry about that paranoia later—he just wanted to find his way back to the main causeway.

He turned the corner and spied a busy-looking street several stalls away. Relieved, he headed toward it. But as he approached a stall crammed with barrels of freshly dead fish, a figure popped up in front of him, blocking his way.

"Copper for a juggle?" he asked enthusiastically.

It was the curly-headed riverman *again*, his eyes glittering eagerly. In his hands he clutched a sweet potato, a ceramic cup, and a hen's egg. The Alcoran took a step back and frowned at him. So that was why he'd been watching—he was panhandling. The cheeky youth had probably spotted the well-dressed Alcoran, with his embroidered bolero and fashionably waxed hair, and assumed he could wring a few coins from him.

Well, he was wrong.

"Excuse me," said the messenger, trying to step around him.

"I'm quite impressive," the riverman insisted, moving to block him.

"Young man, I insist you—"

"Sweeten the deal?" The man swiped something from the fish stall and came up with a fourth object—a limp catfish, its mouth gaping open. Before the Alcoran could comment, the riverman tossed it in the air.

"I'll warn you, though," the riverman said cheerfully as he lobbed the sweet potato after it. "Juggling four things at once has never been my strong point."

The Alcoran didn't have time to react. The cup soared into the air, followed by the egg, just as the catfish landed back in his palm.

"Ha!" the riverman crowed, tossing the fish again. The potato came down and then went back up. "Look at that, a full rotation—this has to be worth a silver at least, wouldn't you agree? *Oh . . . !*"

The Alcoran didn't see everything that went wrong, because his eyes closed when the sweet potato came flying out of orbit and struck him on the forehead. He heard the smash of ceramic at his feet and felt the crunch of an eggshell against his shoulder. Yolk splattered across his collar. And then—*splat.* The catfish landed . . .

On his *face.*

"Great blazing Light!" He swiped frantically at the fish.

"Oh!" he heard the riverman exclaim again.

"Hey!" shouted a gruff voice. Before the Alcoran could wipe the fish slime from his eyes, he was engulfed with a towel. "Leave the fellow alone, you no-good scoundrel!"

"I was only . . ."

"Go on, get lost! I oughta cuff you 'round the head—go on! Go harass someone else!"

The Alcoran staggered, blinded by the ministrations of the newcomer, who seemed to be trying to scour his face clean while admonishing the juggler at the same time. Shards of the ceramic cup crunched under his boots. He opened his mouth to protest the assistance and got a wad of towel between his teeth.

"So terribly sorry, sir," the newcomer said loudly. "You mustn't think poorly of all us River-folk—these meddlesome youths have no respect, not even for their kinfolk, let alone our Canyon-folk neighbors . . . Oh, but your fancy jacket—let me help you with that egg . . ." He ground his towel into the Alcoran's collar, which only served to smash the egg yolk further into the fabric.

"It's fine, it's fine, leave it!" the Alcoran finally managed to say amid the man's aggressive assistance.

"Nonsense, my good canyonman. Here, we'll

get that yolk out, don't you worry. Come along." The man dragged the Alcoran to the fish stand. He grabbed a bucket from the counter and splashed it without warning over his collar. It was water—river water, the Alcoran realized—lukewarm and smelling of silt and fish.

The Alcoran jumped back. "Falling stars, man!"

But the stall vendor snatched at him again and began scrubbing his saturated collar. "No respect," he continued. "No respect for a citizen of the Seventh King, none at all . . ."

"Leave it!" the Alcoran said loudly, finally wrenching himself from the vendor's grip. "Great Light, just leave it!" He straightened his now wet and soiled bolero and wiped the last of the fish remnants from his face.

The vendor bowed humbly. "A thousand apologies for the inconvenience, sir."

"And me!" chimed a voice in the Alcoran's ear. He startled away from the juggler, who hadn't fled the scene as he had assumed. "Never meant to hit you with a fish, sir!"

"Ugh!" The Alcoran threw up his hands. "Just keep away from me! Don't come near me again— either of you!"

Without another word, he turned on his heel and fled through the market stalls, his waxed hair sticking up in several places and his embroidered bolero peppered with fish scales.

The riverman watched him go, quietly wiping the fish juice off his own fingers. He hoped the Alcoran wouldn't notice the undone clasp on his bag until much later. But even if he did, it shouldn't matter. The message was safely back inside the bag, the softened wax seal remolded into place, thanks to the heat of the day. He turned his attention instead to the fish vendor, who was neatening his wares.

"Fabian, you're a wizard with a towel," he said warmly.

"Hmph," the vendor grunted. "You're paying for that catfish, Roubideaux."

"Naturally. But not at the moment. Got a scrap of parchment?"

The vendor handed him a square of paper used to wrap fish, along with a charcoal stick. The riverman hurriedly began writing down the message he'd read, word for word, before he forgot any of it.

"Did you get what you were after?" asked Fabian.

"Think so." The riverman read his work. "And what a find, too. Many thanks, Fabian. This could be worth quite a few catfish, I think." He slipped the paper into his vest pocket. "How about a crabcake for the road? I have a message to deliver."

CHAPTER 1

Mae dropped down next to me with a jingle of bells, pink-cheeked and breathing heavily.

"Five months after the fact, and I'm still tallying all the lies you told me," I said.

She fanned herself, looking legitimately surprised. "What *now*? I thought we'd laid everything out."

"You *are* a good dancer," I said. "More so than you let on."

"Oh." She rolled her eyes. "Some people would call that modesty, Mona, not lying. And when exactly on our journey was I supposed to demonstrate my hey-for-four to you?" Her eyes followed her new husband as he wove among his folk to join us at the high table. "Besides—I didn't have the right partner."

Valien climbed the few steps up to the table, straightening the silver circlet that ran across his brow into his thatch of black hair. He, too, was out of breath, though it wasn't surprising given the flurry of exuberant dancing taking place in the courtyard of Lampyrinae. For over two hours now, the Wood-folk had been stomping and spinning, the silver accents on their gowns and tunics and boots gleaming in the lantern light. They bowed to their partners only to immediately re-form their long lines for the next set—and there was no sign of them stopping any time soon.

"Your brothers are threatening anarchy if you don't dance with them next," Valien said to Mae, sliding into his seat next to her. Like her, he made a fair amount of noise as he moved—they both had a slew of tiny bells sewn onto cuffs around their wrists and heavily fringed leather boots. They jingled with every movement, making the two of them easy to find in the crowd.

"Oh, they don't mean it," she said. "And anyway, you used to threaten anarchy right alongside them when we were kids."

"Well, but now *I'm* the king," he said.

"Should have thought of that earlier, maybe. Ugh, *Arlen!*" Mae whisked her silver skirts out of the way as a puddle of blackberry wine bloomed over the tablecloth.

Arlen swore under his breath, his face reddening under his pearled eyepatch. He snatched up his napkin and blotted the spill.

I added my own napkin to the effort. "It's all right," I said quietly.

He hated making these kinds of mistakes. In the

first few weeks after the Alcoran captain's sword blinded his left eye, he had been a walking disaster, toppling vases, missing steps, and generally crashing into any obstacle on his left side. He had since become much better at navigating his surroundings, but he was still a work in progress. Knocking over a wine glass at an event as public as a foreign royal wedding would not be something he'd quickly forget—especially if Mae got a kick out of reminding him about it.

Unfortunately, at that moment, the music ringing from the massive oak tree in the middle of the courtyard eased to a halt. Wood-folk across the courtyard bowed to their partners. Some hurried back to their goblets, but most turned to face the high table as a cluster of folk hauled a groaning wooden cart into the courtyard. I closed my stained napkin in my fist and rested it surreptitiously in my lap as the cart was brought to a halt in front of the new king and queen.

"King Valien and Queen Ellamae Heartwood of Lampyrinae," said a burly man with a deep bow. "A gift from the smiths, in honor of your wedding and the beginning of your reign." He and his apprentices dragged away the shroud of canvas to reveal a set of massive wooden panels: the new gates to the palace, carved with soaring twin trees. The centers of the trunks were inlaid with silver. Valien and Mae's grateful words were swallowed up by the cheering in the courtyard.

"I've been meaning to ask you," I said to her as the panels were hauled away. "This name you both took—Heartwood. A bit flouncy for you, isn't it?"

The look she gave me was a familiar one—that pained expression she wore when I flaunted my ignorance of the mountains. "Heartwood. It's the heart of a tree, the center of the trunk. It gives structure to everything else. It's strong. And it's useful—it can get a fire going."

"Ah," I said. "That makes much more sense. You're obnoxiously clever."

"You're dull and prosaic."

"Well, I like the name."

"Thank you."

The fiddlers and drummers took up their instruments in the tree branches again, and folk turned their attention back to forming their lines. I smoothed my napkin back on the table as the Wood-folk began yet another complex dance.

"A ladies' chain," Mae said, setting her cup down. "Come on, Mona, I'll show you how."

"No, no. I'm perfectly fine watching."

"I didn't ask if you were *fine*. Come on . . . as a wedding gift."

"I already gave you pearls and a song," I said, shaking her hand off my wrist. "Don't make me take them back."

"Well, you can't take back the song, and I'll fight you for the pearls."

"I suppose that's a 'thank you'?"

She fingered the string of green seed pearls looped from shoulder to shoulder, twined to resemble a leafy vine. "I suppose. I feel a little conspicuous. This thing alone could have bought me a month's worth of meals in Paroa."

"Three months', more likely. But it looks well on you."

She unfurled her palm in an automatic gesture of gratitude. "Thank you. And thank you for singing at the ceremony. It was nice. If I lied to you about dancing, then you lied to me about singing. You have a lovely voice."

"Thank you." I watched the chaos unfold before us, sure someone was going to collide with another at every turn. "Though it should have been Colm, not me. His voice is richer than mine. It would have carried better through the courtyard."

As soon as I spoke, I wished I hadn't. Mae's smile became fixed, her eyes on the whirl of color and sound before us. I mentally kicked myself, remembering her reaction the previous day when she realized only Arlen and I had made the journey to Lampyrinae.

"It's not you," I had told her last night as she rested her head against the cold window. "He's not angry at you anymore. He's angry at himself, and a bit lost."

"You said he would come around."

"And he has. But think, Mae . . . everyone here knows he nearly killed you. And Valien was . . . a bit stiff with him in those first few days, when you were mending."

"He's long past that. No one cares anymore. And besides that, half the Guard saw him save my life on the Firefall."

I had shrugged then. "You know Colm. He hates to be the center of any kind of attention. He sends you his best—he really does. He dove for most of the pearls I brought you. But he couldn't bring himself to come."

She had closed her eyes, her disappointment mirrored in the darkening windowpanes.

The flurry of music slowed, and folk applauded the musicians in the branches. They bowed with enthusiasm and then struck up a new tune—slow, lilting. A waltz. Dancers broke from their lines to seek out partners, and soon the courtyard was full of circling couples.

Valien smiled and took Mae's hand in his, but just as she made to rise from her seat, an ambuscade in the form of her brothers descended on her chair.

"Damn the crown!"

"Up Beegum Bald!"

They latched on to her arms and hauled her from her seat. She struggled against them, jingling haphazardly. "You bunch of idiots!"

But the three of them wrestled her down the steps and into the courtyard beyond, where they took turns twirling her between them. They waltzed her away from the high table even as she poured contempt—and laughter—on them.

Valien still had his hand uplifted to take hers. "Ah," he said. "I've been overthrown." He reached across Mae's empty chair to me. "Given the circumstances, Lady Queen, will you grant me a waltz?"

I felt myself color slightly. "Oh, I think perhaps not, Valien."

"Ellamae said you were hoping to dance tonight."

I cast Mae a dark look, but she was absorbed in berating her brothers.

"Now's your chance, Mona," Arlen said with some vindication, giving me a push.

I could hear my mother's voice echoing in my head as it always did. *Don't do something if you don't think you can do it well.* I glanced out at the courtyard. The folk that weren't watching the new queen waltz on the arm of her eldest brother were watching us at the high table. Valien still had his hand stretched out to me. Turning him down would appear cold.

I laid my hand in his and rose from my seat before Arlen could disrupt my poise. Valien led me out into the current of waltzing couples.

"Which foot first?" I asked quietly.

"Right," he said, holding my hand aloft.

I followed his stride, trying to keep my eyes from flicking down to my feet. Over the king's shoulder, Mae's brother led her easily into an elaborate spin, the fringe on her boots flying with each step. I gripped Valien's leading hand a bit tighter. I hoped he would not try to spin me. I could feel the ridged scar tissue on his palm, the childhood injury leftover from his father's abusive temper. Valien had dodged that particular blow, but he had landed with his hand deep in the fire grate, and the burn scars had remained.

"Relax a little," he said gently, giving my hand a bob.

"I'm out of practice," I said. "I haven't had much call to dance in the last four years."

"I won't do anything surprising," he promised.

I wanted to reply that given our history, I doubted he could do anything that would surprise me, but I bit back the words and focused instead on following his lead. *Glide, two, three.*

"How are you enjoying October in the mountains, Queen Mona?"

"Lovely," I said between breaths.

"How goes the progress down on the lake?"

"Slow but steady." I took too big a step and wobbled. His bells gave an extra jingle as he steadied me and led me into the next step. Recovered, I said, "We've deconstructed all but one of the barracks the Alcorans built."

"And the towns closest to the river mouth are being fortified?"

"Yes." I wished he would let me focus on my feet. I could feel the eyes of dozens of Wood-folk watching my graceless show. "Everything we're salvaging is going to that effort."

"Blackshell?"

I shook my head. "Palace defenses will have to wait. There's not enough material."

"Not even with our timber shipments?"

"Timber, yes. Steel, no." I missed a step and took

two to make up for it. "We're dreadfully short on steel."

"I'll see if we can increase bloomery production."

"You can't," I said, unable to spare the words to dance around the subject. "Not in the quantities I need. I need high-quality steel from the Cypri mills, and I need a great deal of it."

"I'll ask my councilor of trade what she thinks about moving shipments from Cyprien through the mountain gaps."

"I can tell you what she'll think," I said. "She'll tell you it's far too expensive to justify, and that it would be a detriment to your own bloomeries. No one is going to waste the effort to move goods from Cyprien overland through Paroa, Winder, and the Silverwood when they could just sail up the southern waterways like they've been doing for centuries."

A few beats of music passed.

"You've been thinking about this for a while," he said.

"I was going to wait to bring it up until our state meeting next month," I said. "But I won't deny I'm a bit on edge, Valien. Every day I wake up wondering if this is the day Celeno will send his warships back to the lake. We need to be ready. But trade over the mountains this summer was much sparser than I anticipated."

"Part of that was the road," he countered. "Tradeway Road and the Palisade Road took a great deal of work. We have plans to widen several of the bridges in the spring . . ."

"Even so, it may still be several years before folk take your routes with any regularity. Traders are used to the sea routes." A familiar knot of dread welled in my stomach, one that had been growing over the past five months of trying to stand my country on its own two feet after years of subjugation. But I pressed on—as I had done and always would do. "And steel isn't the only thing we're having to ration. Textiles, silks from Samna. Salt—we don't smoke our meat as your folk do. We could very well be without either of them by spring."

He rotated a quarter turn. I wobbled again. *Jingle.* Over his shoulder, I saw Mae go into an elegant spin from her eldest brother to her youngest.

"What do you propose?" he asked.

"I don't know. That's what's worrying me." *That and these steps.* "I don't have any answers yet." I watched Mae's silver gown swirl over her boots. "If I had my way, I'd open trade in the waterways with Cyprien."

"Trade with Cyprien means trade with Alcoro."

"Which is why I haven't pursued it, obviously," I said with a hint of sharpness. "Until the Cypri ports are liberated from Alcoran control, I won't have anything to do with them. Unfortunately, I can't see that happening any time soon."

"We could try to send word to the Cypri folk."

"Who would we contact, though?" I asked. "Even before the Alcorans invaded almost sixty years ago, they never had a real monarchy. They had that . . ."

"Assembly, I think it was called."

"Yes. Very decentralized. There's no royal line that might have survived the invasion—which means they have no leaders. No diplomats, no ambassadors." I glowered absently over his shoulder, cursing King Celeno for the umpteenth time for destroying the prosperity of my country and those around it. "And even if they had an organized faction of folk who wanted to liberate their country from Alcoro, they couldn't possibly have the military to make it happen."

I felt him give a small sigh under my hand on his shoulder, though the sound of it was lost to the music. "Ellamae and I have plans to open a timbering agreement with the Winderan monarchy in the spring," he said. "That may help draw folk from the coast over the mountains. I don't deny it may be a sparse few years, and not just for you. Supplying you from our own stores has impacted us as well. But things will get better, Lady Queen, with time."

"Time that I can't afford," I said. "The longer we sit around hoping Celeno won't retaliate, the more time he has to plan a counterattack."

"But we have the upper hand on him now." He checked our progress momentarily to avoid colliding with another couple, and I caught my toe on his boot. *Jingle jangle.* "We'll be able to see his ships coming from miles away, and once the road to the southern lookouts is complete, it should take less than a day for a mounted scout to reach Lampyrinae."

"When *will* the road be complete?"

"Barring an early snowstorm, it should be done by next month."

I blew out a breath. "I worry even that may be too long. I doubt Celeno will wait until spring to launch his next assault. He'll know it's to his advantage to limit the amount of time my folk can spend in the water, and in the dead of winter . . ."

"Queen Mona," Valien said as gently as possible. "Must we solve all our problems on the dance floor?"

I realized then that the music was slowing to its conclusion. To my right, Mae sank into a dip on the arm of her middle brother. I flushed with embarrassment. Valien had begun our dance making polite conversation, and I had turned it into a drill on policy.

"Forgive me," I said. "That was rude."

He smiled mildly as he slowed his step. "On the contrary, Lady Queen. You bring up valid points. I'm fortunate to call you my ally. Grant me a few days with my bride, and then we will lay out all our concerns for the coming winter."

"Yes, yes, of course."

As the final chord sounded, he lifted his left hand and gave me the slightest nudge with his right. To my surprise I found myself completing a twirl of my own, my skirt swirling around my ankles. He guided me to a stop and bowed low over my hand.

"Well done," he said with a smile. He turned over his scarred palm. "Thank you."

I dipped my own courtesy to him. "Likewise."

With that, he slipped back through his folk to Mae and wrapped his arms around her. Relieved, most likely, to put the interruption in their joy behind him. Hoping my pink cheeks would be attributed to the dance, I hurried back to the high table.

"Not too bad," Arlen said. "Though you could have smiled once or twice."

"Quiet," I said, reaching for my wine.

Mae and Valien made their way arm in arm toward the table, but they never reached it. One of the fiddlers in the trees lifted his bow and called in a ringing voice, "A blessing of the Light!"

"A blessing of the Light!" several people cried.

"Blessed be the Light!"

The call was taken up, and the crowd pressed forward to surround the king and queen. I set my wine down slowly as Mae and Valien drew closer together. They turned their hands over, and all across the courtyard, folk followed suit, their palms filled with the light of the lanterns. Their gesture of thanks. Eyes closed, faces turned upward to the night sky, they began, hundreds of voices rising through the branches.

> "Blessed be the Light that guides and
> nourishes.
> Blessed be the Light that kindles and
> inspires.

Blessed be the Light that draws us from the
darkness.
Blessed be the Light, giver of life."

I curled my fingers around the back of the chair in front of me. Next to me, Arlen stood awkwardly with his hands clasped in front of him, his good eye shut.

"Shine upon me. Shine through me. Shine
within me."

Perhaps she felt my gaze. Perhaps she wanted a glimpse of the courtyard in prayer. Whatever the reason, Mae opened her eyes early. It was too late for me to look away. She caught my gaze, saw how I was standing. Her lips gave a little twitch, almost a smile. A sad smile. She knew I wouldn't be praying with the others.

"Blessed be the Light," murmured the Wood-folk, and after that Mae's face was lost from my view, swept up in the many embraces from those around her. The fiddler in the tree began a sweet tune, full of joy and contentment. Folk called their goodnights. The festivities would continue out in the courtyard, but the time had come for the new couple to retreat together, continuing their celebration in private.

As they were shunted up the courtyard to the palace, their jingling growing fainter, Mae turned back once. Her height made it difficult for me to see her through the crowd. But she stood on tiptoes as she walked, offering me one last wave. I waved back, silently wishing her well. I wished her the strength and integrity I knew she already possessed. I wished her the love of her husband and the respect of her folk. I wished her the confidence I didn't have, to place her trust and faith in something higher than herself.

Hours after the festivities had quieted, I was rattled from sleep by a pounding on the door of my guest room. I jerked upright, clothed in the darkness of the bed hangings.

"Queen Mona Alastaire!" shouted a muffled voice.

I wrenched the hangings aside and met a wash of cold air—even with the fires lit, the palace of Lampyrinae was frosty in the autumn night. I drew my dressing gown around my shoulders and slid my slippers on my feet as I hurried to the carved wooden door.

A palace attendant stood in the hall, clutching a lantern. Her hair was mussed—she looked as though she had only just been roused from sleep. "King Valien and Queen Ellamae request your presence."

Still fighting the fog of sleep, I glanced over my shoulder to the window, wondering if I had somehow overslept. It was inky black outside. Moonless. "What time is it?"

"Nearly four."

"Four?"

"In the morning," she said unhelpfully.

"It's their wedding night," I said, thunderstruck.

"It's urgent," she replied. "A party of scouts has arrived from the southern wood. They're reporting a fleet of Alcoran ships is moving north through the Cypri waterways."

Great Light, I thought, before another, more urgent thought came to me.

Colm.

I pulled the door wide. "Where are they meeting?"

"In the king's study. I'll take you there."

I glanced up the hall. Arlen's room was around the corner from mine. "Has someone told my brother?"

In response, a piteous groan echoed off the walls.

"Good," I said.

"Follow me," said the attendant.

I drew my dressing gown closer around my shoulders and belted it at the waist. My heart beat against my chest, but as my groggy head cleared, I realized I didn't need to panic just yet—a ship spotted from the southern lookouts would take several days to get to the mouth of the river. There would be enough time to travel down the Palisades to the lake. Enough time to organize a front. Enough time.

Not like before.

The attendant led me out of the guest wing and across the main body of the palace. The halls echoed with silence—folk were sleeping off their jubilation. Despite my edginess, I stifled a yawn. I had slipped away before most of the Wood-folk, but I couldn't have been asleep more than a few hours. I smoothed my hands over my hair and cheeks.

Out of the corner of my eye, I saw the attendant steal a glance at me. I rubbed my cheek again, wondering if I had pillow marks.

"Lady Queen?"

"Yes?"

She took a short breath. "That . . . that was lovely, the song you sang at the ceremony. Me and a few others, we listened from behind the courtyard."

"Thank you."

"Are they somber affairs, Lumeni weddings?"

"Somber?" I turned to regard her. She had the copper skin of her folk, though it was several shades lighter than Mae's, and pinker now that she was flushing.

"The song, it seemed very somber. Not . . . not sad, just . . . serious."

"Oh." We started up a handsome staircase. "It's not supposed to be somber. That must have been my own doing."

"Well, we liked it. You made Miria cry."

Splendid. The last time I had sung that song was at Colm and Ama's wedding. Clearly I hadn't been able to keep that memory from affecting my voice. Being reminded of my sister-in-law's death did nothing to ease my anxiety.

We came to a wing protected by a pair of Palace Guards and arrived at a set of recessed double doors.

The king and queen's chambers. The attendant opened one and led me into a large parlor draped in rich green and silver. The country's banner hung on the wall, a silver tree on a green field, the roots embellished with blue pearls to represent the Woodfolk's beloved fireflies. Next to this hung the portrait that had been presented to Mae and Valien earlier in the day—he in his embroidered emerald cloak, she in her shining silver gown. I noticed the artist had painted the scar over Mae's left collarbone where Colm's atlatl dart had had to be cut out five months ago. I wondered if she had specifically asked for it to be included.

Several doors were set into the far wall, with one cracked open a few inches. In front of it lay a bell-covered cuff. I just caught a glimpse of a carved poster bed, its linens tousled, before the attendant led me to one of the other doors. She knocked.

"Enter!"

Valien was spreading maps of the Silverwood, Lumen Lake, and Cyprien over a heavy wooden table. He had on trousers and a belted robe, but his feet and chest were bare. Mae was curled up in one of the cushioned chairs, clutching a silk dressing gown across her chest. She glowered, her face black as night.

"I will murder King Celeno," she said when I entered.

"Welcome to sovereignty," I replied. "Cutting short your wedding night for the security of your country."

She growled, drawing the dressing gown closer around her shoulders. There was a red mark on her neck—and it wasn't the atlatl scar.

Across the table stood a scout I recognized, her rank denoted by a silver cord running over her shoulder. It was Deina, the Woodwalker who had raised the palace to our escape from the king's dungeons. I wondered if she and Mae had made peace yet over the havoc we had wreaked during our journey through the Silverwood. Her presence here, at least, was a good sign in that direction.

The door opened behind me and in staggered Arlen. His good eye was red-rimmed and bleary, and the strap to his pearled patch was twisted across his forehead. He hated waking up before the sun on any occasion, but doing so after a night of revelry was borderline miraculous. His sandy hair stuck up all along one side of his face.

"Alcoro is a nation of unwashed hogs nose-deep in puddle scum," he spat.

"Have you been working on that the whole way over here?" Mae asked him.

"No, it struck me in a flash. Tell me, had you actually gone to sleep yet?"

"Wouldn't you like to know," she snarled.

"Where were these boats spotted?" I asked, cutting off the banter and coming to stand over Valien's shoulder.

He tapped a squiggle on the map. "The Rooftops."

"How long ago?"

"Four days," Mae said.

Deina shifted slightly at her tone. "We would have been quicker," she said. "But the road to the look-outs . . ."

"Isn't done," Valien said. "I know." He rubbed his face. "Four days."

"How long do we have until the boats reach the lake?" I asked.

He looked at Mae. "Another four?"

"From the Rooftops? Try two."

I frowned. It would take almost a full day of travel to make it down the Palisades from Lampyrinae to Blackshell. That would leave us barely twenty-four hours to form any kind of counterattack.

"Why didn't you turn these boats away like you did the other few you've spotted?" I asked Deina.

"These are different," she said. "The others were small, little personal crafts meant for spying. A few pitched arrows were enough to deter them. Seems like they took that as an invitation, though, because these new ones are warships, and they came on us at dusk. By the time we got down to the foothills and within firing range, it was the dead of night, and they were long gone up the river. I doubt we could have deterred them at all."

"Two days." Valien drummed distractedly on the table. "We can't move any significant force down to the south in that short amount of time." He looked at Arlen. "What can you muster?"

"Between the arms you've supplied us and what

we've been able to forge in the last five months, probably fifty swords and a hundred bows, tops," he said, fidgeting with his twisted patch strap. "But we've got another three hundred atlatls, at least. They're a poor match against ballistae and crossbows, but if we line the banks with javelins and trust the chain to keep the ships in the river, at least briefly . . ."

I traced the waterways and then looked at Deina. "How many in the fleet?"

"Three."

"Just three? You're sure?"

"Positive."

Valien glanced up at me. "You think perhaps they're not planning on attacking?"

I pursed my lips. The memory of the invasion flashed through my head—the smoke, the screams, the absolute helplessness. But another detail stood out. "They sailed in with twelve ships four years ago. It took that many to cut off all the channels."

"Don't underestimate him," Mae said. "Remember, Alcoro is a nation of engineers and strategists. Celeno's unlikely to try the same thing twice."

"I know. Just as he'll know you're watching the waterways for us."

"So what do you think he'll do?" asked Valien.

"That's what I *don't* know, and that's his advantage. But we know he's coming, and the river is chained off. That's *our* advantage."

A moment of silence passed, except for the drumming of Valien's fingers. Eventually, he spoke again. "You don't think he's hoping for diplomacy?"

I frowned. Mae picked up a rather ugly ceramic buck with bulging eyes from the table and turned it idly in her hands.

"No," I said finally. "What on earth could he say to me?"

"Maybe he'll try to apologize," said Arlen.

"The man believes he's carrying out a divine plan," I said sharply. "He's not likely to apologize for it. No. Even if he *wanted* to apologize, I wouldn't accept it. The last time I misjudged him, he murdered sixty-four of my citizens. It will not happen again."

"So we forget the southern slopes," Valien said, sweeping away the topmost map to reveal a different one underneath. "We can't get a force down there quickly enough anyway. Instead we bring a contingent down the Palisades with us. We can position the Armed Guard on the shore and the Wood Guard on the western slopes."

"We should still send archers to the south," Mae said, twirling the buck by one of its antlers. "If things go awry, at least Celeno's soldiers can't escape back down through Cyprien."

"Yes," I said decisively. "I don't want a single Alcoran to get back to their king."

"Very well," Valien said. "Ellamae, you can put out the order for the Guard to wake early. In the meantime, I'll need to meet with our councilors."

"We need to leave as soon as possible," I said. "We have to get down to Colm before tonight."

"Yes—definitely. Can you give me until seven?"

I pressed my lips together. Every second gone was a second wasted, but without the Silvern army, those seconds were moot anyway. "Seven is fine."

There was a thump and a crack. We all looked to Mae, who had dropped the ceramic buck onto the wood floor. Both of its antlers and one of its legs had snapped off.

"Sorry," she said.

Valien looked down at the figurine. "It's all right."

"It was ugly."

"Yes. It was my father's."

"Then I'm not sorry."

"Ellamae . . ." His face was weary in the lantern light. "I'll make this up to you."

"The buck?"

"Our wedding night."

"I would hope so." She kicked the bits of the buck under the table. "In the meantime, I hear Lumen Lake is a marvelous place for a honeymoon."

CHAPTER 2

At five minutes before seven, the four of us were bundled onto our mounts, their noses turned down the newly reconstructed road connecting Lampyrinae and Blackshell. We ate breakfast from our horses' backs, licking sugar off our fingers from hand pies leftover from the wedding feast. Mae had given her orders to her scouts, archers, and swordsmen, directing each unit to their assigned post. They had scrambled to do her bidding, and I remembered, just a few months ago, when she had been worried about being the right person to lead her folk. I smiled slightly as I watched the Royal Guard's natural, genuine respect for their new queen—she had always been their leader, well before she wore a crown or Woodwalker insignia. She'd been a leader from the moment she set her sights on righting the injustices within her country—something her folk knew, even if she didn't.

We passed through the settlement that bloomed outward from the palace, the winding track flanked by sturdy cabins, many of which were built right against the trunks of ancient trees. A few domestic turkeys pecked here and there, and garden patches spilled over with the last of the autumn squash. The carved posts and lintels of the town were still decorated with swaths of colorful autumn leaves in celebration of the king and queen's marriage. Mae had carried a similar bough of leaves in the crook of her arm during the ceremony.

That already feels like ages ago.

Not to everyone, though. Folk moved about their early-morning tasks with a distinct drag in their step from the revelry the night before. Most did double-takes when they saw us. I couldn't blame them. By all rights, the newly married king and queen should have been cloistered away together for the better part of a week, certainly not riding down the mountain just hours after their wedding. Some folk called out to them. Valien responded with practiced poise, but most of Mae's replies were halfhearted waves, her shoulders hunched in fatigue.

"You're not presenting an overly regal image, Mae," I said after a particularly expansive yawn.

"Tell it to my horse's backside."

"Sit up straighter," I hissed. "At least until you're away from the settlement. Folk are going to think something's wrong."

"Something *is* wrong," she grumbled. "The finest night of my life was cut short by a palace attendant pounding on my door. I swear Deina lagged an extra day to arrive at the most wretched possible hour."

"It happened, it's done. Move on. Folk are going to think something went wrong with you and Valien."

"I loathe you," she said. But at the next cluster of homes, she sat up a little straighter and returned her folk's greetings with more enthusiasm.

The crisp morning chill eased away on the exposed slopes of the Palisades. I was profoundly thankful I didn't have to traverse the patchy scout footpath leading down these cliffs as we had after our flight from the palace dungeons. The old trade road had been rebuilt, its ways wide and smooth. My heart warmed as we crested the head of the cliffs to see the misty lake spreading away before us, the many peaks of the islands breaking into the sun.

At the very edge of sight shone one particularly noticeable landmark—the Beacon. Of the many waterfalls that spilled down the Palisades and the cliffs flanking the southwestern lakeshore, the Beacon was positioned in such a way that it caught the earliest rays of sun that shot up the river channel. It always lit first in the mornings, its towering cascade and billowing mists reflecting the sunlight to the point of brilliance, so bright it hurt to look straight at it. I breathed in a deep draught of mountain air. I would never grow tired of this sight, not after years spent aching for my country. The view only hardened my determination.

Celeno would *not* wrest the lake from me a second time.

We rode swiftly down the Palisades, urging our horses around the tight switchbacks. The ride soon became monotonous, and I managed to lose myself in thoughts of defending the lake. But by the time evening fell, the energy brought on by anxiety had dwindled away. My thighs ached from gripping my horse's flanks at every precarious turn, and my eyes were heavy with fatigue. Mae and Arlen were grousing at each other from either end of my mount. Even Valien was stiff and silent, his usual easy smile set into a thin line. It was with great relief that the land evened out and we urged our horses through the village clustered against the wall of Blackshell. The heavy double gates were thrown open, no longer barring the palace from the Silverwood, but guards were posted on the wall all the same. At my wave, they ran ahead of us to raise the palace attendants.

My valet was the first to appear, running down the steps to take hold of my horse's reins. "You're back early, my queen."

"I am, Eavan." I slid gratefully off my mount's back. "I have urgent business to take care of. Have someone gather my councilors together in the map room. And have Grainne prepare a room in the guest wing for the king and queen of the Silverwood."

"Yes, my queen. Right away."

"Before you go—where is Colm? Asleep?"

"The library, I believe."

As usual. "Thank you, Eavan. I'll be in the map room in half an hour."

I led the others into the entrance hall. The night was cloudy, with no view of the stars through the large rose window. Palace attendants hurried ahead of us, turning up the lamps, casting glimmering light on the mother-of-pearl tiles paneling the hallways. We crossed the hall, making for the southern wings. Hanging prominently in this passage, positioned to catch the changing rays of the sun, hung a handsome chandelier of mirrored silver, a gift from Valien's smiths upon our reformed alliance. That had been a grand ceremony, held at the head of the Palisades, where the mountains opened up to the view of the lake. With a great deal of fanfare and formal speeches, we had presented Valien and Mae with several cases of meticulously matched blue pearls, to replace the knots representing the sacred blue fireflies in their banners. They, in turn, had gifted us the elegant silver chandelier. I had accepted it with all the grace and praise my mother would have expected of me. It helped that Mae had somehow found the tact to keep silent on my disdain for any flashy thing meant to remind me of the Light. We passed under it now, and the only thing it reminded me of was what I was up against—Alcoro's corrupted belief that the Light was somehow guiding them to take my country away again.

The attendants hadn't yet reached the hallway to the library, but the cracked door flickered with firelight. I pulled it open to find Colm in a familiar state, bent over the great polished table and surrounded by heaps of parchment and heavy books. Ink stained his fingers as he copied a lengthy passage. The Alcoran invaders had left a great deal of literature behind, and Colm had taken it upon himself to cross-reference many of our own historical accounts, educational texts, and collections of folklore. I hadn't been particularly pleased with this endeavor, but I let him go about his work all the same. His research was—regrettably—useful, and far be it from me to criticize the one thing distracting him from the ghosts echoing through the halls of Blackshell . . . and his own guilt.

He looked up as we entered, and his gaze slid over each of our faces. In his place, Arlen would have launched into some obtuse debate about how I wasn't supposed to be back for at least another day, how Mae and Valien were supposed to be reveling in newly married life. But Colm just set down his quill and straightened.

"What's wrong?" he asked.

"Alcoro," I said, joining him at the table. "They're sending three ships up the Cypri waterways."

He frowned. "How close?"

"A day, roughly," said Mae, coming to study his work. "'The historical evolution of Alcoran ladies' hair ornaments'?"

"A vital piece of cultural anthropology," he said seriously. "How was your wedding?"

I thought she might launch into another tirade

against the interruption in the festivities, but instead she gave a small shrug. "Lovely."

The barest moment of too-long silence ticked by. "Sorry," he said.

"I just said it was lovely."

"I'm sorry I didn't come."

"Me, too." She flicked both of her hands in dismissal and dragged a map of the eastern world out from under a pile of scrolls. "But it doesn't matter. Let's focus on what's at hand."

"Have you summoned the councilors?" Colm asked me.

"Yes. They'll be in the map room in half an hour. But I want to have options sketched out before then." I smoothed the map. "I want the folk on Perch and Fourcolor Islands to evacuate to their northern shores. I want ships in the coves ready to bear them to Oisin's Bow if the fighting gets out of control."

"Archers on the boats, or on the islands?" asked Arlen.

"I want archers on a blockade at the mouth of the river. Atlatls and swordsmen will be divided between the riverbank and the islands. I don't want our folk unprotected like they were last time."

"That leaves the shore open," said Colm. "Even if we remove those folk to the islands, we don't want the Alcorans ransacking the villages."

"The Silverwood will cover the shore," Valien said. "Our folk won't be much good on the islands anyway. We'll have archers on the lower slopes and our swordsmen in formation along the lakefront."

"Good. Now, before we meet with my councilors, we need to discuss where all of us will be. Under no circumstances should we all be in the same place at once," I said firmly. "Arlen, you stay with the atlatls on Fourcolor."

"No."

I looked up sharply. He licked his lips. "Not Fourcolor. Put me on Grayraen."

"Fourcolor is a better location . . ."

"Fourcolor is where Sorcha's family lives," he said, his ears red. "And my aim isn't as good as it was."

I shot him a glare before returning to the map. For all his pining for Sorcha during our exile, he was irrationally jittery about her affections now that we had returned. But I didn't have time to worry about his love life at the moment. "You're on Fourcolor. End of story. Colm will be on the riverbank. As for you two . . ."

"Val's the better swordsman," Mae said. "I'll go up with the Wood Guard. He can take the shore."

"Good. And I'll be on the blockade."

"You should stay at Blackshell," Colm said quietly.

I rounded on him. "Do *not* say that again, Colm. I will not be caught here like I was last time. If Celeno's ships breach the chain, this is the first place they'll head. I'm no safer here than anywhere else, and I want to be at the mouth of the river." I straightened, rolling up the map. "I want to look Celeno's folk in the eyes when they knock on the door to my country."

My sleep that night was plagued by a never-ending mental list of additional tasks and alternate plans. I lay on my back, staring up at the pattern of fish scales on my canopy, until I couldn't bear to stay still a moment longer. I shoved off my coverlet, turned up my lamp, and stood over my desk, scribbling my excess thoughts across sheets of parchment. I paced, muttering aloud, stopping occasionally in front of my mirror to debate some sticking point in our plans. For the more thorny problems, I talked through them while standing before my mantelpiece, above which hung the portrait of my mother and father. The painter had very accurately captured that look of lofty disapproval my mother so often bore—the look that said she was both disappointed and too poised to let it show. That look often accompanied her most frequently repeated phrase:

You are a country.

It had been my waking mantra and evening benediction, a reminder that nothing I said or did existed in a void. That I acted and spoke for several thousand other people, that I held their lives and livelihoods in my hands as surely as I held my own. It was a phrase that had chased me down the southern waterways after Alcoro attacked and haunted me up and down the coast of Paroa in our exile. It became my recurring nightmare—the harsh anthem of my failure to protect my folk. It had spurred me over the Silverwood Mountains at Mae's heels and sustained me as I held my breath under the pitching hull of the Alcoran ship, driving the auger's bit into the sodden wood.

And it fueled me now. Standing in front of my mother's portrait with that phrase in my head had always successfully pushed me to reexamine my thoughts, think through my words and actions more carefully. It didn't fail me this time. I let her unwavering stare scrutinize me, which forced me to adapt, strengthen, and solidify my strategy, until I was sure even she wouldn't be able to find fault.

When weariness found its way among the anxiety, I slouched down in the armchair by the fireplace, resting my aching head against the cushion. But I was up again fifteen minutes later, the memory of ballistae repeats thundering me from my sleep. I staggered for my desk again, breaking two quills in my haste to write down my thoughts. Throughout the night, the same two words echoed through my head.

Never again.

It was impossible to say when I finally fell asleep, but somehow I did. I woke to find myself curled on the settee against the bank of windows facing the lake, my forehead pressed into the frosty glass. I didn't even remember sitting down in this spot, wrapped in the blue and white brocade hangings. The world outside my window was a drifting mass of mist. The lake faded in and out of view beyond my balcony, slate gray in the faint morning light. I lifted my head away from the window, stretching out my frozen limbs. Immediately, my mind began whirling again. I needed folk to fill troughs and buckets to douse their homes. I needed to be sure the chains in the river had not rusted in their bolts. I needed to walk. I needed to move.

I need to swim.

I pulled my heavy woolen cloak from my wardrobe and strode from my bedchamber before I could change my mind. I passed through my parlor for my private staircase—the guards on the landing snapped to attention as I swept past them, as did the ones outside the doors to my lakeside patio.

"As you were," I murmured before they could say anything that might make me stop and think twice. Shedding my shoes, I made my way forward, the cold stone stinging my feet. I draped my cloak over the railing and descended the steps that disappeared into the lake. Ignoring the fact that I should have changed into my heavy diving cover, I swept my arms over my head and arced into the water.

The cold shot through me, tightening my skin, freezing my muscles. I sank, my body shrinking into itself, constricting to find a shred of warmth. My fingers clenched on my shoulders; my knees knotted up at my chest. A shiver ran through me, and in a sharp movement I stretched myself wide, forcing my limbs to straighten. I swept my arms backward, pushing the water behind me, propelling myself deeper into the weak light. The shadowy lakebed fell away beneath me, its grasses drifting in the gentle current. I twisted in the water, loosening every tight place in my body, scooping my hands forward again and again until the first thread of heat found its way into my muscles.

I shot out into the channel between Blackshell and Grayraen Island. I sailed over the Moon Beds, the mussels invisible in the gloom. During the day, the light would reflect in satiny waves against the shells, but at this hour the darkness was absolute. I spiraled down into the depths, enjoying the cleansing rush of water against my skin. The light from the surface faded away, and I stretched out my hands to feel the endless ridges of shells lining the bottom, their fringes flicking away as my fingers roved over them. *Like a dragon's back*, Ama used to say. *Like a sleeping lake monster. Like a giant pimply face.*

Ama. She had the innate ability to pluck out incongruous shells and split them open to reveal pearls of huge size, or incredible luster, or unique color. She once found a specimen the exact size and color of a blueberry. She had given it to Colm, who set it into a cloak pin to wear at their wedding. I hadn't thought about that pin since we returned to the lake. What had happened to it? The Alcorans had shipped most of my jewelry down the waterways during their reign. Had they done the same with Colm's pin?

I drifted onto my back, gazing up at the early-morning sky filtering through the surface. My limbs buzzed, the cold of the water mixing with the heat from my exertion. This was what I had needed—immersion in the heart of my country. I almost thought I could fall asleep drifting through the depths. I stretched my hands in front of me, white in the gloom. I would not let Celeno cause me or my folk any more grief. Let him try to take my lake away from me again. I was not the unprepared, unconcerned queen of four years ago. He would find me ready and waiting, and he would suffer for it.

I reached down, plucked up a mussel, and kicked back to the surface. The air streamed across my wet skin as I stroked back toward the shore, clutching the mussel in my fist. The mist was beginning to rise off the lake, the sky blushing pink behind the mountains. As I neared my patio, I saw a figure stealing along the lakeshore on silent feet, a dark shadow in the mist.

Mae.

"You're crazier than a wobbling possum," she said as I rose out of the lake, my nightdress clinging to my skin. "What on earth possessed you to get in the water at this temperature?"

"I needed to think."

"I find a mug of tea to be more helpful than the chills."

"I'd have at least ten more minutes before the chills set in." I picked up my cloak from the railing of my patio and shrugged it over my shoulders. "What are you doing up so early? This is supposed to be your honeymoon."

She kicked a rock into the water. "I haven't been on many honeymoons, but I doubt most of them involve scouting for blinds to place cadres of archers."

I wrung out my hair. "Oh."

"He rode away to survey the riverbank before I even woke up. He left me a note and a squashed hand pie." She scowled at the water, now reflecting the pastel light.

I tossed her the mussel. "Want to find your first pearl?"

"Can I hock it for a boat to the coast?"

"Mae."

"I know, I know." She pressed her hand to her eyes. "'Shape up.'"

"Valien needs you right now. He needs your skills and your support. He needs you not to blame him."

"I know. I'm sorry. I've made a rotten queen so far. I just . . . I had seen our marriage as the official end to all the uncertainty in our past. No more hundred-mile treks to meet in secret. No more seedy innkeepers ready to sell us out. No more sneaking around his father. No more goodbyes." She sighed and dropped her hand. "But you're right. I'm being an idiot. I'm done now. No more whining."

"Glad to hear it."

She looked at the mussel clutched in her fist. "How does this work?"

"Use your knife to pry it open."

"Does it hurt the thing?"

She would worry about that. "Do your snares hurt the grouse you catch? Do your arrows hurt the rabbits?"

"We catch rabbits and grouse for food."

"We eat mussels for food. We trade their pearls for food."

She frowned but took out her knife and slid it into the crack between the two shells. We walked along the lake as she worked, moving slowly down the tiled pathway at the water's edge. Even while concentrating on the mussel, she made no noise when she walked, unconsciously stepping around any windblown leaf that might crunch underfoot. I had tried mimicking her once, a few weeks after returning to the lake, walking barefoot around my room on the outsides of my feet. But the only thing I had accomplished was jamming my little toe against the bedframe—and making considerably more noise because of it.

The mussel cracked open, and I showed her how to loosen the flesh inside and squeeze it through her hands, which she did without so much as a flinch.

"Anything there?"

She dug her finger into the mess and pulled out a little white crescent.

"Look at that," I said. "A waxing moon."

"It looks like a nail clipping," she said, wiping it off.

"Folk like to say the nature of a person's first pearl says something about their future. There's a book with all the different meanings of color and shape and size.

Yellow means wealth, green means joy, black means sorrow, that kind of thing."

She held up the crescent. "And white?"

"Chastity."

She gave a tremendous groan. "Are you serious?"

I smiled. "No. It means health."

She lobbed the mussel waste at me; it landed *splat* on my sleeve. I laughed at her, my anxiety washed away in the wake of my swim and her companionship. We continued down the path, bickering good-naturedly, while I picked bits of mussel off my arm. As we rounded the bend of the shore, the southern stretch of the lake opened up before us. Mae pulled up to a halt.

"How is it," she said, "that without even speaking, he can make me feel petty?"

I glanced up from my sleeve. We were at the edge of the great terrace that led down to the lake. Standing ankle-deep in the water, his trousers rolled up around his calves and his hands deep in his pockets, was Colm, gazing out into the mist.

"He has that effect on everyone," I said.

"I see you've finished it," she said quietly as we moved closer.

Behind Colm stood a new statue carved from marble mined in the quarries near Rósmarie. It had traveled over the reconstructed Tradeway Road as a great white block, but over the past five months, it had been carved into a figure standing atop a smooth platform. We descended the terrace, coming to flank the statue. Colm turned at our approach.

"Morning," he said.

Mae peered up at the statue's face. "Does it look like her?"

"Sometimes," he said.

I knew what he meant. The stonemasons had done a good job of replicating the ripple of Ama's honey-colored hair and the elegant lines of her face. But they couldn't capture everything—not the crinkle of her eyes when she smiled or the infectious sound of her laugh. Not the quick cleverness of her hands, now clasped demurely in front of her. My gaze fell to the carved folds of her gown pooling around her feet. AMA DONAGHU ALASTAIRE. Her name headed five long columns of text. The list of our dead. Scattered over the platform were tokens—mother-of-pearl carvings, bundles of dried flowers, and pearls of every color and size.

"That blueberry pearl Ama gave you," I said to Colm. "Did the Alcorans take it?"

"No."

"Where is it?"

"On the bottom of the lake," he said. "I was wearing it when they attacked."

He was looking back out at the mists, away from the statue. He did this often, coming to stand near it but not actually looking at it, as if he couldn't bear to do both at the same time.

I mourned every one of the sixty-four men and women Celeno had murdered in Lumen, but this was the greatest casualty he had left me. The Seventh King had taken my brother and buried him deep inside himself, burned with the vivid image of Ama's execution. He had taken Colm's deep, still pool of quiet confidence and muddied it, each day finding new ways to keep the silt from settling. He had made the lake into both a graveyard and a prison. Haunted and fettered.

The fifth column of names carved into the marble was shorter than the others. *Room for more.* My determination kindled in me once again, and I swept my wet hair over my shoulder. "I expect the councilors will be awake soon." I turned back up the terrace. "I'm going to change. We should be sailing for the mouth of the river by midmorning. You'll both be ready then?"

"I'll be ready," said Mae.

Colm didn't turn around. "I *am* ready."

So was I.

Valien came back from his reconnaissance just minutes before the ranks of Silverwood Guardsmen marched out of the forest. He and Mae gave directions to their officers on the splitting and ordering of their soldiers. When this was done, we boarded the flat-bottomed *Spindrift*, its high curved bow bobbing at the dock. Colm and Arlen helped Cavan cast off, and he maneuvered us into the channel, the bow leading us into the south.

"I thought Cavan was a boat-builder," Mae said, nodding to the helm.

"He's a sailor, too. The Alcorans didn't want any Lake-folk in charge of their own vessels, so the sailors were assigned different crafts. Cavan Conlaugh is good at building boats, but he's even better at sailing them."

A gust of wind blew across the water, rocking the *Spindrift*. Mae's hand jumped to clutch the railing, her eyes closed.

"Boats," she said with the tiniest groan. "*Water*."

"We've *got* to teach you how to swim," I said, grinning at her discomfort.

"If we as humans had been meant to swim, we would have been born with fins," she said, pinching Valien's sleeve in her fingers. He was leaning against the hull, facing inward, only slightly more at ease than she. They were dressed in gleaming Guard uniforms, their embroidered moss-colored tunics cinched at the waist with tooled leather belts. Their brown breeches were tucked into their usual soft-soled boots, though these were less elaborate than their wedding finery, with only a double band of fringe on the calves. She had the silver cord of a Woodwalker running over her shoulder, while his was white in the manner of their officers. Belted to their waists were quivers packed with turkey-feather arrows.

I looked across the boat to Arlen and Colm, who were leaning on the rail, watching the shore slip by. They had on the deep blue tunics of our spearmen, each with a pouch of darts buckled to their belts. I was wearing a similar tunic, though longer and embroidered with seed pearls along the neck and sleeves. I'd have preferred a gown for an occasion of this magnitude, but a tunic and trousers would be much easier to maneuver in—and easier to swim in, if things went terribly wrong. Arlen twirled his atlatl idly in his fingers. He had not replaced the missing pearl in the Bird of Prey's face, bursting with pride at the significance of its one gleaming eye.

The boat rollicked again, and Mae turned away from the water to face the deck, taking slow breaths.

"You must have sailed through Cyprien when you traveled west a few years ago," I commented.

"I hated it then, too."

Sailing down the shoreline didn't take long. The town of Lakemouth was really only an extension of the settlement around Blackshell, charged with being our main hub of trade and our first line of defense. I was glad to see the streets were nearly empty, its citizens evacuated to the islands, but it was also a bit disheartening. *Once more we're forced to fight Celeno for our homes.*

I shook off that thought as we hurried to take our positions. Colm and my councilor of defense directed our spearmen along both sides of the river. Arlen boarded another boat and sailed with a contingent of atlatls out to Fourcolor Island. Valien arranged his swordsmen along the lakeshore. Mae clambered up the mountainside, disappearing into the tangle of trees

to find the best vantage point for the southern waterways. As the light turned golden, while Valien and I
discussed the range of the archers, a distant bird call
made him swivel his head toward the slopes.

"That's Mae?" I asked, straining to hear.

"Golden-crowned sparrow," he said, nodding.
"They're close."

Things started happening very quickly then. Soldiers fell into their ranks. Darts were loaded into
atlatls. Silverwood archers wedged themselves into
crooks of trees, their arrows trained down the river.
I boarded a skiff that rowed me away from the shore,
back to the *Spindrift* anchored just out of range of the
river's mouth.

"Last chance, my queen," Cavan said quietly as he
helped me board. "Perhaps you should take up position on Betwixt instead?"

"Hold steady, Cavan," I replied, striding to the helm.

For ten, then fifteen, then twenty minutes, there
was little sound save the water lapping at the hull.
I gripped the railing, my gaze on the river. Spears
and javelins bristled up and down the banks, the sun
glinting off their barbed heads. A few cryptic bird
calls rang through the forest's edge, Silverwood archers finalizing their positions.

And then she burst around the bend, her bowsprit
puncturing the clear autumn sky.

"A ketch," Cavan said with some surprise, noting
its two masts.

I was surprised as well. Instead of the burly triplemasted ships from four years ago, the ketch that sailed around the bend was barely bigger than the *Spindrift*. But that wasn't all.

"Look," said Cavan, pointing.

I followed his finger and saw, on the mainmast, the Alcoran banner—a bright patch of russet against the sky.

Fixed above it, streaming in the wind, was a much larger swath of white.

"What's this?" I murmured, my brow furrowed.

As the ship approached the chains, a figure appeared at the bow. On the riverbank, I saw Colm lift his arm. Javelins tensed in the sun. The trees shifted with archers finding their marks. But the Alcoran in the bow acted first, raising not a crossbow, but a white flag. The ship reached the chains and ground against them, the bowsprit jerking at the impact.

For a few moments there was only a ridiculous standstill. Colm had his javelin fitted to his atlatl, poised for the ship. I could see Valien astride a rise at the head of his swordsmen, trying vainly to determine what was happening at the river. Mae and Arlen were lost to my sight, but I knew they were equally alert. I pictured Mae's arrow trained on the Alcoran in the bow.

"He's shouting something," Cavan said.

From the deck of the ketch, the Alcoran was indeed calling out. But I couldn't make out his words from our position in the blockade.

"Take me closer, Cavan," I murmured.

"My queen . . ."

"Closer."

We edged out of the blockade, drifting carefully toward the mouth of the river. The wind picked up, and the Alcoran flag snapped forward. Soon we were close enough for me to make out the white prism surrounded by seven turquoise stars.

"Hold," I said.

We bobbed in the water, out of crossbow range but well within striking distance of ballistae. But I didn't see any such weapons on deck. Why? Were they hidden? Had the Alcorans developed different weaponry I couldn't yet see? I moved to the port rail, leaning out to hear what the Alcoran was shouting. He was still waving the white flag. Finally the wind shifted, carrying his voice to me.

"Parley!"

CHAPTER 3

"Rivers to the sea," I said sharply. "They want diplomacies."

"They can't be serious," Cavan said, extending a spyglass and squinting through it.

On the shore, I saw Colm approach the edge of the river with a pack of spearmen, still poised to strike. The Alcoran with the white flag leaned over the rail of his ship, calling out to him.

"Shall I take you closer, my queen?"

"Let's wait a moment."

The spears on the riverbank lost their bristle, no longer all pointing at the same sharp angle. Folk shifted among themselves. Colm was conversing with the Alcoran, calling over the half a dozen yards of flowing water that separated them. I squinted at the ketch, bobbing against the chains, then scanned beyond it, waiting to see the flurry of an ambush at any moment. Would Colm have time to react? His javelin was still set to his atlatl, but it wasn't poised for a throw. Would they be quicker than he to lift their weapons?

Around the bend, the two sister ships sailed into view, of the same rigging and size as the first. They ground to a halt in the middle of the river, dropping their anchors to keep from ramming the stern of the ketch straining at the chains. I saw spears spike briefly into formation at their arrival, but in another few moments, folk had relaxed once again.

A runner detached herself from the press on the shore and made her way to Valien, still standing astride the rise, probably somewhat confused—*just as I am*. At the same moment, Colm strode down to the water's edge and boarded one of the skiffs at the docks with a handful of others. They bent over the oars and rowed out to meet us. The Alcoran ships bobbed placidly, waiting.

"They can't actually want a parley?" I asked, offering Colm my arm as he clambered over the rail.

"They do. They've invited you on board their vessel. I told them you refuse."

"I should hope so."

"So now they're requesting permission to send one emissary to speak with you, wherever you think it most appropriate."

I stared at him. "What on earth do they want to talk about?"

"Trade, I assume, or some kind of alliance."

"Why did they bring three ships if they only want to talk?"

"That I don't know. But if we move Valien's swordsmen up to the riverbank, we should have enough folk to cover all three of them."

I frowned, thinking. Part of me wanted to send the ships away pockmarked with spearheads. But part of me was truly curious to hear the words that Celeno had chosen for his emissary to bring to me. Words, I told myself, that could only be fruitless. Words that would only serve to elicit a laugh and a dismissal. But still, I wanted to hear them. I wanted to know how severe the Seventh King's delusion had become. And besides, there may be information I could use for my own purposes.

"Well, we certainly will not receive their message at Blackshell," I said. "And not in Lakemouth. In fact, I don't think I want them leaving the riverbank."

"We can escort their emissary out of range of the ships, and hold the discussion in one of the boathouses."

"Yes, I think something like that would be our best option. Bring word to Valien to move his swordsmen to the river."

"And Arlen and Mae?"

"Have someone send word, but leave them where they are for the moment. I still don't want us all in the same place."

Ten minutes later, I climbed out of the skiff onto the docks. Ranks of Silverwood soldiers were hurrying past on their way to flank the river. In one of the boathouses, folk shifted canoes to clear a place for us to gather. Out on the water, the blockade held steady. Folk were tense, but the ugly anxiety of battle was already easing away.

I strode to the boathouse, my mind awhirl. I didn't know what to think, and as a result, I compensated by jumping from one possible outcome to the next. Valien found me frowning into the empty space beside the canoes.

"Unexpected, this," he said. "Though I'd be lying if I said I wasn't a little relieved."

"I'll be relieved when I can see the sterns of those ships in the river," I said. He didn't reply, merely checking the looseness of his sword in its scabbard and adjusting his white shoulder cord under its epaulet.

Five spearmen filtered into the boathouse, arranging themselves around Valien and me. Four Silverwood archers took up positions in the corners. Two swordsmen flanked the spearmen. I pulled my pearl pendant out of my tunic and let it rest on my chest. I smoothed the flyaways from my hair and touched my crown—for whatever reason, my crown was among the few jeweled items the Alcorans had not stolen. They had hung it up on a wall in the throne room, the beasts, between two russet banners, like some kind of trophy. I had made sure to burn those particular flags first.

A few moments later, I heard the tramping of feet, and around the wall of the boathouse strode Colm, his atlatl in his fist. Behind him, flanked by three spearmen and two Silverwood archers, was the Alcoran emissary.

She was just a shade overpolished. She was not dressed in military uniform, but typical garb one might expect from an Alcoran noblewoman. Her black hair was held back by a band of three white gems. Dark charcoal skirt over shining black boots. Crisp white shirt under a charcoal bolero. Sash of russet silk. A ring set with a small turquoise stone around her middle finger. Enough to denote her allegiance, but not enough to appear overly zealous. She was cloakless, perhaps to emphasize the fact that she carried no weapons. I did not ease my glare, though—everything about this woman was calculated.

She bent into a deep bow, her right foot extended.

"Queen Mona Alastaire," she said. "I offer you my thanks for receiving me."

"Save your thanks," I replied. "I have a feeling I will not earn it. Tell me, what message did your Seventh King give you to bring to me? Be quick. I want you gone before sunset."

She didn't ruffle at my sharp tone. In fact, she didn't even answer me directly—how *dare* she. She turned instead to Valien, standing to my left, his posture crisp but milder than mine.

"King Valien Bluesmoke, I offer you my thanks as well."

Valien didn't correct the erroneous name she used. "Please answer Queen Mona's question."

"My name is Atria Coacotzli," she said, straightening. "I am an ambassador of King Celeno Tezozomoc, the Seventh King of Alcoro, Fulfillment of the Prophecy of the Prism, Crown of Stairs-to-the-Stars, may he be blessed in the Light."

"May he be struck with blindness and bad joints," I snapped. "Don't you dare parade his titles in front of me. You know perfectly well what I think of your king. What is your message?"

"I bring you an inquiry most humble and hopeful," she said in the same evened-out voice. Too smooth, too polished. Too *long-winded*. "King Celeno extends his greetings to you and your folk and asks that you may consider his proposal."

"I might," I said through gritted teeth, "if you would *get to the point*."

"King Celeno deems to make you an offer of recompense and reconciliation. He implores you to meet with him face-to-face to discuss the future of our great nations, the jewels of the eastern world."

"You cannot be serious," I said flatly. "Celeno asks that I meet with him? He spent three years content with the thought that he had me publicly executed. How can he possibly think I would trust him not to make a second attempt at assassination?"

"The Prophecy of the Prism is revealing itself in mysterious ways," she said calmly. "Strategies that once upheld the Prophecy have now been found to be faulty."

My indignation flared. "Is *that* supposed to be an apology? You tried and failed to enslave an entire country, and so now you must crawl back, hoping to barter. Yes, your strategy appears to have been faulty."

"King Celeno hopes to impress upon you that as his stratagems have evolved, so he hopes yours will as well. He implores you not to close your country to the partnership we may be able to forge."

"This is absurd," I said. "Stop hiding behind your fabricated justification. Speak plainly. How does he expect me to agree to this? Does he think I will come riding into Alcoro as if I'm sightseeing in the canyons?"

At that moment, there was a rustle and a murmur from beyond the ranks of spearmen guarding the wide boathouse entrance. The armed folk around the room bristled, but then an irritated voice cut through.

"Oh, earth and sky, get out of the way."

Valien raised his eyebrows as Mae elbowed her way through the spearmen. Her flatbow was slung over her shoulder. She had patches of dirt on both her knees and a yellow leaf in her hair.

"Ellamae, I don't think . . ."

"Started without me, have you?" she asked, striding into the room. "That's all right. I'll catch up quickly."

She was angry. "Mae," I said, "I didn't want us all together . . ."

"Well, then, get out. Or have you forgotten that of the five crowned heads, I'm the only one who's actually held convincing diplomacies with one of Celeno's finger puppets?"

"You were bluffing," I said stiffly. I wouldn't let her rankle me now.

She laid her bow against a canoe and hopped up on the overturned hull. "Imagine what I can do when I'm being honest."

For the first time, Atria Coacotzli seemed to lose a fraction of her composure. "You are . . ."

"That's right, my lady canyonlands, I'm the grubby woodwoman who double-crossed your captain. They'll make anyone a queen nowadays, won't they?"

She frowned, breaking her placid mask. Her information on the monarchy of the Silverwood was out of date. She clearly had not been briefed on how best to appeal to a Silverwood queen.

If I wasn't so irked at Mae, I would have hugged her right then, because after a moment, Atria turned back to me, choosing to ignore the new queen in the room. I couldn't help but smirk. Mae would not allow herself to be edged out, and if it was going to undo the ambassador's composure, neither would I. I was glad she had come, after all.

"How much of a fool does your king think I am," I said, "to ask me to go all the way to him and meet face-to-face?"

"He does not ask you to come to Alcoro. He and Queen Gemma are already en route to the capital of Cyprien in Lilou. He hopes you will join him there, in neutral territory."

"You've occupied Cyprien for over fifty years," I said. "I hardly call that neutral."

"He offers you passage on his fleet, if you desire it, with as many of your soldiers as you deem necessary. Though he asks that your meeting be conducted without the presence of armed soldiers."

"That's fine, as there will be no meeting to conduct."

"He is prepared to compensate you handsomely," said Atria patiently, ignoring the fact that I had told her no in eight different ways. I could almost respect her if it wasn't so infuriating. She continued on. "The three ships in my fleet are loaded with a great deal of goods that may interest the folk of both the lake and the mountains. Goods you will soon find scarce without access to Cypri trade routes."

"We have alternate access to the eastern coast," I said. "I don't need the Cypri trade routes."

But she was prepared for this argument as well and spoke my own silent trepidations aloud. "It's true that the mountains gaps are open once again to trade, but it has been decades—over a century—since folk have used Tradeway Road regularly. Folk trust the sea routes. The city of Matariki exists solely to support the merchants who use it as a hub. That kind of industry is not something that can be easily rerouted, particularly when the new route is tedious, snowy, and heavily taxed."

"And what is *your* tax, canyonwoman?" Mae asked hotly. "What do you charge the folk of Cyprien to use their own ports?"

"I'll note, too, that the merchants who have come through the Silverwood in the last five months have found our taxes to be fair," said Valien quietly. "Comparable, at least, to the fines King Celeno has levied on the waterways."

"And I'm sure it will play out well for you in your coming reign," she said with cloying diplomacy. "But it does not change the fact that this winter, and the winters to come, may prove to be lean for the folk of the lake, who have long relied on river trade."

She then turned back to me and launched unprovoked into a list. "Sugarcane. Salt. Coffee. Textiles. Rice. Cotton. Wool. Steel. Spices. Herbs . . ."

"Enough," I said, waving her down. With each item she listed, it added to my growing bank of goods we would have to do without. "Our lack of these things may make for a meager winter, but it's a price we're willing to pay to sever our ties with Alcoro. I will not meet with Celeno face-to-face. You may tell him this plan of his is just as faulty as the first."

"This was not King Celeno's plan," Atria said.

"What?" I wasn't sure I had heard her correctly.

"This was not the king's plan. An attempt at diplomacy was Queen Gemma's idea."

"I couldn't care less if it was his pet canary's idea . . ."

"An effort," she overrode me, "to deter the king from moving a fleet of two dozen warships up the waterways. An effort to cut out the need for bloodshed."

I saw Colm shift over her shoulder, but I was not about to let this woman cow me. "Send your warships," I said to her. "Load them with your ballistae and your soldiers. I will set fire to them as they pile up in the river."

"I urge you, I implore you, Lady Queen," she said, and I was surprised to hear a shred of concern in her voice. Was this part of her performance? "King Celeno will not be so unprepared as he was four years ago. He has a great deal of resources available to him, and his arsenal is constantly expanding. Will you risk the safety of your new allies in the Silverwood without ever making an attempt at diplomacy?"

"Now you threaten me—and my allies," I said. "We had diplomacy between Lumen and Alcoro for ninety-five years. *You* were the fools who put an end to it." I pointed to the door. "We're done here. Get out."

Her jaw worked, but the spearmen and archers in the room tensed their weapons, and she gave a short sigh of concession.

"I regret it, Queen Mona." She bowed to me. "Thank you for your time." She bowed to Valien, and after a moment's hesitation, inclined her head to Mae. She frowned in return.

As she turned to leave, Colm cleared his throat. "We'll deliberate amongst ourselves, Ambassador Coacotzli, and pen you a missive to bring to your king. Don't sail away just yet."

My gaze flew to him, stunned. The Alcoran paused and then bowed to him as well. She straightened and allowed herself to be escorted out of the boathouse by the entourage of soldiers. The archers and spearmen surrounding us filed out after them, taking up positions along the docks.

Tension crackled in the room. Valien went to stand by Mae, who was bouncing one foot up and down on the lip of the canoe. I kept my gaze on Colm, staring him down with indignation.

"What's wrong with you?" I asked him. "I have no intention of penning a response, and I want her ships gone immediately."

"We need to think this over more carefully," he said steadily, his eyes locked with mine.

"We need to do no such thing."

"You're being too quick to pass judgment."

"That's what you said about trusting Mae in Tiktika," I said hotly.

"Well, and I was right."

Mae glanced down, twisting her mouth to smother a grin.

"Half-right," I said.

"Sophistry," he said, waving his hand. "This is different, and you know it. I just feel this is an opportunity we won't get again."

"I sincerely hope we don't," I said fiercely. "Celeno is a usurper and a murderer, and I will not ally with him. Don't you accuse me of sophistry."

Someone burst through the row of soldiers guarding the wide door. Mae's hand jumped to her bow, but it was only Arlen, red-faced and windblown.

"And just when exactly were you planning on including me in all the talk?" he demanded.

I clapped my hands to my forehead. "Great Light, you're all idiots! This isn't some council meeting on mussel harvest! There are three enemy ships anchored on our front step. One long-range ballistae shot, and Celeno could neatly wipe out the monarchies of two separate countries. This is dangerous, volatile business with a dangerous, volatile monarch."

"Which is why I think it's worth our time to take it slowly," Colm pressed. "You heard the ambassador. It wasn't Celeno's idea to open up diplomacies. It was his wife's."

"If you care to believe that! And besides, why on *earth* should it matter whose idea it was?"

"Because," he said, "it means that Celeno's motives aren't the only ones at work in Alcoro. It means there is division, division that runs all the way between the king and the queen. That is not insignificant, Mona."

"Did you see the way she squirmed when she said Celeno's arsenal is expanding?" Mae said. I whirled to her. Now she was siding against me, too? "She doesn't want war. She was trying to convince you as much for her country's sake as yours."

"Convince you to do what?" asked Arlen. "What did she say?"

"Celeno's asking Mona to meet with him in Cyprien," Colm said. "To discuss the reestablishment of trade."

Arlen, surely, would disapprove. Hotheaded, impulsive Arlen, ready to fight any stranger who looked at him wrong. For the first time, I found myself willing him not to listen to his older brother.

But he furrowed his brow. "Or what?"

"Or he resumes his efforts to overthrow us, and destabilize the Silverwood, I imagine," Colm replied.

"Two dozen warships," Mae added. I could have throttled her.

"The number doesn't matter," I said, trying to keep the anger out of my voice. "The Silverwood scouts will see them coming. We'll line the river with pitched spears and arrows. The chains will hold the ships. We'll set fire to them. We'll sink them."

"The chains aren't meant to hold more than a few ships at bay," Arlen said. Trust him to choose this moment to discover a sense of forethought. "And twenty-four ships will stretch a long ways down the river. I imagine he'll send them in waves. The first ship will be sent to break the chains. The others will sail into the lake unhindered."

"We'll sink them before they can do any harm."

"They'll fire right back on us," he said, fingering his atlatl. "The only reason we were able to sink them the first time was because they had no idea what was happening. They'll shoot us in the water if we try to dive under them. And besides that, unless he plans to wait until spring, we'll be diving in the dead of winter. Folk will have only a few minutes in the water before they have to start worrying about the chills."

"Valien," I said, turning desperately to him. "Tell me you haven't lost all reason. It's not in your interest to open up trade on the river."

He was frowning, leaning on the canoe, his hands

68 EMILY B. MARTIN

curled around his elbows. "Trade in the river won't benefit the Silverwood," he said, and I let out a breath of relief. "But," he continued, "war and ruin will help us even less. If Celeno retakes the lake, he's unlikely to leave us alone as he did the first time around."

"You were ready enough to march into battle this morning!"

"We didn't know there would be an alternative," he said patiently. "I will always reach for diplomacy before I consider the prospect of war. I pledged you the support of my banner, Queen Mona, and I will give it to you if you ask for it, but I don't warm to the idea of sending my folk into a massacre."

I could have screamed in frustration, but Mae overrode me before I could speak. "We're overlooking one very big thing."

"Besides the fact you're all bordering insanity?"

"Yes," she said. "Besides that."

"What?" I asked through clenched teeth.

"Cyprien," she said. "We're overlooking Cyprien. With our new alliance and no trade upstream, Alcoro's hold on Cyprien is more vulnerable than it's been in fifty years. I passed through it as an ordinary traveler years ago, but I doubt any of us would be able to approach it now. Celeno is giving us an opportunity to get inside and get a feel for the loyalties of the River-folk."

Valien took his wife's hand and squeezed it, not quite hiding the pride that flashed across his face. I

ground my teeth even harder, knowing he was recalling what I said while dancing with him just two
nights past. I *did* want to know where Cyprien's loyalties lay. But that alone was not reason enough for
me to think this a rational plan.

I turned again to Colm, standing as calmly as he
ever had.

"Celeno murdered your wife," I said to him.

"Yes," he said. "And I won't let him murder anyone
else's."

Silence settled throughout the room. Arlen scratched
his head wearily with the Bird. Valien ran his thumb
over Mae's fingers. Colm didn't move.

I took a deep, slow breath and unclenched my fists.
"Well. It seems I'm outnumbered."

Everyone except Colm had the decency to glance
away.

"Now comes the part where we argue about who's
going," Mae said.

"Send me," Colm said. "I'll go in your place."

"I will not send you," I snapped. "There's no argument to be had, at least not from this end. Celeno
wants to meet with *me*. If he wanted an ambassador,
he'd have sent one in his place."

"He just did send one," Arlen pointed out.

"I mean to Lilou," I said sharply—I was still irritated at his sudden wellspring of levelheadedness just
when I needed him on my side. "The Alcoran king
and queen are both heading to Lilou themselves. Dip-

lomatically, it would be poor protocol to merely send them an ambassador. I will not allow them to continue looking on our folk as a bunch of uncultured rubes ready to be subjugated."

That logic was sound enough, but the truth of the matter was that if this was really happening—if my country and theirs were going to meet in parlance after everything they had done—then I wanted to be the one to go. I *had* to be the one to go. I wanted Celeno to see me, not someone speaking for me—the person he thought he executed. I wanted to be the one to hear his words and counter them, to draw him out and make him fidget in long silence. I didn't want him to think me intimidated—not politically, not personally. When his future thoughts turned again to Lumen Lake, wondering how else he could leach us dry, I wanted it to be my face he saw.

You are a country.

I narrowed my eyes at Colm, daring him to argue. He twisted his mouth in dissent but didn't say anything. Valien sighed.

"I'll go with you . . ." he began, but Mae cut him off.

"You won't, Val. I've barely been a queen for two days. You can't leave me to run the country for weeks by myself. And don't say it's too big a risk," she said as he opened his mouth. "You sent me to win the trust of a hostile monarch mere months ago."

"Ellamae Heartwood, my quick-tempered queen," he said. "Let me finish. I was going to say I'll go to

Cyprien if you're unwilling. Of course you're the more logical choice. When did you imagine I stopped trusting you?"

She mouthed wordlessly for a moment, as if still thinking she needed to argue her case.

"Oh," she finally said.

He kissed her fingers. "Of course, it doesn't mean I'm happy about it."

"Well, *I'm* not going," Arlen said. "Even if I thought you lot would let me. I might want to avoid all-out war with Celeno, but that doesn't mean I wouldn't snap and chin him unconscious."

"Ah." Valien turned back to Mae. "He has a point. Don't do that."

She smiled seductively at him. "He ruined our wedding night. My love, I am liable to do anything."

"Please don't be angry with me."

I stuffed a gown into my trunk. "I'm not angry. Why would you think I'm angry?"

Colm watched me from where he was leaning on my doorframe. "You're crumpling your gowns."

I exhaled and removed the gown, smoothing it out on my coverlet. "Okay—I'm a *little* angry. But it's with Celeno, not you. When we drove out his ships, the last thing I thought I'd be doing is negotiating trade with him again."

"Our folk need it. The ambassador was right. It

will take time for merchants to take the mountain gaps with any regularity, and the snows won't make it any easier."

"I know. Believe me, I know." I laid the tightly folded gown in my trunk and tucked the matching pair of shoes alongside it. "But to turn right around and reach out to Alcoro . . . I suppose I'm just surprised the idea came from you. You, who can barely stand to look at Ama's statue." I shook my head. "You're a better person than I am, Colm, if you can look past what he did."

"I'm not."

"You always have been. Selfless, honorable, all of Father's good traits. You're my moral compass."

"I'm *not*," he said, and the urgency in his voice made me look up from my work. He looked as though he had just swallowed something bitter. "I'm not looking past what he did. But if we can open up trade on the river, someone will have to oversee it. Someone will have to travel away from the lake to Lilou and Matariki several times a year. Celeno killed our old councilor of trade. The position's open."

I stared at him. Even as he spoke, his face was lined with self-disgust.

"You want me to negotiate trade with Celeno so you have an excuse to *leave the lake*?" I exclaimed.

"Let me go instead, Mona. Please."

"No."

"Please."

"*No*. If you go, there won't be any negotiation involved. He could ask for ten barges of all-white pearls every month, and you'd offer to make it a dozen." I threw a turtleshell comb into my trunk, knocking askew the shoes I had just packed. "No. I'm packing. I'm going. I'm going to open up the barest amount of trade we need to get by, and I'm going to do it for the sake of our folk, not you."

I bundled up a cloak and wedged it down next to the shoes. The buckles on the shoes snagged the fabric, pulling up a few loops of thread. I balled my fists and drew in a deep breath. In the silence of the moment, I looked up. Colm was leaning his head against the doorframe, his eyes squeezed shut.

I let out my breath. Colm didn't deserve my unkindness. He didn't deserve my parting words to be harsh ones. If he was at the point of bartering with his wife's murderer, he was suffering far more than he had let on.

I crossed the room and threaded my arms under his, resting my head on his shoulder. Without hesitation, he hugged me back.

"I'm sorry," he whispered.

"Don't be sorry. I should have seen something like this coming. If I can work things out, I'll consider appointing you councilor of trade. But don't leave us yet. We need you here."

"Nobody needs me here."

I sighed into his shoulder. "*I* need you here, no matter how mopey you get. You're my moral compass."

"I don't point north anymore."

"Well, it's about time you started being selfish." I

went back to my trunk and pulled out the rumpled cloak. "You were making the rest of us look bad."

My brothers weren't done with their surprises, however. The following morning, I hurried from one task to the next, eating breakfast as I went. I had absolutely refused passage on Celeno's ships, so now Cavan and his hands were bustling around the *Spindrift*, preparing her for the journey to Lilou. After seeing that my trunk was boarded, I met with my councilors to secure the running of the country in my stead. Colm was there, shouldering responsibilities without so much as a frown. I rushed from the council room to check on the folk rowing the goods from Celeno's ships down the lakeshore. But as I strode toward the main hall, Arlen scuttled out of the corridor to the armory.

"I think I should come with you after all," he said breathlessly. There were two bright pink patches on his cheeks.

I stopped in my tracks. "Why?"

"So I can protect you."

"There are ten spearmen and eight Silverwood swordsmen going with us," I said, eyeing his discomfort. "What's the real reason?"

He twisted his hands. "Sorcha wants to get married."

I wanted to throw back my head and laugh, but I settled for raising an eyebrow. "Does she? What brought this on?"

"She saw how nobly I ran to protect her family on Fourcolor yesterday."

I continued to fight back the laugh. He seemed legitimately distressed. "And you were worried you couldn't throw well anymore."

"I don't . . . I don't think I would be a good husband."

That brought me up short. What had gotten into both of my brothers, that they were spouting words I never thought I'd hear them utter? When had Arlen gone from a gangly boy with scratched knuckles and too-big ears to a man worried about being a good husband? I realized with a start that he was now the same age Colm had been when he married Ama.

"Arlen, I don't have time to list the ways you'd make a good husband. The fact that you're concerned about it already makes you better than most." I wasn't used to being philosophical with him. "For now, content yourself with the fact that I will absolutely not allow you to get married without me present. That should buy you a few weeks. Will that satisfy her, do you think?"

"I suppose."

"Queen's order."

"Yes."

"Good." I studied him. "Listen, do me a favor. Go check that the cargo from the Alcoran ships is being inventoried."

"All right."

"And then find Colm. Tell him he doesn't have to oversee the demolition of the barracks on Button

Island. I want you to do it instead. Can you make sure we salvage everything we can?"

"I'll try."

"Excellent. We cast off in an hour. I'll see you on the dock?"

"Sure."

I watched him walk away, shaking my head as he rounded the far corner. I turned and headed back up the hallway to wrap up my last few tasks before we set sail. I hoped Mae was still surly about leaving Valien, because I wasn't sure how much more personality development I could handle.

CHAPTER 4

The *Spindrift* and the *Halfmoon* were packed and tugging at their moorings. Mae and Valien emerged tousle-haired from the wings of Blackshell. Colm and Arlen stood on the docks with a handful of other folk. Without further ado, we made our goodbyes and boarded the ship. Cavan and his hands scurried across the deck, casting us off to waves and calls of good fortune from the dock.

At the mouth of the river, we were greeted by the sterns of the Alcoran ships, already on their way downstream. I breathed a sigh of relief. So far, Atria Coacotzli had not deceived us. Her ships had unloaded their cargo and made their retreat with no hidden armies or surprise ballista repeats. Still, I gripped the railing as we entered the river. If this diplomatic meeting ended in any kind of violence,

I would never consider an Alcoran anything but an enemy for the rest of my life—if I survived it.

Mae watched the mountains slide by, her stance wide at the frankly minimal rocking of the boat. When we listed port without warning, she swayed, her hand jumping to her middle.

"Earth and sky," she muttered, closing her eyes. "I think I'll go below deck and drink for the next five days."

"It's worse down below."

"You're not listening: I plan to be drinking."

I smiled, shaking my head.

The journey was as uneventful as we could hope for. We made good time, the favorable winds and downstream current bearing us swiftly into the south. The weather was crisp and clear, save for a brief but gusty autumn storm that saw Mae retching over a bucket.

"You know," I said as I set a glass of water down at her elbow. "A less kind person might remind you of an incident with a rat snake, where all you did was laugh at me."

With no breath to spare for a cutting remark, she gestured rudely at me and went back to clutching her bucket.

I left her in relative peace.

Despite the blaze of color on the mountainsides and the free, clean breeze, I did not spend much time at the rail myself. The last time I had traveled these waters, I had been swimming, diving under patrolling Alcoran ships, urging my brothers to move faster. Mourning Ama and dozens of others. Seething with hatred for the Seventh King who had ripped my crown from me. I remembered landmarks as we passed them—a stretch of pines where we had passed a night, shivering with cold. A stand of rocks where we had hidden from Celeno's soldiers, submerged up to our noses. A scrubby beach where Colm had vomited lungfuls of water that he had sucked in as he wept, swimming arm over arm, blindly following my orders. After a few such reminders, it became too much.

So instead I spent the time below deck planning with Mae, discussing how much trade we should open without impacting the new routes over the mountains. We debated how we should treat Celeno himself and where to station our soldiers. We talked, too, about how we might gauge the loyalties of the Cypri folk—whether they had fully resigned themselves to Alcoran supremacy, or whether there was some measure of unrest.

"It's going to be difficult," I said on the fourth day while poring over a text on Cypri history. "Theirs always was a strange country. They never had a monarchy, you know."

"So I've heard." Mae was lying on her cramped bunk, working a splinter out of the pad of her thumb. "They had some kind of council, right?"

"The Assembly of Six," I said, squinting at Colm's cramped notes in the margins of the text. "One representative for each of the six provinces in the country."

"Six people? An even number? How did they make any collective decisions?"

"Honestly, I have no idea," I said, thinking of my own council. There had always been an odd number of councilors, to provide a basic majority on divisive issues—and there were many divisive issues. I couldn't imagine the headache of an even split.

"But it was hereditary, right?" she said, peering at her thumb. "Those representatives—they were basically just monarchs of each little province, right?"

"Apparently not," I said. "They were elected."

"Elected? By whom?"

"Popular vote," I said. "The citizens of Cyprien. Any Cypri sixteen and older could vote their candidate to the Assembly, and they could vote them off the Assembly, too."

"Really?"

"Really." I shook my head. "They kept it up for centuries, apparently. Popular elections every five years."

"That's *incredible*." I glanced up at the emphasis in her voice. She'd forgotten the splinter and was staring at me with a look of stunned admiration. "For common folk to have a say in their government? What a system."

"'What a system'?" I echoed. "You're a monarch, Mae. Charged with running and protecting your country. How would you feel if you could be ousted from your role just because a faction of folk disagreed with you?"

"Um, I *was*, Mona," she said, furrowing her brow.

"Thanks for that. And it was *because* of a monarch—Vandalen was totally unfit to be king of the Silverwood, but since he was related to the *previous* monarch, he got to wear the crown. What if we'd been able to vote him out? What if we'd been able to replace him?"

"I'll tell you what would happen," I said. "Civil war is what would happen, or instability at the very least—which leaves a country vulnerable to stronger political systems. Cyprien's system worked until Alcoro needed its resources, and then look how well the River-folk's Assembly fared. Monarchs aren't always popular, Mae, but at least we keep a country united."

"I could be *really* mean and point out that your country didn't fare much better when Alcoro decided it wanted it."

I turned a page with a curt slap. "I made it back, didn't I? Lumen Lake spent almost four years under Alcoran rule, until someone showed up who folk were used to following—me. I'm not bragging, Mae, or saying I'm a perfect monarch, but the system *works*. Yes, there are people who shouldn't be monarchs—Celeno and Vandalen among them—but a bad monarch eventually reaps the implications of their poor decisions. Vandalen was a warmonger, and it cost him his life. He abused his son, and it cost him his legacy." I closed the book. "Celeno, hopefully, is starting to feel the ramifications himself. That's why he's reaching out for diplomacy. His previous actions have failed."

She *tsked* her tongue and went back to the splinter.

"It's just interesting to hear of folk actually having a say in who they answer to."

"Well, they don't anymore," I said. "You're *sure* you didn't pick up on any unrest when you traveled through the country?"

She huffed—I'd asked her this question before. "Nothing. Nobody's out shouting the Alcoran prophecy in the streets, but there wasn't any sign of conflict, either. Alcorans control the ports and industry, and the Cypri just seem to take it in stride."

"And what about Alcoro?" I asked. "Did you get a sense of how the Canyon-folk feel about Celeno?"

She shrugged, her gaze on her thumb. "I only made it as far as Parnassia, on the other side of the mountains that border Cyprien. They're certainly more overt, though. They plaster his banner everywhere, and the words of the Prism. 'We are creatures of the Light, and we know It is perfect.' It's painted on buildings and carved into posts."

"What about Queen Gemma?"

"No idea. Not a whisper of her."

I pursed my lips. "I wish I knew more about her. I wish I knew why she was chosen to be Celeno's queen, especially if she's disagreeing with him now."

"Is it so far-fetched to think they might actually love each other?"

I pulled out another book on Alcoran history. "Yes. Celeno was born into far too powerful a role to have the freedom to marry someone he loved."

"Val managed it."

"He wouldn't have, if his father had had anything to say about it," I said. "Half the reason you were exiled was to keep you and Valien apart."

"But we still managed it," she said crossly. "Despite everything."

"Yes, and you must know your story is an anomaly. For most monarchs, romantic attraction is a luxury for commoners."

"I *am* a commoner. Ha! Little bugger." She spat the splinter out of her teeth into her palm.

"Which is probably why you never thought twice about it," I said, skimming Colm's notes in the text. "You were raised without the restrictions of politics."

"Ah, this is another mother thing, isn't it?" she said, wiping her hand on her breeches. "What was her mantra on this topic? 'Only go for the good-looking ones'?"

"No," I said, feeling my cheeks flush despite myself. "It was 'distance your heart from your head.' Every suitor, no matter how casual, must be regarded as a potential monarch. If they wouldn't make a good monarch, then I didn't have the luxury of pursuing that relationship. That was the standard I had to abide by."

"Great blazing Light," she said. "Your mother told you these things when you were a kid. You're a grown woman now, Mona. You're allowed to start straying from her advice just a little bit."

I kept my eyes on the page. "I tried that once. Guess what? It was a disaster."

In a swift move, she swung her feet over the edge of her bunk and sat up ramrod straight. "*Really?*"

I glanced sharply at her. "Really."

"What happened? Did you break his heart?"

"No."

"Her heart?"

"*No.*"

"Did he leave you for someone else?"

"No, Mae . . ."

"Did *she* leave you for someone else?"

"*No!*" I turned over a book page with a slap. "Great Light, let it be!"

She leaned back against the wall of her bunk. "Oh, I'm asking Colm when we get back."

"Don't bother. He won't tell you."

"Why?"

"Because he promised me he wouldn't tell anyone, ever."

"Oh, Mona," she sighed. "Everyone's had their share of romantic woes. It doesn't make you silly or emotional."

I snapped the book shut. "You're in the wrong universe, Mae. Here's a lesson on being a monarch: everything you do affects someone else. Sometimes everything you do affects your whole country."

Mae studied me, her head tilted. "What happened?"

"I told you, it was a disaster, and everyone involved will tell you exactly the same. Now leave it alone. Let's talk about something more practical." I straightened the stack of books on the table. "What are you going to wear when we meet with Celeno?"

She shrugged. "I hadn't really thought about it. My Guard uniform, I suppose."

"I don't think you should. I don't want to appear overly militant. Besides, you're a queen—you should look the part. What else did you bring? Tell me you brought something besides traveling tunics."

She glared at me. "In case you'd forgotten, we left the Silverwood in a bit of a hurry after a night of no sleep. I packed for battle, not tea and cookies."

"Rivers to the sea." I pushed back my chair and stood. "You'll have to borrow something of mine."

"Impossible."

"Why?"

"Three reasons." She pointed to her breasts. "One. Two." She slapped her hips. "Three. And you'd have to hem about a foot off the bottom."

I went to my trunk. "We'll make it work."

"Never."

"You doubt my sewing skills."

"I do. You're not a miracle worker. Just let me wear my uniform."

"I saw it when we met with Atria. The knees are filthy. Tell me, what color is the cleanest pair of breeches you brought?"

She sighed and propped her boots up on the end of her bunk. "Probably brown. Most of them are brown."

"Do you have gray?"

"No, I don't have gray. What does it matter?"

"Brown's a bad color for you. Muddies you."

She fanned herself in mock distress. "Oh, you cruel thing. To think I've gone this far in life not knowing . . ."

I pulled out the richest color I had brought, a midnight blue gown with a square neckline. "You should consider wearing reds, or pastels."

"*Pastels?*" She spit the word out as if it tasted bad.

"Something other than olive drab and brown."

"Maybe I'll just go naked, so Celeno's not offended," she said vehemently. "And don't slam green—it's the color of our banner."

"Then let it stay on the banner. Get up," I said, dragging a chair into the middle of the floor. "Let's get to work."

"I thought we were supposed to be talking about something practical?" she said.

"On the chair."

She moaned, she whined, she griped, she berated my frivolity as I tugged my gown over her head and shoulders. I finally got her to quiet down and stand up straight by suggesting that a pair of my heeled shoes might improve her posture. It was much easier to fit her without her slouching.

The dress was indeed a tight fit in the bust, but the fabric had some give to it. The long torso I could shorten, and she could hide the seam with a belt. I secured the fabric in place with straight pins and took out a pair of shears. As I brought them to the skirt, she broke her silence with a screech.

"Stop! What are you doing?"

I paused. "I'm shortening the skirt, of course."

"I thought you'd just tack it up! Don't cut it! You'll ruin it!"

"You can have the gown. I have others." I brought the shears to the fabric. She lashed out and grasped my wrist. I was surprised to see anger kindling in her eyes.

"Mona, this gown has a blue-zillion pearls on the neckline. The fabric probably traveled from the far side of Samna. This thing is worth more than my sister's entire wardrobe. You can't just cut it up."

I set the shears down. "I know you think me petty, but remember that Celeno hasn't received word that Valien has gotten married. If any of his soldiers were at the lake the day we sank their ships, they may recognize you. They'll remember you as a patched-together messenger."

"So?"

"So you have to look the part. This kind of thing is important in court. Stupid and extravagant, yes. Welcome to the throne."

"That's not the kind of queen I want to be."

"Trust me, Mae, you'll have the opportunity to rule your country with mud on your hands and knees, but that time is not now. Another lesson on being a monarch: *everything matters*, right down to what you're wearing."

She puckered up her mouth in a frown but let go of my wrist. She held still as I lifted the shears, but then she yelped again.

"Great Light, how high are you cutting it?"

"Up to your thighs."

"My *thighs*?"

"So you can wear it over your breeches. I'm making it into a formal tunic."

"Why? I thought you wanted me in a gown."

"I want you to look like the queen of the Silverwood." I made the first snip in the fabric. "I want to show off your boots."

She held still as I made my way around the skirt. "I see."

"I'm not a *complete* monster," I said as the fabric fell away.

"Liar," she whispered.

We sailed into the outermost docks of Lilou just as the sun was setting on the fifth day. I came above deck and was hit with the first waft of marshy air.

"You look splendid, my queen," Cavan said.

"Thank you." I loved this particular gown, blue-gray with mother-of-pearl clasps and sleeves that fell away gracefully at the elbows. It seemed like the right balance between elegant and severe. I just hated that I had to wear it on *this* occasion.

I approached the rail. "How soon?"

"Just a few minutes, my queen."

Out of the corner of my eye, I saw Mae ascend the staircase.

"Well, look at you," I said, turning to face her. The

midnight blue gown had transformed marvelously into a formal tunic. She had insisted on belting it with her tooled leather belt rather than one of my lengths of pearls, but with her fringed boots, it looked distinctive rather than out of place.

"I admit I doubted you," she said, smoothing the skirt over her breeches. "How is it you're so good at tailoring? I'd have thought you'd always had someone to do it for you."

"Not for three years," I said. "I was always good at needlework—nice tangible task, where attention to detail is visibly rewarded—but when we were exiled, it became a necessity, not just an art. I was constantly piecing together scavenged clothes for the three of us. Especially for Arlen—he was always blowing out his knees and elbows. And you know me—do you think I'd let myself be seen in an ill-fitting tunic, even in exile?"

"Never." She held up a handful of pins. "Do my hair?"

I smoothed her dark hair, winding it around the silver circlet running across her brow. As I pinned her curls up at the back of her head, we rounded the bend of the channel leading into the city of Lilou. I glanced past the bow to the skyline.

At the sight, my hand slipped on a pin and I stabbed Mae's scalp.

"Ow! Watch it!"

"What in the world . . ."

The whole city was on fire, glowing red against

the darkening sky. Embers swirled into the night as far as the eye could see. The water flickered orange. Smoke clung to the breeze.

"Oh!" Mae exclaimed. "First Fire! I've heard of it, but I've never seen it. Their autumn festival—they douse all their fires, sweep out their hearths, and re-kindle them with new fire."

"What for?" I asked, riveted by the spectacle before us. "It's not as if fire goes stale."

"It's *symbolic*, of course, Mona. It's all about start-ing fresh, letting go of things in the past." She watched a firework burst over the water. "They celebrate for a whole week. It's where they see the Light, you know. Fire."

I looked harder. So the city wasn't burning down. But it was an easy mistake to make, given the glow pouring from every street, every dock. As we grew closer, the music reached us—pulsing drums and wild fiddles, coupled with shouts and snatches of song. We glided through the channel, staring at the scenes on either side of our ship. The docks were packed with River-folk, weaving from one astounding display to the next. Braziers burned every few feet, some spit-ting colored sparks and smoke. Two jugglers threw flaming batons over the heads of delighted bystanders. Folk cheered a man walking barefoot across a bed of live coals. A woman danced with two torches, holding them to her lips and spouting a cloud of fire into the air. Children twirled flaming hoops around their hips and arms, shrieking with laughter.

Mae shook her head. "Incredible."

"Terrifying," I said. "How do they keep from burning the place down?"

"Luck?"

The colors were overwhelming, jewel-bright purple, emerald, crimson, and gold. Many folk wore masks over their eyes, painted gold and rimmed with sequins to reflect the endless firelight. Women wore bold gowns dripping with fringe and tassels, while men wore colored sashes around their waists, many with loose tails that must surely be fire hazards—but with so much flame, it was impossible to determine what *wasn't* a hazard. I swiveled my head this way and that, staring at the light and color and movement, sure at some point someone was going to catch fire and plunge into the glowing water. But no one did. Either they were skilled enough to avoid injury, or they were so caught up in the revelry that they were immune to the danger all around them. That said, I did see a few folk look away from the festivities to watch our ship sail past, eyeing the banner of Lumen Lake fluttering on the mainmast.

What was going through their minds as they saw my banner? My country and theirs had been allies once, but now everything was marred and muddled by Alcoro. Did the River-folk regard my country in the same light as the Canyon-folk? Or was there something else at work? I craned my head to watch a man spinning a flaming staff under a row of Alcoran flags. I hadn't considered the country might be reveling during our visit. Would Mae and I be able to discern *anything* about Cypri loyalty while we were here?

We sailed into a stretch of docks that were relatively quieter and darker than the rest of the city. A cluster of folk huddled around a single lantern shielded with red-tinted glass and flickering on their plain charcoal tunics and russet sashes. Alcorans. They hailed our ship, gesturing for us to berth where they gathered.

I took a breath, trying to shove the whirlwind of activity from my mind. Now began the negotiations. I gazed at the Alcorans with narrowed eyes as they caught the lines Cavan's deckhands tossed down to them, securing us to the dock.

"Ah," Mae said. "I just realized."

"What?"

"I'm nervous."

I smiled grimly. "Me, too. Don't let it show, understood? Stay in control."

"I'll try."

"And remember what I said."

"Which part?"

"Everything."

The gangplank was fed down to the dock, and a small number of our armed folk descended to the Alcorans at the bottom. Mae and I stood at the rail of the ship, surveying the group. Many of the men bore waxed mustaches, and the women all wore similar jeweled bands in their hair, which must denote some kind of rank. The torchlight glinted off their shiny black boots and turquoise rings. From what we could see, they were unarmed.

Atria Coacotzli stood at the forefront, and our handful of folk spoke to her. She nodded in assent, but before she could move toward the gangplank, another request was made of her. I saw the Alcorans shift a bit, perhaps offended, but Atria quietly held her arms out to her sides. Our folk ran their hands along her wrists, up to her shoulders, down her waist and thighs. They prodded her stiff boots. When they were assured she had no hidden weapons on her person, they flanked her and led her up the gangplank.

If she was miffed at her brusque treatment, she didn't show it. As much as I resented it, I felt a grudging respect—at least for her diplomatic skill— growing for Atria. When she stepped onto our deck, her face was arranged with the same formal mildness as before. She bowed deeply.

"Queen Mona Alastaire of Lumen Lake and the Twelve Islands," she said. "And Queen Ellamae Heart-wood of the Silverwood Mountains." So she had scavenged information on Mae. That must mean Celeno knew as well. "Welcome to Lilou."

"Thank you, Ambassador Coacotzli," I said, inclining my head. Mae gave the barest flash of her palm.

"If you're ready, we will take you to King Celeno's ship," she said.

"No," I said. "Queen Ellamae and I will receive him here, on the *Spindrift*."

Once more I had to give Atria credit—she was a well-trained diplomat and a quick thinker. She didn't raise her eyebrows or balk at this unexpected and significant command. She offered another slight bow. "Lady Queen, my king and queen have arranged a formal reception for you on their ship, with refreshments and samples of our finest coffee. There will be no armed folk on board, save his two personal guards."

"We appreciate the gesture," I said. "But we will not meet him on his ship."

"You may have your soldiers make a brief search of the deck and hold, if it would ease any concern."

"It would not," I said. "We will *not* meet him on his ship. We have already sailed into Alcoran territory. If he is truly interested in diplomacy, he will meet us on our ship."

She glanced at the deck of the *Spindrift*, where my folk had quickly set up a plain table and four chairs. The Lumeni and Silvern banners flanked the affair, the only semblance of adornment. "My king has two others with him," she said. "To help with negotiations."

"We have more chairs," I said.

"Lady Queen, I must entreat you. There is no threat to you here." Back was that odd flicker of genuine concern I'd seen briefly in the boathouse—I still couldn't decide if it was a calculated slip or an unintentional one. "My king means you no harm."

"And I mean him none," I said. "But when I say no, Ambassador, it means no."

"He will not be pleased," she said. "This was not what he envisioned."

I settled into silence.

Silence is a powerful tool, one my mother had drilled in me—we had once gone close to an hour, standing just a few feet from each other, staring each other in the eye until a servant had unwittingly interrupted the exercise. After her death, I'd used it to draw folk out, holding their gaze until they shifted and looked away or jumped to fill the void with words—often conceding vital information. *Words are power*, my mother used to say. *But silence is control.*

Yes, Atria was good. I wouldn't mind having an ambassador as cool as she. She didn't let her tongue tie itself in knots to break the silence. I glimpsed Mae's gaze sliding away before hers did. The distant sounds of the River-folk's revelry drifted around us. Somewhere close by, a fiddler played a slightly eerie melody. Atria remained still, and calm. It could have been the start of a very long standoff.

But ultimately, she sighed, nodding a curt acquiescence. "I will speak to my king. I shall bring you back his message."

"No," I said. "Bring me back *him.*"

She bowed once more to each of us and headed down the gangplank to her folk. They clustered around her. A few cast dark looks at the rail. But the ambassador led them away without any delay.

Mae let out a breath. "Well. A little warning would have been helpful. That was uncomfortable."

"Successful, though." I began to turn away from the dock, to give the command for two more chairs, but the words paused on my lips. I stopped, looking across the stretch of water to the next dock over. A small crowd had gathered, sparse enough to see through. It was there that the fiddler was playing that eerie melody, full of minor runs and dissonant chords. And accompanying the music, set apart from the rest of the burning festivity, was easily the most extraordinary display I had seen yet.

A young man was gracefully stepping this way and that, spinning a pair of slender chains that ended in twin flames. They left glowing streaks in the night, circling him in wheels of fire. He twirled them in impossible patterns around his body, arcing them over his head and illuminating his mop of curly hair. I'd seen street performers and dancers during my wanderings, and even some who performed with fire, but I'd never seen anything quite so arresting as this. The man's movements were both energetic and fluid, almost hypnotic—my tense grip loosened on the ship rail. For the barest moment, my mind eased, filled only with the fiery patterns slicing through the darkness. We were too far away, and the spinner was moving too quickly, for me to get a good look at his face. But for the span of just a few seconds, he stood still, his stance wide on the dock, facing the ship. Through the whirling pattern of fire, he looked at me across the water. A second later, however, I was sure it must have been a trick of the flames flying about his head. He twisted them in the air and turned his back to me.

"So . . . chairs, right?"

I turned around, blinking. "What?"

Mae gestured to the austere table. "We need two more chairs, right?"

"Yes. Chairs. Yes." I shook my head to clear it and called to Cavan. "Please have one of the hands bring up two more chairs."

"Wish Cockaleekie—or whatever her name is—had told us Celeno was bringing advisors," Mae said. "I wouldn't mind having our councilor of trade here with us. I'm good with silver production and tradable goods, but I'm still learning the finer details of allotment and shipment tax and such."

"Leave it to me." I looked sideways at her. "And if you can't remember her name, just call her 'Ambassador.'"

"Cockaleekie is a delightful soup; she should be honored . . ."

"'Ambassador.'"

"Great Light," she said. "You're *no* fun when you're full-tilt diplomat."

Ambassador Coacotzli was gone almost twenty minutes. Mae stood at the hull, watching the city burn in its revelry, but I sat at the table so I couldn't see that fire spinner. I could hear the fiddle music, so the man must have still been performing, but I forced myself to concentrate, trying not to picture glowing circles wheeling through the air. Instead, I pictured my mother, gazing down from the mantelpiece. It was enough to sharpen my focus. I stared into space, running over everything Mae and I had discussed on our journey, turning over each minute point of interest and examining it fully. I was beginning the process a second time when Mae said, "They're coming."

"All of them?"

"All of them. That one in the middle must be the king, and the queen beside him. Hard to tell, though—all their lanterns are red. Red glass." She coughed. "Bit ominous."

"They tint all their lights red," I said. "It comes from their star-gazing heritage. Keeps them from ruining their night vision."

"How can you possibly know that?"

"Colm found out after reading all the literature they left behind in Lumen."

"He would. But maybe he got it wrong. Maybe they're just trying to mimic the way a forest fire looks before it burns your house down."

"Don't say that in front of them, all right? Don't let them think you're intimidated." I beckoned. "Come back here with me, so they can't see you staring from the hull."

When Atria ascended the gangplank once more, she found us standing resolutely next to the table. If Celeno had given her grief about my stipulations, she didn't let it show.

"My king and queen regret your refusal to accept

their hospitality, but they acquiesce to your request," she said, bowing slightly. "They have several requirements before they board. Our soldiers shall make a sweep of the ship. As before, the only armed presence on the ship will be two personal guards, and weapons shall be sheathed and unloaded—unstrung," she continued, correcting her slip, as only Alcorans used newfangled crossbows—heavy, tedious things to load, crank, and shoot. But as usual, the Canyon-folk had forgotten the antiquated, puny weapon my folk had quietly revived during their slavery. An atlatl didn't need to be cranked or strung and would fire a dart before they could fumble a quarrel into place.

Perhaps she took my slight smile as a sign of agreement, because she pressed on with a bit more ease. "As for the rest of our soldiers, they shall take up position with the same access to the ship as your retinue."

"How many in yours?" I asked.

"Thirty, Lady Queen."

"Send half back to your ship," I said, "and we have an accord."

Things unfolded as I ordered. The two Alcoran guards made a quick but thorough sweep of the deck and hold, accompanied by two of our spearmen. Down on the docks, I heard both their folk and ours organizing themselves into factions on the dock. Over their noise, the fiddler was still playing. I tried to ignore it.

When all was satisfactory, the guards took up position on either side of the table. Our two guards, the best marksman and markswoman in our contingent, stood opposite, their hands clasped behind their backs, where each gripped an atlatl to accompany the darts at their belts. The Alcorans let their unloaded crossbows rest across their waists, but I was sure they had knives within easy access. I would be a fool to think they'd not have some means at their disposal, just as my guards did.

Ambassador Coacotzli disappeared back down the gangplank. Mae and I took our places by the table again, our banners lolling in the marshy breeze. Bootsteps thumped up the gangplank. Heads appeared over the rail, and finally the king stepped onto our lantern-lit deck.

My first impression was that the man looked astonishingly average. Skin neither light nor dark. Hair an unremarkable brown, combed backward in thick waves. Eyes of a medium, indeterminate shade. No crisp, waxed mustache. In fact, all his colors melted together, with nothing striking standing out. That is, unless one counted his garb. He seemed to be compensating for his lackluster image with his apparel—a black bolero heavily embroidered in crimson and gold over a matching waistcoat and sash. Stretching from shoulder to shoulder was a chain of deep turquoise stones, at the center of which hung a faceted white gem. A matching gem was set into his crown, surrounded, I noticed resentfully, with seven iridescent pearls.

Our pearls.

The rest of his party had filed on after him while I looked him over. Atria moved to their forefront and bowed low before her king. She was going to introduce us first, as if we were his guests rather than the other way around. I didn't let my irritation show.

"I present to you Queen Mona Alastaire of Lumen Lake and the Twelve Islands, and Queen Ellamae Heartwood of the Silverwood Mountains." Atria straightened and turned to us. "Lady Queens, may I present King Celeno and Queen Gemma Tezozomoc of Alcoro."

My gaze slid to the queen then, standing at her husband's shoulder. She had a pretty face, youthful and soft, with a similar complexion to the king's, though her hair was a darker brown. Her rich russet gown and jeweled crown would have appeared elegant if not for the rather fussy lace shift that ran from her wrists up to her chin, so that only her hands and face were bare. It seemed oddly out of place under that graceful ensemble, but perhaps it was the style of the canyons.

"Welcome to Cyprien, Lady Queens," Celeno said. His voice was overloud, as if this, too, was meant to bolster his nondescript features.

"Welcome to the flagship *Spindrift*," I replied, unwilling to let him claim host dominance.

"I trust you had a pleasant journey?" he asked.

Better than last time, I wanted to say. *No deaths to*

mourn. No weeks of starvation and cold. "Yes, thank you."

"May I congratulate you, Queen Ellamae, on your recent marriage," he continued. "My well-wishes to you and King Valien."

I heard her swallow a snort of incredulity. Even if he didn't know that he had fully disrupted their celebrations, he had nerve. She curled her lip ever so slightly. "Thank you." She did not offer him her palm-up gesture of gratitude. I tightened my lips. I was glad he had given her something to get fired up about, but I hoped he wouldn't push her past the threshold of civilized discourse. I didn't want this to end with the Seventh King nursing a black eye.

To the side of the king and queen stood the two additional advisors. One was a portly man, who shifted from foot to foot, clearly impatient to be introduced. The other was a tall, thin woman in an immaculate black overdress and russet bolero, with the same jeweled headband as the other canyonwomen on the dock. I might have admired her sense of decorum and poise if she hadn't been watching me with a shrewd, slightly disconcerting stare.

Ambassador Coacotzli gestured to the man. "We're joined by Algon Catzomoc, the governor of Cyprien."

His waxed mustache quivered with importance. "Pleased to make your acquaintances, Lady Queens."

Governor, indeed. I wondered what form of execution had been chosen for the Assembly of Six when

Alcoro had taken Cyprien for its own. "Likewise," I said stiffly.

"And Most Reverend Shaula Otzacamos, Prelate of the Prophecy of the Prism," the ambassador said with a slight bow.

I honestly didn't know how to respond. He had brought his religious advisor with him? For what possible purpose, other than to remind me just how baseless his country's governance really was? I nodded curtly to her stoic half-courtesy.

Celeno's eyes swept the stark table and chairs, backed by the two banners. "It is not too late, Lady Queens, to adjourn to our flagship. We prepared an excellent reception for you, with one of our finest drone flautists and a selection of coffees of exceptional quality."

"No, thank you," I said. "Coffee is too bitter for my taste. Besides, Queen Ellamae and I did not travel this distance to be entertained. We wish to discuss our business so we can return back to our respective countries."

Celeno opened his mouth as if to press his point, but beside him, Queen Gemma inclined her head slightly. "Thank you. We shall."

Cut off, Celeno shut his mouth and instead flicked his hand at Ambassador Coacotzli, who bowed to us all and retreated down the gangplank. Without looking at Gemma, he moved toward the table. Someone else was looking at the queen, however—the Prelate,

Shaula. Her eyes narrowed just slightly as Gemma followed Celeno to the table.

Interesting.

Mae and I sat across the table from the four Alcorans. Gemma sank down on the king's right, and the Prelate settled on his left. The governor scooted his chair close to hers, as if determined to remain relevant to the conversation.

"Queen Mona," Celeno began, his voice still a shade too loud. "I commend you on constructing an alliance with the Silverwood monarchy, who until recently have sided with no one. The tradeways through the mountains will be a boon to the economy of the eastern coast."

I didn't say anything. He may begin by dancing around the subject, but I was not going to let him keep it up for very long. Distantly I heard the fiddler finish the tune, followed by a smattering of applause.

"I regret the collapse of our trade partnership," he continued. His face was tense. Despite his youth, he already had furrows creased permanently into his forehead. "I regret the losses it has brought to both of our countries."

Quietly, steadily, I held up my hand. "King Celeno," I said. "I ask that you do me the courtesy of speaking directly. Please do not pretend that the events of the past four years were unhappy coincidences or mere interruptions to our trade schedules. You usurped my country and murdered many of my folk—folk innocent of any crime against you. Folk with husbands and wives and children. You must know what I think of you and your beliefs. If you are indeed interested in discussing renewed partnership, I recommend you do not gloss over these things as if they were accidents. If you continue speaking this way, Queen Ellamae and I will excuse ourselves, and there will be no amity between our nations for the rest of my reign. Do you understand?"

The effect on the Alcorans was subtle but marvelous. Celeno kept his face stony, though a flush crept up from his embroidered collar. Gemma's eyes dropped to the tabletop. The governor's hand jumped to his mustache, smoothing the waxed hairs with vigor. My mother would have been proud of me. Only the Prelate remained impassive, gazing coolly at me.

The king shifted, resting his gloved hands stiffly before him. "Very well." His voice lost the formal volume, and it sounded harsher for it. "Very well, then, Lady Queen. We shall jump right in, if that's what you wish."

If that's what you wish. As if my wishes had anything to do with why we were here right now. I wished to hear him plead his remorse and admit to being wildly unfit to bear a crown. But that would get us nowhere. I folded my hands in a mirror of his own. "Tell me what agreement you had in mind."

He coughed slightly. "My ministers of trade have suggested beginning small, with monthly shipments of basic textiles, rice, sugarcane, and salt in return for fifteen cases of matched pearls and five cases of mother-of-pearl."

"We can do without the rice and sugarcane," I said. "I will take bimonthly shipments of Samnese textiles, along with twenty pounds of salt and fifty steel billets. For this I will offer six cases of pearls matched in either color or size, but not both."

He lifted an eyebrow at my absurdly low price. "Samnese textiles require careful packaging and a week-long passage over the sea. I will not accept less than ten cases for that alone, and the pearls must be fully matched."

"Matching is a tedious process. Six is my offer for the textiles. I will compensate the salt and steel with two cases of mother-of-pearl."

"Six will get you eight bolts of fabric and no more."

"I want at least fifteen bolts. They don't have to be dyed."

The Prelate leaned over and whispered something in Celeno's ear. I narrowed my eyes. This woman was not a councilor of trade—she had little place advising the king on negotiations. As I reassessed her role in these negotiations, I noticed Queen Gemma was still staring fixedly at the tabletop, her shoulders tense.

"I will accept six cases of pearls for a maximum of twelve bolts of Samnese textiles provided they are matched in color and size," Celeno said, straightening. "With this, I request ten pounds of silver bullion."

"For twelve bolts of cloth?" Mae asked, raising her eyebrows.

"For the cloth and salt and steel."

"Perhaps you misunderstand me," I said severely. His gaze jumped back to mine. I let several long beats of silence pass—*silence is control*—just to make him feel the weight of my next words. A muscle in his jaw clenched at the unexpected pause.

"I do not intend to pay you fairly for these goods," I continued. "Your advisors have suggested starting small. I must agree with them. You shattered the trust between our nations, and it's going to take much more than five months of silence to undo that damage. If you're seeking trade in order to fatten your treasuries, I'm afraid you will be disappointed. Consider how many shipments of our pearls you've already taken without giving anything in return but subjugation? No, Lumen Lake will not be the conduit that forces your prophecy to come true. I will trade with you only if you intend to rebuild our alliance— slowly, incrementally."

His bland brown eyes blazed. "You forget your position, Queen Mona," he said sharply. "I certainly do expect fair payment. I am extending my hand in alliance to negate the need for violence. Peaceful trade is a privilege for your folk, not mine. Or shall I send word that you have requested my warships to revisit your lake? What will your folk do then?"

"So already you threaten me, just minutes after sitting down," I said coolly.

Before Celeno could speak, Gemma shifted slightly, her arm moving under the table as she placed her hand on the king's knee. His eyes still burned, but he sat back, his fists clenched on the tabletop. I focused my attention on her, and before Celeno could respond to my last comment, I said, "Tell me, Queen Gemma. Your ambassador said this meeting was your idea. Was she telling me the truth?"

Her eyes rose from the table to me, and for the first time, I could make out their color. They were a deep blue, but her irises were surrounded by a ring of gold. It was a striking combination, and framed by her long lashes, they gave her otherwise youthful face an air of grandeur. This was offset, however, by her quiet response.

"Yes."

"Yes, this all was your idea? Then tell me—what are your thoughts? Why are you seeking trade with my country? Why are you prodding your husband toward peace, when Alcoran monarchs have been invading other countries for fifty years?"

Celeno ground his teeth, but he had the decency to let his wife respond for herself. Next to the king, the Prelate stared down the table at the queen without turning her head. I couldn't tell if Gemma felt her sidelong look or not, but if she did, she ignored it. She rearranged her hands in her lap and said simply, "I don't want any more bloodshed."

"No?" I studied her with open skepticism. She returned my gaze impassively, her face showing neither anger nor fear. Only the tense line of her shoulders gave any indication that she was not perfectly at ease. "No more bloodshed? What a kind, selfless queen you are. Strange that this should start now, when I suddenly have a well-armed ally, rather than four years ago, when all I had was a handful of spearmen. Tell me, whose blood are you concerned about?"

She regarded me—not with hostility, but with something very close to sadness in her eyes. But Celeno overrode her before she could respond.

"Enough," he snapped. "You will not bully my wife. It was her suggestion to meet with you, but I was the one to make it happen. I am offering you trade because you will need it in the coming winter, and because under the Prophecy of the Prism, I have a right to share in your wealth. Do not think I will roll over and allow you to swindle me."

I snapped, my thin scaffold of propriety collapsing under my fury. "*Swindle* you? You wretched fool. How dare you say such a thing to me? Your country is built on a mountain of lies, and yet you hold them high as if they're something to be proud of. There is no Prism. There is no Prophecy. There is no Light. You are acting out of greed and disillusionment, and it has corrupted you inside and out. You are a murderer, Celeno, unworthy to call yourself a king . . ."

His face contorted. "You have little place to call me a murderer, when you yourself orchestrated the deaths of a hundred of my folk the very day you returned to the lake. Have you thought of that, in your self-righteousness? By your own standards, you're no better than I."

I stood up, blazing with anger, scraping my chair on the deck and rocking the table. Mae's hand jumped to my arm. I tugged at her grip, thinking she was trying to restrain me, but then I saw her creased brow.

"Something's wrong," she said.

"Wha—"

The gangplank burst into flames.

Gemma screamed. We all collectively threw ourselves away from the hull, shielding our faces with our hands. The flames shot into the night sky, white, roaring, brighter than any fire I'd ever seen. Shouts rose from the dock below. I heard the clang of metal on metal. Darts materialized in our guards' atlatls. But before anyone had a chance to act, a sharp crack cut through the air, and my vision went white. I stumbled, clapping my hand to my eyes. They burned, tearing up amid a storm of flashing spots.

"Mae!" I shouted. I lowered my hand, blinking furiously. My sight was a blurred mess of light and dark. "Mae!"

"Here!" A hand collided with the side of my head and then jumped to my arm.

"Can you see?"

"Not a thing! Come on, to the water!"

I gripped her sleeve as we ran blindly toward the starboard hull, away from the waves of heat rolling off the gangplank. I rubbed my eyes and wiped at the tears seeping down my cheeks. I heard the clatter of chairs hitting the deck, the clang of a metal pole as one of our banners toppled over. The world slowly melted back into focus, but the shouting and smoke continued to disorient me. We reached the hull just as a sail caught fire above us.

Mae threw her leg over the rail. Before I could join her, though, fire erupted between us in another blinding flash. I staggered backward, tripping on the hem of my gown and crashing down to my side. Pain streaked up my right arm. My nose filled with the scent of burning hair. I cried out, rolling away from the burning planks, trying to smother the flames that were clinging to my clothes. Smoke billowed through the air. I clambered to my hands and knees, coughing forcefully, my right arm scorched and bleeding. My vision was gone again—I drove the heels of my hands into my tearing eyes.

"Mae!"

There was no answer. I groped for the hull, trying desperately to ignore the pain searing across my arm. As my sight returned, I looked up to the rail, and my heart caught in my throat—Mae was gone. I hauled myself over the edge and looked down at the rippling water. A figure thrashed under the surface.

Mae, sinking into the depths.

"No!" I clawed over the hull, my arm screaming in protest, but at that moment, a pair of hands wound around me and pulled me back onto the ship.

"No!" I was hysterical now. I writhed, kicking my feet, scrabbling with my hands to find something to grab. My fingers closed on something curved, something hard, something with a protrusion and two holes—a mask. I yanked, and the figure holding me staggered. But the next moment, he clapped a wet sponge to my face. I gasped, gagged, and the burning world fell away, suddenly and absolutely, into profound emptiness.

CHAPTER 5

The *Spindrift*.

I was on the *Spindrift*.

Had I overslept?

Were we in Lilou yet?

Why hadn't Mae woken me?

I furrowed my brow. Mae.

Mae.

I shifted, and pain shot through my arm. Tears sprung to my eyes.

I was lying on my left side on wooden planks. A rough blanket was draped over my shoulder. Lying a few inches away from my face was a sponge, similar to the ones my brothers and I used to dive for on the coast during our wanderings. It was wrapped in a bit of twine. As I stared at it, a tendril of scent reached my nose, and comprehension hit me—the thing had been bound to my face. It had plunged me into sleep.

I jerked backward, away from it, but my back was already pressed against a wooden slat hull. The floor rocked gently beneath me. The only sound was the quiet brush of water. So I was on a boat after all, but it was not the *Spindrift*.

No, because the *Spindrift* had been set on fire.

I craned my head, trying to determine my surroundings. The darkness was thick—there was no flicker of torchlight or glimmer of moonlight. But I thought I could make out the far hull, just a few feet from me. A small boat, then. I twitched my wrists. They weren't bound. I flicked my head, trying to wipe away my disorientation. Out of the corner of my eye, someone shifted in the bow. Someone standing up, shadowed in the dark.

Someone who had set my ship on fire and left Mae to drown.

With one tremendous push, I lurched to my hands and knees, rocking the boat. The figure in the bow jerked in surprise, but before he could move, I flung myself backward against the hull, rolled over the lip, and dropped into the water below.

The water was disgusting, ripe with rot and slimy with growth. I swept my hands out in front of me and drove immediately into a tangle of roots. My burned arm scraped against the slick bark, sending spikes of pain through my shoulder. Some slippery bulbous thing slid against my mouth and cheek. Nauseated, I fought down the instinct to thrash. I placed my hands on the soggy bark and pushed backward, shuddering in the press of weeds. But I was snagged, caught by my hair and elbows and ruined gown. My arm throbbed. My stomach churned from the noxious sponge that had been pressed to my nose. I twisted, trying to slide free.

A hand closed around my ankle and my panic flared. I kicked, slipping from the hold of the roots and driving into soft, rotten muck. But the hand didn't let go. With a great heave, my captor pulled me back toward the boat. I bent my elbows, preparing to drive one into my captor's face, but as he lifted me bodily from the water, he closed his grip on my right arm. I gasped at the pain, and in my sudden debilitation, a second pair of hands wound under my armpits. I was hauled back onto the boat.

I hit the wooden boards and rolled, trying to shake off the hands holding me down.

"Take your hands off me!" I snarled.

"*Torchfire*. Get that sponge back in place, before we're heard!"

"Don't you dare!" I twisted against my captors' grips. "Take your hands off me at once!"

A figure straddled me, holding me down.

"I'm sorry, lolly," said a quiet voice.

That smell hit me once more. "No—"

Nothing.

I woke with the same disorientation as before. My stomach churned with nausea, and my head was groggy and aching. I was lying on my left side again. Dappled light pressed against my eyelids. I smelled rot, and burnt hair, and honey.

Honey?

Someone was holding my burned arm. Someone was spreading something thick and sticky over my skin.

Someone was putting honey on my skin.

My eyes flew open. A figure was bent over me, his face less than a foot from mine. I lurched away, wrenching my arm from his grasp. He uttered some exclamation, grappling with the open honey pot clutched between his knees. I scrabbled backward into a canvas wall, my legs tangled in a mess of sheets. Pain raced up my arm, but I braced myself against the plank floor and staggered to my feet.

I had to bend at the knees and tilt my head—I was in some kind of low tent, the thick canvas stretched over a pitched frame. A faded curtain was strung up the middle of the space as a partition. Morning light shone through the loose tent flap. But sitting between me and the flap was a man, trying to stem the flow of honey dripping over his hand.

A man with nut-brown skin and a thatch of coarse, curly hair.

"You," I blurted.

It was the fire spinner I had seen from across the dock. He stoppered the pot of honey, awkwardly, because his hand was still sticky.

"Morning, lolly," he said. "Let me finish dressing that burn for you."

I took a tiny step toward him, cupped my palm, and slapped him across the ear as hard as I could. He sprawled sideways across the wooden floor.

"*Torchfire . . .*"

I darted past him in the cramped space, wrenched the tent flap aside, and sprinted out into the sun. A quick, disoriented glance told me I was on a porch in the middle of a forest. A figure crouching on the planks scrambled to his feet at my appearance, but I raced past him before he could stop me. Still foggy, still confused, I skidded to a halt at the edge of the porch.

Where there should have been solid ground was sluggish, rust-colored water. Trees marched away from us on all sides, their sweeping trunks rising out of the water. Beards of ghostly, grayish moss trailed from every branch. A fish drifted lazily out from underneath the wooden boards at my feet.

Not a porch. I was on a boat. A tent on a boat. In a forest of water.

An arm crossed over my chest and jerked me back from the edge. I twisted against the hold, but he adjusted his grip on me, winding his arms up under my armpits.

The curly-haired man emerged from the tent clutching his ear. "Easy, Lyle! Don't break her skin!"

My captor gave me a little shake. "Don't you go

bolting over the edge, you hear me? There's gators in these waters bigger than you are and snakes that'll kill you with one bite. Understand?"

I had no breath to spare for a reply, so agonizing was the pain radiating through my arm. When it became clear I wasn't going to respond, he released me and moved toward the bow of the boat to bar any escape in that direction.

For a moment, it seemed my head was groggier than I previously thought. I was seeing double, flanked on both sides by the same angular, nut-brown face. I gave a flick of my head, blinking, before realizing they were twins. But where the man standing by the tent had his mop of dark corkscrews, the one standing in the bow was bald as an egg, shorn smooth.

I stared between the two of them. Honey dripped down my wrist.

"Who are you?" I finally asked. "Where am I? What in the name of the Light have you done?"

"You're on the *Swamp Rabbit*," said the curly-haired twin. "In the bayou of the Lower Draws."

I glanced at the landscape sliding by. The bayou. I had heard of this place, the maze of water and swampland that made up a large portion of Cyprien. It was not welcome news. I clenched and unclenched my hands. "Where are you taking me?"

"Toadhollow, for the moment. Not the most sophisticated town in Cyprien, but it's off the main channel, so we should be safe there."

"*Safe?*"

The curly-haired man gestured to my arm. "Please, lolly. Let me bind your arm before you drip honey everywhere."

I was indeed dripping honey onto the deck, but I didn't care. To my right, the shorn brother—Lyle—picked up a pole. He leaned it over the side of the boat and nudged us away from a tangle of weeds.

"Who are you?" I asked them. "What do you want with me?"

"You ask too many questions at once," said Lyle, setting the pole back down. "Pick the one you want answered."

I gritted my teeth. "Who are you?"

"I'm Rou," said the curly-haired twin. "That's Lyle. We're . . . what would you call us, Lyle? Emissaries? Ambassadors?"

"You're assassins," I spat at them. "Do you have any idea what you did last night? You murdered the queen of the Silverwood." My throat closed on these words, their reality sinking in. "You killed her, and her husband is going to string you up like butchered hogs, if I don't get to it first."

"She's not dead," said the curly-haired twin. "She swam to a skiff."

"You're lying," I said fiercely. "She can't swim."

"Dark-headed, fancy tunic? Wearing half a deer on her feet?" He swatted at a wasp that buzzed around his sticky hand. "She swam to a skiff—not well, mind you, a lot of splashing and coughing. But she made it. Some folk inside pulled her in."

"Who?" I asked. "Who pulled her in?"

"I don't know. I was focused on getting away before another sail caught fire."

I glared at him, desperately wanting to believe him but unwilling to do so. "What about my guards? The folk who came with us, who were on the dock with the Alcorans? What did you do to them?"

"Nothing. We didn't need to. Nobody was on the gangplank when it lit, and the flash grenades took care of everything else. We didn't want to hurt anyone. We were only coming for you."

"Why?" I asked. "What do you want with me?"

He tugged on his ear. I hoped it was ringing like a bell. "Me, personally? I want to dress your arm so you don't attract yellow jackets."

I looked down at my arm. The skin from my wrist to my shoulder was raw and blistered. My long, graceful sleeve had been cut away at the seam.

I brought my gaze back up to the curly-haired twin. What had he called himself? Rou.

"What do you want with me after that?" I asked.

"Your help," he said.

"My help with what?"

"Liberating Cyprien from Alcoran control," he said.

My eyebrows snapped down. "You drugged me, abducted me, and are holding me captive on a tiny boat in the middle of the swamp. Why on earth would I feel compelled to help you?"

"Cypri independence benefits your country as

well as ours," Rou said. "And besides, we have something that might interest you."

"What is that?"

He pulled the tent flap aside and gestured to the other side of the partition hanging from the ceiling. I hesitated, and then joined him, looking down at the floor.

On a mat, unconscious and bound at the wrists, was Queen Gemma.

"Great Light," I said, gripping the tent pole. "What have you *done*?"

* * *

Official greetings to Queen Mona Alastaire of Lumen Lake and the Twelve Islands.

We must begin by offering our sincerest apologies. We regret the uncouth manner employed to procure your assistance, but time is short, and our previous efforts to contact you have failed. We place our strict trust in the Roubideaux brothers to see that your utmost comfort and well-being is assured for the remainder of your journey.

After fifty-six years under Alcoran control, the country of Cyprien has come to a long-awaited crossroad. In light of the admirable liberation of Lumen Lake, King Celeno Tezozomoc's hold on our country is weakened and vulnerable. The time has come to put our careful plans into action. As you will have learned by now, these involve leveraging the release of Queen

Gemma Tezozomoc to her husband, King Celeno, in return for the full liberation of the Cypri people.

We need not detail to you the impact this independence promises not only for Cyprien, but for Lumen Lake as well. Most significantly, upon reclaiming our waterways from Celeno, we will act as the first line of defense for you and your folk. There shall be no more bloodshed in Lumen for Alcoro's gain once the waterways are back under the Cypri banner. Additionally, it is our hope that together we may draft a trade agreement that will prove profitable to your country as well as ours.

With a show of your support, the stand against the brutality of Celeno becomes formidable. Our request of you is this: assist the Assembly in drafting an agreement joining our countries in alliance. Then, if you are so inclined, stand with us against Celeno during negotiations.

We regret that we cannot offer you the immediate opportunity to refuse our request. With Celeno alerted to our true loyalties, much of the bayou will now be impassable. There is a network of loyal folk on a pre-planned route who will assist you in your journey. Deviation from this path may prove disastrous for you and for our mission. Necessarily, we must respectfully insist that you accompany our emissaries to Siere. If, at that point, you find our request unreasonable, you may stay as our guest until the waterways are safe from Alcoran retaliation, at which point you will be escorted in safety to your country.

Do not hesitate to make any request of the Roubideauxs. They are as much at your service as ours in this endeavor, and they are instructed as such.

The Assembly of Six extends our gratitude for your consideration of this matter and offers our wishes for a safe and comfortable journey. We look forward to our official meeting.

> Senator Eulalie Ancelet, the Lower Draws
> Senator Odilia Dupont, Lilou
> Senator Josephine Moreaux, Siere
> Senator Ives Charbonneau, the Crescent Coast
> Senator Arnau Fontenot, Alosia
> Senator Leila Garoux, Tugalu

I looked up from the letter, written on heavy parchment and stamped with the antiquated seal of Cyprien, a plume of fire pressed into purple wax. Rou was unwinding a length of linen. His brother Lyle was standing in the stern, behind the tent, guiding us through the water with the long wooden pole.

"Your Assembly of Six wasn't killed off in the Alcoran invasion?" I asked as Rou took hold of my burned arm.

"They were, in fact—publicly executed in the capitals of their respective provinces. But there are measures in place to ensure the replacement of a representative until the next round of elections. All it meant was there were six new people making up the Assembly."

"But . . . surely Alcoro put an end to all that?" I said. I was no more pleased with this man and his brother, but the only alternative to listening to his tale was sitting in the tent with my hands over my ears. "How could they allow you to maintain your own government?"

He wiped my sticky hand with a wet cloth. "They didn't. They banned free elections and removed any infrastructure traditionally used for voting. For the first election, our folk simply met elsewhere, campaigning on public docks rather than in the town halls. The Alcorans responded by criminalizing unapproved public speaking. So our folk moved inside, holding campaigns and elections in private homes. The Alcorans ended up outlawing any meeting of ten or more people in any private place—that law is still in effect today."

"How have you gotten around it?" I asked.

He started winding the linen around my arm, beginning at my shoulder. "We haven't. There are Alcorans in nearly every town, and it becomes fairly obvious if all the River-folk suddenly disappear to meet in secret. For fifty-six years, we River-folk haven't gathered in groups behind closed doors. There are public places, of course, where folk congregate—the steel mills, the docks, public markets. But the Alcorans are closely tied to all those things, all our industry and trade. But there's one gathering, the biggest of any year, that they take no part in."

"What's—oh."

"Right—First Fire," he said with half a grin. "They

hate it. Fire always makes them twitchy anyway, and for a whole town to be lit up like a furnace on blast . . . they've never wanted anything to do with it. It was the logical choice to facilitate elections, and it's worked for over four decades. I think the Alcorans reasoned there was only so cohesive we could be in one week and figured that wouldn't be enough time to organize a country-wide vote."

I had to agree with that reasoning. "So how *do* you make it happen?" I asked, wincing as the linen touched my burns.

"Representative hopefuls campaign through the week, mostly by distributing secret pamphlets that can be burned after being read. Fortunately, there's plenty of fire to take care of that—we're never in want of tinder during an election year. On the last night—that's five days from now—folk cast their votes."

"And is this an election year?"

"It is, which is part of what makes this so important. Folk are ready. We're done with the Alcorans tampering with our customs and lifeways. They'd abolish First Fire if they didn't think it kept some measure of control over us. That's pretty much all we have left, though. They've changed the structure of our industry, our economics, our education. Folk are through with it."

"Queen Ellamae came through your country just a few years ago," I said. "She said there seemed to be nothing wrong."

"Well, of course not—we're careful to keep it hidden, especially from strangers. And don't forget—a few years is a lot of time. Things have already changed drastically just in this past year alone. Regardless, we've been fighting back in one way or another for half a century. If the Alcorans suspected any kind of unrest, they'd put an end to it. And for a while, it almost didn't matter. Most issues are solved at the province level— once we got elections back under control, provincial governance was never affected by an Alcoran central government. I'm sure we've come off as being especially mild, never having any disputes to bring to their leadership in Lilou. But that's changing now, and rapidly, too. We need the Assembly back in place as our central government, not just in the provinces."

"Why?" I asked. "Why are things at such a breaking point so suddenly?"

"Several reasons. You popping up out of the blue and wresting Lumen Lake away from Celeno is a significant one. Folk saw it could be done, and what's more, it's weakened the Alcorans' hold on us. With no trade upstream, all their usual schedules have fallen apart. Our weaponry, too, has grown and evolved—largely thanks to our poleman here." He nodded to his brother in the stern. "But the biggest reason is the draft."

"What draft?"

"The Alcorans are instating a draft on any able-bodied person sixteen to twenty-eight. The only exceptions are pregnant women and single parents." He wrapped the last of the linen around my wrist. "They have their sights on Paroa next. If they can control the coast, they can control everything that happens inland."

"How do you know this?" I asked sharply. "And why would they seek out diplomacy with me if they were already planning to attack the coast?"

"A question we hoped you might be able to clarify for us," he said, pinning the end of the linen.

"I may have been able to," I said with disapproval, "if you hadn't interrupted our meeting and set my ship on fire. I barely got anything out of Celeno I didn't already know."

"Well, things didn't seem to be going so hot for you before then," he said.

I bristled. "How *dare* you? How dare you assume anything about my actions . . ."

"Sorry." He waved both hands. "I'm sorry—that came out wrong. I just meant that Celeno didn't seem particularly open to strategic negotiation, did he? Especially not with that creepy religious lady there. And this draft may be one of the reasons for that. If Alcoro already has plans to attack the coast, I wonder why exactly they wanted you to come to Lilou? What if they were planning something a bit more sinister than they let on?" His face split into a grin. "Who knows—maybe we saved your life!"

I glared at him stonily. His grin slid a bit—but it didn't fully go away.

"About the draft," I said coldly.

The corners of his mouth still curled upward, he shrugged. "About the draft. In September, orders of the draft were spread through all the province capitals, courtesy of that sausage-fingered idiot Catzomoc, the governor. That same week, I intercepted a message off an Alcoran messenger by hitting him in the face with a fish. It was the missive from King Celeno laying out his orders for your rendezvous in Lilou. With the Assembly suddenly drowning under cries of rebellion, they saw their chance to finally connect with you."

I looked back down at the letter in my hands. "Had you tried before? What does the Assembly mean when they say their previous efforts have failed?"

"We tried to send word to you," Rou said. "For months we tried. The few times we could get a boat into the northern waterways without arousing the suspicions of Celeno's folk, we were driven back by the Silverwood archers. Our hulls have the pockmarks to prove it."

I pursed my lips, remembering the scouting boats Valien's folk had seen from the lookouts.

"In September, we sent a messenger to Matariki to try to approach the Silverwood Mountains from the south." He shrugged. "She's probably still working her way north. But once the Assembly got word of Celeno's request to meet with you, the opportunity was too good to pass up. I'm sorry about your arm— you weren't supposed to get hurt. We wouldn't have drugged you, either, but we couldn't risk any noise. Until we were safely in the denser part of the bayou, Celeno's folk could have easily followed us from the docks."

"What *was* that thing you put on my face?" I asked, eyeing him beadily.

"A soporific sponge. Alcoran healers use them for surgeries."

"And the projectiles? The weapons you used to set the ship on fire?"

"Liquid fire," Lyle said from the stern. "Little shells of quicklime compound. They burn on water."

"They burn *on water*? How is that—"

Rou flapped his hand to silence me.

"—possible?" I finished.

With that, words began spilling from Lyle's mouth.

"An extreme exothermic reaction, buoyed by oil. They produce significant heat energy when they're hydrated, to the point that they'll set anything remotely combustible on fire. They burn incredibly hot."

He then launched into some explanation on the reconversion of the quicklime by reversing the hydric reaction, but Rou overrode him. "Lyle's a chemist," he said loudly. "Downright wizardly with creating fire that'd singe the teeth off a gator, but the real danger is letting him build up a head of steam."

I touched a finger to my bandaged arm. "So is this a natural burn? Will it heal?"

"Oh, yes, it'll heal just fine," Rou assured me. "It'll hurt for a while, but as long as it doesn't get infected, you'll still have all your freckles. We're lucky, though, that your face was shielded by your hair. Quicklime does ugly things if it gets in your mouth or eyes."

"My face was . . ." My hand flew to my head, and I sucked in a sharp breath. The hair framing my face was long and unharmed, but behind my right ear was a gaping space covered with matted tufts. My hair had been burned away. The clumps left were singed and uneven.

And what was more . . .

"My crown," I said. "Where's my crown?"

Rou glanced up and then back down at the medical kit as he bundled his supplies away. "Were you wearing a crown?"

I ground my teeth, this extra indignity pushing me over the edge. Rou looked up from his medical kit in time to grasp my wrist as my palm sped toward his ear once again.

"Hot damn, lolly, don't you hit me again, or you'll blow out my ear!"

I struggled against his grasp. "I'd just gotten it *back*, you witless churl . . ."

"I *said* we were sorry," Rou said hotly. "We didn't mean for you to be rolling around on the deck."

"And I didn't mean to be abducted by a couple of indecent, asinine—"

"Look, there's no need for fancy name-calling.

Perhaps someone recovered your crown before the ship went down. As for your hair, we can cut it, if you like, or cover it, or leave it—whatever you want, we'll make it happen. Soon as we get to our host's house."

I pried his fingers off my wrist. "Who's house?"

"Well, it depends. If the Alcorans turn west at Marvert, we'll stay in Toadhollow with the Doucets. Good family, very kind. About a million kids. She's a master pastry chef, runs the finest patisserie in the Draws." He clutched his stomach appreciatively. "Wait until you taste her pecan torte, Lady Queen, it'll make your mother cry . . ."

"How will we know if the Alcorans turn west at Marvert?" I asked, irked by his chatter. I wanted to go home, not eat dessert. "How do we know if the way is clear?"

"We have someone scouting ahead of us, of course. We'll be meeting up with him outside Toadhollow in about a half an hour." He saw the surprise on my face. "Didn't you read the Assembly's letter? We have a whole network of folk ready to sneak us through the Draws and up to Siere. Folk are waiting to throw their doors wide for you. They know how important this endeavor is." He quirked a half-smile. "What did you think, that I was going to make you sleep in this rickety old punt for the next week?"

I frowned at his amusement. "Yes, I had assumed it would be something like that."

"Oh, no, Lady Queen. We have to move quickly

and quietly under Celeno's nose, but we're going to be doing it in as much comfort as we can afford. You're the crowned head of Lumen Lake, after all. You'd be riding down the open waterways on the *Ember of Lilou*, if that wouldn't be overly conspicuous."

"I am the *crowned* head."

"Look, how many times do I need to apologize?"

"Unfortunately for you, continuously," I said. "On a related note, what am I supposed to wear on this foolhardy trip?"

"Skunk leather and reed skirts." He shook his head at me. "Gowns, of course. They'll be waiting with our riverman. I imagine they're stylish, too, if you're worried."

"I will be more inclined to look kindly upon you if you stop teasing me. Shall I remind you once more that you *abducted* me? You've broken every rule of civilized politics. You've insulted me, endangered my allies, destroyed my property, and undone my own plans. If it hasn't sunk in yet, I am *not* pleased with you or your government. I don't think it's out of the realm of possibility that my treatment would be as undignified as this whole situation has been."

"Lady Queen." He leaned forward slightly, opening his palms on his knees. "I know what we did was wrong, and I'm sorry for the harm we caused you. You've got every right to be angry. But surely you can understand the plight of our country? Didn't yours just overcome a similar challenge? We heard tales of you bushwhacking across the Silverwood

Mountains and sinking a dozen Alcoran ships with nothing more than a few hand tools. Were those stories true? Didn't you do everything in your power to restore Lumen Lake's banner? Didn't you need the help of an outsider to get it accomplished?"

I didn't ease my glare, but my knot of anger relaxed—a little. While his words did nothing to wash away my indignation, they were true. I had employed equally unorthodox methods to retake my country just a few months ago. And if I was honest with myself, the idea of allying with Cyprien against Alcoro was far more appealing than haggling over trade goods with the Seventh King. In reaction to this thought—and to look away from Rou's now-earnest face—I turned to the closed tent flap.

"What happens to Gemma?" I asked.

"She'll be locked up and guarded each night. She's on a tincture right now—I figured we owed you an explanation before she came to. But I'll need to let her wake up before the hour's out or she's going to get dehydrated. I'm hoping she'll come around once we're safe at Lady Doucet's. So you'll have to decide before too long whether you're with us or not."

"Tell me your plan," I said. "Carefully, in detail. What *exactly* are your terms?"

He ran a hand through his curls. "We bring you up through the Draws and across Alosia—"

"What are the Draws?" I interrupted. "You keep saying that word. What is it?"

"You're in it." He fished a roll of parchment out of

a satchel and unrolled it to reveal a map of Cyprien. "The Lower Draws is this whole southern reach of Cyprien, made up mostly of bayou and marsh. Boggy, buggy, dense—not our most pleasant country—but the Alcorans have never been able to penetrate it beyond the main channels. They opt instead to take the road along the Alosia River to get from Lilou to Siere." He traced the river, well to the north and east of us. "We're planning to swing west, keeping mostly to the small backwater towns, before turning north. We'll pick up a cart outside Dismal Green and head overland across the Hills of Lime to Siere."

"So it's one of the provinces." I looked at the letter in my hands again. "And Eulalie Ancelet is its representative. Senator."

He grinned. "You catch on quick."

I waved away his levity. "So we get to Siere."

"So we get to Siere. The Assembly will be waiting for us there—they'll congregate as soon as elections are over at the end of this week. We'll probably take a bit longer to get there, but it's in our interest to get as far as we can before First Fire ends. It will be much harder for the Alcorans to track us down when the whole country is celebrating, so we're hoping to at least be through the Draws by the time the week is out. Anyway, you'll hold council with them and negotiate—if you're willing—some form of alliance between Cyprien and Lumen Lake. I imagine they'll at least ask for a show of arms in the event of war and your official recognition of Cyprien as an independent country, in return for mutually beneficial trade. Once you reach an agreement, we'll send word to Celeno that we are playing host to his wife and are prepared to negotiate the terms of her release."

"Do you really think that leverage is sufficient?" I asked. "Do you really think he'll put her before Alcoro?"

"Have you not heard about their partnership? No, I suppose you've been in the dark for a while. They're famously close. She always takes part in council meetings, even though she's not the blood monarch, and he defers to her on homeland affairs." He shrugged. "Unless that's all been propaganda over the last few years. But it's significant, don't you think, that they traveled together to Lilou? It would have been safer for one of them to stay home."

"It's significant that she seems to be disagreeing with his foreign policy," I said, remembering Colm's deductions back at the lake. "But it can't be helped now. So you notify Celeno. Then what?"

He leaned back on his palms, crossing his legs at the knees. "When we receive his response, we'll meet a delegation of Celeno's folk in Siere—again, if you're willing. We'll declare our alliance with Lumen Lake, and the Silverwood, too, if you think you can speak on their behalf. We'll emphasize the strength we now possess in the waterways. You'll refuse to acknowledge his sovereignty in Cyprien and make it clear you won't trade directly with his folk. Let's face it—that was a bold request for him to make of you in the first place. And don't let him deceive you—he *needs* your trade, badly. Without your pearls, trade down the river collapses, and there goes their most stable source of income. We'll offer to keep the tradeways of Cyprien open to him, operating in our own right, under our own banner. We'll demand he remove every last Alcoran from our borders and renounce his authority in our country. For this, we'll open our trade routes to a small number of his ships each month, and we'll return the queen, unharmed." He took a breath. "Reasonable enough?"

I thought over his words carefully. There were flaws, of course, things I would take up with the Assembly when we began our negotiations. But even in light of these things, I felt much more at ease with this political route than I had with bargaining directly with Alcoro.

"Reasonable, yes," I said. "But remember that Celeno cannot necessarily be called a reasonable man. What do you do if he refuses?"

"We keep Queen Gemma—civilly, of course, but in prison, probably in Bellemere—that's the capital of the Draws, halfway between a hub and a backwater. We halt all compliance between our folk and the Alcorans and evacuate the main waterways to avoid Alcoran retaliation. And then . . ." He shrugged wearily. "And then we more or less declare war on Alcoro and begin assaulting Celeno's ships. We're hoping he finds that undesirable."

"Are you sure you can stand against him? Do you have the numbers?"

He nodded to Lyle in the stern. "What we lack in manpower, we make up for in firepower. We have grenades that can set a ship on fire in a downpour. We have flares that can temporarily blind an attacker. You've seen them both now. We can create glorious, debilitating explosions. And we know the bayou like a rabbit knows its warren. We'd stand a fighting chance." He raised one corner of his lips. "And if you stood by our side, well. We'd be dead near unstoppable."

I weighed his words. I thought of the surety my folk would have if we could quickly and effectively set fire to a ship in the river or generate explosions like the ones that rocked the *Spindrift* this night past. If these two brothers got me safely to the Assembly of Six, I would be sure to include a weapons contract in my terms. I looked back to the tent, but Lyle was hidden behind it. I would have to discuss matters with him further, figure out the details of these strange new devices and what else they could do. My heart beat a little faster—he could be the key to finally securing protection for my folk.

I turned back to Rou, looking at him for the first time as a potential ally rather than a threat. I studied the details of his appearance I had overlooked in my uneasiness. He had a patch of stubble on his chin. He wore a loose white shirt tucked into a wide burgundy sash. Over this hung a green vest embroidered with gold thread—a nice green, I noticed appreciatively, a pleasant emerald—an appealing contrast against his dark colors. *See, it can be done, Mae.* A cord ran under his collar, the pendant hidden under his shirt. Instinctively my hand jumped to my chest, and I let out my breath—my heirloom pearl hadn't slipped off, a welcome relief. My gaze slid down his rolled-up sleeve to his right hand, where there was an old pink burn scar on the fleshy part between his thumb and first finger. The ring circling his little finger was thick and unadorned, like a seal without a stone. A family ring, perhaps?

I looked back into his eyes. They were lighter than I had originally thought, almost the same color as the honey he had spread over my arm. I stayed silent for several more seconds, wanting to see his reaction to this tactic. He didn't squirm or chatter. He gazed back, his eyebrows raised. For such a talkative person, I wouldn't have expected that amount of restraint. I felt the same stirring of grudging regard I had toward Atria, but I tamped it down—despite his self-control and appreciably stylish clothing, I was not in the mood to grant this man any extra goodwill.

Finally I asked, "Who are you?"

He grinned, his smile a white crescent against his brown skin. "I thought I'd already told you."

I twitched the Assembly's letter at him. "This says your surname is Roubideaux."

"It does."

"Your name is Rou Roubideaux?"

He laughed. "My name is Theophilius Roubideaux, but that's a mite pretentious, don't you think?"

"Why don't you go by Theo?"

"I'm named for an uncle. Theo was *his* nickname."

From the stern, Lyle's pole thunked against the hull. Rou shifted on his palms. "As for titles, that's a bit trickier. Most of the time Lyle and I serve as the Assembly's go-betweens. We bring state messages between the senators and official instructions to the right people—we help coordinate diplomacy, engineering, reconnaissance, military action . . . you name it, we do it."

"And how did you come by these roles?" I asked.

"Oh," he said with a shrug. "Unbridled talent, I suppose, at least from Lyle's end. He's something of a genius, if you hadn't figured that out. Built a reputation for himself manufacturing incendiaries. Most of his job now is arsenal development and expansion. One of the families we'll stay with is his quicklime supplier."

"And you?" I asked. "What do you do?"

He gave a half-grin. "What don't I do? I play spoons and juggle fruit for kids. I buy pastries from dock vendors and drink spiced coffee with nobles. I gossip with fishmongers and bow over ladies' hands. I curse coking ovens with steelworkers and discuss independent banking with land barons. Mostly, I'm charming."

Don't flatter yourself. "A diplomat," I remarked.

"On a good day, I suppose. Except when I'm hitting foreign dignitaries with catfish or hauling them out of swamps."

"And you spin fire," I said.

His jaunty expression eased into something more candid. "I do. Poi. I spin poi."

I remembered the graceful way he had moved among the wheels of fire. "That was . . . remarkable."

He looked legitimately pleased. "Thank you."

"Coming into Hunner Drown, Rou," Lyle said from the stern.

"Oh, good." Rou pushed himself to his feet. He extended his hand to me. "So. Do you think you can trust me just yet, lolly?"

I was met suddenly with a memory of Colm sitting at a table in Tiktika, his chin in his hand as he eyed Mae, bedraggled from her slip into the ocean. *You're being too quick to trust,* he had said to me.

Well, I thought back. *I don't have much choice at the moment, do I?*

There would be time to form a more accurate opinion of this man and his brother, and of their strange, decentralized government. At the moment, all I could do was take control of my predicament.

"Let's get two things clear." I stood as well, ignoring his offered hand. "First, if this is really happening—if you really are going to escort me across your country to meet with your government, then you—and your brother—need to act like it. You address me by my title, and you keep your jokes to yourself."

He dropped his outstretched hand. "My apologies, Lady Queen."

"Secondly, about my trust. I have been told it comes too easily. I can assure you my forgiveness does not."

He gave a deep bow, grinning again. "Then let's hope I'm never in need of it."

CHAPTER 6

We glided into the area Lyle had called Hunner
Drown. It was a deep, dense place, a maze of gnarled
trees and curtains of moss. A long-legged, crook-
necked bird startled as we drifted around a boggy
rise, its wings beating the humid air. There was a
mighty splash somewhere in the gloom, far larger
than a frog or fish. I inched away from the hull.

Rou had taken up a second pole in the bow of
the boat, nudging us away from knobbly wooden
growths that rose up from the murky water.

"What are those things?" I asked. "Are they trees?"

"Cypress knees," Rou said, tapping one with his
pole. "When it's foggy, they look like arms rising up
out of the water. That's why folk call this place Hunner
Drown. Looks like a hundred folk trapped under the
surface."

I shivered despite the warm, damp air. Combined

with the deep, dappled shade and the trailing moss, the knees gave the bayou an eerie atmosphere.

"And where are we going?" I asked. "Is there a town here?"

"Not here, no. We're just outside Toadhollow, but here's just an old dock. A good place for a private meeting."

It struck me that they could be taking me any-where, to anyone. This could all be a ruse, and they could be delivering me straight to Celeno, for all I knew. "Who is this riverman we're meeting?" I asked sharply.

"Oh, don't you worry," Rou said, sweeping aside a beard of moss. "He's a gentleman of insurmount-able skill and character. A finer ally you won't find anywhere this side of the sea."

"He's right touched," Lyle said from the stern.

Rou threw a glance over his shoulder. "And in-valuable to the success of our mission, *brother*." The *Swamp Rabbit* jarred against one of the knees, and he turned around, dipping his pole back in the water.

I frowned at their banter and the use of the phrase "our mission." I was still turning over the Assembly's letter in my mind, and for the brothers to assume I was already fully behind them needled me. I turned my head, observing the bayou around us more closely. Being stuck here with no other op-tions frustrated me to no end, but perhaps at some point I could get away—I couldn't be *that* far from Lilou. Mae and my folk were surely looking for me—

assuming Mae was still alive. Uneasy at that thought, I eyed the dark, murky water. If I could get under the surface before the brothers caught me, I could swim away from them in no time.

There was a low hiss from a rotting log on our port side.

"Ho!" Rou gave a little hop on the deck and shoved hard at the log with his pole. We lurched to the right. "Blazing cottonmouth! Give a good push, Lyle, he's ticked!"

I sprang to my feet with a gasp and scrambled for the middle of the punt. Lyle's pole sloshed in the water, and I watched as the coiled snake slid past, its deadly white mouth gaping wide.

"Fire and smoke!" Rou said with a laugh. "He dang near got me! You can sit down, Lady Queen— they're good swimmers, but they don't usually chase folk down."

Too rattled to be embarrassed, I moved slowly back to the hull and sank onto the crate, grinding my teeth in both alarm and aggravation. Gone were any thoughts of diving into the water. Curse this place and its abundance of murderous creatures.

In another few minutes, a shadowy dock and run-down outbuilding emerged in the gloom. Roped to it was a short punt loaded with a variety of bundles and crates. At first, I didn't see anyone accompanying the boat, but as we got closer, I realized that the form I had taken for the scraggly remnants of a tree was in fact a man. I bit back a sharp comment to Rou as we glided within earshot.

"All right, Fisheye?" Rou called out.

"Git here'n help me with this load, y'durn tom-fool."

He was a scarecrow, a stringy, bent man with a beard of white whiskers identical to the moss trailing from the trees. He was one of the lighter-skinned Cypri, though one could only tell by virtue of his watery blue eyes—the rest of his face was the color and texture of a baked apple. On his head was a blown-out straw hat, and his shapeless clothes hung off his frame like laundry on a wire. He caught the rope Rou tossed him with a hand as knobbly as the cypress knees, securing us to the dock.

Rou offered me his hand, the muscles in his face jumping as he worked to keep his grin contained. I ignored his hand—I'd been getting on and off boats all my life—and took a large step up onto the dock. The riverman stood with his head thrust forward from his gnarled shoulders, staring at me. Rou joined me on the dock.

"Queen Mona, I present to you Cleophas Meaux, better known to most of us as Fisheye."

"Very pleased to meet you," I said evenly.

Some unintelligible string of words tumbled out from behind his beard.

"I beg your pardon?" I asked.

"I say, yer hair looks like gophers been rootin' in it."

I tucked my ragged strands behind my ear. "Yes. It got singed."

"I say it surely did, like a durn foxtail. Got the other one, did you?" he shot at Rou.

"Queen Gemma is on board, yes. She'll be waking up soon."

"Wellen, best git yer mess loaded. Here, lolly, you can take the tacklebox." He thrust a wooden chest into my arms. The corner grated along my bandaged burns. I swallowed a cry.

"Ah." Rou quickly lifted the box from my arms. "Fisheye, I think we'll let a person of Queen Mona's stature sit out loading the cargo. Besides, she's got a nasty burn."

"Pah, f'you say so. Go on, sit down so yer not in the way."

I lifted my chin and made to move past the bizarre man, when the thick gray fur along his shoulders twitched of its own accord. I startled backward. "Rivers to the sea . . ."

What I had taken for part of his shapeless wardrobe was in fact a live creature—an opossum, curled around his neck like a collar. Its long bald tail disappeared into the man's beard. It turned its wicked little face to me and hissed.

"Mirabelle! You be sweet," scolded Fisheye. "Don't pay Mirabelle no mind. She don't take to strangers."

Behind him, Rou bent over a stand of crates, bracing himself to keep his fit of laughter silent. I gave a noncommittal response and hurried to a splintery post that was well away from the pile of cargo. I perched on it, trying to smooth out my jangled nerves. I couldn't decide if I should be appalled or bursting with laughter.

As Lyle and Fisheye swung boxes down onto the *Swamp Rabbit*, Rou approached me with a wide trunk in his arms.

"Your wardrobe, Lady Queen," he said, his voice still edged with mirth.

"I thought I told you to keep your jokes to yourself," I said as he set the trunk down.

"Ah." He shook his head, grinning. "Don't jump to conclusions just yet. Fisheye lives and breathes the bayou, and he's got no love for Celeno's folk, who've dredged up some of the waterways to accommodate their ships. This is a man we absolutely want on our side. He'll be traveling ahead of us, checking which ways are clear and notifying the folk who'll be housing us."

"And the possum?" I asked.

He shrugged. "The possum. What's there to say?" He lifted the lid off the trunk. "You should have a handful of both fancy gowns and day dresses." He rifled among the layers of lace and fringe. "And boots, somewhere. A cloak. Underthings. Two pairs of shirts and trousers. A hair brush and mirror."

"And how long before we get to our hosts' house?"

"Only a few minutes, after this. Then you can change clothes."

"Roubideaux!" clamored Fisheye. "Quit lollygaggin'!"

With another grin he hurried back to the punt to help Lyle load the crates. I picked through the top few gowns, pursing my mouth in distaste at the fancier ones. These were frilly confections of layered lace, many with tassels on the hems and heavily beaded bodices. I had always preferred starker gowns, letting the tailoring and few well-placed embellishments convey their finery. But I couldn't be picky now. At the moment, I was feeling fortunate not to be tied up in a sack and tossed into the swamp.

I closed the lid, and as I did, a cockroach the size of a hen's egg scuttled out from the splintery post I was sitting on. It ran *over my knee*.

I jumped up and swiped the thing away, biting back a shriek. It flew off the dock, where it floundered in the water. Reflexively, I shuddered and brushed my arms and neck. Mae would have huffed and rolled her eyes at me.

Mae. What had happened to her? I closed my eyes, my anxious thoughts settling on her like a heavy fog. Could she possibly have survived the fall into the deep water of the channel? The only water I had ever seen her submerged in was the roiling ocean and a foaming river. Had she found some amount of control over the still water off the docks? Rou had certainly described *her*—no one else near the ship matched his description. But then, he must have seen her on deck before she fell overboard. Perhaps he hadn't seen her swimming at all. I didn't trust him on this—I *couldn't* trust him. Not on something as weighty as a friend's death. My stomach twisted, a wash of uncertain grief mingling with my other uneasy emotions.

What would Mae do in my situation? She would probably sneak away into the bayou with nothing but her compass and a bit of shoestring, alligators and snakes be damned. No one would see or hear a whisper of her until she turned up in Lilou, unharmed and well-fed. I did not have the same likelihood of survival on my own in this maze of water. I might be able to swim the channels Mae could not, but I didn't know how to set snares or forage or heal wounds with inconspicuous weeds. I didn't know the benign creatures from the deadly ones. No, I was bound to the plans of the Assembly and their eccentric collection of aides after all—for good or for ill.

Rou pattered back up the dock, rolling up his map. "We're clear for Toadhollow," he said. "Ready to go?"

Does it really matter? I glanced at the water. The cockroach was still floundering on the surface, until a large, shadowy mouth emerged out of the gloom and gulped it down whole.

"Ready," I said.

Rou hoisted my trunk in his arms and carried it down the rickety dock. I hurried after him to the punt, which was now loaded with crates.

"What's all this cargo for, if we're staying with

River-folk each night?" I asked as he settled my trunk against the hull.

"We have a few errands to run along the way. Most of them are empty to take the bags of quicklime we'll pick up in a few days. Some of them have incendiary prototypes to drop off to manufacturers. And then there are a few basics in case we get stuck somewhere hiding from the Alcorans."

"We're not going up in a blaze of fire and smoke, are we?" I asked.

He offered me his hand again. "Not if you don't strike any sparks."

I ignored his hand once more and stepped back down onto the *Swamp Rabbit*. Fisheye watched, scratching Mirabelle under her pointed chin.

"You can check the channel past Toadhollow tomorrow?" Rou asked him.

"Meet'chou at that sandbar on the far side," he replied. "You best git movin' early, though, afore the Alcorans have time to think too much."

"We will." Rou picked up his pole. "A pleasant afternoon to you, sir!"

"Don't be stupid," he said in return.

With that, Rou and Lyle shoved us off the dock, and we glided between the cypress knees and back into the bayou.

I went to sit on one of the crates, but Rou glanced at me over his shoulder.

"Begging your pardon, Lady Queen, but I'm afraid I have to ask you to get back in the tent, just for a few minutes. We'll be coming in to Toadhollow soon, and not everyone is privy to the Assembly's plans. The fewer people who see a suspiciously regal passenger with us, the better."

"What if Gemma wakes up?" I asked.

"We'll pole fast," he said.

Reluctantly, I stood, went back to the tent, and slipped inside. Gemma was still lying on her side, and she looked a mess. Her rich brown hair fell every which way around her face and shoulders, and one side of her elegant portrait neckline drooped down her scorched lace shift. She was missing an earring, though I noticed with a scowl she had managed to keep her crown of white gems.

Carefully, I settled down just inside the tent flap, as far away as I could get from her. I didn't want her to wake and find me here, in *literally* the same boat as she. Granted, she looked entirely harmless, her young face relaxed, not tense as it had been the night before. How old *was* she? What kind of life did she lead, being married to such a reckless zealot? What did she really believe? I studied her a moment longer, as if I could read the answers to my questions in her face. But I discerned nothing, and she didn't stir, her chest rising and falling in shallow breaths.

My mind drifted back to our ill-fated meeting the previous night. I had derailed the negotiations, I realized. I had let my temper get the better of me. For a meeker adversary, this might have had effect, but Celeno was likely used to people being angry at him.

Even if the discussion hadn't been interrupted by the Roubideauxs, he probably wouldn't have budged on his trade demands. Perhaps it was better this way, then. I would get a second chance to treat with him, this time with significantly greater leverage. I would stay cooler, more aloof. He had chafed at my silence—I would use that to greater effect. Yes, next time, with the Assembly of Six and an alternative to accepting Alcoran trade, I would be armed with the right weaponry.

I turned my gaze from Gemma's face to the world outside the tent flap. The trees had started breaking up, and the bayou seemed to be feeding into a proper river, broad and slow-moving. We passed a few punts dotting the water—Rou returned the greetings his folk called to him. The bank rose and dried out, and the trees became thick and gnarled, draped with bearded moss. The first outbuildings emerged through the trees, and the tangled brush of the riverbank gave way to docks and walkways. These jutted out into the waterway, narrowing the navigable water to a few lanes of punts. Soon the docks were lined with businesses, their wooden facades painted in vibrant colors—emerald green, sunflower yellow, purple with golden trim. Bold merchant signs hung over the waterway, many strung with bells that jangled when they were struck with errant poles. I craned my head to get as good a look as I could through the narrow opening. *Live hellbenders, ten silvers. Madame Cleoma's Fire Theatrics*

*Supply: fans, hoops, poi, staves, and more. Now hiring
sous chef—inquire within.*

Purple and gold bunting was stretched from post
to post—First Fire, I remembered. Open braziers
lined the busy docks, and even in the light of day, they
were burning heartily. As we glided down the river,
I saw someone moving from one brazier to the next,
carefully replenishing the oil inside. I craned my
head, searching for any hint of the election process
taking place. But nothing stood out. Nothing gave
the River-folk away.

What I did see was a different kind of subversion, one I might have dismissed if I wasn't looking
for it. Even in this town, far smaller than the city
of Lilou, there were signs of Alcoran presence, but
they were all quietly undermined by subtle handi-
work. A burning brazier sat directly next to a red-
tinted lantern, negating the point of the lantern's
shields. A wooden beam loomed over the bell at the
town center, carved with the words of the Alcoran
prophecy. But it was draped with purple and gold
bunting, so every other word was obscured. An Alcoran flag hung from a post a few yards away, but
someone had tacked a cup to the wood, a cup which
evidently held some kind of seed, judging from the
streaks of bird droppings sullying the russet fabric.
I smiled slightly. Rou hadn't lied. Fifty-six years an
occupied country, and the Cypri had been fighting
back all along.

A small offshoot joined the main river, and from

the bow, Rou navigated us into the little outlet. Soon we were passing among homes, elaborate two-story houses with sweeping porches and wrought-iron accents. Like the shops, these, too, were painted cheerful colors, and most had intricate, overflowing gardens leading down to the bank. We rounded a bend in the river and pulled up alongside a dock in front of a peach-colored house. Rou set his pole down and looped our tether around a post. Our hull scraped against the dock.

I gathered myself to get to my feet, when on a whim I looked back over my shoulder.

Gemma was awake.

Her eyes were open, and she was staring straight at me from the shadows. She didn't move; she didn't speak. Just stared, blinking once.

"All right, Queen Mona," Rou called. "Lyle will take you up to the house. We're going in the side door, through the kitchen—best move quickly."

I didn't need any persuasion. I practically jumped back onto the deck. Lyle gave a short jerk of his head and started around the small side path, hidden from the river by a bank of azaleas. I hurried after him. At the kitchen door, I looked back down to the punt. Rou was just pulling aside the tent flap.

"Lady Queen!" My attention was pulled away from the boat, and I turned to see a woman in a gauzy lilac dress bobbing a courtesy to me in the middle of a large, cluttered kitchen. The buttery aroma of fresh pastry engulfed me as I stepped through the door. The woman reached out, and I automatically extended my hand to shake, which she did by clasping it in both her hands. "I'm so relieved you've made it safely. I'm Maude Doucet. I beg you to excuse the mess, but it's safer than bringing you in the front door."

"Of course," I said, still rattled from the morning and Gemma's stare. "It's a pleasure."

It was an automatic lie—nothing about this journey had been a pleasure, least of all Gemma seeing me in ragged tatters, little more than a glorified captive.

"Welcome to Toadhollow," Maude said. "Come with me—I'll show you to your room."

I followed her through the kitchen, past cooling racks of exquisite pastries waiting expectantly for a dusting from the bowl of powdered sugar nearby. My stomach growled—I had lost all track of time, and I realized I hadn't eaten since before we had sailed into Lilou. I imagined reaching out and snatching a fat turnover, the sides bursting with berry preserves. Before my impulses won out, we left the kitchen and its fragrant goods behind and entered a sunny hallway. Maude led me up a carpeted staircase to the landing, where a door was cracked open just an inch and filled with a column of bright eyes. There was a sharp giggle followed by a round of shushing.

"The children," Maude said, hurrying me down the hall. "I've told them you and Queen Gemma are visiting dignitaries from Samna, but the only person they're really interested in is Master Roubideaux." She opened a door for me.

It was a small room, but tidy, hung with plum-colored drapes. As Maude insisted I ask her for anything I might need, Lyle sidled in with my trunk. He set it down, and with that, they both left the room, closing the door behind them.

I looked at the trunk for a few seconds, and then strode to the window. It faced the river, and I craned my head to see down to the sidewalk. Rou was hurrying for the kitchen door, cradling Gemma tightly in his arms. Her head was on his shoulder—she looked for all the world like she was asleep.

I shook myself and went back to my trunk, picking through the dresses inside. Most Lumeni gowns laced or buttoned up the torso—though usually lake-women wore a skirt or trousers and a chemise for daily wear, when they weren't wearing diving suits. But the Cypri style, from what I had seen on the docks in Lilou and Toadhollow, involved a loose, sleeveless overdress cinched under the bust by a matching sash, designed to hang over a closer-fitting shift. I had glimpsed a few women wearing a variation of Rou's trousers, vest, and sash, but I left these options in my trunk alone. Since returning to the lake, I had relished the opportunity to wear gowns again, and I preferred the decorum of one now. Ultimately I pulled out a dusky blue over-dress—in all the uncertainty of the morning, it was comforting to wear my country's color.

I struggled out of my ruined gown, my burned arm hindering me every step of the way. Wincing, I slid it through the long sleeve of the shift, trying not to agitate my bandage. I pulled the overdress over my head and clasped the coordinating sash under my chest. There was quite a bit of excess—Mae would fill out this gown much better than my scant curves. I groaned in dismay—it would suit her height better, as well. The skirt was too short, falling unfashionably above my ankles. I moved to the mirror next to the bureau to survey the damage.

Great Light, I looked a mess, too. Why hadn't anyone told me my face was smudged with soot? There was a washbasin under the mirror, and I bent over it, scouring my face until my nose and cheeks were pink and shiny. I rummaged for the brush Rou had promised in my trunk and attacked my disastrous hair. But no matter how much I smoothed it, that singed patch stuck out from behind my right ear like fur on a wet dog. I considered trying to braid my hair over my head as I had on my journey with Mae over the mountains, but I could barely hold my burned arm in the air for more than a few seconds. Frustrated, I settled for sweeping it over one shoulder. I thought I might have to tie it off with a bit of string or some other oddment, but then I found a satchel in my trunk with a selection of colored ribbons inside. A tiny—*very* tiny—modicum of my indignation eased.

From the hall came a sudden round of shrieking and a clatter of little feet on wood. As I finished tying the blue ribbon around my hair, someone rapped on my door. I opened it to find Rou draped with children. They hung off his back, arms, and legs like barnacles, all shouting over one another. A little girl with two poufs of dark hair on either side of her head was hugging him around the neck.

"Gemma's awake," he said, cocking his head to look past the little girl in his arms.

I stepped out into the hall with him. "Was she awake when you brought her in?"

"No, still asleep. She came to when I put her on the bed."

She was awake before that. What had gone through her mind when she saw me in the tent with her? Somehow I needed to be sure she understood the differences in our positions.

The little girl turned to me, still hugging Rou. "What's on your face?" she asked.

"It's just soot. Did I miss any?"

"Yeah—you have little spots all over."

I blanked for a moment, wondering if I had missed something in my reflection. I was about to turn back to the mirror when Rou said, "They're freckles, Anouk. You've got some, too, but they're harder to see." He tapped her nose and then began to free himself from the children's grips. "All right, ladies and gentlemen. Miss Mona and I need to talk to Miss Gemma. Why don't you all head downstairs? I'll be down in a few minutes. If you find me some apples, I'll juggle for you."

They squealed their delight and tumbled over one another for the stairs.

"Sorry," he said as he led me down the hall. "They're not used to seeing anyone lighter than the Canyon-folk."

"Oh, of course." I was probably the palest person they'd ever seen.

He stopped in front of the door at the end of the hall. "Queen Mona, have you decided what you're going to say to Gemma?"

"Not word for word," I said. "Why?"

"Will you stand with Cyprien? With the Assembly? Will you present a united front against Alcoro, starting here and now?" His hands dug absently in his pockets. "I wouldn't ask, but . . . I feel as though I've asked a lot of you in a short period of time."

"Yes. You have." I thought of the weapons contract, and the promise of never having to trade directly with Celeno ever again. "But I'll stand with you, at least before Gemma. I will reiterate that I'm still not pleased with you, and I have matters I want to discuss at length with the Assembly about their tactics. But I *do* want to see Alcoro driven out of your waterways as much as you."

Slightly chastened, Rou nevertheless smiled in relief and turned the knob to the door. I followed him over the threshold.

Gemma sat hunched on the bed, clutching a cup of water in trembling hands. Lyle came in a moment later, carrying a trunk that was much smaller than mine.

She lowered the cup to her lap, her hands still bound at the wrists. "What are you doing here?" she asked quietly.

I looked down at her through narrowed eyes. "I'm answering a summons from the Assembly of Six to negotiate an alliance between their folk and mine. As it turns out, you didn't manage to wipe out the Cypri government. That makes two countries where you've tried and failed."

She flinched, but she didn't try to counter me like I thought she might. Instead she asked, "What happened to your hair?"

I frowned at her. "It was burned in the attack on my ship last night. Regrettable, but then, your husband has made secrecy and violence a necessity."

She straightened slightly and spoke in a voice soft but direct. "You don't know what you're talking about."

"No," I agreed. "Only the things made clear to me in the past four years."

Her lip twitched as she bit the inside of her cheek, and she tugged unconsciously on the sleeve of her fussy lace shift. She looked from me to Rou. "What are you going to do to me?"

"We mean you no harm, Lady Queen. None at all. We want very much to return you to your country." I was surprised at the gentleness in Rou's voice. He crouched down before her. "But we can't do that just yet—I'm afraid you have to stay with us a little while longer. But it shouldn't be all bad. My name is

Rou, and this is my brother Lyle. We'll be your escorts to our representatives in the city of Siere."

"Why are we going to Siere?" she asked.

"To meet with the Assembly. We're hoping you'll inspire your husband to agree to our demands to liberate Cyprien."

She looked from him to me and then back again, her lips slightly parted. "You can't be serious," she whispered.

I stirred in anger. "Can't he? Did it never occur to you that perhaps the countries you invade are not pleased to be sharing your banner?"

"You don't understand—this is coming at the worst possible time." Her voice rose slightly. "You have to let me go—you *must* let me go."

"We're not asking for your alliance, Queen Gemma, only to act as part of our leverage," Rou said. "Willing or unwilling is up to you."

She shook her head. A few more locks of hair spilled out from underneath her crown of prisms. "My husband will *not* barter for my life. He can't—it's simply not possible."

A few ticks of silence slid by at this blunt statement. "Why do you say that?" Rou finally asked.

"Because he must see the Prophecy of the Prism fulfilled," she said simply. "And no Alcoran's life carries more weight than that. None. Certainly not mine. We're taught this from an early age. In all the years my folk have been among you, didn't you *once* listen to our words?"

"All respect, Lady Queen," he said dryly. "We had to listen to them a lot."

"Then you should understand. The Prophecy matters more than any one life. We're all just conduits for it—even my husband."

"He hasn't heard our terms yet," he said. "We believe he'll find them reasonable."

"You're going to be disappointed," she said with certainty. "If you keep me, this won't end in your liberation—it will end in disaster."

"Well, we're going to take the chance anyway," Rou said.

"No—you *have to let me go*."

"No, Lady Queen. I'm sorry, truly, that it's so distressing to you, but we can't do that." He put his hand on hers, and she flinched. "I'm just going to untie your wrists. I recommend not trying to flee. Even if the bayou wasn't full of creatures bent on eating you, we're too far out for you to get very far on your own." He loosened the knot and slid the rope off her wrists. "We're going to lock your door, but someone will be up with food in just a few minutes. In the meantime, we do want you to be comfortable." He opened the lid of the trunk to reveal a stack of plain but neat overdresses and shifts.

"Master Rou!" called a little voice from down the hall. "We got you some apples!"

Rou stood. "Perhaps Queen Mona will help you out of that gown."

"Wait . . . what?" I asked. He gave me an entreating look as he beckoned Lyle out of the room. The door closed behind them, and I was left standing over Gemma. She looked up at me, worrying the left sleeve of her lace shift.

"This isn't going to work," she said again.

"Perhaps you'll be surprised," I said shortly. "There's more at work in this world than your prophecy."

She was silent for a moment, biting her lip. I looked her over, my mouth drawn in a tight frown.

"Did you plan this, then?" she asked, her voice soft but steady. "Even after Celeno asked to meet with you peacefully?"

"No, actually, I didn't. I had every intention of meeting with him. The River-folk's attack was as much a surprise to me as it was to you."

"And yet you're planning to ally with them? When they've treated you as a captive?"

"I'm not pleased with their methods, and I will make that displeasure known to their Assembly. But the Roubideauxs have been straightforward with me so far." *I hope.* "Besides, they've hardly treated me half as poorly as your folk have."

My harsh words reached her—she cut her eyes away and drew in a quick breath, her shoulders taking on that tension she had showed on the ship. Vaguely I thought I should be kinder to her, befriend her, even, but I hadn't forgotten Celeno's words the previous night, their infuriating callousness exacerbated by her misguided convictions just a moment ago. Even if she was having second thoughts now, this woman had had just as much chance to push for peace when her country invaded mine four years ago. I was not inclined to grant her any sympathy.

"Have you considered they may be using you, as they're using me?" she said, bringing her gaze back to me. "What's to stop them from trading *you* to my husband in return for their liberation?"

Obviously I had thought about them using me, but the angles all seemed to point to a mutually beneficial exchange. This new idea, though, was one I hadn't fully considered. Aware of how vague it sounded, I said, "They know they have more to gain from my alliance than my enmity."

"Then why did they leave the Silverwood queen?" She gripped the knees of her ruined gown. "Your new strength comes from the Silverwood army. Why would the River-folk not want to negotiate with Queen Ellamae as well?"

"I imagine they were pressed for time and assumed I could speak on her behalf."

"Why would they assume that? I would no more expect you to speak for them as you might speak for Celeno." She tilted her head. "Have you considered they might be seeking to drive a wedge between your folk and the Silverwood? It's not as if all of your interests are the same. Your folk will negotiate with your safety and release in mind, but the Wood-folk won't be so driven. As I said—you're not their queen."

"The Assembly and the Cypri people have nothing to gain from undoing my alliance with King Valien and Queen Ellamae."

"Except reclaiming all trade in the eastern world," she said quietly.

I stared at her for a moment, unnerved by this obvious motive I had overlooked. She raised her eyebrows just a fraction of an inch at my silence. For all her whispering and softness, the Alcoran queen had a sharp mind that I had clearly underestimated. Irked, I twitched my hand. "That's nonsense. Come, let's get your silks off so you can put on a fresh shift."

She startled away from my reach, tugging on her sleeve. "No . . . no, thank you. I can manage."

"I'll at least undo the sash in the back."

"No, don't bother," she said.

"Really, a dress like this can't be easy to get out of . . ."

"I don't need your help," she said, her voice a bit higher. "I don't *want* your help. Please leave me alone."

I stood in front of her, my hand outstretched for the scorched shoulder of her gown. Her cheek jumped as she bit the inside of her lip.

"Please leave me alone," she said again.

I sighed sharply and turned for the door. Without a word, I passed back into the hallway, leaving Gemma to struggle out of her ruined clothes by herself. The key to the room was in the keyhole. I swung the door closed and turned it decisively in the lock.

I strode down the hall and started down the staircase. Lyle was in the foyer, kneeling over one of the crates we had picked up from Fisheye. I stopped in front of him.

"Lyle," I said. "If you want to negotiate with the Silverwood as well as Lumen, why didn't you bring Ellamae with us?"

He didn't look up. "We only brought two sponges."

That seemed to be a method, not a reason. "I don't think I can speak for King Valien and Queen Ellamae. It would be a disservice to their folk and their interests. You should have brought Ellamae as well."

He shrugged. "Oh well."

"Is there a place on our route I can send a message? Some way to let my brothers know I'm safe?"

"No." He slid the top back on the crate. "Could be intercepted. Can't risk it." He stood, hefted the crate in his arms, and started back out the door. "Stay inside."

I stared after him as the front door swung closed in my face.

They're seeking to drive a wedge between your folk and the Silverwood. What strategy would benefit Cyprien more—allying with Lumen Lake against Alcoro, or offering me to Celeno? Surely the Assembly could not think my council and my brothers would stand for my being used as leverage. But that was the point Gemma was making. My folk might not stand for it, but would Valien's? He had promised us the support of his banner, but did that extend to declaring war on a neighboring country that posed no direct threat to the Wood-folk?

My thoughts settled back on Mae. I decided I was glad they hadn't abducted her, for whatever reason. She had recently spent a great deal of time and effort getting me safely over the Silverwood Mountains to form the alliance between our two countries. She wouldn't let a brief conflict of interests undo that. She would make her way back to my brothers and Valien, and they would all orchestrate some mutually beneficial strategy.

Assuming, once again, that she was alive.

An assumption I still didn't trust myself to make.

A series of giggles filtered down the hallway. Fists clenched, I turned from the front door and headed toward the sound. In a parlor off the hall, Rou stood in front of a settee, his eyes fixed on the air in front of him, where three apples were flying from his hands in synchronized loops. The Doucet children were draped over the settee, watching him earnestly. He circled the apples first one way, and then another. He leaned forward and tossed one behind his back, catching it deftly over his shoulder. The smallest girl—Anouk—clapped her hands, her poufs of hair bouncing with her excitement. And then, he made a sharp movement. The children squealed with delight. One of the apples flying through the air now had a crisp bite mark in it, and he was chewing on a too-big piece of fruit.

Anouk grasped a fourth apple and tossed it up

with the others. Rou stuck his tongue between his teeth, altering his pattern. He had nearly completed a full round when one apple went rogue—he lunged to snatch it, but two collided in the air, and then everything fell apart. Apples bounced off the cushions of the settee and rolled across the floor. The children scrambled after them, laughing.

"Ah," he said with disappointment. "They'll never take me in the circus." He accepted the bitten apple from Anouk and took another bite.

"Rou," I said.

He looked to the doorway. "Oh, hello. Did you see my act? Would you like an apple?"

"May I talk to you, please?"

He sighed at the children now piling the apples back into his arms. "Ladies and gentlemen, I must ask that you skedaddle. Why don't you go hound your mother to wrap me a galette for tomorrow?"

They begged and pleaded, but he shunted them out of the parlor and closed the door behind them. I took a few steps into the room. The large bay windows were open to the afternoon, letting in the warm, marshy breeze.

Rou took another bite of his apple and made a face. "Bruised." He sighed. "I never lose my grip like that . . ."

I turned and looked him square in the eye. "Tell me, Master Roubideaux, have you been fully honest with me?"

"No, I'm sorry. I've never been able to juggle four things at once."

I wasn't amused. "I just spoke with your brother. I asked him about a few of the finer details of your plan, and he was not . . . overly reassuring about things."

"What do you mean?"

"He couldn't give me a good reason for not making off with Queen Ellamae last night. If you're really interested in allying with the Silverwood, you should have brought their queen along on this bizarre journey." He paused mid-chew, his brow furrowed. "Furthermore," I said, "he denied my request to send a letter to my brothers because it could be intercepted. But you must understand—if they think something has befallen me, they will not look kindly on your folk or the Assembly at all. Considering that my folk—and Queen Ellamae's—were on the dock in Lilou, word of my disappearance will certainly reach my country as soon as the *Halfmoon* gets back to the lake, which means we only have a finite amount of time. Colm has the authority to make decisions in my stead, and I wouldn't put it past him to mobilize our forces down the waterways."

Hurriedly, he swallowed the half-chewed bite of apple in his mouth. "Oh, Queen Mona. I should have warned you, but I thought it would be apparent. My brother is, ah, not the most sociable of fellows. Downright surly on a good day. Balancing long chemical reactions is his idea of a two-way conversation." He shook his head. "Of course you may send a message to your brothers, so long as we word it carefully. They have every right to know you're safe. As for Queen Ellamae . . . I knew who she was only by virtue of spying on your negotiations with Celeno. Up until last night, we had no idea the Silvern king had gotten married, and there was nothing to indicate he was sending an embassy to Lilou with you. We planned to capture two queens and no more. In retrospect, yes, we most certainly should have invited Queen Ellamae to join us."

My heart pounded with relief, but I continued to glare at him. "And you are *certain*, without a doubt, that you saw her climb into a skiff? She's my friend, Rou, not just my ally, and if I were to find out she had drowned . . ."

"She's alive," he assured me. "I saw her. I heard her, too, after she got in the boat, swearing a blue streak—something about earth and sky in that twangy mountain accent. Trust me, Lady Queen, I wouldn't lie to you about that. I haven't lied to you about anything. We've already made ourselves enemies to Celeno—it would cross the line into stupidity if we were to set Lumen Lake and the Silverwood against us as well."

My fists eased on my tasseled gown. He cocked his head at me. "You believed me on the punt. What made you change your mind?"

"I *didn't* believe you on the punt. I'm still deciding if I believe you. I simply accepted what you said for the sake of argument. But now I've had time to actually think about things, and not everything is making sense."

"I understand. I know this whole thing isn't ideal. I didn't relish the idea of attacking your ship and forcing your hand, either. Not especially civil, or diplomatic. But like you said to Gemma, Alcoro has necessitated using drastic measures." He gestured to me, palm out. "Please, if something else is bothering you, don't hesitate to tell me. Lyle's useless to talk to—believe me, I know. Come to me instead."

It would have been nice to trust him that easily. He had a rather insufferable air of approachability. But that was the job of a good diplomat—to win trust, and then use it. That talent was probably exactly why he'd been chosen for this role.

But two could play that game, and I had been playing it from the cradle, surrounded by a country of people who all needed something from me. A law passed, a decree made, a favor granted. Influence. It was the only thing ever sought from me—even Mae had needed it to accomplish her early goals. And now this man needed it—but he wouldn't get it without proving himself first. I allowed a length of silence, looking him over coolly. Again, he didn't speak. He didn't squirm. He only made one movement, heavy with purpose. Slowly, deliberately, his gaze not leaving mine, he lifted his hand—and took another bite from his apple. I arched an eyebrow, resisting the sudden urge to laugh.

"You joke too much," I said.

"I haven't said a word I don't mean, Lady Queen." He took another bite. "But I am beginning to understand you take more to actions than words. So tomorrow morning we'll sketch out a letter to your brothers. We'll have to do it cleverly, so we don't give away our route in case it's intercepted, but it shouldn't be too difficult for a couple of cunning folk like ourselves. Will that aid my cause?"

"It will aid mine, and that's the one I care more about at the moment. But it will suffice—as long as you write better than you juggle."

He grinned again. "The fourth apple threw me off." He tossed his apple core out the open window and crooked his arm to me. "Shall we adjourn for lunch? Lady Doucet's marinated mushrooms are not to be missed."

I rested my arm in his, in part to let him think he'd won a small victory—that way he'd be more likely to make a mistake later on. He patted my hand.

"You clean up nicely, by the way," he said. "Loveliest straggle-haired queen in all of Toadhollow."

I jerked my head to him, and he waved his free hand with a smile. "Sorry, sorry. Jokes to myself."

CHAPTER 7

I woke early the next morning, still full from the sumptuous dinner Maude had prepared the night before. Quietly, I gathered up the notebook and quill I had requested from her and settled into the chair by the window to begin organizing my thoughts. The first thing I had to write down were questions for Lyle, so I would be ready to copy down his answers when we got back on the punt. Specifically, I was interested in inventories and descriptions of his incendiary weaponry, including their worth, so I could estimate the cost of our agreement. I pulled back the curtain to let in the soft morning light.

I paused. I was not the first one awake. My window looked out over the river, misty at this early hour. Down on the dock was Rou, surrounded by golden arcs of fire. His shirtsleeves were rolled up to his elbows, and his feet were bare as he stepped around the path of his spinning poi. He looked different than he had the previous night, when he bantered jovially with the Doucet children at dinner. His jaunty crescent grin was replaced with a look of quiet, almost meditative focus.

I watched him move for a while, feeling almost as though I were seeing something private. I shook myself and looked down at my blank notebook, trying to remember the litany of notes that had been streaming through my head all night. I touched the quill to the paper, made a mark, and then looked back out the window. Rou was spinning his poi in tandem, creating parallel lines of fire. I looked back to my paper. I wrote the date. I looked out the window again. He swept the flames up over his head, passing them just inches above his mass of dark curls. I closed my notebook.

The morning slowly brightened, the sun slanted through the bearded moss and glanced off the river, and still I watched Rou spin, mesmerized. I came to my senses when a floorboard creaked somewhere down the hall. One of the children called for her mother. The house was waking up. Around the bend of the river, a solitary punt appeared. Rou must have seen it, too, because he extinguished his poi by snapping them through the air with a swift jerk. He bundled the chains neatly into a bag and returned the greeting the riverman gave him.

There was a creak behind me as my door opened unsolicited. I swiveled my head around. It was Anouk, dressed in a ruffled nightgown.

"Miss Mona." She held out her little fist. "I made you a fire wand."

I looked at the mass of ribbons in her hand. "Oh," I said. "Thank you."

She pattered across the room and put it in my lap. "Happy First Fire," she said.

She was halfway out the door before I thought to respond. "You, too."

I examined the little stick, wrapped with a tassel of golden ribbons. I had no idea what it was for. When I looked back out the window, Rou was gone.

As soon as I was dressed, the morning began to rush. As per Fisheye's instructions, Rou and Lyle wanted to get us moving down the river as soon as possible. Rou sat down with me in the parlor to check my burn and word a letter to my brothers. He dabbed at my blisters with salve as we debated how to phrase the message without giving away our route and intentions. After he bound up my arm again, I hastily dashed off a letter that amounted to *don't panic, I'm not dead, I'm seeing to urgent business.* I also gave them my hurried hopes that Mae had made it safely back to them and ordered them not to declare war on anyone until I got back.

Rou took the letter and posted it—I craned my head against the front window as I watched him slip it in the cast-iron mailbox down by the river. He even peered into the slot to be sure the letter was all the way in. A little spark of begrudging gratitude flickered briefly—actions did, indeed, speak louder than words. Perhaps he was not altogether untrustworthy.

Breakfast was a hurried affair, with little time to linger over the exquisite raspberry pastries Maude laid out before us. Rou brought my trunk back out to the *Swamp Rabbit*. Gemma was let out of her room, dressed in a gray overdress and—to my surprise—the same high-necked lace shift as the day before. She hurried through the kitchen, but she paused on the walk outside, trying to look over the bushes shielding the door. At a growled word from Lyle, she put her head down and continued to the punt. I moved through the kitchen to the door, glancing over my shoulder just before I stepped outside. Rou was accepting a mauling of hugs from the Doucet children, smiling with his eyes closed as Anouk squeezed him around his neck. He stood and returned an embrace from Maude, groaning with delight when she placed a generous bundle of wrapped pastries in his arms.

"You're not related, are you?" I asked as he joined me outside the kitchen door. "To the Doucets. Are they family?"

"*Umf*, I wish," he said wistfully, unwrapping a corner of the bundle.

"They seem to like you very much."

"And aren't I lucky for it." He broke off the corner of a turnover, popped it in his mouth, and held out the bundle to me. "Pastry?"

We hurried down the walk, and at the bequest of Rou, I climbed back in the tent, my fingers sticky with the piece of turnover I'd accepted from him. Gemma was sitting wedged in the corner, hugging her arms across her knees. I settled down again at the tent flap.

"Do the shifts in your trunk not fit?" I asked.

"No," she said.

"I can alter them, if you want."

"No," she said again. "I like mine."

I shrugged. If she wanted to wear a dirty shift, so be it. I ate the turnover. Apple, with a hint of ginger. It was delicious—I licked the crumbs off my fingers surreptitiously.

We drifted down the little river toward Toadhollow until we joined back with the main channel. The town showed remnants of revelry from the night before. Purple and gold streamers lay tiredly along the docks. Faint wafts of smoke clung to the morning breeze. A sequined mask sat forgotten on a windowsill. Amid the quiet, however, the braziers along the docks still burned steadily.

"Queen Mona," Gemma said.

I didn't turn around. "What?"

"Did you mean what you said on the ship the other night?"

I kept my eyes on the town. "I mean everything I say. Which part are you talking about, specifically?"

"When you said there is no Light. Do you really believe that?"

I narrowed my eyes. "Yes. Would you like to hazard a guess as to why?"

A few seconds passed, during which I avoided turning around to see her expression. Then she spoke.

"Don't base your beliefs on the actions of one imperfect person."

"No?" I said, still looking out the tent flap. "What if I base my beliefs on the actions of one imperfect *country*?"

"If you do, then you do not understand the Light."

"I understand that belief in such a thing has led to the subjugation of two countries and the destruction of hundreds of lives," I said sharply. "I have difficulty overlooking that fact. And does the Seventh King know you call him imperfect? That seems a bit damning of you."

"I see you do not understand marriage, either."

I jerked my head around. Her arms were clasped around her knees, her chin slightly tucked, but her gaze held steady on mine.

"Obviously," I said with force. "As I had few opportunities to *get married* while wandering the coast of Paroa for three years, fighting just to stay alive."

She opened her mouth to reply, but I turned away before she could. "Please consider not speaking to me again."

She kept her silence.

In just a few minutes, we left Toadhollow behind us. The riverbank gave way once again to mossy trees, and the sluggish current picked up. In the bow, Rou put his pole down and approached the tent.

"Coast is clear, Lady Queens," he said. "You can come out."

I joined him on the deck. He crouched down at the opening. "You can come out, too, Queen Gemma."

There was a barely audible response from inside.

"Lady Queen, once the sun gets above the trees, it's going to bake you like a sugar bun in this little tent. Come on out."

A few more seconds passed, and then she emerged onto the deck. She sat down on one of the overturned crates, clasping her hands around her elbows.

Rou stretched his arms over his head. "On the river for most of today," he said. "Blissfully little in the way of poling."

In the stern, Lyle put down his pole and circled the tent. With no word to the rest of us, he rummaged in one of the crates and pulled out a thick notebook stuffed with papers covered in garbled sums and chemical notations. Silently he disappeared again behind the tent. With the slightest eye-roll, Rou nudged a crate and dropped down onto it, leaning his elbows back on the hull.

It struck me that I should spend this time writing, too. I still hadn't managed to organize my questions for Lyle. I opened my trunk and pulled out my own notebook. Underneath it was the tassel of golden ribbons Maude's little girl had given me.

"Oh," I said, straightening. "Anouk gave me this, Rou. What is it?"

His face broke into a grin. "She made you a fire wand!"

"What's it for?"

"Nothing especially." He took it from my hand and shook it. The golden ribbons flashed in the sun. "Little kids who are too small to be trusted with burning torches make fire wands for First Fire. This is good." He shook it again. "Now we can celebrate on our own." He sighed. "To think we're spending all of First Fire avoiding the best towns! All the music and food we'll miss—though Maude Doucet's pastries make up for some of it. Is she not the most heavenly chef?"

I sat down on my trunk, my notebook in my lap. "She's quite good."

"'Quite good.'" He placed his hand on his chest. "Oh, you sovereigns. So diplomatic. She's a magician with a whisk, and nothing less."

My mouth twisted in amusement as I opened to the page I had written the date on earlier that morning. "Where are we going today? What magical being will house us tonight?"

"Puddlewelle tonight. Lord Comeaux. A painter. A magician with a brush. Don't walk down his halls in the middle of the night—you'll think the pictures on the wall will reach out and snatch you, they're so realistic."

"What does he use?" Gemma asked suddenly.

Rou looked at her. "Use for what?"

"His medium. What kind of paint?"

"Search me. Oil, isn't it? I'm not sure."

"Does he use inks at all, or charcoal?"

"I don't know." He cocked his head. "Are you an artist, Queen Gemma?"

She dropped her eyes to her lap, fiddling with her left sleeve. "No, not like that. I don't do paintings. I do illustrations."

"Illustrations?"

"Scientific illustrations. Entomology, mostly, but some botany."

"A biologist!" Rou exclaimed, as if this was the most delightful thing he'd ever heard. "I had no idea. I love biologists! Trustworthy folk, in my experience, and chatty, if you know their topic." He jerked his head toward the stern, where Lyle was hiding with his notebook. "Though you have to know how to make them quit, as with any scientist."

"What was the first thing you said?" I asked Gemma. "Before botany?"

"Entomology," she said, flicking her eyes up to mine and then back down to her lap. "Insects."

"*Bugs.*" Rou recrossed his ankles, grinning. "What kind of bugs, Lady Queen?"

"I sketch all kinds," she said quietly. "But I mostly study cicadas. Well—I used to."

"The things that screech all night in the summer? Tell me, do they purposefully find the most atrocious pitch possible for the human ear, or are they just that tone-deaf?"

He brought a smile to her face, though it didn't last. I shivered slightly, trying to imagine the desire to sit down and draw an insect, especially one as ugly as a cicada. More interesting, though, was the fact that he'd garnered a reaction from her—charmed her for just a fleeting moment. Perhaps he would be more useful than I had given him credit for.

"Maybe we can borrow some materials from Lord Comeaux," Rou continued to Gemma. "So you can draw swamp bugs."

She smoothed the knee of her gray overdress and looked away. "Don't bother. It's been . . . a while since the last time I sketched."

"Perfect timing, then—there's a whole heap of nothing between us and Siere." He swept his gaze to me. "And what's *your* secret talent, Queen Mona?" I looked up from my notebook. "Do you play a wicked upright bass? Do you mix unusual cocktails? Do you noodle for catfish?"

"I sing," I said.

"Oh, everyone *sings*," he said, and I felt a sudden, surprising flurry of irritation. "*I* sing."

"Maybe I should have been clearer," I said hotly. "I sing *well*."

He clutched his chest. "Oh, my pride."

I looked back down at my page. "Your pride, from what I've gathered, is much too inflated to be brought down by one comment."

I could hear his grin in his voice. "Thank goodness for that. But come now, what's your secret talent? Your parlor trick?"

"I don't have one."

"You must."

"I *don't*," I said again, glaring at him. "I have no time for talents or tricks. My mother used to tell me not to do something if I couldn't do it well."

"That's absurd."

"I beg your pardon?"

"I said, that's absurd," he said, scratching his stubble. "What a thing to tell a child." He stood up. "Come on, we'll start with a headstand."

"What? You can't be serious."

"I'm always serious. Think what a joy you'll be at formal parties," he said, getting on all fours on the deck. "The queen who can stand on her head."

"I'm wearing a dress."

"Oh, there's no one around." He put his curly head onto the wood. He drew his knees to his elbows, and in a smooth, controlled movement, he lifted his waist and legs into the air.

He gave me an upside-down grin. "What do you think?"

"I think you're ridiculous."

He pointed his toes, his bootlaces dangling. "Don't you want to invite me to your state dinner now? I find noblewomen swoon when I perform inane tricks."

I put my hands on the hull and threw my weight against it. The boat rocked in the water. His legs broke apart, swinging wildly, and then he arched down, landing on his back on the wooden boards.

Gemma's hand jumped to her mouth in alarm. But Rou drew in a short breath and laughed, his hands on his chest.

My own smile died on my lips. In his fall, the cord under his collar had slid out from under his shirt. The pendant now rested on the deck beside his ear. My eyebrows snapped down. The sun flashed off of several cut faces. A prism.

"What is *that*?" I asked. "Do you really wear a token of the Light?"

He craned his head to see what I was pointing at. "Sure, like most of my folk." He looked up at me. "Why? You have your own."

"I do not."

"That pearl you wear."

I plucked my pendant off my chest. "This is *not* a token of the Light. This is a royal heirloom, and nothing else."

He raised himself up on his elbows, one eyebrow quirked. "What's the matter?"

"She doesn't believe in the Light," Gemma said quietly, her shoulders drooping.

"Really? Not at all?"

"No," I said, irritated that we'd landed on this subject again in such a short period of time. "Not at all."

"Torchfire, what's that like?" he asked.

"It's simple," I lied. "It's easy, and it's logical. I don't have to give up my own worth to archaic rock carvings. I don't have to feel like I'm being judged by some sort of distant power."

He dropped back down onto the deck. "Well, I wouldn't believe in it, either, if that's what I thought it was."

"What do you think it is?" I asked.

"The Light isn't some distant outside force," he said, waving his hands in the air to illustrate. "The Light is internal, and individual. It's the divinity in each person. We're each harbors for it, and together we create the greater entity."

"That doesn't make any sense," I said. "Who's 'we'? Who's a harbor?"

He looked up at me. "Everyone."

"*Everyone*? Every single person? Even the bad ones?"

"What person is all bad? What person is all good? Yes, everyone. You. Me. Gemma. Lyle. King Celeno."

"What a pleasant thought," I said irritably. "To think we're each little bundles of divinity. That seems like just a way to bolster our own egos."

He gave me a look of incredulity. "Until you realize that if each person is a little bit divine, then our greatest calling is to honor the Light in others. Because honestly, without the Light, what makes us worth anything? Our worth comes from recognizing our own Light and the Light in others."

I stared at him. I had never heard of anything like this before. "Do all the River-folk believe this?"

"More or less." He rolled off his back into a sitting position.

I looked at Gemma. "Do you see the Light this way, too?"

"Not exactly," she said. "We still think of it externally, as a guiding force. We are creatures of it, and we know . . ."

"'. . . it is perfect,'" Rou finished, rattling off the first line of the Alcorans' prophecy. He shook his head. "That's something I've never been able to sink my teeth into, Queen Gemma. Seems like an awful tall order, claiming that anything associated with humanity is perfect."

"But the Light is not humanity. The Light is what guides us. It's our own fault we don't always interpret it the right way."

"What do you mean, 'interpret'?" I asked. "What's there to interpret?"

"The Prophecy, of course," she said. "Folk have postulated for years about what it means. The whole job of the Prelate is to dedicate their life to illuminating the meaning of the Prophecy. They fast, they pray, they meditate, they research and theorize, all to divine the meaning of the Prophecy."

"Is it *that* difficult to understand?" I asked.

"Well, folk have had to fill in the missing pieces through the years," she said.

"The *what*?" I said.

"The parts of the petroglyphs that have worn away over time," she said, looking up at me. "There have been centuries of research done to determine exactly what they—"

"They're not even *complete*?" I exclaimed. "You pillage and manipulate and usurp other countries based on a set of rock carvings that *aren't even complete*?"

"No! No, Queen Mona, that's what I'm saying . . . the Prelate and a legion of acolytes and scholars spend their whole lives trying to interpret the meaning . . ."

"So you fill in the gaps with mere conjecture?" I asked angrily.

"They're inspired by the Light, it's guided and directed by . . ."

"And just when did the Light direct you to the country of Cyprien?" I asked, gesturing around me. "When did it direct you to mine?"

I thought it was a scathing rhetorical question, but she smoothed her skirt, her shoulders tense once again. "Cyprien, about sixty years ago, around the time our turquoise mines began to fail," she said quietly. "Lumen Lake, seven years ago. When Celeno's mother died and he was crowned."

My mouth dropped open, my rage surging inside me like a bitter storm. I dragged my shocked gaze to Rou, who was sitting against the hull with his elbows on his knees.

He rubbed a few fingers over his stubble. "And what exactly does that look like, Lady Queen?" he asked Gemma. "Does the Light reach out and put a little *x* on the map for you?"

She looked between the two of us, and then back out at the water. "It's revealed to the Prelate. I won't even bother explaining how, as I expect it won't matter to either of you."

"What matters to me is the Light's impeccable sense of *timing*," I said with vehemence. "Your turquoise dries up, and *then* the Light points you to Cyprien? Your queen dies, the Seventh King is crowned, and *then* it points you to Lumen Lake? Convenient, that the Light makes these things known any time your country is at a political or economic crossroad."

Gemma splayed her fingers in her lap as if holding an invisible bowl, frustration written on her face. "The Light made these things known because the answers were *sought out* at those critical times. When such important decisions come up, the Prelate retreats to the petroglyphs to perform a fast—at the most recent one, she was there for almost a week, praying and meditating, eating nothing, drinking only sacred tinctures . . ."

"Which would make anyone hallucinate any number of things," I snapped. "Lack of food alone is enough to make anyone go a bit witless—believe me, *I know*. Five days swimming down the southern waterways on an empty stomach, and I was convinced I was seeing bodies floating in the water alongside me. Not the best mental state to base your decisions on strategy and politics, I would have thought."

"The Prophecy is what drives our strategy and politics," she said doggedly. "It's not as divorced as you seem to think it is. We have always had great minds in Alcoro—engineers and scientists, healers and artists. My folk have been fueled through the history of my country to strive for excellence, to better themselves, all because we knew it was going to further the Prophecy."

"Which makes it self-fulfilling," I said sharply.

"It hasn't been fulfilled yet," she replied.

Rou passed his hand through his curls. "Seems to me your folk could have done a lot more with your wealth of knowledge than use it for war."

"Your schools have benefitted," she said almost inaudibly. "Alcoro has the best academics this side of the sea. The collaborations that have been done by our scholars—"

"How dare you take that line?" I cut in. "How dare you use that as justification? We in Lumen Lake are cleverer about trade than Alcoro. The Silverwood trumps us all in caring for their resources. Does that give either of us the right to claim *your* country under the pretense of running it better than you? Look." I waved to Rou as he leaned both elbows back on the hull. "The Cypris don't want you here. They're risking their safety to be *rid* of you. Do you really think you do everyone a favor by denying them the right to their own government? By making them fight and die for your own cause?"

I thought at first I had finally aroused her anger, the way she stared fixedly at me. But then her gaze swung to Rou. "What do you mean, fight for our cause?"

"Your draft, of course," I said. "It makes me a bit skeptical, you know, of your good intentions if in the same stroke you're planning to send Cypri mercenaries against Paroa. Did the Light reveal this to you as well?"

Her eyes flew back to mine, her lips parted. "When did this . . ."

"A few weeks ago," Rou said, his eyebrows raised at her growing consternation. "Your acting governor disseminated the orders to all the provinces. It's supposed to begin the day after First Fire."

She stared a moment longer. Then, in a slow movement, she lowered her head and pressed her hands to her cheeks. "Oh, great Light," she whispered.

"Didn't you know?" I said sharply. "Or was your husband acting without your knowledge?"

She didn't answer right away. Her hands slid from her cheeks to tent over her nose. Rou and I glanced at each other just as she lifted her head again.

"You've got to let me go back," she said. "This plan of yours isn't going to work. The longer you keep me here, the more dangerous things will get— for everyone. Cyprien, Alcoro—great Light, the rest of the eastern world!"

"No, Lady Queen," Rou said. "That's not an option."

"Celeno won't give up Cyprien," she pressed. "He can't. He'll take war before he lets it go. More bloodshed. More lives piled on his."

"I would think he'd have numbed to it by now," I said harshly.

"No," she said. "Oh, no, Mona. Perhaps you're numb to the lives you took the day you reclaimed your crown. I assure you he is not."

"Of course he's not!" I shot back. "They were *your* folk!"

She wiped her eye. "It's not just them. He's not . . . he's in so much pain, all the time. Oh, Mona, if only you knew what he's gone through."

"Stop," I said. "Don't try to impress upon me the suffering of your husband. He's caused me more grief than any person living or dead. His actions killed my best friend and dozens of my folk. His actions cost one of my brothers his eye and the other his emotional stability. He's cruel and probably mad, Gemma. Don't you dare defend him to me."

She bowed her head against my glare, her face in her hand. She sniffled. I huffed, aggravated at both her meekness and her misled convictions, and looked instead at Rou. He was gazing down the river and agitating the thick ring circling his little finger. After a few beats of pregnant silence, he raised his hand and called out over the water.

"A fine morning to you, sir!"

"Late, as usual, slower'n a daggum cooter stuck in a honey pot, and makin' enough noise to run out the gators!"

I looked to the bank to see Fisheye standing astride his battered little punt. Rou took up his pole and maneuvered us into the shallows. Lyle emerged from behind the tent and tossed our tether around a tree trunk.

"What have you got for us today, Fisheye?" Rou asked.

The gnarled old riverman flapped a map in his hand. Mirabelle clung to his shoulders, her beady eyes watching our arrival.

"Way to Puddlewelle's clear," he said. "But Bog-fire mebbe trickier tomorrow."

"We'll worry about tomorrow," Rou said, unrolling his own map.

"I'm thinkin' you'll have to route through Temper Crik."

"We won't go through Temper Creek," he said absently, glancing over his map. "We'll swing east."

"You're a durn fool."

"I'm aware." Rou rolled up the map. "You can check Bogfire?"

"Pah," Fisheye spat in some kind of agreement. "Be waitin' fer you on the far side near the big ol' loblolly." He turned his watery eyes to me. "Hair still raggedy."

I pursed my mouth in irritation. "Yes, of course it is. There hasn't been time for me to tend to it properly. Please don't bring it up again."

"No promises." He picked up his pole. "And no promises fer Bogfire, neither," he said to Rou.

"Aren't the Alcorans going to get suspicious if they see you popping up in all the towns along the waterway?" I asked him.

"They don't bother me, lolly," he said, unwinding his tether. "They think I'm crazy."

With that, he thrust his pole against the bank and scooted out into the slow current.

I balled my hands and raised my voice as his punt floated away. "You may call me Lady Queen!"

He lifted a gnarled hand to his ear. "Eh?"

I drew in a breath, preparing to shout, but the current moved quicker than I anticipated. Before I could admonish him again, he was out of earshot.

Rou chuckled and stuck his map in his back pocket. "Finest man alive, Fisheye Meaux." He bent to pick up his own pole, missing my withering glare—perhaps intentionally. "All clear for Puddlewelle, then. Let's go see the portrait painter."

Lord Comeaux's house was powder blue and slightly lopsided, the porch railings engulfed by masses of climbing jessamine. Rou hoisted my trunk in his arms and led the way up the walk. I followed him, and Gemma followed me, her eyes on the walkway. She had been silent most of the morning, ignoring Rou's further attempts to draw her out. Instead, she had spent the time staring out over the river, her hands clenched on her knees.

I had managed to get a bit of writing done, but not as much as I would have liked. Fortunately, we had a few hours before dusk, and I planned to sit down with Lyle during that time. I held my notebook under my arm and waited while Rou kicked the front door several times in lieu of knocking, his hands occupied with my trunk.

The door opened, and Lord Comeaux beckoned us inside. With many bows, he ushered us into the parlor and then hurried away to take Gemma upstairs. We headed toward the coffee table, laid out with a steaming pot and a platter of pickles, cheese, and toast. A handful of scrubby flowers sat in a glass jar that looked like it usually housed paint water.

"Safe," Rou said with a sigh, putting my trunk down and dropping onto one of the settees. I sat down opposite him. Lyle didn't sit, but began piling food from the tray into his palm, presumably to take away to eat somewhere else. Rou plucked up a piece of pickled okra. "Should be a quiet evening," he said. "We're on the edge of Puddlewelle, not a lot of folk around . . ."

"Roubideauxs," said a voice from the parlor door.

Both Lyle and Rou reacted at once. Lyle dropped his handful of food back onto the platter. Rou lunged to his feet. Both of them clapped their palms over their chest as they swung to face the figure in the door.

"Senator Ancelet!" Rou exclaimed. "We didn't know . . ."

"Of course not," she said smoothly. "I wasn't sure I could make it myself until this morning." She looked past them to me. "Queen Mona. It's an honor to meet you. Eulalie Ancelet—I represent the Lower Draws."

I rose from the settee as she made her way into the room. Her skin was a shade darker than Rou and Lyle's, and her long black hair hung straight down her back. She was dressed for travel, opting for a vest and trousers rather than an embellished overdress. I extended my hand. Like Maude Doucet, she clasped it in both of hers—belatedly I added my left hand to the gesture.

"The honor is mine," I said. "I'm relieved to hear about the survival of your government throughout Alcoro's occupation. It's an admirable accomplishment."

"Hardly as admirable as actually driving them out," she replied. "But with your input, and likely a great slice of luck, we'll be following your example." She looked at Rou. "No trouble so far?"

"None yet," he said. "We cross the channel tomorrow, but we shouldn't stick out. I admit I'm surprised to see you, Senator—aren't you on the campaign trail?"

"All week," she said with a hint of weariness. "I'd stay here longer, otherwise. I would very much like an in-depth conversation with you, Lady Queen. But there will be time in Siere for that, with the rest of the Assembly. For now, my focus has to be on reelection, or my time in Siere will be short. I'll be in Bellemere tonight—perhaps my most important stop."

"How's the opposition?" Rou asked.

"Tough. Ines Deschamps knows how to stir up a crowd, and she's run a top-notch campaign. The folk who support her are totally dedicated, very hard to sway."

Rou snorted. "Deschamps couldn't negotiate her way out of a cloth sack. She'd set fire to the sack while she was still inside."

"Never underestimate an opponent, Rou. Folk know she's got a strong backbone. They'll be looking for someone rock solid to stand against the Alcorans."

"And we've *got* someone," he said. "You've held office for five years, and folk trust you. And you're First this year—that's got to work in your favor."

"First of what?" I asked, interrupting their conversation.

"Of the senators," Rou said. "First Among Equals."

"We rotate," Eulalie explained. "Each year, a different senator takes the role of First Among Equals, to act as speaker, and to take charge in case of crisis."

"Is that how you make decisions?" I asked. "Queen Ellamae and I were wondering about that. With an equal number in the Assembly, does the First make final decisions in case of a split?"

"Oh, no," Eulalie said, adjusting her cuffs around her wrists. "The office doesn't make my voice any more important. It's more of a formality, and a safety net in case of emergency. But it does give me a bit more visibility."

"How do you make collective decisions, then?" I asked.

She looked up at me. "We talk. We negotiate until an agreement can be reached."

"And that always works? No one ever holds out until their demands are met?"

She shrugged. "Sometimes. No system is ever perfect. Eight times in our history, there have been issues that the Assembly hasn't been able to resolve within itself."

"What happened?"

"It goes to popular vote," she said. "There's a special election to decide a verdict. But that takes more time and effort to organize than a senatorial election, and we don't have the capacity to pull it off under Alcoran control. It's made those of us on the Assembly more reliant on collaboration—and that's a good thing. The provinces create the whole of Cyprien. We're all parts of one body. What hurts one hurts the others, and what benefits one benefits the others. Our history has shown us that self-preservation is a waste of effort."

I dropped my gaze suddenly, fighting against the flush that crept up my neck. Her words rang boldly true, and not in a pleasant way. My mind was suddenly full of flashes of my past I usually tried not to think about—but that was hardly something I could mention in casual conversation with a new political acquaintance.

"What about industry, Senator?" Lyle asked. "Did you see my drafts . . ."

"Mill design is going to have to wait, Lyle," she said. "If this effort against Alcoro fails, it's not going to matter whether we have fancy new furnaces. We have to focus on one thing at a time, and we have to do it carefully."

"Which, I still maintain, is not Deschamps' forte," Rou said with satisfaction. "You've got my vote, Senator."

"I'd better not, Rou," she said sternly. "On voting day, I expect you to be holed away upriver, well away from any town center." She looked at Lyle again. "Are the prototypes ready to bring to the Brasseauxs?"

"They are."

"Very good." She smiled thinly at me. "I suppose it must seem fairly haphazard to you, Lady Queen, this system of ours."

"It's certainly different," I said. "A different mindset entirely."

"I've always been proud of Cyprien's representative government," she said. "But I admit I envy a monarch's surety. There's nothing quite so rattling as attempting to sell your merits while a horde of people hurl defamation and denouncement— especially while trying to keep things from reaching Alcoran ears. But such is politics." With a sigh, she selected a piece of okra from the tray and popped it in her mouth. "Now I'm afraid I have to be off, or I'll miss all the slander Deschamps has ready for tonight. Stay safe. Thank you for your alliance, Queen Mona. I look forward to seeing you in Siere."

"There's no alliance yet," I reminded her. "But I'm hoping we may craft one. In the meantime, good luck in your campaign, Senator."

She nodded once at Rou and Lyle. "Blessed First Fire."

"Blessed First Fire, Senator."

She left the room, throwing her cloak around her shoulders as she did. We heard the front door swing closed.

"Well." Rou dropped back down onto the settee. "I'm glad you two crossed paths, even if it was just for a moment. She's a brilliant thinker, Senator Ancelet, and she understands her folk."

"I look forward to talking to her more," I said, sitting as well. "And the rest of the senators."

Lyle didn't sit. "Deschamps, though," he said thoughtfully. "She's a force to be reckoned with."

"Yeah, the way a rampaging gator is," Rou said, stretching his arms over his head. "This is a sticky situation we're in. Senator Ancelet has shown she's got the finesse for it."

"Hm." Lyle frowned absently at the pickled okra.

Rou eyed him. "You're not thinking of voting for Deschamps, are you?"

"Probably won't matter. You heard the senator—we'll be in hiding on voting night." He shrugged and swept the handful of food back into his palm. "If I had the option, though . . ."

Rou was about to press his case when Lord Comeaux bustled into the room.

"Terribly sorry for the wait, Lady Queen!" he wheezed. "Turns out the Alcoran queen is an artist as well. Inks! For scientific articles! I shall have to compare notes with her. But later. Did the senator leave? She said she couldn't stay long." At our affirmation, he clapped his spotted hands together. "Well then! Shall I give you a tour of my studio?"

Dutifully I rose to follow, seeing Lyle slip from the room out of the corner of my eye. Another chance to question him lost. I frowned, but quickly put on a neutral face.

Rou, however, didn't hide his displeasure as he watched his brother go.

Once again, Rou had not exaggerated our host's talent. Lord Comeaux was indeed an extraordinary painter, specializing in animals and bayou landscapes. He took me through his studio and gallery hall, pausing in front of each work and describing their process in great detail. I learned more about oils, color schemes, egrets, and snapping turtles than I ever thought I would know. I listened as attentively as I could, but my mind kept wandering to my half-finished notes on Lyle's incendiaries. I thought about jotting down my new thoughts on the pretense of copying Lord Comeaux's words, but that would be insincere, and it would probably only lengthen the amount of time we spent in front of each painting.

I got away as soon as I politely could, having decided in front of the exquisitely detailed bullfrog that I would just take down Lyle's information and organize it later. Notebook in hand, I made my way from Lord Comeaux's porch down the weedy walkway to the dock. The afternoon was waning, the late light slanting through the mossy trees. I could see Lyle on board the punt, sitting among a nest of crates, each piled with papers. He hunched over his own thick notebook, occasionally riffling through the notes scattered around him. He glanced up at my footsteps on the dock.

"Yes?" he asked.

"Do you have a moment?" I said.

"For what?"

"I have questions about your incendiary devices," I said, opening my notebook. "The different kinds you've created, their uses, the cost of their manufacture . . ."

As I spoke, his eyebrows snapped down over his eyes, and inexplicably he turned back to his scattered work. He huffed in aggravation. "Sorry," he said without sounding like he meant it. "I'm busy."

I stared down at him, affronted by his rudeness. "I need this information to draft my agreement with your Assembly," I said. "Knowing their properties and value will ensure an accurate contract—"

"I'm *busy*," he said again, jerking his hand at his pages of notes.

I pursed my mouth, gripping my notebook in my hand. He kept his gaze determinedly on his work, his quill scratching out a long, cryptic sum. I almost reprimanded him—no personal work of his should take precedent over state business. But I stopped myself. There was no sense in antagonizing him—yet. I'd give him the chance to react more professionally.

"Tomorrow, then," I said.

He gave a noncommittal grunt. I tutted my disapproval and turned on my heel, stalking back up the curving walk to the house. The porch was hidden from view by a bank of magnolias, and I stormed around it, running through a variety of reprimands I would use tomorrow if his attitude didn't change.

"Lolly, you look like you'd punch a gator for looking at you crossways."

I halted in my steps. Set into a gap in the magnolias was a whitewashed bench, and sitting on the bench was Rou, tuning a mandolin propped on his knee.

"Everything all right?" he asked, his fingers pausing on the tuning keys.

I let out the breath I'd been holding. "I . . . yes, everything's fine." I gestured curtly back down the walk. "Your brother."

"What's he done now?"

"Nothing, he was just . . . a little short with me. He says he's busy."

Rou rolled his eyes. "He's a beetlehead, is what he is. What do you need?"

I lifted my notebook. "I need details on his weaponry, to draft my agreement with the Assembly."

"Oh." He glanced at his tuning keys, plucking a string to test its pitch. "Unfortunately he's the one to give you the best information in that respect. I know how to detonate them without blasting my face off, but as far as engineering goes . . ." He shrugged. "I can have a word with him, if you want."

"No, I'll just try again tomorrow." I blew out another breath, looking out at the riverbank. "Perhaps I just caught him at a bad time."

"Yeah, the last two decades, give or take," he said. He plucked another string, its pitch curving into tune. "How's your arm?"

Painful, and stiff. "All right," I said.

"Tell you what." He set his mandolin down and patted the bench next to him. "Let's take the bandage off, let it air out awhile. Just don't let Lord Comeaux see, or he'll start talking about what colors he'd use to replicate the blisters."

I resisted the urge to make a face as I sat down next to him. He took my wrist and unpinned the linen. As he worked, I caught a dull glint. The sun was shining off the silver ring he wore on his little finger. This close, the thing looked ancient, its surface pitted and dented. It was an odd width, reaching almost to his knuckle, with no stone or seal on its flat face.

"Is that a family ring?" I asked, gesturing with my quill. "Lyle has one, too."

He straightened his fingers and looked down at it. "This? It's my steel."

"Your steel?"

"My firesteel."

"You mean for starting fires?"

He squinted at me, as if trying to tell if I was joking. Then he fished inside his collar and pulled out the pendant I had seen earlier. In a swift motion, he struck his ring against the pendant. A burst of sparks jumped from his hand.

"Flint," I said. I reached out impulsively and took it in my hand. "Your pendant is a flint?"

"You saw it earlier," he said. "Why so surprised?"

"I thought it was a prism." Without the sun flashing off it, it was easy now to see that it wasn't a clear gem, but a polished brown stone, veined with gray. "And you said it was a token of the Light."

"Well, it is." He wound my bandage around his hand. "That doesn't mean it can't be useful, too. Fire is the most sacred symbol for us—and it's the most useful. Our country would be nothing without fire—it's how we forge, how we cook, how we vote . . ."

"How you vote?" I said. "What do you mean?"

"Back before the Alcoran invasion, we used a paper ballot for voting. No big deal. But those were outlawed along with everything else, and they were too obvious to use safely. We had to switch to something more discreet. Now we use braziers." He settled against the bench's backrest. "On the last night of First Fire, after the candidates have campaigned all week, braziers are set out in each town, one for each candidate. They each start out half-full of oil. They're lit at the same time. Voters come and get a vial of oil and add it to their candidate's brazier. Folk monitor them all through the night. Last one burning is the winner."

I stared at him. "Just like that?"

"Well, then all the towns from each province have to be tallied," he said. "It's usually a few days before the winners are declared."

"What if someone cheats?" I asked. "What if someone tampers with the braziers, or adds extra oil? What if the folk monitoring them mix up the braziers?"

"You heard Senator Ancelet—it's not a perfect system," he said. "Once we're back under our own flag, I'm sure it will be abandoned for legitimate ballots again. But there's never been any real problem, as far as I know. Perhaps a slip-up here or there, where they both burn out around the same time, or where one eats fuel faster than the other. But tampering with votes is not something that's taken lightly. This is the most important thing we do in Cyprien, and it only comes every five years. And the very fact that it's now interwoven with fire—it's made the process sacred. It's too important to think about tampering with something so closely tied to the Light."

I looked back out at the river. The sun had slipped behind the line of trees, leaving the sky with a heavy golden glow. It reflected off the water, creating a path of solid gold snaking through the trees. Sun on water—my folk's Light.

"I have another question, Rou."

"Hm?"

"I've been thinking about this philosophy of your folk. Seeing the Light in each person, and so on." Thinking about it too much, in fact, when I should have been planning my negotiations with the Assembly.

He crossed one boot over his knee. "Yes?"

"It's so . . . I mean, it seems so fanciful," I said. "You say everyone is a harbor, that no one is all good or all bad. But all I can think about is King Celeno. Think of what he did here, to your folk. Think of what he did to mine. Do you really see the Light living inside him?"

He plucked a few strings of his mandolin where it lay next to him on the bench. "Whenever I struggle to find the Light in someone, I try to unwind their circumstances. Think about it—from the *second* Celeno was born, from the moment the healer announced he was a boy, he was elevated as some kind of savior of Alcoro. Can you imagine what that kind of pressure would do to a child? To a teenager? Especially one who didn't *feel* particularly capable? Do you think he actually considers himself extraordinary?"

"You saw him on my ship, did you not?" I replied. "You saw the ostentatious wardrobe, the blinding crown. You really think he doesn't believe himself an extraordinary person?"

"What does a praying mantis do when it wants to look impressive? It fans out its wings and waves its stupid little arms around." He wiggled his pinkie finger in illustration. "You think it really believes it's ten feet tall? No—it's all show. And I doubt Celeno is any more self-delusional. He's just an ordinary person expected to fulfill wild expectations with absolutely nothing more than his plain old self." He dropped his hand back to his mandolin and plucked another chord. "I'm not justifying what he's done, and I'm not saying I particularly like the man. But yes, I can see the Light in him. I imagine he struggles. Who wouldn't, given his situation?"

I frowned at him. "*I* was born under similar circumstances, Rou. My parents were old when I was born. My father's health was already failing. From day one, my parents knew they would die when I was still a child. I was expected to lead a country before my twelfth birthday."

He smiled. "And you've taken to it famously. More importantly, though, you're not Celeno. Your strengths aren't his, and your weaknesses aren't his. We're not all identical clones dropped into different circumstances. Not even those of us who are identical," he added mildly, plucking another string.

I gazed out at the river. As if someone puffed out a candle, the sky darkened, and the golden color of the river faded to twilight blue. He plucked out a melody on his mandolin and then glanced at me. "Still bothering you?"

I sighed and shook my head. "I just don't understand."

He lifted himself off his elbows and picked up his mandolin. "Don't beat yourself up about it. It's not your folk's custom."

"But even my folk . . .." I rubbed my forehead. "As a

child, I turned to the Palisades each night to see the sun hit the waterfalls out of habit. But I never really . . . I didn't *really* believe it was something divine. I just don't understand how other folk can be so sure of something that seems so abstract."

He settled his back against the armrest, now sitting sideways on the bench so he was facing me. "Have you ever considered you might see the Light somewhere else? That maybe in a different form, it might resonate more for you?"

I turned my head to him. He strummed a few quick chords on his mandolin.

"No," I said. "I've never heard of anyone who saw the Light differently from their folk."

He shrugged. "Me neither. The Light is a cultural thing—we revere it the way we do because we were raised that way. But like I said, we're not all identical. Think of it this way: light can have different brightness and color, right? Even two candles side by side will be different. So it stands to reason the Light wouldn't be the same for everyone, either. Maybe you're drawn to it in a different way and just don't know how, yet."

"Have you ever heard of someone like that?"

He grinned. "Maybe you're a trendsetter."

I looked back out at the river, now almost invisible in the gathering darkness. "I don't know where else I would see it."

"You seem like a fairly practical person, Lady Queen."

"What's that supposed to mean?"

"Just that maybe you need to look for the Light in practical things," he said, plucking his strings. "Consider this: your folk see the Light in reflections. The Sea-folk see it in the sunrise, and the Hill-folk see it in the moon. The Wood-folk see it in their fireflies, and those what-d'you-call-'ems—the glowing mushrooms."

"Foxfire."

"Yes, that. Canyon-folk see the Light in the stars. Island-folk, lightning. I've heard the Tree-folk see it in the rainbow, if hearsay is to be believed." He strummed his mandolin. "And we see it in fire. What's different about fire?"

I looked back at him. He played a few nonsensical chords. As his fingers moved, I caught the glint from his ring again. Ah.

"We can *create* fire," I said.

"Right. We can make it, and we can use it. If we're careful, we can control it." He strummed again. "That's why a flint and firesteel are tokens of the Light for us. Their usefulness doesn't undermine their sanctity. It enhances it. Maybe that's something that makes more sense to you." He shrugged. "It's a thought, anyway."

I looked back to the river. "It's a thought."

We didn't speak again. Rou picked at his mandolin. As if in reply, the frogs down by the river began chirping their evening song. My notebook lay closed on my knees. As the night fully fell around us, he bound up my arm again, and we went our separate ways. I lay awake for a long time in the strange bed in a foreign house, staring at the deep shadows on the ceiling.

Thinking.

I woke early again the next morning, but it was only half in the interest of writing. I stole through the house until I found a window that peeped out to the river where the *Swamp Rabbit* was tethered. Sure enough, Rou was standing barefoot on the dock, looping the ends of his poi around his fingers. I settled down at the very edge of the sill, trying to stay as hidden as possible. I still wasn't sure this morning routine was something he wanted me spying on, and I didn't want him to change his pattern on my account. So I hunched behind the curtain, my notebook empty in my lap, while he struck his steel to his flint to light his poi and begin their golden circles through the air.

After bidding goodbye to Lord Comeaux, we met Fisheye at his appointed tree and were informed in his eccentric vernacular that Bogfire was being watched by the Alcorans.

"Sinkpot's yer best bet," he said, scratching Mirabelle behind the ears. "Only take the north channel crossing, not the south. Coupl'a suspect boats in the river."

"The south is about three hours faster," Rou said, bent over his map. "Otherwise we get spit out above the bend in the channel. We'll be quick. We can get by a few Alcoran boats. There's no reason for them to single us out."

"Don't say I didn't warn you. After Sinkpot you can head up through Fogwaller and Temper Crik."

"We're not going through Temper Creek," Rou insisted again, his face furrowed in a frown. "We'll scoot over to Sinkpot and try our luck with Belle-mere."

"Bellemere's crawlin', y'tomfool."

"Well, then we'll circle it for Dismal Green."

"You cain't pole up to Dismal Green from the east, s'too dense, and the riverway's bein' watched."

"But we have to go there—the Benoits are expect-ing us. They have our quicklime order."

Fisheye spat. "Wellen, you can git there from the west."

"I told you, I won't take these ladies through Temper Creek."

"Yer a daggum fool, Roubideaux. What's the use in ferretin' out Celeno's folk if yer not gonna listen to me?" He jerked his tether off of the tree he was moored to. He stalked to the stern of his punt and dipped his pole in the water. "Don't be stupid now, y'hear? Got enough stupid on my plate."

"Why don't you want to go through Temper Creek?" I asked Rou as the riverman poled away into the bayou.

Rou rolled up his map. "Because it's a festering armpit of misery and shame."

"Have you spent much time there?" I asked as he picked up his pole.

He dipped the pole in the water. "I grew up there." He shoved us off, directing us in a slightly different direction than Fisheye had taken. "Not only is it an armpit, it's a tad out of the way—it would probably add an extra day to the trip, and we need to be through the Draws before First Fire ends. To top it off, our contact there is tentative at best—our uncle. He's a kind old thing, but a little batty. I'd worry he'd let something slip in casual conversation without meaning to."

I looked at Gemma, who was sitting against the hull with a book of thick parchment open in her lap. Though she'd been locked in one of Lord Comeaux's spare rooms, they had spent a great deal of time discussing the differences in their methods and materials when he brought her evening meal. She was probably a much more gratifying audience than I had been. As we prepared to leave in the morning, he had furnished her with the book and a set of inks to bring with her on our journey. Now she held it and some swamp weed she had plucked from the bank in her lap, but she wasn't illustrating just yet. She was staring out over the water, her mouth set in a thin line.

She was still wearing her fussy shift. The delicate lace was not meant for the rough treatment of the past few days. The hems of her sleeves were dirty and fraying, and several spots were almost worn through. I took a seat on a crate across from her. She glanced at me and then back out over the river.

"How are you?" I asked, hoping to sound friendlier than I had the previous day.

"Fine," she said shortly.

"You look troubled."

"Well, I am. I wish you all would listen when I tell you this journey is a mistake."

"It's in motion now," I said. "It can't be helped, for good or bad. If *you* would listen, you might find the benefits to the rest of the eastern world outweigh the costs to your husband."

She turned her head away, her fingers tightening on her notebook and potential subject material, crushing a few of the leaves. "I *am* listening, Queen Mona. I have been listening my whole life. But I've told you, this effort has come at the worst possible time, and the consequences are going to be more drastic than you anticipate."

"I have learned to anticipate quite a lot," I said coolly. Her lips tightened, and not without difficulty, I stopped myself from provoking her further. Perhaps I should avoid talking about Celeno anymore, if I wanted to bring her around. I gestured to her dirty sleeves.

"We can get you a shift that fits, you know," I said. "Why do you keep wearing that one?"

"None of them are long enough," she said, still looking away from me. "They don't come up my neck."

I wracked my brain, trying to think if this was an Alcoran custom, if folk were expected to cover their skin. All the Alcorans we had seen in Lilou had been wearing boleros with stiff collars, but I had assumed it was just part of a uniform. Clearly I didn't know as much about them as I had thought, which unsettled me. Did Colm know these things? Or were they missing from even our cultural literature?

"I might be able to sew collars onto the ones in your trunk. If I could do that, would you wear them?"

She looked back at me. "Is it bothering you?"

"Frankly, yes. You and I already look like a couple of ragdolls. No sense in making it worse if it can be helped."

Rou chuckled from the bow. Gemma glanced down at her fraying sleeve. "If the shift came high enough, I would wear it."

"Excellent. Rou, do you have a sewing kit on board?"

"Affirmative, Lady Queen."

"Fetch it, if you please."

He set down his pole and crossed the deck, disappearing into the tent.

"You look fine, you know," Gemma said quietly.

"I have a head full of singed hair and my gowns are too short. My arm is swaddled like an infant. You'll forgive me if I don't agree with you."

"No one would doubt you're a queen," she said.

I studied her. She kept her gaze out at the river, her art materials still clenched in her lap.

"Posture," I said. One of my earliest lessons. I tapped the back of my fingers under my chin. "Sit up straighter. You have lovely eyes, Gemma—don't cast them away like you're apologizing to someone. Roll your shoulders back, and the chin will follow." I repeated my mother's words. "'Display confidence, and folk will believe it.'"

Rather than taking my advice, however, she closed her eyes in a slow, almost aggrieved movement. I heard her breath stream out her nose.

The tent flap rustled, and Rou came back out with a flat box in his hand. He handed it to me. "The lady's sewing kit."

"Thank you." I took it and waited a moment, but Gemma didn't open her eyes or speak again. Well, she'd solicited my advice—or I thought she had, anyway. It made no difference to me whether she took it or not.

Wordlessly, I left her with her inks and went into the tent to open her trunk. There were four shifts inside. I brought them out to the deck and spent most of the morning snipping one of them into strips, hemming them into shape, and topstitching the seams. The bayou slid by around us, the stands of cypress and tupelo trees slowly thinning out as we progressed. The humid air warmed significantly.

"You lied to me," Rou said near midday.

I looked up from my work. The sluggish current had picked up, and he was leaning on his pole, watching me. "When?"

"Yesterday. When you said you didn't have a secret talent."

I looked back down at the almost-completed collar in my hands. All that was left was to snip one of the buttons off the shift and sew it on the altered one.

"Well, you didn't seem especially impressed by the singing."

He was silent for a minute, and I thought he had gone back to poling. But then he said, "I'm sorry."

I looked up again. "What for?"

"I didn't mean to put you down. My jokes, you know, sometimes they fall flat."

"Yes, I've noticed—and I thought we agreed you were to keep them to yourself."

He grinned. "I do try, Lady Queen, honest. And I'd like to hear you sing. Will you sing now?"

"No. I'm busy." We jarred against a fallen log. Lyle swore from the stern. "And you should be, too. Get to work."

"All right, then. I'll sing." He lifted his pole, shoved us away from the log, and launched into a long, elaborate, and off-key song about a goose, a gator, and a disastrous twelve-course banquet. I hunched over my work to keep my amusement hidden from sight.

He had nearly gotten through the eleventh verse of the song when his voice abruptly cut off.

"Oh," he said. "Coming up on the channel."

I looked up. The trees had thinned to nearly nothing, and looming in front of us was a massive open waterway, wider than any river I'd ever seen. The nearest trees were nearly a quarter mile away, perhaps more, separated from us by the expanse of muddy, mulish water.

"You can't possibly pole across that?" I asked with surprise. I don't know what I had expected—just another river, I suppose. But this was almost as wide as the distance between Blackshell and Grayraen Island, wide enough for many ships.

"No, it's too deep for a pole. We have to pay a toll, and a paddle boat will take us across. You can see the punts up that way lining up. Hm, lots of traffic—we may be waiting awhile." He sighed. "Lady Queens, I'm afraid you have to get back in the tent. I know it's hot—I'm sorry."

I bundled up the sewing kit and gathered my work. Gemma trudged through the tent flap. I followed. "Hot" was an understatement. It was stifling inside, thick with the smell of baking canvas and brackish water. I left the flap open as much as I dared and settled down on the floor.

"What do you think?" I asked, holding up the first completed shift for Gemma to see. "Will this work for you?"

She looked it over without any enthusiasm. "Yes, it's fine. Thank you."

I eyed the dirty collar of her current shift. Her skin above the lace had a touch of red, as if the fabric had been chafing her. "They must be uncomfortable, these high collars," I said lightly. "Especially in such hot weather."

She shrugged and looked away.

"Well, look who's washed up," said a female voice outside, and we both tensed. "A couple of Roubideauxs up to no good. Here for a tow?"

"Naturally, Miz Rosaline."

I peeked out the tent flap to see Rou toss our tether to a woman standing on a long, narrow dock. She caught the rope and attached it with a slip knot to a cable that ran parallel to the dock, leading toward the channel. Punts crammed the water ahead of us, all tethered to the cable, waiting their turn for the paddle boat. I tried to get a look out at the channel, to see what such a boat looked like, but the view was blocked by the press of punts and the remaining cypress trunks.

Rou rummaged in his pocket. "Two silvers, isn't it?"

"Don't fool with me, Roubideaux. You know it's four. Though today I ought to make it ten, great Light—what a morning."

"I don't suppose you'd take six in return for a shortcut in line?" he asked, counting out the coins in his palm.

"Can't, sorry. And don't try to sweet-talk me— I'm not in the mood."

"Eight?"

"I *can't*, Rou—the Alcorans are mucking up the crossing, going through every boat, making things take three times longer than necessary. Folk are already riled. On that note, I sure hope you don't have campaign material on board—had to dump a whole crate of pamphlets for Senator Ancelet in the water just an hour ago . . ."

The coins spilled from Rou's palm and pinged off the deck. "Did you say Alcorans are searching the boats?"

"Got here a few hours ago, been holding everything up. Why, you don't have contraband, do you?"

"Great blazing Light!" He swiped up his pole. "Untie our tether—we've got to get out of here!"

I didn't have a chance to see more. Without warning, I was shoved to one side from behind. I fell into the loose tent flap, the heavy canvas flopping over my head. Gemma sprang out onto the deck.

"*Help me!*" I heard her shriek over the water. "In the name of the Light and the Seventh King, help!"

I ripped the canvas off my head and scrambled to my feet. Rou jumped forward and latched on to Gemma's wrists, but she twisted in his grip and continued to shout. On the punt ahead of us, a curious head poked around the deck cabin.

I glanced past the jumble of boats for the distant shore.

It was very far.

I lunged forward and caught Gemma around the middle, jerking her from Rou's grasp and propelling her to the bow of the punt. We hit the low hull with force, pitched forward, and plunged into the murky water.

Great Light, it was like trying to swim Colm away from Lumen Lake the day the Alcorans attacked. She thrashed in my grip, fighting me tooth and nail. But she was smaller than Colm, at least, and with a few strong kicks I directed us under the line of punts. The water was no less disgusting than my last trip into the bayou, warm and smelly and thick with growth. Silt and decay clouded up from the murky bottom as Gemma struggled against me. But I was long used to swimming with only my legs, though it was normally with a basket of abalone rather than a thrashing queen. Still, I drove us quickly under the line of boats, trying to clamp Gemma's arms by her sides as I went.

The weedy bottom began to fall away, and the remaining tree trunks disappeared. The water took on a slight current, pushing against us from the right. At that moment, Gemma's struggling became different. Her hand found my forearm—my left one, thankfully—and squeezed tightly, her fingernails cutting into my skin. I heard her whimper through the water.

Can't surface now, I thought, irritated by her meager supply of air. I increased my pace, though, drawing my left arm out of her grip and sweeping it in front of me. We swerved around a slimy log jutting up from the muck. It was only when a school of dull-colored fish startled from its shadow that I remembered the threat of alligators and snakes. I carried us forward, convincing myself the river was too wide and deep for such animals.

I knew we were passing under the Alcoran boats when anchor chains stretched down to the riverbed. Their hulls, rounder than the flat-bottomed Cypri punts, forced me to arc downward. Silt clouded my eyes. The stink of the water rushed up my nose.

Gemma whimpered in earnest. With one, two, three determined kicks, we sailed under the blockade and into the sun on the far side.

Gemma reached up and tugged sharply on a lock of my hair. Praying the Alcorans would be facing the trees and not the channel, I angled toward the sunlight. I put my hand under her chin and thrust her face above the surface.

She dragged in two frighteningly loud draughts of air and coughed explosively. Before she recovered enough breath to scream, though, I pulled her back under. She fought me with renewed strength, but the brief respite had allowed me to get a better grip on her. Clutching her again with both arms, I swam further out into the channel as quickly as I possibly could.

It was unnerving, this water—when I swept my arm out in front of me, I could barely see the tips of my fingers through the murk. Not that there was anything to see—when we surfaced again a moment later, we were well beyond shouting distance of the shore, surrounded by endless dirt-colored water. Gemma choked and spluttered as she drew breath.

"How good of a swimmer are you?" I asked.

She didn't answer, her head tilted back as she drew ragged gasps of air.

"Think you could make it back to your folk's boats?" I asked, nodding toward the shore we had come from.

When she still didn't say anything, I released my grip on her and propelled myself backward, leaving several feet of water between us. As I expected, she went under. Perhaps I was misinformed about Alcoran culture and politics, but I could make inferences about growing up surrounded by desert. She emerged with significant splashing, coughing out dirty water.

"Wait," she gasped. "No, I can't—not that far. And my dress, my shoes . . . don't leave me here."

I swam back to her side and hoisted her above the surface once more.

"Then listen," I said between my own breaths as I fought to keep us afloat. "This is a big river. I'm going to get us to the other side. But it's going to be a lot easier if you stop fighting me. If you slip my grip, I can't promise I'll be able to find you again in this water. Understand?"

She coughed again. "All right . . . all right, fine."

Her crown was askew on her head, snagged in her wet hair. "Here," I said, reaching up and working it free. I closed her fingers around it. "Hold on to that." Hopefully it would keep at least one of her hands occupied. "All right. Deep breath."

She dragged in another gasp, and I pulled us under again.

Yes, good—it was much easier without her thrashing. I continued to swim us forward, using the current to gauge my direction. But it wasn't always easy to determine, and I had to surface more than I would have liked to be sure we weren't straying off track. On one of these occasions, I finally saw the paddle boat crossing the channel from the far dock. It had a paddle wheel as big as a person, powered by two River-folk cranking levers on either side. A punt bobbed along in its wake, towed by a stout cable. We passed underneath it on our next dive, the wheel churning with the force of a waterfall and filling the water with bubbles and froth.

I'd swum much farther and longer before—my very life and livelihood had depended on it more than once, after all—but dragging a person was tiring, and the long Cypri shift and overdress I was wearing did me no favors. I had chosen a dress with beading on the hem that morning, and it tugged me downward, into the depths. My boots, too, were a burden, but they were the only pair in my trunk, and I didn't fancy meeting the Assembly of Six in bare feet. I kicked with all my strength, driving us through the endless, opaque river.

There were Alcorans checking the boats on the far shore, too, so before we got within shouting distance, I angled downriver. I was thoroughly relieved when the first tree trunks began to rise out of the water. I stroked toward a massive cypress, its roots sweeping out from the trunk like the train on a gown. I latched on to it and hauled Gemma up alongside me. We both breathed heavily for a moment, gripping the slimy bark. My right arm sizzled with pain, but I ignored it, squinting across the water. The paddle boat was starting another tow from the far dock, but the *Swamp Rabbit* had been far back in the line. It could be an hour before Rou and Lyle were able to cross. We needed to find a place to wait—preferably out of the water—where we could see the channel.

Gemma suddenly shrieked and hauled herself up the tree, practically climbing on my shoulders. I was pushed under the water with no breath, but before I could surface and admonish her, I saw what must have startled her—a large shape wending through the gloom. I pushed her knee off my shoulder and broke back into the air.

"Something touched my leg!" she gasped.

"Get up, get out of the water," I said, pushing her higher onto the cypress roots. I scrambled after her. It was a steep pitch, hardly a comfortable platform, but we leaned against the bark and pulled our feet up after us.

"What is it?" she asked breathlessly. "An alligator?"

I peered into the water. If it was an alligator, it was a relatively small one—too small, I would think, to prey on humans . . .

"Great Light!" I exclaimed. "It's a *fish*."

It drifted to the surface, its gray, whiskered lips probing the flakes of bark and slime we'd disturbed in our retreat.

"A catfish," I said.

"It's *huge*," she said faintly, clutching her crown in her fists.

It was—bigger than any fish I'd ever seen, five feet long if it was an inch. After gulping down a few oddments, it sank back into the depths, ghostlike.

Gemma let out a shaky breath. "I liked it better when I *didn't* know what lived in the river."

"Mm," I said, turning my head away, unwilling to grant her a smile of commiseration. "I'd have liked it best if we could have stayed on the punt."

She sighed and leaned her head against the bark. "Queen Mona, I've told you. This isn't going to work, and the sooner I can get back to my folk, the sooner I can undo some of the damage."

"'Undo the damage'?" I repeated. "By maintaining your hold on Cyprien? By invading Paroa, and Winder after that? What damage does that undo? I'm doubtful that would even inch your Prophecy forward. It's not going to bring you prosperity—it's going to bring you ruin, and everyone else besides."

She closed her eyes. "The Prophecy is going to come true no matter what method we employ. I'm trying to find the way that won't destroy my husband."

I stared at her, my anger rising. "You realize you're putting the worth of one person above several countries? No one is worth that."

"I don't expect you to understand."

"I understand *plenty*," I said sharply. "No single person is worth more than a country's well-being, and to pretend otherwise is, simply put, an abuse of your power and privilege. I know that for a resolute fact. I learned it a long time ago."

She opened her eyes and drew a breath, as if preparing to press her point, but then she stopped. She squinted out at the channel.

"Is that them?"

I looked out at the river, where the paddle boat was nearing the tree line. Sure enough, bumping along behind it was the *Swamp Rabbit*, evidenced by the patchy tent jostling on board. While they were still a few feet from the tow dock, a recognizable figure leaped from the paddle boat and hauled at the tether for the punt.

"They must have moved up in line," I said. "Come on. We need to get somewhere they'll see us."

She took a quick breath, her eyes flicking to the water. "Well, but . . ."

"Our other option is starving at the base of this tree," I said irritably. "Catfish don't eat people." At least, I didn't think they did—even if they were *hulking, monstrous catfish*. I tried to mask my own apprehension with cool indifference.

She whimpered nervously, but followed after me as I slithered back in the water. I pulled her deeper into the trees, trying to catch glimpses of the dock while staying far enough away to keep her from shouting for her folk. Soon the water grew shallower, turning from river back into bayou. But when I tried to stand, my feet only sank into the mud. So we continued to swim, vainly trying to keep our eyes and mouths out of the leaf-stained water. Twice I saw snakes, but they fled at our approach, gliding over the water with eerie, serpentine ease. A dragonfly the size of my palm landed *on my head*, the insolent fiend—I lost my grip on Gemma briefly as I swiped it away. Unprepared, she got a mouthful of swamp. I couldn't say I cared. It was her fault we were in this mess.

By the time the far end of the tow dock came into view, my stomach was in knots from the disgust and trepidation. Fortunately, there were fewer punts in line on this side of the channel, and the end of the dock was quiet . . . save for Rou, bent double as he ran as fast as he could while dragging the *Swamp Rabbit* alongside him. He didn't slow when he reached the end—he jumped back to the deck, rocking the punt, and plunged his pole into the water. Lyle moved his own pole from the stern.

"Deep breath," I said to Gemma. "We're going under again. It'll be faster."

At least, it would have been faster, if I didn't have a blasted forest in my way. Regardless, in less than half a minute, I was alongside the hull of the *Swamp Rabbit*—I could tell because I could hear the brothers arguing on board. I surfaced next to the hull and narrowly avoiding being impaled on Rou's pole. He yelped at our appearance.

"Flaming, fiery, blazing Light and sparks a-flying!" Recovering his senses, he flung his pole down and dropped to his knees. He leaned down and hoisted

Gemma bodily onto the deck. I hauled myself alongside her, shedding water.

"Great blazing Light!" Rou said again, sitting with a *flump* on the deck. His eyes were wide as saucers—and his cheek had a fresh cut on it. He gripped his head in his hands. "Are you all right?"

"Fine," I said. In truth, my right arm was burning viciously, and my limbs buzzed with weariness. Gemma knelt on the deck, hugging herself and drawing deep gasps of air.

"Are you hurt?" he asked, bending down to see Gemma's face. She shook her head. He looked to me and took hold of my burned arm. "Are you?"

"No. *Your* hands are shaking, though."

"I was sure I'd have to resuscitate one of you, or pick bits of you from between a gator's teeth, if we ever saw you again!" he said. "Great Light, Lady Queen!"

The punt bumped gently against a tree—Lyle had dropped his own pole and was storming around the tent. He stopped in front of Gemma. "That was some fine foolery you pulled," he spat, glaring down at her. "We've got irons and a gag in one of the crates, you know."

She looked up and wiped her eyes. "This whole thing . . . everything you're doing is a mistake. This isn't going to work like you hope it will. If you let me go now, I won't breathe a word of you or the Assembly. I'll tell Celeno I got away without knowing anything about you."

"Balls," growled Lyle.

Rou sighed and shook his head. "No, Queen Gemma. We're not going to do that."

"Folk are going to die," she whispered.

"Folk already *are* dying, Lady Queen," Rou said. "Alcoro wants Cyprien for two reasons: our trade access and our steel mills. Have you looked at the reports from our steel mills in the last fifty years?"

"Production has increased," she said quietly.

"Yes. You know what else has increased? Worker injury and death." He leaned forward so he could see her face again, hidden by the curtain of her wet hair. "I've worked in the mills, Lady Queen. I've been running around the bayou delivering messages for much longer. Folk are getting restless, and if we don't try to solve this diplomatically, you're going to have a full-fledged uprising of angry, repressed people, and you saw how well that played out for you in Lumen Lake. Listen. If you cooperate, this trip will be quick and painless for all of us. And once we get to Siere, I promise I will secure you an audience with the Assembly. Perhaps you can talk them into altering their strategy, if you have a better idea. But you have to cooperate."

She sniffed and dashed her thumbs under her eyes. Without another word, she rocked onto her hands and knees and crawled into the tent. The flap swung shut behind her. Rou ran his hands over his face and left them there, pressed over his eyes.

"Did anyone see?" I asked.

He let out his breath and dropped his hands. "Only Rosaline and the fellow in the punt ahead of us. But they're all right—she's used to sneaking folk around under the Alcorans' noses, and he turned out to be a bootlegger. No allegiance to the Canyon-folk."

"Helped that we threw them each a billet's worth of silver," Lyle said irascibly.

"Yes, well, no real loss," Rou said wearily.

"What happened to your cheek?" I asked.

"Punched," he said. "By the bootlegger."

"Punched?"

"Not hard," he said quickly. "But he was wearing a steel."

"Why . . ."

"Saved our skins," he said. "Nobody else saw what happened, but plenty of folk heard—heard Gemma shouting, and then a mighty splash. People were hopping onto the dock to see what the ruckus was about. Another minute and the Alcorans would have come poking around. I was trying to explain to Rosaline the extremity of our situation without broadcasting it to everyone, when the bootlegger hopped onto our punt and punched me in the face. I dropped like a rock." He glanced up at Lyle. "What was he shouting at me?"

"Something about you calling his mother a plucked pintail," he said.

"Yeah, I thought that was the gist. Anyway, Rosaline caught on and dragged us to the front of the line to 'separate the fighting.' Then we just had to get by the Alcorans."

"Did they search the crates?" I asked.

"No. They were looking for Gemma, not illegal cargo. They only cared about spaces big enough to hide a person. They thumped the deck a bit, and pushed stuff around, but they didn't open anything." He heaved a sigh and ran his hands over his face one last time. And then he looked at me—looked at me with the strangest expression.

"What?" I asked.

"You swam all the way across the channel."

"Yes . . ."

"Dragging a person."

"Yes."

He shook his head. "Never let me say again that the Lake-folk's greatest strength is napping on the beach. What possessed you?"

"It's a kneejerk reaction, I suppose," I said, wringing out my hair. "'Get to the water.' So far it hasn't failed me."

He opened his mouth, then closed it again. He ran his hand through his curls. He almost seemed embarrassed. Finally he cleared his throat and said, "Are you all right?"

"You've already asked me that."

"Yes, and I imagine you're fibbing. How's your arm?"

"A little sore."

"I bet. I'll clean the swamp out of it, but not here." He got to his feet. "Let's put some bayou between us and Celeno's folk first." He extended his hand to me.

I took it and stood, but he didn't let go. His mouth was open again, as if searching for the right words.

"What?" I asked again.

He dropped my hand, shook his head once more, and turned back to the bow. "You're a good swimmer."

"Of course," I said.

He shook our tether loose. Lyle circled back to the stern, and Rou directed us away from the trees. I swayed on the deck, staring at Rou's turned back, wondering what he had actually been trying to say.

CHAPTER 8

Gemma didn't come out of the tent the rest of the afternoon. I sat on the deck, leaning against the hull with my notebook open in my lap. Now was a good time to question Lyle, and I held my quill determinedly in my fingers. But I was exhausted from the swim across the channel, and the breeze was warm, and the boat rocked gently . . . and the next thing I knew, Rou was crouched in front of me, his hand on my arm, quietly speaking my name. The sky held the first blush of evening. Someone had rolled up a cloak and set it behind my head to keep it from lolling.

Someone. Well, it certainly wasn't Gemma, and Lyle didn't quite seem the type for personal comfort.

"Sorry to wake you," Rou said.

"Not at all," I croaked. My throat felt lined with silt, and I reeked of swamp. I took his offered hand and struggled to my feet. I accompanied him unsteadily up the walk to our hosts' house. Gemma trudged in front of Lyle with her head down.

I felt better after bathing and changing into a shift and dress that weren't crusted with mud. It's amazing what simply being *clean* can do to raise your spirits. Renewed, I went in search of Lyle, notebook in hand. But he was nowhere to be found—not on the punt, not on the porch, not in the parlor or workshop or dining room. When I finally found him sitting against the coldhouse, his quill flying across his parchment, Rou was calling me for dinner.

"He's *avoiding* me," I said indignantly.

"I find him at his most pleasant during those times," he said, crooking his arm to me.

"But why?" I asked, taking his arm. "Why won't he talk to me?"

"Because you're a living, breathing human being who might require him to emote."

"I don't want to chat with him. I'm trying to accommodate your Assembly's requests, and he has information I need."

Rou sighed. "I'll have a word with him once he comes back. He won't care what I say, but maybe if I keep at him, he'll give in to make me stop."

Our hosts that evening were the Brasseauxs, a pair of sweet old ladies who used their modest hatmaking business as a front for running covert goods around the waterways for the Assembly. They took the crates of Lyle's incendiary prototypes from us and promised to deliver them to the folk we had to bypass on our route. They then tried to foist a dozen different hats upon me, delighted by the conundrum my ragged hair presented them. They spent an hour pinning bits of lace and sweeps of silk to a variety of brims to cover the singed patch behind my ear. I had never been one for wearing hats unless it was snowing out, as I almost always had a crown on my head, but it was entertaining hearing them quibble back and forth. Rou sat crossways in an armchair in the corner, plucking absently at his mandolin and flashing me that crescent grin from across the room as the hatmakers fussed around me. His amusement was infectious, and I gladly tilted my head down while the ladies measured a brim, aiming my own unyielding smile at the floor.

The next morning, I left my notebook tucked into my traveling bag when I snuck downstairs. The Brasseauxs had no servants, so I didn't have to worry about making excuses to anyone about why I was sitting at the riverside window. I was late—Rou had already lit his poi when I settled down on the settee and twitched back the drapes. I watched as he began their pattern, starting with slow, alternating arcs on either side of his body. The dock he was standing on had gaps between the slats, and I could see the reflections of the fire in bright lines on the river's surface. Something about this was especially beautiful to me, and as he moved his feet over the dock, it looked like he was stepping over a bed of gleaming coals.

A part of me felt foolish. I could see Colm lifting his eyebrows at me, could hear Arlen's snide comment. I could feel the sharp nudge Mae gave me to the ribs. At the moment, I couldn't make myself care. There were plenty of times in my life that I had wept or giggled at some triviality, always tucked carefully out of sight from prying eyes. Those stolen moments helped me keep my head during heated debates with my council. They helped me keep my composure as I expressed condolences to a citizen's family. The quiet enjoyment of watching Rou spin might later help me keep a civil tongue if talk on the punt turned to Celeno. I pushed away the foolishness and rested my chin in my hand, following the graceful pattern of Rou's fire as it danced over the river.

I watched until the sun warmed the surface of the water and he snapped his poi through the air to extinguish them. As he bundled them away in their bag, I crept back to my room. I packed up my trunk, tucking the feathered, netted hat the Brasseauxs had gifted me inside. I brushed my mangled hair, worrying the singed wisps behind my ear.

As ragged as the burned patch looked, I couldn't bring myself to cut it. I was being stubborn, and vain, but my hair had always been long. As a spindly, stick-straight girl, it was one of my few physical features I thought was truly beautiful. And besides, it was fashionable. I liked wearing it loose or pinning it up in elegant chignons. I liked wearing pearl pins and silver combs. And I couldn't make myself give all that up—not yet, anyway.

As I stowed the brush in my trunk, there was a knock at my door, and I opened it to find Rou with his medical kit tucked under his arm.

"Morning," he said. "Time to check that burn."

I sat in the chair by the window, and he perched on the footstool and unpinned the linen on my arm.

"Sleep well?" he asked.

"Yes, thank you. And you?"

"Like a rock—the bullfrogs drowned out Lyle's snoring. I talked to him, by the way—told him to quit making our folk look like a bunch of backwater drivelers and tell you what you need to know."

"And?"

"Oh, he went off on some impassioned rant about how his career and reputation are riding on his current work, and that the world could wait a few days until he was done. He always likes to paint himself as some kind of national hero. And I guess, in a way, he is," Rou said grudgingly. "But it doesn't mean he couldn't contribute even more by being a decent human being. I'll try him again later today—he's got no right to put you off."

He unwound the linen at my wrist. I sucked in a slight breath as the bandages stuck to one patch of my burn. He cradled my arm and blew gently on the raw spot, easing the sting.

"Sorry," he said. "I know it hurts."

"It's not as bad as it was," I said, wincing as he carefully lifted away the remaining linen.

"Yesterday did it no favors." He held my wrist and elbow gently, peering at my blistered skin in the morning light. "No infection. That's good. I'm going to put honey on it again, so don't go running around foolheaded like you did the first day."

I twisted my mouth to hide my smile while he took the stopper out of the honey pot. As his hand moved in the light, I saw the old burn mark on his hand.

"You have a burn scar," I said.

"Where?"

"There, on your hand. On the back of your thumb. What's that from?"

"Oh, right," he said, glancing at it. "That's old. And it's a double. Two in the same day." He turned over his right wrist, where another light-colored divot stood out against his brown skin. "Breaking blooms."

"Breaking . . . ?"

"Iron blooms—the chunks of iron right after they come out of the furnace. To get all the slag off them, they have to be broken apart with axes while they're still hot. Flying shrapnel was expected. I was lucky it was just my hand—there are plenty of half-blind folk who got hit in their eyes. Torchfire, it hurt, though, and it had to be wrapped, so later that evening, when I was spinning my poi, I fumbled my pattern and slapped the back of my hand with one of the wicks." He turned his left hand back over to the scar by his thumb.

"Ouch."

He bent his head over my arm. "People get worse."

"So that's what you did in the mills?"

"Sometimes. I was working the blast furnace, mostly, but some in the coking ovens and the forge when they needed extra hands."

"This was in Temper Creek? The town you don't want to travel through?"

"It was. Middle of blue-eyed nowhere."

"How did you wind up as a diplomat for the Assembly of Six?" I asked.

"Um. Good question." He cleared his throat. "The easy answer is I was a tagalong to Lyle's incendiaries. The Assembly wanted his skill, and I sort of got thrown in the mix as an added bonus."

"And the long answer?"

"Oh." He drizzled honey on my arm. "The long answer is I hated working at the mill—I mean, everyone hates it, but I was less resilient than most. Or maybe more resentful, I don't know. The Alcorans took over all the management positions in Cypri industry, you know. Meaning we're just manpower. The fellow in charge of the mill was good at maximizing production, but he had never had to run like a madman from molten iron boiling over a trough, spewing fire and slag like a belching dragon. Something about doing the work yourself gives you a better appreciation for your fellow workers."

"I didn't realize," I said. "About the industry, I mean. I suppose I knew it must be difficult work, but . . ."

"It isn't the worst job imaginable, but it's sure close. My brother was better about it than I was. He put his head down and stuck with it after I quit to scrounge up other jobs." His hands suddenly paused, his fingers near the crook of my elbow. I tilted my head to see where he was looking, in case he was examining some worrying part of my burn he'd missed before. But when he saw me move, he shook himself and continued. "I was a mail carrier the longest. Ran all around the backwater towns delivering messages. When Lyle went to work for the Assembly, they didn't really know what to do with me, so they just let me keep being a messenger."

"Is that what you want to keep doing?" I asked. "Or would you have chosen to do something else?"

"Oh, no, I like it. I like people. And people like me. I can put my stupid tricks to good use. I can do something worthwhile."

"Like spinning poi."

"Like spinning poi, though that's perhaps my one lone talent I don't consider stupid."

"I wouldn't, either," I said, and wondered if I was blushing. "When did you learn?"

"Long time ago. Sixteen, seventeen years, I can't remember. Took me a while."

"Is it very difficult?"

He smoothed out the last of the honey near my wrist. "Oh, a bit, but it took me longer than most because I didn't have much time to practice. Fortunately it's a skill that's best learned at night, so I could do it after work and school."

"What about your family? Do you have other family?"

"Just Lyle. But enough about me. All you really need to know is that I can stand on my head and I like pastries. Tell me about you. Because you've already turned out not to be the queen I was expecting."

"You were expecting the queen from four years ago," I said as he stoppered the honey pot once again. "But a lot of things changed during our exile."

"Apparently. In preparing us to host you, Senator Ancelet was under the impression you commission a new gown made of Samnese silk for every solstice."

I looked out the window. "I used to. But you might imagine, in light of everything that's happened, some of my past pursuits strike me as a bit . . . superficial."

"Hotter fire, stronger steel. That's what my mother would have said to you."

"Would she? What was your mother like?"

"She was the pinnacle of humanity. But we're talking about you now." He unwound a clean length of linen. "I suppose you had to care for your brothers?"

"Well, to a point. They weren't children any more than I was. But Colm, my middle brother, was grieving his wife, and my youngest brother, Arlen, developed a wild temper. So yes, I had to be the one to make things happen. We worked odd jobs, like you, for a while."

"Diving?"

"Some. But I worked as a seamstress in Sunmarten for almost a year. The tailor I worked for was ready to make me a partner." I smiled slightly, remembering the dismally amusing conversation. "She liked my leadership skills."

He laughed, winding down to my wrist. "Who'd have thought?"

"I might well have taken the job, too, if we hadn't had to flee north after Arlen shouted out our real identities at midwinter. I could have strangled him then, but of course, if he hadn't outed us, we'd never have met Mae."

"That's a story I do want to hear," he said, pinning the end of the linen. "But I smell eggs Roemere, and I'd hate to deprive the ladies of their opportunity to squabble over your hair again." He got to his feet. "Have you decided whether you want to cut it?"

I ran my hand over the singed patch, rough and matted despite the thorough brushing I'd given it. "I'm not sure. I've been avoiding mirrors. I suppose I should do something to it before I meet the rest of the Assembly. Does it look awful?"

"Lady Queen, you could have bulrushes sprouting from your head and you'd still look regal. On the subject, though . . ." He glanced at the half-open door. "Just so you're aware, when someone's about to light a flash grenade, we yell *blind*. That tells whoever's in the know to shield their eyes."

"Blind."

"Yes. Hopefully we won't be lighting any on the trip, but just in case things go amiss." He held out his hand. "Breakfast?"

I laid my hand in his and stood, debating whether to voice the request on my mind. As he bundled up his medical kit, I said, "Rou."

"Hm?"

"I liked seeing you spin in Lilou. Maybe I can watch you again sometime?"

He tucked the bag under his elbow and crooked his other arm to me. "If I get my poi out, I'll let you know. Hard to find time for it, you know."

I stopped myself from mentioning that I was often awake before the sun. The fact that he'd sidestepped the question meant that he wasn't open to the idea of me sitting in on his quiet morning routine. Why? Was it a reluctance to perform for others? I recalled his juggling for the Doucet children, his careless picking at his mandolin, his launching into song on the punt—and I dismissed the idea of stage fright. No, it was something else I couldn't discern, and I couldn't think of how to pose the question without giving myself away. I'd have to give it more thought.

I took his proffered arm. Together we walked to the door and out into the hall, following the smell of frying eggs and ham.

Gemma looked distinctly more polished in her fresh shift. I still hadn't been able to interpret her preference for such conservative clothing—whether it was a cultural norm or simply a fashion trend, I couldn't say. She spent the morning on the *Swamp Rabbit* with her inks again, filling the pages of her book with detailed illustrations of plant life and determinedly ignoring the rest of us. Early in our journey, Rou snatched up an insect from the hull—a damselfly, apparently—and brought it to her. She underwent a short-lived transformation, her silence falling away as she exclaimed over its size and iridescent color, taking it from his hands without reservation and examining the struggling thing this way and that. I shuddered, still unable to wrap my head around the Alcoran queen. She had already proven she had a sharp mind, with obvious skills in science and strategy. And yet she clung to her folk's Prophecy with a blind, illogical devotion. What was really at work here, and more importantly—how could I guide her to see sense?

We met Fisheye, who once again advised us to take the western detour through Temper Creek. He admonished Rou in a variety of ways for his stubbornness, his white whiskers quivering in irritation.

"We'll cut up to Fogwallow tonight," Rou said, overriding the riverman's litany of rebukes. "Then tomorrow we'll cross the river and head up to Dismal Green."

"*Y'cain't pole to Dismal Green from the east, y'snakebit waterdog!*" Fisheye exclaimed with vehemence, making Mirabelle sway on his shoulder.

"We'll manage. We've had good rains. The basin will be full."

"Pah!" He stomped back onto his punt. "F'you git snapped up by Celeno's folk, I'mma stand in the crowd at yer execution and shout that I told you so." With that, he stabbed the bank with his pole and shot away into the bayou.

Fogwallow, Rou said, would be an enjoyable stay. "Delightful family," he said. "The Toussaints. Their oldest daughter, Heloise, is smitten with me—we should be treated well." I arched an eyebrow before struggling to hide the expression, surprised at the sudden spark of irritation that flared in me.

Fortunately, he didn't notice. "They live on a bit of a rise, too," he continued, "so we may be able to see some of First Fire down in the village." He gave a hearty sigh. "There's an amazing staff spinner in Fogwallow who always puts on the best displays—I wish you could see her, Queen Mona. It's a sight, all of it. Coal-walkers and fire-breathers, and the food." He groaned and threw an arm over his stomach. "It's such a shame that we have to miss it all."

"Maybe I'll come back next year," I heard myself say.

"You should. Things will all be righted by then. We'll take you through the classiest towns on the *Ember* riverboat line, and you can eat all the jubilee tarts and drink all the spiced coffee in the waterways."

"Watch it."

"Sorry, am I overstepping—"

"Watch it," I repeated, pointing.

We bounced off a stand of cypress knees while he leaned wistfully on his pole. There was a soft exclamation from the hull—Gemma's ink had slopped from its bottle. A dark splotch marred an illustration she had been working on, but she was looking at the sleeve of her new shift, which was now stained with black speckles.

"Ah, I'm sorry," Rou said, hastily maneuvering us away from the knees. "I'm an idiot."

I was about to quip a response to him when something caught my eye. Gemma was dabbing at her sleeve—her left one, the one she was always worrying. It slid up briefly, and I caught a glimpse of a mark on her wrist. A purple mark. Very distinct. Very dark.

Very much like a bruise.

My heart jumped in my chest, my easy mood gone. I recalled the way she had recoiled from me when I offered to help her out of her gown on our first morning together. I recalled her tugging on her sleeve, checking to be sure it wasn't riding up. Her desire for high collars . . . was she marked there, too?

What kind of injury would inflict such marks?

Why should someone of her stature be so bent on hiding them?

My hands clenched on my knees, my stomach roiling. It was well known in Lumen Lake that I had no tolerance for domestic violence. Fortunately, my folk were reliably levelheaded, but once or twice a year I had to address the occasional drunken altercation, and I did not look kindly on the perpetrators. I studied Gemma sidelong as she sought to right her inks and parchment. Any shred of lenience I had granted Celeno in the past few days evaporated. I recalled how she flinched at a raised voice and how urgently she spoke about the consequences this journey may have. Was her husband, lauded as the most worthy man in Alcoran history, nothing more than the most cowardly of thugs?

I itched to share my thoughts with Rou, but of course there was no opportunity to speak privately to him on the punt. For the rest of the day, I tried to carry on normal conversation, but I couldn't keep my eyes from flicking down to Gemma's ink-stained sleeve. I tried to analyze her movements and her past behavior. I tried to think through what this might mean for our endeavor.

Because when it came right down to it, the idea of sending her back to an abusive husband did not sit well with me at all.

"I've been admiring your crown," I said to her in the late afternoon. It was true, and I decided I may as well voice my admiration. "It catches the light beautifully."

She lifted a hand from her notebook and touched it. "All Alcoran women wear them."

This was news to me. "They all wear crowns?"

"We call them star bands. Mine is just more elaborate than most. A common woman would wear cut glass, a noblewoman might wear diamonds."

I recalled the jeweled hair bands I had seen the Alcoran women wearing when we first arrived in Lilou. "So they're not meant to be prisms?"

"Not originally. Nowadays, yes, that meaning is often associated with them, but in our early history, they were meant to honor the stars. Back when the notion of the Seventh King was an abstract, futuristic idea, my folk cleaved more to the stars than the words of the Prism."

I gave a sudden, involuntary laugh. She looked down, her shoulders hunching at my response.

"No," I said, trying to control my smile. "No, I'm sorry. I'm not laughing at you. I'm laughing at my brother."

"Your brother?"

"Colm, my middle brother. He's something of a scholar in history and culture. Before I left for Cyprien, he was working on transcribing a text on Alcoran ladies' hair ornaments. He said it was a vital piece of cultural anthropology."

"He was right. Our earliest records are the petroglyphs, and they clearly show them. It's how male and female figures are distinguished." She put her quill to her parchment and drew a circle, followed by a stem and angular branches—a stick figure. Over the head she put three dots. "In all the petroglyphs ever found in Alcoro, women are always depicted with dots above their heads. We in modern history have developed star bands to mimic that flourish."

"How do you know they're women?" I asked. "How do you know they're not something men wore, or leaders wore?"

"Because many of the figures are doing distinctly female things. Giving birth, for example." She drew another figure, this time with stick legs splayed apart and a smaller circle and line emerging between them. "Births used to be momentous events to our ancestors, and any time a woman had a child, her partner would carve this mark near their home. Other figures are shown pregnant." She drew a third figure with a distinct swell in the middle. "Or breastfeeding. Or menstruating. All have dots above their heads. We believe the feats of women's bodies were highly revered in our ancient society."

"I've heard that's where the concept of inner Light began," Rou said from the bow, poking the bank with his pole.

I looked at him. "You've heard of this?"

"We share some of the same past. The line between Alcoro and Cyprien wasn't always there. Folk up toward Siere tend to be more sandy-colored, like the Canyon-folk, instead of dark like us lowlanders." He waved his bare forearm vaguely to illustrate.

"Your folk have kept more of the old practices," Gemma said to him.

"How so?" I asked.

"Their matriarchy, for one thing."

"Matriarchy?" I looked back to Rou. "You take your mothers' names?"

"And then we take our wives'," he said, nudging the bank again. "My father went from being Jules Jejeune to Jules Roubideaux when he married my mother."

I was beginning to wonder if I had paid any attention at all in my international history lessons, or if our information was just woefully inadequate. "I had no idea." I looked back to Gemma. "But that's not your folk's custom, is it?"

She looked back down at her illustration. "No. In theory, a couple decides which surname they'll take upon marriage, but it usually ends up being the husband's name."

My eyes flicked to her sleeve again. I cleared my throat slightly. "Gemma, did you . . . have much say in your marriage to Celeno?"

She smiled thinly at her parchment. "No. Not much." She must have realized what had just come out of her mouth, because she jerked her eyes up to mine. "Not that I'm unhappy with it, of course. Not at all."

"Of course," I said coolly. She swallowed and took up her quill again, turning the page on her stick figure drawings.

Alcoro was a country that literally crowned their women, yet was led by this woman—hushed, cryptic, paradoxical. Under the thumb of her husband, but ready to give up everything to save him.

I was going to get to the bottom of this.

The Toussaints did indeed have a grand house, furnished with balconies on all three stories and surrounded by ornate gardens. I balked, however, the moment the front doors opened—every surface and wall was festooned with the colors of the Alcoran flag. The prism and seven turquoise stars glared down from a russet banner hanging prominently over the rail of the sweeping staircase. Gemma lifted her head somewhat hopefully.

"We're so relieved to see you, Lady Queen!" Lady Toussaint exclaimed—to me, not to Gemma. She nodded to the butler. "Show . . . *her* . . . to her room, please, Eustis, and see the door is locked." The butler obediently directed Gemma to the staircase, her hopeful look replaced with dismay.

"Appalling, isn't it?" Lady Toussaint said in a hushed voice as she shook my hand in both of hers. "Russet clashes with all my mother's furniture."

Rou heard me stuttering my first few questions as she guided me to the parlor. "Sorry," he called after me. "I should have explained."

They were land barons, it turned out, owning much of the arable land in Fogwallow. They'd kept it that way by being vocal supporters of Alcoro—on the outside.

"The Alcorans levy high property taxes designed to reduce the number of Cypri who can legally own their land," Lady Toussaint explained as she gestured for me to take a seat. "We require our tenants to pay only sixty percent of that tax, while we make up the rest."

"Don't you lose money?" I asked.

"Every year," she said with forced lightness. "Our folk pay extra when they can, and we get our own subsidies from the Assembly, but we're always short. I must ask you not to poke your head into too many of the upstairs rooms—most of them have been stripped bare over the years to compensate. My family's belongings . . ." She waved a hand. "Still, we have enough to keep up the appearance, at least for another few years." She smiled warmly at Rou and Lyle as they made their way into the parlor. "How about Ines Deschamps, then, boys? A real champion of industry . . ."

Rou's grin faltered as we were led to the dining room.

We were treated to yet another remarkable meal—oysters on the half-shell, shrimp in red sauce, blackened catfish, bread pudding, custard, cream tarts. I did notice that the butler was also the server, and Lady Toussaint dismissed him after dessert to join his family for First Fire.

"He doesn't live here," she explained when she caught my glance. "He only comes in when we have guests."

The Toussaints' oldest daughter, Heloise, was conspicuously overdressed, wearing an ecru gown full of lace and ribbons. Similar embellishments were wound into her black hair, which was meticulously arranged in an ornate braided whorl. She sat next to Rou at dinner, hanging on to his words, laughing when he laughed, and finding every tiny opportunity to touch him—striking his shoulder in delighted shock when he said something particularly witty, or resting her fingers on his arm as she spoke to him. To my irritation, he seemed to encourage her, leaning his head close to her when she made some quiet comment, or offering her lavish, flowery praise. I couldn't say why this should irk me so much except that Heloise had a distinctly high-pitched giggle that grated on my nerves more and more as the evening wore on.

"Will you come to First Fire tonight, Rou?" she asked breathlessly as we retreated to the parlor for drinks. "Please say you'll come. They've managed to book a juggling troupe tonight, they're supposed to be magnificent . . ."

"Ah," Rou sighed, patting her hand where it rested in the crook of his arm. "I'd love to, Heloise. But Lyle gets lonely out on the punt in the evenings, and I have a few tasks for the Assembly that I need to see to before we leave the Draws. You go for me, and let me know tomorrow just how good the jugglers are."

She was crestfallen, but despite her begging throughout coffee, he declined her request. Whenever Rou addressed me, she pursed her mouth, eyeing my ragged patch of hair with a sulky glare. After coffee, I watched through the window in the front hall as she trudged down the hill behind her brother and sister, her mask clutched halfheartedly in her hand.

I returned to my room late in the evening with every intention of cornering Lyle and demanding answers to my questions. But just as I gathered up my material, I found that the nib of my quill had split sometime over the last few days. Irritated, I took my notebook and ink and headed out of my chamber for the staircase. Lyle had mentioned the library on the top floor, asking Lady Toussaint if he could use it to do some work. Surely there would be a spare quill there, and maybe I would find him as well. I climbed the stairs and made for the end of the hall.

The door was ajar, and I pushed it open to find what must have once been a handsome room, paneled in wood and boasting an ornate fireplace. Now, however, the bookshelves were nearly empty, and two cloth-covered armchairs sat forlornly in the corner. But my eyes immediately went to the glassed doors at the far end, opened up to the night. They led out to a balcony overlooking the river, and the sky flickered golden with the light of First Fire below. Leaning on the rail, silhouetted against the light, was Rou.

There was an old desk by the doors, scattered with a variety of quills. I headed for it. But instead of picking up a quill, I set my notebook down. I went to the open doors.

"Hello," I said.

He turned his head, his tendrils lit by the glow. "Hello, Lady Queen." Below us, the ground swept away to the river, and the mossy trees danced in the flickering light. Music and cheers filtered up from the banks.

I joined him at the rail. "Not down on the punt?"

"Sometimes I need some time alone."

I paused as his words sunk in. "Oh," I said. Thankful that the darkness hid my flush, I turned back for the door.

His hand jumped out to touch my elbow. "No, I didn't mean you . . ."

"It's all right, I need to write anyway . . ."

"I didn't mean you," he said again. "It's Lyle. He drives me crazy. Please stay. We can watch the jugglers."

I paused again, and then joined him once more at the rail. "Can you see them from here?"

"Down there, by the docks. I think that's them. Hard to tell with all the torches."

I watched the flares of firelight rising in the night. "You know, you don't have to feel obligated to stay holed away in our hosts' houses, at least not for my sake. Why didn't you go with Heloise?"

"Lady Queen, are you trying to talk me into insubordination?"

"No," I said. "I just don't see what the fuss is about."

He chuckled. "Oh, it's better that I stay here. We've got some dense bayou to pole through tomorrow, and I don't want to be tired. And besides, I like Heloise well enough, but not to the extent that she likes me. It wouldn't be right to lead her on. Anyway, I'd have to buy her drinks, and then she'd want *me* to drink, and I'm a chatty drunk. I might slip and accidentally ask her to marry me."

"Does that happen often?"

"At least once or twice a day."

I looked away, twisting my mouth in amusement.

"Why do you do that?"

I turned back to him. "Do what?"

He leaned on one elbow, his head slightly tilted. "You bury your smiles. You always look away, or purse up your mouth, so they don't show."

I looked back out at the glowing riverbank. "Another adage of my mother's. 'Don't show the emotion you're really feeling. Show the emotion that will let you stay in control.'"

I could feel him staring at me. Down at the river, a plume of fire burst over the treetops, followed by a round of cheering.

"I would be a terrible monarch," he said.

I smiled slightly, my gaze still on the riverbank. "Probably. But then, my upbringing was more stringent than most. If your mother was the pinnacle of humanity, then mine was the pinnacle of sovereignty. Her most frequent words to me were 'you are a country.'"

He spluttered. "But . . . that's . . . but you're *not*. You're a person in charge of a country."

I looked sideways at him, still smiling. "No, Rou. I'm Lumen Lake. I can't act as if I'm independent from it. My mother knew that, and she knew it would be difficult for a child to comprehend. Hence all the mantras, hence all the rigor. She knew what was at stake for me."

"And it's worked out marvelously for Lumen Lake," he said. "But all I can think about is a mother telling a little girl not to smile."

"My father made up for it," I said, looking back out at the riverbank. "Even after he had to stay in bed, Colm and I used to crawl up with him. We'd put the blanket over our heads, and he'd read us fairy tales." I remembered that dark, safe space under the sheets filled with the sharp herbal scent of Father's tonic. "He kept sock puppets under his pillow to tell the stories."

"When did he die?"

"When I was eight, but he was sick for years." His image in my parents' portrait came to mind—the artist had tried to mask the pallor of his face, but she had unwittingly depicted his hollow cheekbones and thinning beard. Thankfully, though, she had captured the dogged twinkle in his blue eyes.

"What was wrong?" Rou asked. "Consumption?"

"Cancer."

"Oh." He sighed. "Damn cancer to the sun and back."

"Yes." I tucked my ragged strands of hair behind my ear. "There's another mother story for you. Before the funeral, she brought me to my room and said, 'if you have to cry, cry now.'"

Rou shook his head. "And did you?"

"For hours."

We were silent a moment. Over the treetops, flaming brands soared through the air, buoyed by appreciative applause.

"I remember when the ships came through, you know," he said. "The Alcoran warships. On their way to Lumen."

I looked at him in the dim light. "You do?"

"They came up the channel from the coast. We didn't know where they were going. To Lilou, we thought, though we couldn't think why. But then they sailed on past, all twelve of them, and we realized what must be happening. And when the news came that Lumen Lake had fallen, there was the strangest hush through the entire country. I remember folk in Lilou whispering the whole day we found out."

I jerked my head back to the festivities down by the river, because out of nowhere my throat had closed up and my eyes began to burn. I scrunched up my nose, trying to force the unwelcome feeling to pass.

Fortunately he hadn't noticed. He was looking back down at the river, too. "I've never had so many messages before or since to deliver. The senators were frantic, because Alcoran control to our west *and* north practically negated the possibility of ever winning back our independence. Celeno had validated himself. Folk who remember a free Cyprien are getting old, you know. Another decade or so and they'll be all gone. A lot of people were worried we'd forget what it meant to live under our own banner."

I turned my head away on the pretext of coughing and wiped my eyes. "I swam through Lilou," I said. "When we were escaping to Matariki."

"I was there," he said. "Maybe I saw you and thought you were a mermaid."

"We didn't stay long," I said. "Although I think Arlen may have stolen a pie for us to eat."

"My pie!" he exclaimed.

A laugh broke from me before I could stop it, helping to clear away the last of the constriction in my throat. Rou sighed, his mouth crooked in a resigned half-smile as he watched the riverbank.

"Hotter fire, stronger steel," he said.

"Yes." I wiped my eyes a final time. "What happened to your mother, Rou?"

"She died in the consumption epidemic," he said. "Six years ago."

"I'm sorry."

"Me, too. Consumption is a vile, hateful disease—damn it to the sun, too. Sucks the strength right out of a person." He leaned on both elbows. "It was . . . difficult watching her go that way. She had always been the backbone of our family."

"And your father?"

"Long gone."

"Passed away?"

"Walked out. A year after I was born. I don't remember him at all."

"But you know his name. You said his name was Jules."

"Yes. My mother never tried to pretend he didn't exist. She wanted to be sure we understood what he had done."

I looked back out over the river. A thought prodded the edges of my brain. "Do you see the Light in him?"

He smiled without looking at me. "Still stuck on that, are you?"

"Yes. Have you unwound his circumstances, and found him worthy?"

"Have I found him worthy? You're speaking the wrong language, lolly. Sorry—Lady Queen. The Light doesn't live in folk because they're worthy. It just does. It just *is*. It has nothing to do with how good or bad a person is. It's our own tendency to judge a person's goodness that makes us unable to see it in others. Jules Roubideaux was cowardly and self-serving and unworthy to share my mother's name, but the Light still lives in him, wherever he is. If I someday crossed paths with him, I would search for it."

I stared at him. The golden light from the riverbank flickered over his skin. He flicked his gaze sideways to me and grinned.

"I can feel you judging me. You must think I'm a sentimental ball of kitten fur."

"Actually, I was thinking that if I could see the Light in anyone, it would be you," I said. "You're more generous with your goodwill than anyone I've ever met. You see it in everyone."

The grin on his face slipped away, and he turned back to the river. "Oh, look," he said. "They've set a dock on fire."

I looked. Figures were rushing among the spreading flames, slapping at the dock with cloaks and splashing water over the wood.

"Must not have been very good jugglers after all," he said, scratching his stubble. "Doesn't sound like anyone's hurt, though. That's good. Hope that white dress of Heloise's doesn't get soot all over it."

In a blinding rush, the memory of Gemma's shift and bruises came flooding back to me. I gripped the balcony rail. I didn't want to talk about it now, but there wouldn't be another chance once we got back on the punt.

I cleared my throat. "That reminds me, Rou. There's something I've been wanting to talk to you about."

"What's that?"

I drew in a breath, my gaze on the activity below. I realized with some trepidation that his reaction would have a significant effect on my regard for him. "Today when we ran into the cypress knees, and Gemma got ink on her sleeve . . ."

"You want me to be more careful, so I don't keep ruining clothes?"

"No. I saw her sleeve ride up when she was cleaning it. Her left one, the one she's always pulling down. She has marks on her skin. Dark ones. Like bruises."

Slowly, he half-turned to face me. "Maybe she was hurt when we blazed Celeno's ship?"

"If she was hurt, she wouldn't be trying to hide it," I said. "And she was already wearing that silly lace shift before you attacked. It didn't fit with the gown at all. She was already trying to cover her skin."

He didn't say anything. I pressed on. "I think she may be abused, Rou. She didn't want me anywhere near her when she changed clothes, and she's always trying to hide that arm. And you've seen how she reacts to threats, how she recoils and tries to protect herself. I think Celeno may abuse her."

Another moment of silence slid by. When he did speak, he chose his words carefully. "That's a serious allegation to make. It wouldn't be right to jump in with accusations if we weren't absolutely sure."

Dismay flared up inside me. Was his first reaction to rush to Celeno's defense? I turned to face him fully. His easy posture had taken on a hint of tension, and he returned my gaze in full.

"I don't stand for this kind of thing, Rou," I said. "I imprison people for domestic violence."

"You can't sweep in and accuse Celeno of beating his wife," he said. "Think of the outcomes. You have to be careful."

"*Think of the outcomes?* The outcome is a battered woman! How can you say that?" My stomach twisted with anger. "Even if the Alcoran prophecy was true, and Celeno was the savior of all humankind, I wouldn't stand for it . . ."

His eyebrows lifted toward his hairline. "I'm not talking about Celeno," he said. "I'm talking about *Gemma*. This could be an emotional subject for her. She may be so used to protecting Celeno that she'll deny it even if you were to roll up her sleeve. You have to do it carefully, quietly. She's already under stress. Trying to force your way into her marriage may close her up entirely."

"I need to find out, Rou. This will significantly impact my plans for negotiating with Celeno. I don't feel right sending her back to an abusive husband."

"I don't, either. But we need to be sure first, and to be sure, we need to be kind. No storming into her room demanding she strip off her shift. And if it *is* true, she's going to need a friend who will listen to her, not a bunch of foreign dignitaries deciding her fate."

Relief washed through me, which I told myself was born from his concurrence rather than his gentleness. I waited for a quip or witticism, some punchline designed to lighten the mood, but none came. He looked back out at the river, his mouth pursed in thought. "I won't deny it would significantly change our strategy."

"But perhaps, if we can get her on our side, help her see that she doesn't have to go back to him . . . she could be even more useful to us, if she granted us her alliance."

"Perhaps." He ran his hand over his face. "But we have to start small. No ulterior motives. No digging too deep. We have to push all that away. Right now, we just have to be concerned for her well-being—and we have to show it." The corner of his mouth lifted. "Maybe smile at her."

I looked away, twisted my mouth, realized what I was doing, and looked back at him. His own grin grew. "It's okay," he said. "At least I know when you really think something is funny."

"Rou," I said. "Thank you for taking this seriously. I was worried you wouldn't think it significant."

He shifted and looked back out toward the river. "I find it extremely significant. I've got no patience for domestic violence, either. But ultimately, what I think doesn't matter. I'm just a messenger. It's the Assembly you'll have to deliberate with. Whether I side with Gemma or not is inconsequential."

"It's not," I said.

He looked back to me. The corner of his mouth quirked again in the barest smile. I nearly looked away, but I made myself resist the urge. I smiled back.

He nodded to the river. "Fireworks'll start soon. How about we drag the two armchairs out and watch the show?"

This smile was easier, because it was the kind I was used to—a front, trying to smooth over my real emotions. "Thank you," I said, straightening. "But I came looking for Lyle. I need to talk to him."

His own grin slid somewhat as I turned toward the door. "Thank you for speaking with me, Rou," I said over my shoulder. "Have a good evening."

A beat of silence passed as I headed back into the library. "You, too," he said.

I picked up my notebook and selected a quill, and then I crossed the library and made my way into the hall without looking back. I headed down the staircase. I walked to my room, opened the door, and closed and locked it behind me. I would not be going out again tonight. I would not be finding Lyle. I would just have to draft the other parts of the document first, without the weapons contract.

I leaned against the door momentarily, taking smooth, even breaths. Then I walked to my desk, sat down, and opened up my notebook. I uncorked my ink bottle and dipped the new quill. I held it over the page.

I stayed that way for three, four, five minutes, my quill poised, the ink drying on the nib. My mind was a swirling blank. I couldn't think what I had wanted to include in this document. I couldn't even really remember why I thought drafting this document was so important in the first place. Somewhere in the distance, I heard the pop and crackle of a firework.

I slapped my notebook shut and stuffed it back in my trunk. With sharp, irritated movements, I dressed for bed and bundled down under the coverlet amid the faint sounds of First Fire.

I could tell this was going to be the same kind of night as the one before we met Atria Coacotzli, one where my mind was far too full to sink into sleep. But this time, it wasn't full of logistical anxiety. It was full of a frightening amount of nonsense. Because when it came right down to it, the warmth I was feeling toward Rou after talking with him was not reasonable.

Not reasonable at all.

When I finally did manage to fall asleep, I had a dream, the kind that flashes through your head so quickly you wonder if any time passed at all. In it, Mae was burrowed comfortably in the guest bed I was supposed to be sleeping in. I was pacing the floor in front of her. She peeked out from under the coverlet.

"It's not wrong, you know," she said with a yawn. "Being attracted to someone."

"Hush," I said, my nerves jumpy. "I'm not going to let it happen again."

"Just because it went badly once doesn't mean it'll happen again. You're not a child anymore."

I faced her, my fists balled. "I haven't got time for this kind of thing. I have important matters at hand."

She scratched her nose sleepily. "Yup."

"I don't have the energy to waste. I can't be distracted."

"Nope." She drew the coverlet up under her chin. "Mm. This bed is warm."

"It would be a disservice to Lumen Lake. To my allies. I am a country, Mae."

She chuckled. "He has a nice smile, though."

"Hush," I said shakily.

"Intimacy means lowering your defenses," she murmured, closing her eyes. "Intimacy means being vulnerable. But it's not wrong, Mona, and it's definitely not weakness."

"Well, I don't want it."

She didn't answer. She was asleep, leaving me rattled in the middle of the room.

Because I was pretty sure I was lying to myself.

CHAPTER 9

I was caught the next morning.

I had hoped my late night of mental exhaustion would make me sleep late, but my eyes popped open at the barest hint of light. My mind whirled into anxiety again, and with no other option than lying in bed berating myself, I hurriedly dressed and stole downstairs to a riverside window.

It was comforting, watching Rou spin. I wondered why he did it so privately—why he, such a showman, would move through these graceful, impressive displays so secretly. It wasn't as if his skill itself was a secret—I had first seen him performing for a crowd in Lilou, after all. I rested my chin on my arms, recalling what he had said about seeing the Light in a different way. I tried watching the pattern of his poi, following the glowing streaks of firelight, but every time I did, I found my gaze drawn back to him. This didn't help my anxiety, and at one point I closed my eyes only to find the pattern of the wicks still burning behind my eyelids.

When he finished, I crept back up the stairs, each board creaking in the silence of the house. I reached the landing and tried to move down the hall more silently, but as I passed a closed door, I heard a soft knocking on the far side.

"Excuse me," called a timid voice.

I turned, confused, before realizing it was Gemma's room. She was locked in. I moved toward the door. "Are you all right, Gemma?"

"Mona?" Her voice slid down to the keyhole. "Can you fetch a servant?"

"I don't think there are any in the house. Do you need something?"

"I need bandages."

I crouched down. "Are you all right?" I asked again, more urgently.

"I'm fine. It's my cycle. It began last night."

My concern slipped into sympathy. How long had she been awake, waiting for someone to unlock her door? I stood. "I'll get some."

"You'll have to get the key, too."

"Yes." The butler had given it to Rou and Lyle the evening before. "I'll be right back."

Her soft thanks filtered after me as I hurried back to the staircase.

Rou was gone from the dock when I walked down the stairs to the punt, but Lyle was moving about on board. He saw me coming and straightened warily.

"Now's not a good time . . ." he began.

"I'm not here for that," I said, pulling the cover off one of the crates. "Though we're going to get to it sooner or later. Right now, I need the key to Gemma's room. And where do you keep the linen?"

"Why?" he asked.

"Because Gemma needs bandages."

"What for?"

I sat back on my heels, glaring at him. "She started her cycle last night. She's been locked up in her room with no bandages."

I let him mutter and twitch awkwardly without lowering my gaze. He shoved a crate in my direction, avoiding my eyes, and then fled into the tent, fumbling around inside. I opened the crate and took out several lengths of linen, annoyed at how flustered he was. He emerged from the tent and thrust the key into my hand before stalking back to the stern—hiding, I could only assume, behind the tent until I went away. Shaking my head, I stepped back onto the dock and headed up the stairs, leaving Lyle alone with his social awkwardness.

I moved back through the house, stopping by the kitchen to borrow a heated kettle from the bleary-eyed cook. I hurried back up the stairs and turned the key in Gemma's lock. She was sitting stiffly in a wooden chair by the window—locked, I noticed, with a chain around the knobs. Sitting on the floor next to her, neatly folded, was a bloodstained bedsheet.

"I'm sorry, Gemma," I said, coming to her side and giving her the linen. "These idiot boys would never have thought to include bandages in your trunk."

"I'm afraid I've ruined the sheets," she said quietly, taking the linen.

"It's not your fault. The Toussaints have daughters. They'll understand."

She stood and carefully limped to the changing screen, her day clothes already draped over the top. I poured hot water from the kettle into the washbasin and set it with the washcloth on the chair next to the screen.

"Do you need help?" I asked her.

"No, no. I'm fine. You don't have to stay."

"Pass me your nightdress over the top," I said. "I'll get it scoured before we leave."

"You don't have to," she said again, quietly. She paused. "Why were you out in the house so early, anyway? Is Rou awake?"

"No—what? I don't know," I said clumsily, coloring at her immediate jump to that conclusion. "I always wake up early." I searched for a way to change the subject. "You know, this happened to me, too. At an inn in Pangapa. You'd think I'd set fire to the place, the way the innkeeper railed about the sheets."

She let out a small, breathy laugh and then fell silent. She rested her nightdress over the top of the screen, carefully, with her right hand. "I'm a bit surprised it came at all," she said, so quietly I almost didn't hear her.

"You thought you might have been pregnant?" Would *that* have changed things.

"Oh, no. No, I'm good about taking annelace." She reached for the washbowl, again with her right hand. "I just thought . . . I've been a bit on edge, you know."

"That's happened to me, too," I said, though I refrained from telling her it was during the stretch of months immediately following the Alcoran invasion. Hunger, desperation, and rage had taken a toll on the usual rhythms of my body. "Have you skipped a cycle before?"

"Once," she said in nearly a whisper. She pulled her shift from the screen. "A few months ago."

A few months ago. So it was well after she had married Celeno. "What do you suppose it was?" I asked as lightly as I could.

"It was just . . . personal."

Something personal in the last few months. Well, driving Alcoro out of Lumen Lake had certainly happened in the last few months. Perhaps the stress of that failure had exacerbated her husband's temper. Perhaps it had led to the first bout of abuse, or a particularly bad episode.

"Were you . . . unwell?" I asked carefully.

"No," she replied, pulling down the day dress. "I was fine. Physically, I was fine. It was . . . just stress."

Hm.

I wanted to ask her more questions, but I remembered what Rou had said about digging too deep. It was a start, at least, this conversation. I stood and bundled up the stained sheet and nightdress. "I'll bring these to the laundry. Do you need anything else?"

"No, no, I'm fine." She emerged around the screen, clasping the sash over her overdress. She looked up at me, briefly, and then continued arranging her dress. "Thank you, Mona."

"Of course." I crossed the room, opened the door, and nearly collided with a raised fist on the threshold.

Rou stood poised to knock. He dropped his fist and stepped back as I joined him in the hall, closing the door behind me.

"Lyle told me," he said. "I didn't realize . . ."

"No, of course not," I said, handing him the key. "Even if she had felt it coming, she might have been too shy to ask for bandages. But if she's going to be locked up, someone should at least check in the morning to see if she needs anything."

"Yes. I'll come up first thing tomorrow. Is she all right?"

"She feels bad about the sheets, but otherwise she's fine. Nothing out of the ordinary." I granted him a mild smile. In the wake of Gemma's predicament, the irrationalities from the night before started stealing back through my head. I backed up a few inches, trying to open the gap between us.

Rou shook his head. "I'm sorry about Lyle." He took the bundle of fabric from my arm. "I'll take these to the laundry."

"Thank you. How were the fireworks last night?" I asked.

He turned back down the hall. "Dunno."

I watched him walk away, surprised at the sudden urge to kick myself.

The Toussaints gifted us a generous basket of refreshments to bear us through the upcoming backwater towns—sweet pastries, pitted dates, several links of smoked sausage, and a large bottle of top-quality brandy. Heloise waved morosely to us—or, rather, to Rou—as we poled away from their dock. As we drifted in a brief current, Rou laid out his map on one of the crates and crouched over it.

"We're going to try to shoot north today, toward Bellemere," he said, tracing his route with his finger. "Fisheye's not going to like it—we'll see what new adjectives he comes up with for me."

He took up position in the stern, behind the tent—a good thing, I told myself, because I had only just noticed that as he dragged his pole, the muscles in his forearms tended to flex, creating taut, corded lines against his skin. A flush ran through me like a bucket of water overturned on my head. Hurriedly, I turned my back to the stern and faced determinedly forward.

"Lyle," I said.

He grunted, maneuvering us from his position in the bow.

I opened my notebook in my lap. "About your incendiaries."

He huffed, stabbing a soggy stump with his pole. "Believe it or not, this isn't as easy as it looks."

"Your brother has managed it with continuous commentary," I said dryly. Rou laughed from behind the tent. "You can give me short answers. But I do need answers."

He made a sound very close to a growl, but he didn't protest. I uncorked my ink bottle. "How many types of devices have you created?"

"Four in full production. Three prototypes, and about a dozen schematics that haven't been built yet."

My quill scratched on my page. "And their primary functions?"

He steered us around a stand of cypress knees. "Flash grenades—temporary blindness. Liquid fire—continuous burn on damp wood or water. It can be launched as a grenade or used through a siphon. Smoke sacks—clouds of sulfur smoke. Fire barrels—large-scale explosions. Current prototypes are a self-contained flaming arrow, a standalone rocket—"

"Slow down," I said, scribbling as quickly as I could. "Smoke sacks . . ."

"What was your foundational research?" Gemma asked. She was leaning forward slightly, her hands braced on her own notebook.

Lyle looked over his shoulder at her. "Bellamy and Roe," he said. "Villeneuve, Fabre . . ."

"Fabre?" she said. "Have you read any of her work on mill design?"

"Of course—I was writing a thesis on the development of a refractory converter based on her work before I left my tutor."

"What about Alcoran literature?" she asked.

"I've read all of Cavaco's *Foundations of Alchemy*, and most of Itza's work."

"*A Compilation of Thermal Compounds and Their Properties?*"

"Of course—I've heard there's an eighth edition out, though, with an appendix for saltpeter compounds. My tutor only had the seventh edition."

"Prototypes," I said through their discussion. "What did you say about a flaming arrow?"

"Who . . . excuse me, Queen Mona, who was your tutor?" Gemma asked Lyle.

"Alberio Tecuan."

"I know Alberio!" she exclaimed. "His sister was my physics tutor!"

"You had an Alcoran tutor?" I asked Lyle, my quill pausing on the page.

He navigated us around a tangle of brush. "For a while."

"In Temper Creek?"

He snorted derisively. "Hardly. Bellemere. I left Temper Creek when I was ten."

"Oh." I looked back down, about to press on, but then my head popped back up. "*Ten?* Great Light, what age do children start working in the steel mills?"

He swung his pole across the deck, dripping water. "Usually around then. Ten."

"Oh . . ." I furrowed my brow. "Then . . . when did *you* start in the mill? After Bellemere?"

"I didn't work in the mill," he said.

"You didn't?" I thought Rou had said he had.

"No."

"Never?"

"Never," he said with impatience. "I took lessons with Alberio for six years before going to work for the Assembly." He leaned hard on his pole, squeezing us through a stand of cypress knees.

I was thoroughly confused. Had I misunderstood Rou? No . . . he had clearly said his brother kept working at the mill after he himself had quit. I glanced back to the stern. I could only see the bobbing of Rou's hair over the tent. He was whistling. I turned back to the bow.

"Lyle . . ." I began slowly.

"Come on, Rou," he called irascibly over his shoulder. "We're almost at the dock, but we keep grounding on these shoals."

"Yes, my lord."

With a few strong pushes, we shot out into an open patch of water. A tired old dock slouched among the weeds, along with a run-down shack with two blown out windows.

Rou straightened in the stern. "Er . . ."

There was no punt tied to the dock. Fisheye wasn't there.

"We said the old trappers' dock past Fogwallow, didn't we?" Rou said as he joined us in the bow.

"Maybe he's late," I offered.

Lyle poled us to the dock and looped our tether around a post. Rou stepped onto the warped planks.

"I guess we wait," Lyle said, setting his pole down.

"Hang on," Rou said, striding forward. He crouched down and plucked up a dirty scrap of parchment, held in place by a rusty nail. He unfolded it.

"Is it from him?" I asked.

"It's indecipherable enough to be his," he said, squinting at it. "Yes, there's his signature, or he might have had a seizure while he held the quill."

"What does it say?"

He frowned at the note. "Very little. He says the waterways around Bellemere aren't clear, and that we *have to*—he underlined this a bunch of times—we have to head west at least as far as Spadefoot, if not Temper Creek. He says Temper Creek is still a safe place—whatever that means—and that we're not to leave until he meets us at Gris' house, and that we may have to wait there a few extra days."

"A few days?" Lyle repeated. "Why? Where's he going? And why isn't he here himself?"

Rou turned the scrap of parchment over. "He doesn't say." He looked up. "I suppose he's checking the way to Dismal Green?"

Lyle frowned. "We can't afford to waste time in Temper Creek."

"Well, it's better than poling blindly into another

Alcoran blockade." Rou looked back down at the note. "But then again, we always knew Bellemere was going to be risky. I still think we can sneak through if we travel a little at night."

"If the river past Bellemere is blocked, though, it'll impact our travel to Dismal Green," Lyle said. "It could be several days before we get to the Benoits'."

"Well, then, we'll have to skip Dismal Green—we're meeting the cart a few miles outside town, after all. We don't have to stay with the Benoits—they were just one of our options."

"I have to pick up my quicklime order."

"It's not going anywhere," Rou said with irritation. "You can come back to pick it up after we get to Siere."

"No!" Lyle said with surprising force. "There won't be another chance after we get to Siere. Two of my prototypes are waiting for the Benoits' shipment, and if negotiations with Celeno fail, the Assembly is going to need them."

"So send someone else to Dismal Green," Rou said with sharp edge to his voice. He gestured to the boat. "Getting the queens through the Draws before First Fire ends and safely to Siere has *always* been our first objective, not picking up your quicklime order."

"And you think driving straight through Bellemere will be safer than the backwaters?" Lyle thumped the punt with his pole. "You're being an idiot—again. There is *no sane reason* not to go through Temper Creek except for your own irrationality. You went against

Fisheye's advice once already and nearly ran us right into the Alcorans' hands. Are you planning on Queen Mona swimming Gemma a couple miles upriver until the way is clear?" Rou opened his mouth, but Lyle overrode him, his voice rising. "Shut up. You're not focused on our safety. Stop pretending like you're acting on anyone's behalf except your own."

The ringing silence was punctuated by a few ambient swamp noises—a chirp, a buzz, a soft splash. Gemma and I sat on either side of the hull, our eyes fixed on the two brothers. I hadn't heard Lyle get this worked up about anything in our five days together. Nor had I seen Rou's angled face this tight, his jaw working as he glared at his twin. I glanced at Gemma— she met my eyes briefly, her shoulders bent forward as if shielding herself from their heated exchange.

Rou crumpled the note in his fist and stalked back to the punt. He jumped down to the stern, rocking the deck.

"Fine," he said acidly from behind the tent. "I'll just push then, shall I?"

Lyle jerked the tether off the post and shoved us away from the dock. We slid across the open patch of water and back into the dappled shade of the cypress trees.

Our progress through the morning was silent and stilted. We moved through the bayou with sharp bursts of speed as Rou thrust his pole into the water in quick succession. He didn't whistle anymore. Lyle riveted his attention on steering us around swiftly approaching obstacles now that our pace had quickened. My one halfhearted attempt to revive our discussion was met with surly silence.

Near midmorning, we met the tributary of a small river joining the larger branch. A splintery signpost jutted out from the bank at an angle—SPADEFOOT, TEMPER CRK. Without hesitating, Lyle followed the arrow on the sign. There was no comment from the stern. The little river had a fair current, but it was flowing in the wrong direction, and the brothers were forced to stay at their poles, though Lyle's job got far easier. I got the feeling he was only staying rigid in the bow to avoid having to turn around and make eye contact with anyone.

My notebook lay closed in my lap. Once again, I couldn't write. I was thinking far too much about the scraps of information I possessed about the Roubideaux family. It shouldn't have mattered—I told myself this over and over. If I wasn't focusing on my impending meeting with the Assembly, I should at least be thinking about Gemma and the predicament she presented. But I couldn't make myself dwell on those things. Instead, all my thoughts were fixed on the conversations Rou and I had shared over the past few days.

Around midday, I dug out a canteen and edged around the tent for the stern. Rou was standing wide-legged on the deck, moving his pole in a terse rhythm. His forehead was beaded with sweat, and his shirt front was half-unbuttoned.

He was muscled there as well.

I fought against the same heated flush as before, holding out the canteen. "Tell Lyle it's time to switch," I said quietly.

"I don't care," he said flatly, but despite his stiff words, he accepted the canteen and took a long draw of water.

"I'm sorry we have to go this way."

"I'd really rather not discuss it." He handed me back the canteen and switched his pole to the other side. Reluctantly, I turned to leave him alone. "But," he said in between drags of his pole. "I wouldn't mind you staying." He dipped his pole in the water again. "Tell me about Lumen Lake. Tell me about your brothers, and your trip through the Silverwood. Tell me about the new mountain queen."

So I sat with him throughout the afternoon, regaling him with the story of how we met Mae in Tiktika and how I had convinced her—or, rather, how she had convinced me—to make the journey over the Silverwood Mountains. I told him about the fireflies and the king's prison, about the ships on the lake and the revelation of Mae's true loyalties. When I finished, he asked me other questions—questions about diving, about Blackshell, about Colm and Arlen. I wanted to ask him the dozens of questions on my mind, but he had no breath to spare for lengthy answers, and besides, it was enjoyable telling him about my country. It was a pleasant distraction from my frustrating inability to focus on the pressing matters at hand.

Near the middle of the afternoon, I was answering his questions about the Overwater Feast, when I stopped short. Without warning, houses had sprung up along the banks. It threw me off guard—there had been no other boats in the water, no signs of a town, until buildings had simply emerged from the trees. As we floated through them, however, I realized that they must be abandoned. The once-grand facades were dingy and peeling, and their sweeping porches were warped and rotting. Windows and doors were boarded up. The skeleton of a punt lay disintegrating on a dock.

"Where are we?" I asked.

"Spadefoot," he said. "One of the fever towns. In most places, the consumption was contained to only a few streets or block of houses, but in some of these smaller towns, it ripped right through. The folk that survived had to move away. This used to be one of my main mail stops."

"Didn't Fisheye say we could stay here?"

He gave a half-smile, half-grimace. "Ah, lolly, I'm not going to make you sleep in this rotten old ghost town."

"I've slept in worse," I said.

"Lady Queen."

"What?"

"I said lolly. I meant Lady Queen."

"Oh." I colored slightly, grateful that he was still catching himself. I tried to remember what had instigated the conversation and gestured to the ruins around us. "Really, though—if you don't want to go all the way to Temper Creek, don't continue just for my sake."

"No, it's all right. In all likelihood, whichever abandoned house we'd decide to camp out in would fall into the river in the middle of the night. We're close—we might as well stay in our uncle's house." He puckered his mouth. "Of course, he's a little rickety himself. Means well, but going senile. Half-blind. Thinks Lyle and I are the same person."

In another few minutes, we left the ruins of Spadefoot behind us. The trees on the bank grew thick and gnarled, arching over the water and trailing moss over our heads. After another fifteen minutes, we spotted the first punt up the river.

"Lady Queens," Rou said tiredly. "Best get in the tent. Just for a few minutes."

Gemma and I headed through the tent flap and sat on the mats inside.

"How are you?" I asked. "I'm sorry I left you with Lyle most of the day."

"I'm fine, thank you. And I find Lyle interesting."

"Interesting?"

She tucked a strand of hair behind her ear. "He's an incredible scholar—a real academic. Did you know he's working on a more efficient way to start fires? Little splints coated in sulfur, dipped into jars of phosphorus. But he's not satisfied with that—he thinks there's a way to get them to light without the phosphorus. You should see his notes. He could write half a dozen articles on firestarting alone. And that's just his side work."

"I'm surprised you got him to talk that much," I said. I'd been so engrossed in talking to Rou, I hadn't paid attention to the other side of the boat.

"He warms up if you ask the right questions. He obviously puts a great deal of weight in his education." She wrapped her arms around her knees. "He and Rou are very different, are they not?"

"Yes. Quite different."

"Funny, that two people who look so similar can be so different."

"Yes." I didn't want to tell her that aside from the lines of their faces, I didn't see many similarities between the twins at all. Rou's face had an openness to it, a lightness, that was wholly absent in Lyle's. The dark amber eyes that seemed so lively when Rou spoke were cold and closed up in his brother's face. And his movements, the easy grace with which he stepped and gestured and juggled and spun—these were his alone.

I pressed my palm to my eyes. *Stop it,* I chastised myself. *Stop—you useless, moonheaded child.*

The sounds of civilization grew outside the canvas walls, and through the flap I could see houses and shops spreading away into the trees. But these had a different feel from the other bright, bustling towns we had passed through. Colors were more subdued, architecture more straightforward. Folk moved a bit slower, many wearing similar soot-stained coveralls and caps. A distinct smoky tang clung to the breeze. Despite the tired, industrial feel to the town, the banks were still hung with bright streamers and bunting. Folk were setting up food carts and tables along the docks, and a few musicians were already starting to tune their instruments.

"It's the last night of First Fire," Gemma said quietly, peeking through the flap. "I wonder what it'll be like."

Before we went much farther, though, Lyle took up his pole again and directed us up one of the creeks. The banks squeezed in to meet us. Bearded moss dragged along the top of the tent, and rushes scraped the side of the punt. Just when I wondered how much further we could possibly go, we ground to a halt.

"Safe," called Rou.

Gemma and I emerged to find a rickety two-story house being swallowed up by a towering magnolia. It must have been impressive once, but now it was weedy and ill-kept. It wasn't as dilapidated as the houses in Spadefoot, but the upstairs windows were curtained with cobwebs, and several shutters were missing.

"It won't be the grandest night on our journey," Rou said, tying us off—unnecessarily, as the punt was wedged on the sandy bed. "Uncle Gris has a hard time getting around, and he doesn't have any family left here to help him keep the place up. But he's the oldest friend we've got, and in all likelihood, he won't remember your names tomorrow morning."

The walkway to the house was warped and loose, the boards shifting under our feet as we made our way to the front door. Rou swept aside a spiderweb and knocked. He and Lyle still weren't looking at each other.

The door creaked on its hinges, and a leathery old face appeared in the crack, his filmy eyes blinking behind thick spectacles.

"Hello, Uncle Gris," Rou said. "I hope Fisheye warned you we would be coming?"

"Roubideaux!" He flung the door wide and wrapped his skinny arms around Rou. "Oh, my boy, you don't know what a relief this is . . . they told me you were dead!"

"Just as alive as last time," Rou reassured him, patting his shoulder. "We've brought some important guests tonight. I hope you have a few rooms we could beg from you?"

"All friends of yours are always welcome, Roubideaux," Gris said, dabbing at his eyes with a graying handkerchief. "Come in, please come in."

We filed through the doorway. He peered at me, blinking owlishly, as I moved past him into the entry hall.

"Great fire and smoke!" He reached out and brushed at the singed wisps of my hair. "What have they done to your hair?"

I stepped out of his reach as politely as I could. "It was an accident."

"How awful," he said sympathetically, as if this was the saddest thing he could imagine. He patted my hand. "Maybe we can get you a hat."

To avoid showing my frustration, I looked around the room. A staircase swept down to greet us, draped with tasseled hangings that looked like they hadn't been dusted in decades. In fact, the staircase itself was piled with books and curling papers, with only a narrow path carved through the middle.

"We may have to stay here a few days, Uncle Gris," Rou said. He brushed past Lyle, whose face was lined with an even deeper scowl than usual. "We're waiting to hear which routes are safe for us. Tell me, you haven't heard anything up this far, have you? Anything about an abducted queen, or a reward out for our capture?"

"Not a peep, my boy. You're safe here." Gris closed the door and shuffled ahead of us. He stopped at the base of the staircase. "You'll forgive me . . ." he began, leaning on the bannister.

"We'll take the ladies up," Rou said. "Don't you worry. Which rooms are ready?"

"I think Cecilia opened up the two south rooms and the corner room."

"Perfect." He beckoned to us. "Ladies."

We climbed the stairs after him, every board and post creaking and cracking under our progress. The landing sported a faded purple carpet, worn thin in the middle. But the lamps on the walls were clear of dust, and three doors stood open, spilling dappled sunlight into the hall.

"Does your uncle live here alone?" I asked as Gemma and I followed Rou to the first door.

"He has someone come in from town twice a week to tidy up and cook him a few meals," he said, peeking in the first room. "But yes, he lives in this great big house all by himself. He can't climb the stairs anymore, so he's turned the parlor into his bedroom." He gestured to the room. "Queen Gemma, why don't you take this one? It's got a handsome writing desk."

"Thank you," she murmured, slipping past him into the room. Lyle puffed up the stairs behind us with her trunk and the key ring.

"What was his profession?" I asked, following Rou to the next open room. "How does he have such a fine old house?"

"Our family used to manage the steel mill before the Alcorans took over," he said. "Temper Creek was one of the last mill towns to come under Alcoran control, because it's so far out of the way. Thirteen years, I think it took them. By that point, folk had stopped fighting back—no point, with all the main cities under Alcoran control and our voting system disbanded. The Alcorans kept my uncle on as a worker, but they removed my grandmother from her position as manager. My mother would have taken over the mill once she was old enough, but she had to settle for keeping the books for them." He leaned against the doorframe, looking suddenly weary. "Our family unraveled over the years. Now Uncle Gris is the only Roubideaux left in Temper Creek."

"Gris was your mother's brother?"

"Yes." He shifted to one side, letting Lyle sidle in with my trunk. He set it down with a grunt and disappeared back into the hall. Rou rubbed his face tiredly. "I'm named for him. Theophilus Gris, formerly Roubideaux."

I stood still for a moment, looking at him. He gave me a weary half-smile—even that simple expression was warm and genuine, despite the weight of his words. I hesitated, and then I turned and went to my trunk. I opened it and pulled out the sewing kit I had used to make Gemma's collars.

"Do you need anything?" he asked. "Things are going to be pretty self-serve here."

"Yes," I said, straightening. I pulled the pair of shears out of the kit and held them out to him. "I need you to cut my hair."

He raised his eyebrows. "I'm not sure I'm qualified . . ."

"It's not hard," I said firmly. "I had to cut my brothers' hair for three years. If you can spin flaming wicks, you can cut hair." I shook the shears at him. "I'm tired of folk making comments about it."

He picked himself slowly off the doorframe. "How short are you wanting it?"

"As short as these singed bits. Just make everything even." I pressed the shears into his hand and then marched to the vanity. I sat down facing the mirror, but quickly turned my chair so I couldn't see my reflection. I didn't want to watch.

He joined me, hesitantly. I pinched a lock of my hair in my fingers and held it up. "Cut vertically," I said, demonstrating. "Not across. Don't cut it too short at first. You can always even it up later."

"Are you sure about this, Queen Mona?" He touched my hair briefly and then pulled his hand away. "You've got mighty fine hair, you know, it's a little intimidating . . ."

I picked up the brush that was lying on the vanity and handed it to him. "Yes, I'm sure."

He set down the shears and took the brush. Gently, he pulled it through my hair. "Have you cut it short before?"

"Never." I smoothed my skirt over my knees. "I've heard it's a style in some parts of Samna, though. Perhaps I'll start a trend."

"If anyone could, it would be you."

A moment of silence passed as he drew the brush down my hair. His fingers grazed the back of my neck, and—oh . . . I hadn't fully considered what it would mean, to have him standing so close to me, drawing my hair through his hand. I gripped the fabric of my skirt again, trying to keep my eyes from drifting closed at the sensation.

I cleared my throat, forcing some clarity into my head. "Lyle said something earlier that confused me."

He brushed out another length of my hair. "The trick is to change subjects before he starts using too much jargon."

"It wasn't about his incendiaries," I said. "I asked him about working at the steel mill." I was too full of questions to worry about whether this was going to be uncomfortable for him. And besides, I had shared the losses of my life with him on the punt. "He said he never worked at the mill. But I was sure you said your brother worked in one of the furnaces."

His hand paused for the briefest second on my hair, and then it continued. "I certainly did, didn't I?"

"What did he mean, Rou? What did *you* mean?"

A long moment of silence stretched between us. I wasn't sure if he was gathering his thoughts or if he wasn't going to answer my question. After he smoothed my hair in waves over my shoulders, he set the brush down and picked up the shears. "Short, you say?"

"Short," I said.

Without warning, he slid his fingers through my hair and let it fall from his hand.

"You have beautiful hair," he said.

I swallowed, a bloom of heat washing my body. "Thank you."

He lifted the shears and opened them on a strand. "Lyle and I weren't always twins."

There was a long, slow *sli-i-i-ce* as the shears closed. That wave of heat turned suddenly and profoundly to ice, but it wasn't from the lock of golden hair that drifted to the floor. "What do you mean?"

"We were triplets," he said, picking up another strand. "Born one right after another to Zeline Roubideaux on a wretched hot summer day. As Gris could tell you, if he could remember, she carried big and delivered early—most folk assumed she was carrying twins, but then a third popped out after Lyle. Eloi."

He closed the shears again. Another lock of hair fell to the ground. "A job at the steel mill isn't exactly lucrative, but for most families, it's enough to cover expenses. And it helps if there are older children who can work, or at least watch the babies while the second parent earns extra income. We had none of those luxuries—three boys exactly the same age, needing three times the amount of food and clothes and care. All on my father's single income. Until something inside him snapped, and he found it appropriate to walk away from someone trying to care for three identical toddlers."

He snipped again. "My aunt and uncle Gris helped as much as they could, but even with the wealth they had put away before the Alcorans came, they weren't exactly affluent, and they had to care for my grandmother as well. Still, we squeezed through my childhood, somehow—I've lost count of the number of skills my mother taught herself to earn money." He gave a short sigh. "The pinnacle of humanity. How many instances have you heard of where a mother and all three babies survive a triplet birth?"

"None," I said. I didn't even know any twins where everyone had survived.

"Me, neither. She was strong. Fearless, too—sort of like you."

I raised my eyebrows, but he couldn't see.

"It's funny," he continued, brushing a wisp of hair off my neck. "When you look the same, folk assume you are the same. And for Eloi and myself, that was true. We were the twins—always causing trouble, always being excused from it for being so damn charming. He was my best friend. Lyle was the odd one out. While Eloi and I were running around, chasing chickens and fishing the river, Lyle would cloister himself in the house with his books. We never really understood him, or really wanted to. He wasn't any fun, and he was always surly, especially if we teased him while he was trying to read.

"But then we started school, and it became clear—where Eloi and I were as competent as the other kids, Lyle was years ahead of everyone, even the teacher. Mother saw the opportunity to save at least one of us from the mill, so she scrounged every possible copper she could—I remember her selling her guitar, her best gowns, anything we didn't need. As soon as we turned ten, she sent Lyle away to study with the Alcoran tutor in Bellemere. He was smart enough to go to one in Lilou, but we couldn't afford it. Eloi and I, as expected, started work in the mill."

He waved the shears vaguely next to my head. "None of that really matters, I guess. Point is, Lyle went away. Any spare coin any of us earned went to his tuition. And that's what I meant when I said my brother was better about it than me—I was talking about Eloi. I didn't mean to, it just . . . slipped out. But it's true—he was always tougher than me. I resented Lyle for worming his way out of working in the mill, resented that all the harrowing work I had to do every day went straight to him. Turns out I didn't inherit my mother's backbone, if you hadn't noticed. Probably means I take after my father. That was around the time I first started spinning poi. I just needed something to focus on, something to keep me from running like he did."

He made a few more snips, brushing his fingers through my hair. I could feel the air moving against my bare neck.

"Thing about working in the furnaces is, it's not so much about *if* the job will kill you, it's how long it will take to kill you. The lucky folk get caught in some flash accident without any time to think. Awful stuff—you stick a few dozen kids running around over troughs of molten slag, it's just a matter of time before someone gets burned alive or something explodes. Meanwhile, the unlucky ones while away their lives with bad lungs and seared skin until their bodies just give it up. I decided early on I didn't want to be either. It was a selfish decision—there wasn't another job as steady or well-paid in Temper Creek, but I was determined to make it work. As I told you before, I wound up carrying mail."

He paused, idly brushing the lengths of my hair that were left. Then he touched the back of my neck, right at the base of my skull.

"You've got a cluster of freckles here, did you know that?"

"No."

"It looks like a backward *c*." He brushed his fingers over the spot and opened the shears again. "It probably has some deep, cosmic meaning."

"Probably," I said quietly.

He sliced off another length of hair. "Eloi kept working at the mill," he said. "He started out in the forges, but then he was shuffled over to the blast furnaces after a worker choked to death on poisonous gas seeping from the furnace top. That's how things work under the Alcorans. They just move folk around to wherever pieces are missing. Once those furnaces are started, you know, they run continuously for months. They don't shut down, except for scheduled maintenance. And some folk would prefer to do as much maintenance as possible on the go."

He smoothed my hair. "The Alcoran in charge of our mill at the time was famous for his efficiency. For the two decades he was in charge, it didn't fully shut down once. Not once in twenty years. Oh, he'd take it off blast when the furnace lining had to be replaced, but all that meant was the forges were going even harder, turning out wrought iron. Even over First Fire, he would schedule everyone so there was always a skeleton crew present, keeping things operating. Nothing stopped. Nobody went home. And if somebody wasn't entirely sure how one furnace worked, they learned quick."

He paused again, the shears idle against my head. He was at the singed patch now, making small snips. When he spoke again, his voice was tight.

"There's a bell, this wretched bell, in a tower on the mill. Everyone hates it, because when it's rung, it means there's been an accident. An *incident*, as it's officially called. I've always thought that a funny term, *incident*. It sounds so mild." He waved the shears. "Sorry. Anyway, the bell is there to alert workers to a change in their routine, but it also lets the rest of Temper Creek know that somebody's probably dead or maimed."

He busied his shears again, snipping more quickly. "It was such a stupid, pointless thing. It's one thing, you know, when someone's killed in a hearth explosion or by flying slag—it's part of the unpredictability of the furnaces. But then there are some things . . . some things that shouldn't happen. That just didn't need to happen." He paused. "Do you know about blast furnaces, Lady Queen?"

"Are they at all like bloomeries?" I'd taken a tour of Lumen Lake's one iron bloomery before Alcoro's invasion. It had been deconstructed during their occupation, as they fulfilled all their metallurgic needs through Cyprien. More recently I'd accompanied Mae to the Silvern bloomeries, our only source of metal at the moment. Theirs were charcoal-fired, as the abundance of wood for fuel was a nonissue. I flushed slightly, picturing their small-scale stone chimneys and creaky buckskin bellows. Of course the large-scale industry of Cyprien would be nothing like the Wood-folk's furnaces.

"Actually, they're very similar," he said before I could rework my question. "Same concept, same mechanisms, just bigger. Bigger bellows, usually two, powered by the water wheel, and bigger stacks. Bigger hearths, hotter fires. More output. They've been growing for years under the Alcorans, push-ing the limits of limestone and ore, trying to find that perfect balance between efficiency and quality. More iron, more steel, faster production. Until some Canyon-folk realized they could load their ballistae with iron shot, not just bolts, to achieve a greater spread of mayhem and destruction. And so one year, the orders came pouring in—shot, they needed shot. Not big iron bars to pound into steel blades. Little balls of cast iron.

"Well, cast iron of that size is better suited to a bloomery—outrageously inefficient to make shot with a blast furnace. Do you know why?"

"No."

"Because the damn blast has to be turned off," he said, running his fingers through my hair to sepa-rate a long strand. "Those two big bellows have to stop pumping air, and the furnace has to cool down enough for a worker to get his cursed hand near enough to ladle molten iron into the molds. It's a

ASHES TO FIRE 299

huge waste of energy, all that heat, all that water-power, lost. But, it was shot they wanted, so shot had to be made. Guess which mill got the honor? The smallest, most backwoods one in Cyprien. No real tragedy if Temper Creek lost a few days of output."

His hands began to move more quickly. "It was unusual, this time. Nobody had ever heard of this particular accident—incident—occurring, because normally nobody was ever right up in the mouth of the hearth while the thing was still burning. But that's where Eloi was, ladling molten iron into the shot molds, when the Alcoran manager ordered the blast turned back on."

My fingers jumped to my lips. "*Oh* . . ."

"Roasted," he said, his voice gravelly. "Like a sausage on a stick. Clothes burned off. The damn ladle fused to the bones in his hand."

"How . . ."

"How indeed. The manager insisted he'd checked the hearths. He insisted he'd sounded the warning bell for the bellows, but even if he had, there are so many other noises in the mill—clanging and crushing and rumbling. Turning off the bellows was so unusual, it's likely even if there was some kind of warning noise, Eloi wouldn't have known what it meant. And if the manager really did check the hearths, he didn't look closely enough. He could have gone down to the floor, he could have asked if shot was still being poured. He could have waited. But he'd allotted a certain length of time to have the blast off, and when that time was up, he had it cranked back on without realizing one of his workers was still halfway in the furnace."

He paused, cleared his throat. The shears creaked as he opened them again. "The worst part," he said, "was that officially, they needed somebody to identify the body. Which was stupid, because there was nothing recognizable. Mother did it herself—she wouldn't let me go. I remember her face when she came home . . . again, this was the woman who birthed three babies one right after the other, the woman who held us together when her husband ran off. She was not a frail person. But I can only imagine that image of my charred brother was something she never stopped seeing."

He held out his right hand, the one with the thick ring circling his little finger. "This was Eloi's firesteel. It was the only thing left on him that wasn't burned away. Mother brought it back home with her. The little dings are from striking it on flint, but all the pitting . . ."

I stared at its dented surface, riddled with pinholes. Drawing it back out of my sight, he came to the last long strand of hair and sliced it without a pause. He worked his fingertips through my hair, fishing out the uneven tufts, and set to work making everything even. I allowed my eyes to close, trying to resist the urge to lean backward into his hands.

"Lyle had to come home," he said. "We couldn't support his tuition without Eloi's income. But Temper Creek was no place for him. He was far too smart to languish out here in the boondocks. Mother picked us up and moved us to Lilou. She thought Lyle could find appropriate work there, and she was right—he was just what the Assembly was looking for, exactly what they needed to increase our chances to drive Alcoro out of the country. I was an afterthought, with no useful skills to offer, but I was glad to get away from Temper Creek. Problem was, now I was stuck with Lyle. Instead of Eloi—my twin, my best friend, who had shared my childhood and all those awkward years afterward—instead of him, I was faced with my *other brother*, who looked exactly the same and yet entirely different. It's hard to heal up when you're constantly wishing your brother was someone else, and then feeling insurmountable guilt over having those thoughts in the first place."

He stood back, probably looking for any places he missed. "And that's why Lyle and I can't stand each other. He knows what I think, and I know he knows. He's always angry he didn't get to finish his education, even though he's risen higher than he ever could have in some dusty old library. I'm always riddled with guilt because I resent that he's not Eloi. And yet, here we are shackled together by association—me riding his coattails because folk will always assume we're a matched set."

He set the shears down on the vanity and ran both hands through my hair. "So there you have it. That's the story of how I'm a rotten brother, and here's your haircut."

I turned slowly and looked in the mirror. Gone were my long golden tresses, replaced by a crop as short as Arlen's. My bangs he had left a bit longer; they swept across my forehead, skimming my eyebrows. The singed patch was barely distinguishable. I passed my hand through my hair, taking in the new sensation. My whole head felt lighter.

I looked back at Rou. He leaned against the wall next to the vanity, his hands in his pockets.

"Maybe you can get it evened up when we get to Siere," he said.

"You did a good job," I said. "Thank you."

"What do you think?"

I looked back to my reflection. "It's going to take some time to get used to. I look like my brother." I ran my hand through it again. "What do *you* think?"

"I think you could wear Mirabelle the possum on your head, and you'd still be beautiful."

I only barely managed to stop myself from looking down and blushing, wondering if this recurring wave of heat was ever going to get less disarming. As I pointlessly smoothed the fabric of my skirt for the hundredth time, a thought occurred to me. I looked back up at him.

"Your uncle," I said. "You said he thinks you and Lyle are the same person."

"You're sharp," he said wearily. "He thinks we're both Eloi. He used to call us all Roubideaux. As a kid, I thought it was a joke, but I honestly don't think he could ever reliably tell us apart. He was undone when Eloi died—my whole family was. They, of course, knew all about running the mill, all its pitfalls and sacrifices. My mother would have checked the hearths, she'd have cleared the furnace before having the blast turned back on. She would never have consciously risked workers' lives in return for efficiency. Eloi's death was so horribly unnecessary. That's the difference between someone who's actually got blood in the furnaces, and someone who just sees it as a machine." He shrugged one shoulder. "Now my uncle's mind is starting to go, and he's forgotten there were ever three of us."

"I'm sorry," I said.

"It's not so bad."

"I'm sorry for it all," I pressed. "I'm sorry for what happened, and for how you carry it. For what it's worth, Rou, I think you're too hard on yourself. Lots of people harbor guilt and resentment inside themselves. Few of them work so hard to overcome it."

He picked up a lock of my hair that had fallen on the vanity and threaded it through his fingers. It was an odd sensation, to see him caressing something that until just a few moments ago had been part of me. "I don't work as hard as I should."

"You spin your poi in the mornings," I said. "I've seen you."

His fingers paused. "You have?"

"I didn't mean to, at first," I said, and now I *was* blushing, dammit. "But then . . . well, I like watching. I've never seen anything like it, and it . . . I don't know, it's very peaceful." *Stop talking. Stop talking now. End the conversation, tell him to leave, go to bed, get a hold on yourself.*

He let out a breath and leaned against the wall, smiling in an almost grateful way. "You could've come out."

"I wanted to," I said before I had fully finished mentally chastising myself. The words hung in the air, and I watched his body change with them—his chest rising with a sudden inhale, his gaze growing just a bit brighter. I drew in my own quick breath, but the words were spoken. So I pressed on, trying to give them alternate meaning. "But I didn't want you to stop, or feel like you had to perform. I know what it's like to have to perform all the time." I went to tuck my hair behind my ear before remembering it was gone. "Does it help? Spinning. Is that why you do it?"

"Oh, I could craft some kind of soliloquy about how it connects me to the Light, but mostly it's an excuse to get away from Lyle." There was undeniable sadness in his voice. "We're both better brothers when we're not with each other." He drew his fingers down the lock of hair as one might feel a length of silk. I suppressed a shiver.

His fingers stilled, and I looked from his hands up to his eyes. It really wasn't fair, that openness in his face, that earnestness. Someone should teach him to hide it better. I saw the exact moment he made the decision, his whole demeanor shifting just slightly.

He straightened away from the wall. He dropped the lock back onto the vanity.

"Let's go to First Fire," he said.

"What? Now?"

"Yes, now. It's the last night. It'll be a sight, Mona, fireworks and jugglers and dancers . . . all the music, incredible food."

"I . . ." I looked at him. The weariness had slid from his frame, and his eyes were kindling with a kind of tense excitement. "I don't know that it's . . . aren't you tired?"

"I'll bring my poi," he urged. "I'll spin for you. I'd like that. I'll show you the town, the post office where I used to work, the road to my old house. You can see the voting, Mona—I'll be able to vote for Senator Ancelet."

"Didn't you say something about insubordination a few days ago?"

"Well, she never actually *ordered* that I do anything, did she? And if Deschamps has such a dedicated following, Senator Ancelet will need every vote she can get."

"Won't folk recognize me? I stand out a bit." I gestured to my pale skin.

"They'll be too busy reveling to notice. And I doubt anyone is actively looking for you, not out this far. You heard Gris—folk out here still haven't heard about Lilou. And even if they had, for all anyone knows, you escaped back to Lumen." He went to my trunk. "You can wear one of these fancy gowns with the long sleeves, and that hat the Brasseauxs gave you. You'll blend right in. And there are no Alcoran ships here, no watchdogs. There's just the Alcoran in charge of the mill, and I imagine he hates First Fire, like most Canyon-folk. He won't be anywhere near the village."

He straightened, holding a beaded gown of rich aubergine, embroidered in gold. Something desperate was flickering behind his honey-colored eyes.

I should absolutely refuse to go, and I should insist that he not go, either. It was a massive, pointless risk. We still had a great deal of distance to cover, and he had been actively poling all day. We both needed rest. Nothing good—nothing good at all—could come from agreeing to such an absurd idea.

So I stood. "Yes," I said. "I'd like that very much."

His face split into that brilliant crescent grin.

CHAPTER 10

We walked up the track to the village, my arm resting in his. He looked impossibly debonair in an emerald vest and deep golden sash and ascot. We both were wearing masks he had unearthed from the back of one of his uncle's wardrobes. They were gold like the other masks I'd seen, but his was lined with black sequins, while mine had a fringe of purple beads along the bottom rim. The feathered hat from the Brasseauxs was perched on my newly shorn head, the lacy netting covering much of my hair. I hoped between it and the mask, I could avoid drawing too much curiosity.

Rou was energized, fervently so, the bag containing his poi swinging from his sash—and that energy was infectious. He talked animatedly as we walked, pointing out houses of childhood friends and tracks that led to the best swimming holes. I strode along beside him, asking questions despite telling myself over and over that this was an absurdly risky endeavor I should never have agreed to. My purple gown shifted and swung as I moved, its tassels and fringe bouncing at our quick pace. The skirt was long—finally—swooping up to fasten to a cuff around my wrist. I had been concerned about my neck—the scalloped neckline cut straight across my chest, and my throat felt conspicuously bare now that my hair was gone—but Rou had found me a sumptuous silk scarf somewhere in his uncle's house. It didn't match the gown, but it was a similar shade of emerald as his vest, and that pleased me for some silly reason. The whole ensemble was a bit excessive, and too richly colored for me. I probably looked like I had been dressed by a group of children who couldn't agree on what I should wear.

I found I couldn't make myself care. Particularly not after Rou had arranged the scarf around my neck, grinning all the while.

"Like a magnolia in May," he said, standing back to look me up and down.

"Jokes to yourself," I said.

"Not a joke, Lady Queen."

Lanterns sprung up along the path. Up ahead, a glow flickered through the trees. Music and cheering filtered to meet us, coupled with the mingling scents of spices and smoke. We joined other folk hurrying down the path, laughing behind their masks.

"I know these folk," Rou said quietly to me as a large group joined the throng. "I recognize them all."

"Rou . . ."

"Don't worry," he assured me, patting my hand in his elbow. "I won't strike up conversation. Inevitably I'd have to introduce you, and then things would get awkward. It's all right. I want to be as anonymous as you tonight."

I squeezed his arm. "Thank you."

We broke out of the trees, and once again, I was struck with the notion that the whole village was on fire. Torches burned on every post, spitting colored sparks into the air. Bonfires burned up and down the streets. Children ran around waving ribbon wands similar to the one little Anouk Doucet had given me in Toadhollow.

All along the riverbank, folk were performing with fire. Closest to us, a woman was spinning a flaming hoop around her body, moving it up and down her hips, along her arms, behind her head, never letting it come to a stop. I watched her, mesmerized, but before we got any closer, Rou drifted toward the nearest vendor, intent, it seemed, on her wares. I followed.

"Have you made your decision?" asked the vendor mere seconds after we arrived in front of her.

I looked down at her wares. She was selling flint, which struck me as odd—Rou didn't need a flint. What's more, they all looked the same, nearly identical. I couldn't think what decision there was to make.

But Rou wasn't looking at the flint. "I have," he said, meeting her gaze. She nodded once, reached under the counter, and produced a vial of oil the size of my little finger.

"Fans," she said, handing him the vial.

"Thank you." With that, he turned and led me away with the vial clutched in his fist.

"Sorry," he said. "I keep forgetting to explain things . . ."

"Nobody here needs a flint," I said. "Even if you all didn't already carry them, the whole place is on fire. Only an outsider would approach that stall wanting to buy something. The rest of you know that's where you get the oil for the braziers."

He gave a delighted laugh. "And how do we know which braziers are the right ones?"

I looked at the riverbank, which was lined with braziers every few feet, flanking all the folk performing with fiery apparatuses of all kinds.

I nodded toward the woman dancing with two flaming metal fans. "Fans."

"Truly exceptional." Grinning, he headed toward the fan dancer, squeezing my hand where it rested in the crook of his elbow.

We approached the dancer, who was performing next to two burning braziers. Only one other person stood watching her, holding what looked like an ink pot and a brush. Rou released my hand and took his vial to the braziers. In the flickering light, I could see letters inscribed into each one.

I.D.

E.A.

Ines Deschamps and Eulalie Ancelet.

Both burned with the same brightness—it was impossible to tell who might be winning. Without pause, Rou tipped his vial into the reservoir for Senator Ancelet. He handed his empty vial to the bystander, who pocketed it and dipped the brush into the ink pot. He drew it across the back of Rou's hand, leaving a smudged black stain on his skin.

"So you can't vote a second time," I said as he rejoined me.

He took my hand and bowed over it, grinning again. "Lady Queen, you outdo your reputation."

"Perhaps you're simply not as clever as you think you are."

"Perhaps I am, and you're just cleverer."

"Do you feel better now that you've voted?"

"I do. It would have eaten me up, otherwise, especially if Senator Ancelet loses." His gaze landed on something behind me, and his eyes lit up behind his mask. "Ah! Spiced coffee, Mona!" Hurriedly he swept my arm up in his again and pulled me toward the vendor, digging in his pocket for coin. "There's no other way to start the night!"

He passed a few coppers to the vendor, who pocketed them and swirled the contents of a metal carafe. I didn't have the heart to tell Rou I didn't like coffee. But before I could wonder how much of the cup I would have to drink to be polite, the vendor lifted an orange peel out of the bowl with a pair of tongs and promptly set it on fire. It ignited in a plume of blue flame.

"Oh!" I said aloud. Rou laughed again. The vendor ladled the concoction in the carafe over the orange peel, setting the whole mixture on fire. He picked up a pot of coffee and poured it over the flames, and then ladled the result into two small ceramic cups. Rou took them and handed one to me.

"A new hearth, swept clean," he toasted me, chinking his cup against mine.

The result was sweet, exotic, and threaded with liquor. I drank it in sips, barely noticing the bitter taste of coffee underneath the cloves and cinnamon and caramelized orange. I soon realized it wasn't just their coffee the River-folk set on fire. Rou pulled me from one cart to the next, delighted with my surprise every time the vendors ignited a stick of liquor-soaked fruit or sponge cake.

At home, I knew exactly how many glasses of wine was too many. I knew exactly how much I could drink on an empty stomach, how much would make me overly talkative, and how much would just make me drowsy. I never lost track. But this parade of liquors, swirled into sweet drinks and soaked into confections, had no rhyme or reason. Before long, my head was pleasantly buzzing, and my remaining anxiety had eased away.

When our spiced coffee was gone, Rou bought us each some kind of cocktail that sent up a puff of pink flames when ignited. Clutching this in my hands, we made our way to a stall next to a man spinning a fire staff. As I watched him make flaming circles in the air, Rou accepted a cloth bag from the stall vendor. He held it out to me.

"What's this?" I asked. "This isn't on fire."

His eyes twinkled behind his mask. "Pralines. Try one."

I did. Creamy, sweet, delicious. I shook my head. "A bit lackluster, if you ask me."

He grinned. "Don't worry, lolly, we'll get a jubilee tart next—soaked in brandy, wait 'til you see . . ."

"Why do you keep calling me that?" I asked.

He blinked. "Call you what? Oh—I said it again, didn't I?"

"You did. What does it mean?"

He pursed his lips. "You know, I'm not really sure. It's a term of endearment. I think it must come from the loblolly pine, though I can't think why—they grow in mud puddles . . ."

"I told you not to call me that," I said abruptly. "You've got to stop."

He paused, a praline halfway to his mouth.

"I can't stand pet names," I said.

He raised his eyebrows behind his mask. "I don't mean anything by it . . . I don't even realize I'm saying it."

"I know," I said. "I just hate pet names."

"Oh." He hesitated with the praline, and then put it halfheartedly in his mouth. "I'm sorry. I'll try not to say it again."

There was a moment of rather stilted silence, his early buoyancy gone. He looked out at the man performing with the fire staff. I clutched my cocktail in my hands.

"It's just," I said, "there was someone, once, who called me a lot of pet names. I didn't realize how demeaning they were until . . . a bit later."

He turned slowly to me, the sequins on his mask glinting in the firelight. "What happened?"

I clutched my cup and took a large sip, hoping to stall, but it didn't help—the sweet, sharp liquor made me want to spill everything out, everything I had told myself I would never, ever tell a soul.

"A lot of things," I said, trying to tame the urge. "None of them good."

He opened his mouth as if to ask another question, then seemed to think better of it. He looked back at the staff spinner. I took another sip of my drink.

"He was after the crown, of course," I said. "But I didn't realize it until it was too late."

"Too late?"

"It just . . . things got a little out of hand. There was a lot of fallout. I made a lot of mistakes."

"*You* made a lot of mistakes? Seems to me there are usually two people in a relationship."

"Not those kinds of mistakes. Bigger ones. Ones

I should have anticipated. But I was too young and foolish to see it coming."

"I hope he at least learned a lesson from crossing you."

"I told you, I was young, and frightened by that point. I never confronted him." I pressed my lips together. The staff spinner finished his routine with a flourish and bowed to the crowd. "I mostly avoid him, even now. He makes me uncomfortable."

Rou was watching me, not the spinner. "What would you *like* to say to him?"

"A lot of things."

He reached up and pushed his sequined mask up his forehead, baring his face. "If it was him, instead of me, what would you say?"

I shook my head and took a too-big gulp of my drink. The liquor stung going down my throat. "That's not . . . it doesn't . . ."

But Rou didn't know how often I thought of this very thing. How many times I had sat, staring furiously into space, running through the litany of things I wished I could say to Donnel Burke. I closed my eyes, seeing those steely gray eyes in place of Rou's warm amber, his aristocratic horsetail instead of Rou's dark tendrils.

"I won't marry you," I heard myself say. "You haven't even got the beginnings of a good king. You don't care about your folk. You don't care about me."

But those were the few things I *had* said to Donnel, and it had gone all wrong. Memories of those frightening days flooded back to me—the shadows on the wall, the trailing footsteps, the whispers behind my back.

"You haven't got a shred of integrity," I said. "You haven't got an inch of common decency. You know exactly what to say to get what you want, and when you don't get it . . ." I opened my eyes, only distantly seeing Rou's face behind Donnel's. "And when you don't get it, you'll cross sea and sky to get petty revenge."

I drew myself up, my stomach surging. "And . . . and don't call me your *pretty little queen*. Don't call me your sweet little songbird. I'm not yours, and I don't want any name you give me."

I drew a deep breath, remembering the terrible fallout, but before I could continue, Rou's hand flew through the air. With a tremendous *smack*, he slapped himself—hard—across his own cheek. I jumped and dropped my half-full cup.

"Sorry," he said. "But he sounds like a real sop."

Something welled up inside me, something big, and without warning I leaned against the praline stand and dissolved into laughter. My building anger, the hot shame—it collapsed away, leaving an endless stretch of hilarity in its wake. I clutched my sides and laughed like I hadn't laughed in years. Rou grinned, rubbing his smarting cheek.

"You can keep going," he said. "I just couldn't help myself."

I gasped through my laughter. "That was stupid."

He tugged his mask back down his face. "Sounds like he deserved it, though."

"I mean it was stupid of me." I dashed at my tearing eyes under my own mask. "How did you get me going like that?"

"I compared Your Majesty to a swamp pine," he said. "But I won't do it again. Look, now, you've dropped your Sizzle Punch." He crooked his arm to me. "I can't take you anywhere, can I?"

I threaded my arm through his, still laughing. Arm in arm, we headed further down the road, sharing the bag of pralines between us. My burning embarrassment at nearly spilling my heart was fully overridden by giddy relief—still seeing Rou's sheepish grin replacing Donnel's fierce scowl.

We passed a group clustered around a bed of live coals, cheering on the folk striding across it, some carrying partners on their backs. We moved on to a woman juggling torches, each one burning a different color. Rou countered my disbelief at the fire eaters, insisting there was no trick, no heatless flame they were putting in their mouths. He placed a fire staff— unlit—into my hands and showed me how to spin it in front of me. It was only after I had made several failed attempts that I realized I had utterly disregarded my mother's mantra. *Don't do something if you don't think you can do it well.* But Rou was so enthusiastic, so eager for me to try again, that I made two more botched tries before finally completing a continuous spin.

"Now we just have to light it!" he crowed.

"Don't you dare," I said breathlessly, thrusting the staff back into his arms.

We toasted bits of bread and cheese in one of the many bonfires. He brought me to the wide-rimmed fountain in the center of town, where folk were lighting tea candles and setting them afloat in the water.

"Sort of like your Overwater Feast," he said, handing me a candle to light. "Without the singing. Maybe you should sing."

"Maybe you should come to Lumen, if you want to hear me sing."

"Maybe I should."

He bought us each a mug of mulled wine, and we strolled along the riverbank toward a cluster of folk sending fireworks streaming over the water. Bursts of red and gold and blue reflected in the surface, their sparks trailing down like rain.

We stood at the water's edge, watching the crackling lights and sipping our wine. My head swam pleasantly, and I took the opportunity to lean a bit more on his arm, enjoying the warmth of his body. Enjoying it so much, in fact, that I wanted to share something else with him—betray another one of my secrets. A few sparks drifted our way. One landed on the wet stones near my feet, hissing.

I cleared my throat, looking down at the stones. "Rou."

"Hm?"

"I have a . . . a confession."

He lowered his mug from his mouth and turned to

me. I glanced furtively toward the group of folk sending the fireworks into the air. I leaned a bit closer. I heard his breath catch.

"I can skip rocks," I said.

With a cry of delight, he tossed his almost-empty mug aside, took my hands in his, and whirled me around and around. "I knew it!" he shouted. "I knew there was something, some stupid useless trick." He crouched down at the water's edge and dug up a variety of stones. "Are you good?"

I crouched down next to him, the tassel on my wrist cuff dangling just above the surface. "I'm *very* good." I pried up a smooth, flat rock. "My longest is fourteen skips."

I rose with a bend in my knees and bent my arm backward. My burn was stiff, but I didn't care. I flung the rock forward. It broke the surface in a series of ripples, muddling the reflection of the fireworks. Three, four, five skips—it struck a stump and splashed into the water.

Rou drew his own rock back and threw it. It gave one gargantuan *plunk* and sank into the river.

"Get lower," I said. "Bend your knees."

"How did you learn this?" he asked, hunting for another rock. "Did someone teach you?"

I found a few suitable stones and handed him one. "Arlen did, but he didn't know it. I was thirteen. I sat with my needlework while he practiced throwing, watching him try and fail and try again the whole morning. When he was gone, I found my own rock and put everything he had been practicing into my throw—and I got four skips."

He flung again, grinning. This one flew promisingly but still sunk after just one splash. "So you never actually did the failing yourself."

"I did have to practice. I did it quietly, off my patio. Now I gather good stones I see along the lakeshore and keep them in a flowerpot next to my steps. Don't cock your wrist so far back."

He threw. It skipped twice. He whooped and lifted his arms in the air as if he had just won a wrestling match. I crouched and threw my own rock. Eight skips. It struck the far bank and bounced into the bushes.

I straightened. "There's a lot more room at the lake. You'll just have to come practice there."

"I will. I'll use the Overwater Feast as an excuse."

"Perfect."

We picked along the riverbank, prying up suitable stones and sending them skimming off the water's surface. Many of his still sunk on their first strike, but he managed three skips on one throw. I fished rocks out of the river, the water lapping at the toes of my boots. As I brushed the mud off a handful, the water beneath my hands stilled enough for me to see a billowing cloud of smoke reflecting in the water. I looked up. I straightened.

We had rounded a slight bend in the river, away from the revelry in the village center. A monstrous brick building marched away down the bank, its many chimneys spilling smoke and steam. Somewhere in the darkness, a waterwheel turned on its gears, filling the air with a grinding racket. On a squat tower, the shape of a bell was just visible in the ambient glow.

"Temper Creek Steel Mill," said Rou, coming to stand at my elbow. He turned a rock in his fingers. "I wonder which poor souls are on rotation tonight." His gaze lit on the bell tower. "Likelihood of injury increases on these kinds of nights, when folk are off their usual schedules." He tossed his rock unceremoniously into the river. "Likelihood of *incidents*."

I leaned into him, spilling my own handful of stones back into the water. He inclined his forehead to mine. Our masks clinked together, and we rested there for a moment, our heads together, my arm in his once more. I felt the puff of his breath against my cheek and the slight shift of his mask as he slid his eyes from the mill to me. Before I gathered the courage to return his gaze—he was too close, much *much* too close—a clanging sound echoed from the mill, drowning out the faint noise of First Fire.

He startled backward. "Ugh," he said, shuddering. "I hate that sound. They're about to tap the furnace. Workers bang on the pipes to tell others to take cover, in case the molds explode." He gave a shake and pulled me back up the riverbank. "Come on. Let's go see if they've started the fire jumping yet. I didn't bring you here to look at this wretched place."

I cast one more look over my shoulder at the

mill, the bell hanging immobile and shadowed in its tower.

We rejoined the reveling crowds. He bought us both a drink he called a Shooting Star. The vendor set the liquor alight and poured it through the air from one mug to another several times, creating a constant stream of fire. Rou handed one to me, and I drank it, my mouth puckering at the sharpness. As I neared the end of the drink, I began to wish we had gone to First Fire in all the other villages, began to wish I had spent the last five days wearing a beaded mask, holding his arm in mine, laughing more easily than I had in years—long before the Alcoran invasion. Perhaps even before I had been crowned queen. I leaned into him, wanting him to rest his mask against mine like he had by the river—and more. I wanted his face close to mine. I wanted to hear his breath catch in his chest again. *I have that power*, I realized, giddy. *I do that to him. I bring him up short, just like he does to me.*

I liked that. Very much.

A distant shred of sanity snuck through my head, and when Rou wasn't looking, I shook the last few sips of the Shooting Star into the bushes.

"No more liquor," I said to him as he turned to exclaim over the fire jumpers.

"Oh, you have to try a Dragon's Tongue, it sparks, wait 'til you see . . ."

"No more liquor," I insisted. I leaned on his arm, my feet clumsy.

He paused and looked at me. "Do you feel all right? Do you want to go?"

"I don't want to go," I said. "But I also don't want to do anything silly." I straightened a bit. "Besides, you still have to spin for me."

"I do. Here." He took my empty mug and filled it from a carafe of plain water. I took it gratefully.

There was a large crowd gathered around a spectacle we had not yet investigated, and over folk's heads I could see the swinging arcs of spinning poi. I pulled Rou in that direction, my elbow linked around his. He laughed jovially and adjusted his hand so our fingers were threaded together. I didn't pause to remedy this too-intimate touch, instead using the extra leverage to drag him more quickly up the track.

All right—so I would have kept our hands like that regardless.

We elbowed through the crowd until we had a good view of the woman spinning in the empty space. At the edge of the crowd, a drummer was putting forth a driving beat, accompanied by a guitarist. I realized with satisfaction that my admiration of Rou's skill was not unfounded. The woman performing now was good, but she didn't move with the same grace he did—her pattern was less imaginative, her feet less light.

"Elva," Rou murmured next to me. "She's the sister of that fellow who choked on the furnace gases all those years ago."

I leaned close to him. "You're better than she is."

He smiled but didn't reply, his eyes on the performance. I rested my head on his shoulder, my hand in his. Without hesitation, he rested his head against mine.

The drummer slowed her tempo, and Elva eased her pattern, finally extinguishing her poi. Folk applauded her. She bowed to them. The crowd began to clamor for someone else.

I nudged Rou. "Go. Go now."

He picked himself off me and unbuttoned his cuffs, rolling his sleeves up to his elbows. But before he pressed through the crowd, he turned back to me. He took my hand and lifted my fingers to his lips. He kissed them, his eyes on mine, his lips moving across each knuckle. I didn't blush, I didn't look away. I returned his gaze in full, smiling, that now-familiar bloom of heat flaring with force. We were the only two people in the world.

He released my hand and dove through his folk into the circle, his arms raised. People cheered, and the drummer began her beat once more. Rou loosened his silk ascot and took his poi out of their bag. He looped the ends around his fingers. Someone held a torch out to him, and he held the wicks into the flame. They lit with a flare.

He held them out to his sides, the flames jumping up the chains toward his wrists. He bowed to the crowd first one way, then the other—they cheered, urging him on. He made one more bow in my direction. I grinned, holding the fingers he had kissed to my own lips.

He began with a few sweeping strokes, letting the drummer's beat leave him behind. He stepped slowly, fluidly, tracing broad arcs in the air. It was a start similar to the one I'd seen him make in the early mornings. The drummer grew more insistent, driving the pace onward. Folk began to jostle and cheer. The guitarist picked his energetic melody back up, and just as the crowd began growing impatient, Rou burst to life.

He plunged to one side, spinning front to back across the open space—folk along one edge scrambled backward to avoid the path of his poi. He pitched forward into a lunge, one knee on the ground, flames wheeling around his body. Folk shouted and hollered, calling to others outside the circle to come and see this new spinner. Rou rose from his lunge, drawing one knee to his waist and spinning on his heel, his poi circling first parallel and then opposite each other. Their paths grew wide—he stretched his arms to their full length and arced them through the air. They twirled in tighter and tighter until they were flying in orbit around his head.

I stood amid the jubilant crowd, my fingers still pressed to my smiling lips. This wasn't his easy, introspective morning routine. I couldn't think of what words I might use to describe this to someone who hadn't seen it—it was more than a dance, more than a series of acrobatics. This was rawness and energy.

It was a celebration.

He whirled the flames over his head before bringing his wrists together, spiraling them in a circle. They twisted, grew closer together, and became a wheel of flame that ran up his waist, up his chest, over his face. The fire skimmed his hair, and I drew in a sharp breath, but of course it didn't light. His poi leaped suddenly outward, one whirling behind his back, the other barely clearing the space around his wrist.

At some point my eyes moved from the flight of his poi to the movements of his body. His wrists turned impossibly fast, his feet stepped around the streaks of flames as if they were a dance partner. His arms never stopped moving, guiding his wicks with the barest movements, never fumbling into each other. His face was intent, alight—his eyes glowed behind his mask. They weren't watching the frenzied path of his poi, fixed instead on some empty space in front of him. He paused the movements of his feet to stand fully facing me in the crowd, wheeling his poi on either side of his body. His eyes met mine. He grinned. Turned out I didn't need the last few sips of the Shooting Star—I knew exactly what I was going to do when he finished.

A hand closed on my left arm just as he turned away into another series of spins. I shook it off, thinking someone was trying to move me aside so they could see better. But the hand closed tighter. I took my gaze away from Rou and turned to find a mask peering at me.

"Let go of me," I commanded.

"Who are you?" asked the man behind the mask. His voice was rough, smoky.

"Let go," I said again, pushing his hand away.

But instead of letting go, he closed his other hand on my right arm—my burned arm. Even through the fog in my head, this hurt. My breath caught in my throat, and I yanked my left arm free and grasped his hand on my burns.

"Let *go*!" I tugged uselessly at his grip. He was huge, hulking, and his eyes narrowed shrewdly behind his mask. I glanced back at Rou—he was following the pattern of his poi, absorbed in his movements. And then, the man pulled me quietly backward. Folk closed in front of me, jostling for a better view of Rou. He and his poi were lost to my sight.

"How dare you!" I shoved at the big man once again. "How *dare* you touch me! Take your hands off me at once!"

"You sure talk like a queen," he said.

I stilled my movements, my heart pounding, but I was having trouble thinking straight. In my pause, the man swept the feathered hat off my head and then jerked at the tie to my mask. It fell off, exposing my face and hair.

He frowned. "Didn't think you'd have hair this short. But it's you, ain't it, lolly? Lady Queen?"

"You're hurting my arm," I said through clenched teeth. "Let go, and leave me alone."

"Come along, now. No fuss."

He began to drag me away from the crowd gathered around Rou. I twisted in his grip, the burns on my right arm searing in protest. I felt tender new skin tear. My eyes tearing, my head swimming, I opened my mouth and screamed.

It was lost in the other sounds of the revelry, but even so, the giant clapped his hand over my mouth. His skin smelled of coal and smoke.

"Hush now, lolly, and don't struggle. Bellemere's a long way to go with a gag on your mouth."

Bellemere. He wanted to take me to the Alcorans. Did he think I was Gemma? I lashed out with my boot, kicking the man ineffectually in his shin. I tried to bite the flesh of his hand, but his palm was so big, it covered my chin and nose, holding my mouth shut. Folk parted around us, absorbed in the sights on either side of the track. I probably looked like an unruly reveler who had had too much to drink.

Which was true.

I regained some sense and dug my heels into the ground. Remembering what Mae described on our journey over the mountains, after we had been found out in Rusher's Junction, I straightened my fingers and drove them sharply into the man's throat. He choked and loosened his grip, but he grabbed a handful of my long skirt before I could get out of reach. He snatched at my arm again and wrenched it behind my back. I staggered at the pain, my head swirling with fright and too much drink. I buckled to one knee, my rich gown splitting where I fell.

"Get off!" I shouted, terrified, enraged, on the edge of panic. "Get off me—*leave me alone!*"

The air around us blazed bright. A train of fire

slammed into the giant's face, sending a shower of sparks raining down on me. He screeched in pain and staggered away just as I looked up to see Rou whip his other poi toward him. The burning wick wound several times around the man's arm, setting his sleeve alight. Rou hauled him away by his collar and loosened his fingers from his poi strap. The man rolled on the ground, scrabbling to unwind the burning wick from his arm.

Rou dragged me upright and pushed me back toward the village. "Go, go!" he urged. "Back to my uncle's . . ."

He had no time to finish. The big man extinguished his shirt and picked himself off the ground, a shiny burn kissing one cheek. With an angry shout, he lowered his shoulder and barreled into Rou, bringing him crashing to the dirt. Rou was quick, rolling away and flinging his wrist still connected to his lit poi. But the man was quick, too, and he lashed out and grasped the chain—surely it must have scorched his hand, but he didn't flinch. He jerked it off of Rou's fingers and flung it to the ground, stomping the flame out with his boot. Rou was scrambling to get to his feet, but the man closed his hand on Rou's loose collar. He cocked his other arm back, his hand curled into a fist . . .

I jumped forward.

It was foolish, something I never would have attempted without the recklessness brought on by the parade of liquor. I latched on to the man's arm and jerked him backward. He was too big for me to shift, but he faltered briefly, giving Rou enough time to twist out of his grip. He swung himself around the man's back, looping his elbow around his neck.

"Alderic," he said fiercely into the man's ear. "Calm down."

By this point, folk were starting to press in around us, trying to break up the brawl. The man cursed and twisted, trying to pry Rou off his back. Then he stopped short, staring at me crouching in the dirt.

He flung out a massive finger. "This is the queen of Lumen Lake!" he shouted. "There is a thousand-silver price on her capture, and I'll be *damned* . . ." He lashed back and drove his fist into Rou's jaw. It was a glancing blow, but Rou's grip slipped, and the man dragged him off his shoulders and threw him flat on his back on the dirt track. Brushing interceding folk off like flies, he slung a heavy leg over Rou, pinning him down. He put one massive hand on his collar again and pulled the other fist back.

"Alderic," Rou choked under the man's crushing grip. He fumbled at the tie to his mask. "Alderic, it's me, it's—"

The other fist plummeted down, smashing into Rou's face with a sickening crack. For one terrifying moment, I was afraid he had split Rou's skull, but then I realized the crack had come from the mask fracturing in two. I was shouting, pulling uselessly at the giant's arm. Other folk joined me, dragging him away from Rou, who was lying frighteningly still amid the trampling feet. I scrambled to his side, trusting that the crowd would subdue our attacker for the moment. My heart plunged into my stomach. Rou's mask had split vertically across the left eyehole—one side had fallen away from his face, but the other side had been driven into his forehead. The sharp edge was buried in his skin. Blood welled up over the black sequins.

"Rou." I knelt over him, my hands hovering over his body. I didn't know what to do first, whether I should move the mask or leave it. I didn't know the first thing about treating wounds. Great Light, Mae would know. "Rou," I said again, resting one hand on his chest. He was breathing. His heart was beating. He hadn't been killed. But he wasn't moving. I put my other hand on his face. "*Rou.*"

He regained consciousness, his eyelids fluttering. His hand jumped to his forehead, and vaguely he tore off the fractured mask. Blood flowed freely down his nose, into his hair, into his eye.

With trembling hands, I pulled off the emerald scarf around my neck and pressed it to his forehead. Blood began to seep immediately through the fine fabric. I lifted his head and knotted the scarf in place. Behind me, Alderic was still yelling about the queen of Lumen Lake, and I realized folk were starting to shift uncomfortably around us. Rou realized this, too, and he pushed himself off the ground, staggering to his feet. He gripped me under the arm and tried to drag me through the crowd. Someone reached out halfheartedly to grasp his shoulder, but he shook them off. I clearly heard the name *Roubideaux* being muttered from one person to the next.

Alderic had either escaped the folk subduing him, or had convinced them I was worth apprehending. He pushed after us, shouting for folk to stop us, shouting my name and title over and over again. The track before us was cut off by confused folk. A man with a thin, scrawny look stepped directly in our path. Rou clamped me tightly to his side and reluctantly drew his fist back, aiming for the man's face.

The fountain in the center of town exploded in a cloud of white flame, roaring into the night sky, lighting the village like the surface of the sun. Folk wheeled—some gaped, others cheered, thinking it was some festival spectacular. I had seen such flame before, however, on the gangplank of the *Spindrift*. Rou didn't hesitate. He pushed through the distracted crowd, dragging me along with him. I put my head down, now conspicuously bare, and hurried to keep pace with him.

People flocked to the fountain to watch the flames dance on the water. We squeezed through a press of folk and Rou staggered. I looped my arm through his again, trying to steady him. We hurried back through the village and down to the river's edge. The folk near the braziers were gazing up the track, but they were looking at the burning fountain, not us. Even still, I saw several folk do double-takes, first at me, and then at Rou.

We reached the track leading into the forest and hurried into the darkness of the trees. Rou was breathing heavily, and his feet slipped on loose stones and exposed tree roots. When the glow and noise of the town had faded behind us, he suddenly flung himself away from me and staggered against a tree trunk. He clutched his stomach and vomited into the bushes.

I didn't have anything to give him, no water, not even a handkerchief. I placed my hands on his back, trying to steady him.

"Are you all right?" I asked breathlessly.

He straightened, putting his back against the tree. The silk scarf on his forehead was already saturated with blood. "I think I've been concussed," he said lightly, as if discussing the weather. He touched his forehead, swaying slightly.

"Let's get you back," I said, taking his arm in mine again. "Let's get you in bed."

"We can't stay," he said, his hand sliding from his forehead to his eyes. "Great Light, am I an idiot . . . ." He looked up at me. The skin above his left eyebrow was beginning to swell. "I'm sorry, Mona. I may have just undone everything."

"It wasn't your fault . . . you thought it was safe, we both thought it was safe. How folk found out about a reward all the way out here . . ." I cut off as the crunch of running footsteps melted out of the darkness. I started, but Rou didn't look up.

Lyle stormed into view. Without a word, he

grabbed Rou under the arm and dragged him away from the tree, marching him forcibly up the path.

I scurried after them. "Lyle," I said shrilly. "Lyle, slow down, he's hurt . . ."

Lyle threw his brother in front of him. Rou staggered in the dark.

"You stupid ass!" Lyle shouted, his fists balled. "What infantile part of your brain thought going to First Fire was a good idea? Going with *her*?"

"Lyle!" I pushed past him, threading my shoulder under Rou's arm. "It doesn't matter. It happened, it's done. It's my fault, too."

"It *does* matter," he said angrily, jabbing his finger at his brother's face. "You were *recognized*! Word's going to spread that the Lumeni queen is in the company of a couple of Roubideauxs, and folk will assume we've got Gemma as well. Did you even stop to think? Did you even think about Gris? They'll tear down his house tonight!"

"You were the one who thought going through Temper Creek was a good idea," Rou said angrily, swatting his brother's hand out of his face.

"Great flaming Light, I didn't think you'd leave the house! It's all or nothing with you, all the time, isn't it? You can't just sit by and leave well enough alone. You've got to be in the middle of the crowd, you've got to have everyone applauding you. I'm curious, does it ever work? Is it ever enough?"

"Lyle!" I said angrily. "How about we work on getting home, instead of shouting spite?"

He whirled on me. *"Spite?* I beg your pardon, *Your Highness,* but respectfully, you know nothing. Or did he tell you, amid all the flirting and drinking, why we can't call him Theo anymore?"

Rou spun suddenly, his arm around me, striding furiously away from his brother. But Lyle wasn't done shouting.

"Things don't stay in one place, Theo! You're the same person everywhere else that you are here!"

I stumbled along next to Rou, resisting the urge to look back over my shoulder. Much of the fog in my head had been burned away in my fright, but the world was still blurry around the edges as I tried to make sense of Lyle's words. Rou fumed next to me, walking as quickly as his unsteady feet would carry him. Questions buzzed in my head, pressed against my lips—but neither of us said a word.

By the time his uncle's house materialized out of the darkness, Rou was leaning on my shoulder, his toes catching on the broken walkway. We hurried up the steps to the porch, and I pushed open the front door.

I had no desire to attempt the staircase with him wobbling like he was, so I steered him to a frayed old day couch shoved along one wall in the entry hall. A lamp burned dimly in a sconce above it. I turned up the wick and guided Rou down onto the faded cushion.

"I'm sorry," he said thickly.

"Hush," I said, my heart thumping. I was a swirl of confusion and second-guesses. I fumbled with the emerald scarf, now stiff with blood, and peeled it away from the gash on his forehead. I bit my lip—it was a frightening sight. His skin was swollen and mottled, and the edges of the wound gaped open.

"Where's the kitchen?" I asked, trying to keep my voice steady. I had no confidence where blood was concerned. "Where can I find a towel and water?"

"Round the corner, down the hall."

I hurried that way, the fringe on my ruined gown as jumpy as my nerves. The hearth in the kitchen was banked, and I swirled up a few glowing coals and settled a kettle down among them, hoping it would heat. I searched for clean towels and found a few lengths of linen used to wrap cheese. I bundled them up. Between my arm and Gemma's cycle, I didn't know how many bandages we had left—these would have to do. From the entry hall, I heard the front door slam and a pair of heavy boots stomp up the stairs. Lyle must have returned. His footsteps strode up the hallway above us, making the ceiling creak and crack. I heard him open a door to one of the south rooms. He was going to rouse Gemma.

He was getting us ready to leave.

I gathered up the kettle and cloth and hurried back out to the day couch. Rou was holding the scarf to his forehead again.

"I'm still bleeding," he said vaguely.

"Yes," I said, wetting a towel with lukewarm water. I pulled his hand away and dabbed at his bloody forehead. Rivers to the sea, we were lucky the mask hadn't driven into his eye. I thought of Arlen with his patch. And then, as I steeled myself against the open gash on his head, another image of Arlen came to me—his face all bloodied from his first misjudged dive on the Brown Beds, the dive that had left him with the smile-shaped scar under his right eye. He had had wide-open lacerations, too. They had to wrap one whole side of his face in gauze, and they had to . . .

"Rou," I said. "I think you need stitches."

"That's inconvenient."

"Is there . . . is there someone I can fetch? Is there a healer nearby?"

Up above us, the floorboards creaked with two sets of feet. Gemma was up. There was a scrape of a trunk on the wood.

"Not nearby, no. And everybody's at First Fire, anyway." He shifted and probed his swollen wound with his fingers. "S'all right, lolly, I'll be fine . . ."

"Don't call me that," I said, taking a sharp breath. Blood was still leaking from the gash. I took his hand and set it firmly in his lap. "Don't touch it. I'll be right back."

I dashed up the stairs. Lyle was coming down the hall with Gemma's trunk in his arms. I ducked into my room. Everything was as I had left it. The floor around the vanity was still littered with my locks of hair. The sewing kit was still resting on my trunk. I grabbed it and threw open the lid, rooting around for the bottle of brandy the Toussaints had given us. It was wedged down at the bottom of the trunk—I closed my fingers around it and ran back out into the hall.

Back at Rou's side, I splashed the brandy onto a cloth.

"Ah, brandy," he said. "It always goes to my head."

"Hush," I said again, bringing the cloth to his forehead. I had very little idea what I was doing, and I wasn't in the mood for him to make bad jokes. I dabbed at his wound. He jumped.

"Torchfire!" he exclaimed, groping for the bottle. "Great fiery gator teeth, that hurts a lot." He popped the cork off and took a long draw.

"Hold still." I cleaned the gash, immensely grateful for the dregs of recklessness still swirling around inside me. I would never have the courage to attempt this when sober. I picked through the sewing kit, pulling out the finest needle inside.

"Have you done this before?"

"Of course not," I snapped. I threaded the needle. He swilled the brandy bottle and took another draw. I leaned forward, peering at the wound, trying to decide if I should start at the top or bottom.

"You have a beautiful neck," he said. "It's very slender. And with all your hair gone . . ."

"Lie back," I said. I took the bottle out of his hands and set it on the floor.

He sighed and leaned his head against the cushion. I brought the needle to his forehead, my lower lip clenched in my teeth. I put my other hand on the side of his face. Without waiting a second longer, I pressed the needle into his skin.

I felt him stiffen under my hand, but he didn't speak. I didn't dare drag my eyes from my work to see his expression—now that I had started, there was no way I was going to stop. I gave a gentle tug, trying to bring the edges of the wound together, and made another stitch. *Cloth*, I thought fiercely. *Just a rip in a tunic. A split in a seam.* I pulled the thread and looped it around again.

"I can *hear it*," he said. "That's awful."

"And you talking about it isn't helping," I said shakily. "Quiet."

I was relieved to find that each stitch closed the gash a little tighter. A trickle of blood seeped from the wound, and I reached for the cloth and wiped it away. He took the opportunity to grope for the brandy bottle and bring it to his mouth again. I made another two stitches.

"I suppose you want an explanation," he said. "For what Lyle was ranting about."

I did, but it could wait. "Right now I just want you to lie still."

The front door opened, and Lyle stormed up the stairs again, rattling the whole house. I heard him scrape open the door to my room.

"Giedi Acacali," Rou said, and I paused, thinking he was babbling.

"What?"

"The Alcoran who ran the mill when Eloi and I worked there. The one who never shut it down. Giedi Acacali." He gave a throaty chuckle. "Bizarre names, haven't they, the Canyon-folk? All awkward on the tongue. Though I guess I'm one to talk." He chuckled again. He took one more swill from the bottle. I took it away and set it out of his reach.

"Be quiet," I said again. "Lie still."

He pressed on as if he hadn't heard me. "I had one day off work after Eloi was roasted like a potato packet." I realized with a sinking feeling that talking was helping distract him from my work. "The postmaster couldn't give me more than that. The day I came back on the job, I had to deliver a message from Acacali to the coking manager. It was the incident report. *Incident*." He laughed. The loop I had just stitched closed too tight.

"Hold still," I said, placing my hand on his chest. He rested his hands over it, as if he were reciting poetry to me and not stumbling through his worst memories.

"I remember it exactly. Here's what it said. 'Incident: forehearth explosion. Worker decommissioned. Request spare laborer; proficiency not necessary. G. Acacali.' He was out on the floor of the blast furnace when he handed me the note. I stood there, in front of the furnace where Eloi died, reading this slip of parchment he had just handed me. I couldn't believe it—it wasn't a damn hearth explosion! He'd blown-in the damn furnace while my brother was still pouring his damn shot! Acacali got irritated. He looked right at me—straight in the face. 'Well, get going,' he said.

"He didn't recognize me, Mona. He didn't recognize that my face was the same face as the unnamed worker he had incinerated just two days previously. He had no idea who it was who had died, just that someone had. Some cog in the wheel. So I put my hand on his chest and I pushed him." He laughed again. "It was an *incident*! I pushed him into the troughs of slag running in the floor behind him!"

I paused my work despite myself. "You . . ."

"I mean, I didn't mean to. But like I said, it's just a matter of time before the mill finds some way to kill you, especially if you swing such a good opportunity at it. He toppled right in! He caught fire! It was awful. He was mired down in the stuff, burned him right up. Nobody could get near enough to get at him, it was so hot."

My breath seemed to drive into my lungs in a spike—I held it, my eyes riveted on his torn skin. He lifted my hand in his and kissed my wrist, slowly. I jerked it away and flattened my palm on his face, holding his head still. Just a few more stitches and I would be done. Done, and I could wash my hands and face and neck, get this whole night off of me, all the confusion and fright.

"I ran," he said under my hand.

"Be quiet," I ordered.

"I ran and ran and ran, but I didn't have anywhere to go. I had never belonged anywhere else. So I had to go crawling back to my mother in the middle of the night. The whole village was in chaos—folk had come to her door that evening, looking for me. I think they thought I had bolted for good, or else they'd have kept watch on our house. She packed up all the money we had, a little bit of food, and dragged me away into the bayou that very night. We didn't even get to hold the service for Eloi, didn't even get to light his pyre. We ran far away to Lilou, hid ourselves in the crowds. As an extra precaution, Mother stopped calling me Theo. There were other Roubideauxs, after all. She found us a run-down old place to rent for the time being and then left to get Lyle in Bellemere. I had no job, she had no job—we couldn't keep up his tuition. He had to leave his tutor. At first he thought we left town out of grief for Eloi, but when word got around that the mill manager in Temper Creek had been murdered, he put two and two together. He always was the smart one."

Lyle clattered down the stairs with my trunk. He kicked open the door and disappeared into the night.

"It was a stupid thing to do," Rou said, his words slurred. "Pushing Acacali. I was hardly the first person to lose someone at the mill. Nobody else lost their heads about it. Just a part of life. World needs steel. Steel means folk die."

"I'm done," I said, tying off the thread. I glanced

up and down at my work. I couldn't be sure I had
done it the way a seasoned healer would have, but
the stitches were neat and even, and the wound was
closed. I rummaged in the sewing kit before realizing
the shears were still upstairs on the vanity. I leaned
forward and cut the thread with my teeth.

He closed the distance between us and pressed his
lips to my neck.

I jerked back. "Rou! I swear, by the Light—"

"M'all dark inside, Mona," he said. "There's no
Light in me."

"You're drunk," I said, stuffing everything haphazardly into the sewing kit. Hastily I bound the cheese-
cloth around his forehead and pushed myself off the
couch just as the stairs creaked again. Gemma came
down, wrapped in a cloak. She saw us and paused.

"Moon and stars, is he all right?"

"Fantastic," Rou said cheerfully, his hands clasped
on his chest, eyes closed. "Did you know Mona can
sew up flesh, too? I bet you won't even be able to see
the stitches. Is she not radiant? How are you? Do you
want breakfast?"

I held up the nearly empty brandy bottle to Gemma's bewildered stare. "Torched."

The door to the parlor rattled suddenly, and Gris
limped out, dressed in a long nightshirt, leaning on
his cane.

"What's the ruckus?" he wheezed. "I know it's First
Fire, but you young folk can't just throw a house party
in anybody's front hall . . ."

"We have to go, Uncle Gris," Lyle said, striding back over the threshold. "Folk here are on to us. They may come here looking."

"Let 'em come, my boy!" Gris roared with surprising vigor. He brandished his cane. "They came once before, and I gave 'em what for then, too! They'll get nothing out of me!" His eyes fell on me. "Great Light, look at your hair!"

"Come on," Lyle said, moving to the couch. He hoisted Rou's arm over his shoulder and dragged him to his feet.

"Fire and smoke . . ." Rou wavered, trying to steady himself against his brother.

"Let's go," Lyle said, dragging him to the door.

"Roubideaux!" Gris prodded Rou in the ribs with his cane. "Say hello to your mother for me!"

"I will," Rou said cheerfully. With that, we piled through the door and down the rickety walk.

The punt had been shoved off the sand and back into the creek. "In the tent, all of you," Lyle said, opening the flap and unceremoniously dumping Rou through it.

"Don't you need someone in the bow?" I asked. It must have been the last whispers of drink talking, because I had no place pretending I had any skill with a pole.

Apparently he didn't like the idea any more than I did. "We'll take the river route to Dismal Green. It'll be longer, but we'll avoid the bayou. Get in the tent."

Reluctantly I followed Gemma through the flap.

She curled up on one side of the partition, wrapping herself in her cloak. Rou was already sprawled on the other side. I sat by the flap, my arms around my knees, as tight a ball as I could manage.

"M'all dark inside, Mona."

I cast a quick glance at Rou, lying on his back, his hands limp by his sides. I realized that his poi had been left behind in the village.

"Why don't you try to sleep, Rou?"

"He had a family, you know. Acacali. A wife, and two little girls. He used to take walks along the river with'm. They wore pigtails." He gestured vaguely to his head. "He wasn't a bad man. Just efficient. Wonder if he even liked managing the mill. Most Alcorans hate Cyprien, too boggy and dense. Need their wide-open spaces, don't they, Canyon-folk?"

I looked at Gemma. She was peering at me in the darkness, her eyebrows raised.

"Undid my mother, f'course. You would have liked her, Mona, you'd be two peas in a pod. She was magnificent, she was fierce, like you. At least Eloi did her the favor of only hurting her once, dying and getting it over with. I just lived on, this hollow failure of a son who undid everything. Didn't help her, you know, when she came down with consumption. Think by that point she was just tired. Tired of mopping up my spills. Always wonder if she'd have survived otherwise. Well, of course she would have, 'cause we'd never have left Temper Creek, and the fever didn't hit Temper Creek."

He plucked at a thread on the mat below him, his eyes on the sloping canvas roof. "Know why I spin poi, Mona? All those mornings? 'Cause I'm all dark inside." He flailed his hands through the air around him. "Maybe if I surround myself with the Light, it'll flare back up someday."

His hands flopped down to the floor, and he settled into silence. The water lapped against the hull. Lyle's pole scraped the deck. Ahead of us, the sounds of music and cheering drifted to meet us. The right-hand wall of the tent began to glow—we were passing the village. Folk called out to the punt, wishing Lyle a blessed First Fire. He didn't respond. I didn't hear anyone shouting about a queen or a Roubideaux. Above us, the canvas lit with bursts of color as fireworks crackled in the air.

Rou lifted a hand to his face. He moaned softly. "My head hurts."

I picked myself up and crawled to his side. He slid his hand down his face, his clever angular face, all haggard and worn. I lifted his head and rested it in my lap.

"It's going to hurt worse tomorrow," I said. I cradled his head in my hands. "Sleep. Just go to sleep."

He fumbled for my hand and pressed my fingers to his lips again, his eyes closed. He sighed. His breathing became deeper. His brow relaxed. I stroked his cheek, his hair. Still tipsy, I told myself. I was still wrapped up in the liquor. Because of the liquor, I leaned down and kissed his bandaged forehead.

"Oh, Rou," I murmured. "You idiot."

CHAPTER 11

I startled awake when the tent flap was snapped open. Someone was talking, quickly, urgently, and it took me a moment to wrap my head around the words shooting through the darkness.

"Rou! Rou! Wake up!"

I was sitting propped against the pole in the corner of the tent. Rou's head was pillowed on my lap, his fingers twined in mine. I couldn't see him in the darkness, but I could feel his deep breathing.

Lyle was silhouetted in the tent flap against the moonlit sky. He slid his pole into the tent and unmercifully jabbed his brother's stomach.

"Rou! Shake him, Mona, get him up!"

I blinked several times in the darkness. "Lyle, what . . ."

He reached in and took hold of Rou's boot, giving

a great heave. Rou's head slid from my lap and thunked on the wood floor. He groaned, stirred.

"Lyle!" I exclaimed. "What's wrong with you?"

"There are Alcorans in the river ahead," he hissed, crouching over his brother and shaking him. Rou flailed, his boots thrashing. "Get up, you idiot, I need you in the bow!"

I heard Gemma stir on the other side of the partition. "Alcorans?" she whispered.

"You stay right where you are," Lyle said forcefully, pointing at her with his pole. "I am not above trussing you up to keep you quiet. Don't make a sound." He hauled his brother into a sitting position. Rou's head hung from his shoulders, his arms braced against the floor.

"Lyle," I said urgently. "He can't get up. He's been concussed. He's hungover."

"That's his own fault. I'll be damned if I'm going to drift right into another Alcoran blockade just because he made a couple of stupid decisions." He dragged his brother bodily from the tent. "You two stay in here."

I rolled forward onto my knees and followed them out onto the deck. We were tethered to a wispy stand of brush next to a wide-mouthed creek, the rope taut against the current. Some ways down the river, a flicker of lantern light shone through the darkness.

Lantern light with a distinct red cast.

"What did I just say?" Lyle spat, pulling Rou to his feet.

"Don't presume to give me orders," I said. "Why are Alcorans blocking this river? I thought they were concentrating out on the main channel."

"You can ask them yourself in just a few minutes, if this lackwit doesn't pull himself together." He thrust Rou's pole against his chest.

I came alongside him and put my shoulder under Rou's arm. "He can't pole, Lyle."

"Get back in the tent."

"How close are we to Dismal Green?" I asked.

"Two hours, give or take, but it's going to be dense." He shook his brother's shoulder. "Rou. *Theo.*"

A sound escaped Rou's throat, half-pain, half-plea.

"We need to shoot north into the bayou. There's an outlet here we can take. Do you understand me?" He pushed his brother toward the bow. Rou staggered, his pole scraping along the deck, his hand on his forehead. Lyle pushed past me for the stern, jerking our tether loose.

Rou swayed as Lyle shoved us forward. Our bow turned slowly in a wide arc, aiming for the mouth of the creek. We jarred against the bank in the dark. Rou staggered at the impact.

Lyle cursed his brother from the stern. Up ahead, the red light bobbed in the water. It was getting closer.

I guided Rou away from the bow and lowered him down against the hull. I took the pole out of his hands.

"Color?" he mumbled.

"Rest, Rou," I said, wedging him among the crates so he wouldn't slide.

"Color?" he said again.

"What?"

"Color's the light?"

"It's red. Lyle's right. It's an Alcoran boat. Don't worry. You just rest."

Our bow scraped loudly against the bank as Lyle strove to maneuver us into the creek. I made sure Rou wasn't going to knock his head on anything, and then I got to my feet. I gripped the pole with both hands and shoved it against the bank.

We slid free and shot into the darkness under the trees. The pole dragged in the water, catching on the shallow creek bed. I pulled it free just as we struck another obstacle—a trunk, a rock, I couldn't see in the dark. I thrust the pole again and eased us loose.

I was competent with both a canoe and a sailboat, but I had never handled either one in the dead of night in a scrubby creek, and never after a night of strong drink and little sleep. I soon realized that standing with a pole was entirely different from sitting with an oar. Even throwing my back into each movement, I didn't have the strength for it. My hands slid on the pole—it dragged in the brush and boxed me on the cheek. But my heart was thudding with anxiety, washing away my weariness for the moment. I strained my eyes in the darkness, trying to pick out the next obstacle in the dappled moonlight. A shadowy mass loomed over us, and hurriedly I plunged the pole in the water and leaned all my weight on it. We just barely missed a gnarled old tree leaning over the creek. The moss curtaining its branches caught me full in the face and dragged over the tent like fingers.

We continued on into the gloom. The moon rose higher, a fat slice of light, shining just brightly enough to distinguish water from solid object. Eventually, the creek banks fell away, and the bayou opened up around us, rife with tangled roots, winged trunks, and unexpected patches of boggy ground. My hands began to cramp on the pole, and my shoulders burned as I leaned into each push. My right arm ached and stung.

The cypress knees were the worst, invisible in the patchy light. One dense stand loomed up out of nowhere just as I went to swipe my hand across my sweaty forehead. We hit the knobbly growths with force. With the barest fraction of a second to prepare myself, I only staggered sideways, splaying my legs out to keep myself from pitching over the low hull. But Lyle wasn't so lucky. I heard a sharp curse and a hefty splash.

I dropped my pole onto the deck and fumbled around the tent. I dropped to my knees at the water's edge. He broke the surface, spitting and coughing.

"I'm sorry." I reached out and helped him climb back over the hull. He flung his pole away angrily and sat down hard on the deck. Rivulets of water streamed down his clothes, puddling around him.

Without looking at me, he bent forward, gripping his head in his hands.

I stood over him, confused at his reaction. "Are you hurt?"

"Go away."

"What's wrong?"

"Nothing. Go away."

"The only place I can go is around the tent," I said, irritated. "I'm sorry I ran us into the cypress knees. I didn't see them. Are you hurt?"

"No."

"Okay." I waited. But he didn't move, still hunched over at my feet. "Should we keep going?" I asked. "Or do you want to rest?"

For whatever reason, it was the wrong thing to say. He slid his hands from the top of his head over his face. He sniffed wetly.

Marvelous. A concussed Rou and now an emotional Lyle. I wavered, perplexed.

"Maybe we should just tether here for the rest of the night," I said. "No one would find us here, right? You should rest."

He drew his wet sleeve across his nose. "We can't afford to rest. We have to keep going. We have to get to Dismal Green."

"We can afford a moment's rest, Lyle. I know we were trying to get through the Lower Draws before First Fire is over, but it looks like we're just not going to make it. Why don't we stay here? We can both get some rest, and continue on when it's light out."

He shook his head, covering his face with his hands again. "Once word starts to spread about Temper Creek . . . if folk hear our name associated with yours . . ."

I relaxed slightly. He was worried about our mission. It surprised me—he'd never shown any particular fervor for our journey, but then, he didn't wear his heart on his sleeve like his brother. I knelt down next to him, ashamed at the realization that I'd cast them as polar opposites. Of course Lyle would care about the plight of his country as much as Rou.

Perhaps more. He had more to lose.

"I'm sorry, Lyle. It was my decision, too, and I made the wrong one. But it'll be all right. It was a stupid thing to do, and we'll have to tread more carefully. But only Fisheye really knows where we are. The Alcorans won't have any information on our whereabouts."

"You don't know that."

"Why?" I asked. "Are you worried about someone giving us away? The folk in Temper Creek don't know where we're heading. Are you worried about our next hosts?"

"No."

"Fisheye?"

"No, no." He shook his head again. "None of them would . . . betray us. Great Light. This could all turn out so badly." He blew out a shaky breath between his hands. "So, so badly. I didn't realize before just how wrong things could go. I've tried to be so careful, to keep everything secret, and safe. But now none of it matters. It's ruined. He ruins *everything*."

I fell silent, thinking back to Rou's drunken confession. I'd only really been focused on the consequences for him, not for his brother. But Lyle's life had changed, too. He had had to leave his tutor, the career he was building for himself. For someone as skilled as he was, that couldn't have been easy.

"He told me what happened," I said. "Why you had to leave your tutor. I'm sorry. But it's not ruined yet. And he didn't mean it. He didn't mean it then, and he didn't mean it tonight."

"Of course he didn't *mean* it. He doesn't ever *mean* it—and everyone's going to forgive him for it. He can *literally* get away with murder."

"Lyle . . ."

"Folk would give him *anything*," he continued, his voice rising slightly, "just in return for his goodwill. He always says I'm the smart one, the *useful* one, when he overlooks the fact that folk would take him a *hundred* times before they'd take me. They don't want me—they want what I can do." He kicked the pole with a clatter. "Even you, Lady Queen. No different. I'm just a tool. Next to him—that idiot, that impulsive, selfish *idiot*—I'm worth nothing. And so I have to use it for my own end, just like him—only folk don't pardon me every step of the way."

I stared through the darkness at him. He glared at the deck. I couldn't place his tone, or the inexplicable anguish in his voice—he almost sounded like he was pleading an excuse for some wrong he hadn't committed. But something else did make sense now—his continuous reluctance to talk to me. Gemma had gotten him to open up, by asking him about his methods, his interests and background, the things he was passionate about. But he was right about me. I had just wanted what he could do. I stayed silent a moment longer, thinking.

"I'm sorry," I said again. "You're right. I have only been focused on your weaponry, and I let myself get distracted by your brother. I value your work. I'm impressed by your skill and the breadth of your knowledge. But I'm also grateful for *you*. You got us out of Temper Creek. I might have been dragged away—Rou could have been killed. But you got us away. You kept your head. Thank you for that."

"Don't."

"Well, I am thankful," I said determinedly. "I know it was a risk for you, too."

"You don't know anything."

I sighed. "Maybe not. But I think I understand more than you realize, Lyle. Folk have always wanted me for what I can do, too. I'm not . . . a terribly likable person, either. I don't relate well to people. If someone has an interest in me, it's for my position, my power. Even Queen Ellamae and I wouldn't be friends now if she hadn't needed me to accomplish a goal of hers first."

Voicing these words aloud brought back the old dread Donnel Burke always dredged up, and my thoughts lit briefly on Rou. He needed me for something, too—he needed me to maneuver his country to freedom. I'd known this from the start, but I'd allowed myself to ignore it in the past few days. But now it occurred to me that that could be what this was all about—the flirting, the grinning, the heartfelt monologues. Rou needed me to trust him.

That's what a good diplomat was supposed to do.

I looked down at the same patch of floorboard as Lyle, my heart twisting in my chest. "I've made several significant mistakes lately, in that respect—taking people at face value, without thinking to look for an ulterior motive. It's desperation, I suppose. I certainly wasn't always this way. But it's dangerous. For people like you and me, folk always approach us with some other motivation, don't they? There's always something else at work."

He looked away. "Maybe you should look harder."

I didn't know what to say, the insecurities I'd just voiced clouding my head. The headache chasing the heels of drinking wasn't helping.

So I asked, "What do you mean, 'look harder'?"

But he dropped his head and dragged his hand over his face. It was a movement so like his brother's that it could have been Rou sitting in front of me if not for his bare head. I was suddenly flooded with his meaning, his words from a moment ago echoing back to me in a different light. *They don't want me— they want what I can do. Even you, Lady Queen.*

Rivers to the sea, this was a disaster. I would take

the anxiety of meeting with Celeno a hundred times over the confusion the Roubideaux brothers presented to me. I took a breath and pushed myself off my knees. That's it—I was done.

"Now isn't the right time to do anything except press on, I suppose," I said. "You're right—if we're close to Dismal Green, we should focus on getting there. Then at least we can rest properly. I'll try not to hit anything else."

Without waiting for a reply, I headed back around the tent. Rou was fast asleep, his bandaged head pressed against the crate. Ignoring him and the pain in my arm and hands, I swiped up the pole from the deck. The punt rocked slightly. I stood in the bow, waiting. With no word from the stern, we shoved off, gliding back into the inky darkness.

I pushed downward with the pole, guiding us clumsily around the patch of cypress knees. I tried with all my might to ignore the fact that somehow I'd garnered the attention of two separate men in the span of just a few days, but the only other thing to focus on was the pain building in my arm and palms. I gritted my teeth, trying instead to focus on nothing at all, but that only left me in the grips of my headache.

The Assembly of Six, I thought. The alliance between my country and theirs. I mentally laid out the document Valien and Mae and I had drafted several months ago allying the lake and the mountains, and began substituting appropriate language. *The terms of this partnership shall be as follows: Section A— Expectations in the Event of Conflict, Part One. External Military Threat to the Independent Nation of Cyprien . . .*

Mercifully, the night was later than I thought. Not long after we began moving again, the sky above the mossy canopy began to lighten, washing the bayou with weak gray light. Shapes became more distinguished, and I could see obstacles coming from farther away. I went from pushing us off knees and trunks to guiding us around them. We passed under an arching branch—moss swiped my sweaty face. I uncurled a hand from the pole and wiped my forehead. My whole arm trembled, hollow.

The bayou began to dry and rise around us, and by dawn we were scraping through another creek bed. Just when I wondered how much farther we could possibly force the punt, we wiggled out into a river. This one was different from the other rusty, sluggish waterways we had encountered. The water ran cleaner and swifter. But if I thought this meant I could finally set the pole down, I was wrong. The water was studded with rocks, and the current kept pushing our bow toward the banks. I strove to keep us from turning broadside in the current, my lungs burning with labored breath.

We reached the first docks of Dismal Green as the sun was rising. The place was silent, weary from the night of festivity. Despite the emptiness—and the fact that I was drenched in sweat—I took a moment to dig a cloak out from the tent. I draped it over my shoulders, pulling the hood up over my shorn head. I followed Lyle's quiet instructions from the stern, edging us to the right when the river forked. Houses melted out of the early-morning mist, modest homes with tidy gardens and sturdy docks. We came to a lemon yellow house set back from the river on a long, sloping hill, and it was here that Lyle directed me. The *Swamp Rabbit* scraped tiredly along the dock, and Lyle jumped out to tether us.

I leaned on the pole, my whole body numb and buzzing. Every muscle ached. My burn throbbed. Vaguely I turned my hand over to see a harsh line of blisters running across my palm. I closed my eyes and rested my head against the pole.

There was a deep, shuddering sigh from behind me, and I turned to face Rou. He was still asleep, his knees drawn up tightly to his chest. His bandaged forehead was pressed against the crates.

A call echoed from up the shore. I lifted my gaze to see a rectangle of warm light spilling from the house, its many windows shining pink in the dawn. A figure holding some kind of bundle was silhouetted in the doorway.

Slowly, I set down my pole and knelt in front of Rou, but Lyle waved his hand at me.

"I'll get him. You get to the house. Gemma." He flapped the side of the tent. "Come on, inside."

She emerged bleary-eyed but fully awake, her cloak pulled tight around her shoulders. Together, she and I hurried up the stone walk, flanked on both sides by a cheery garden that spilled onto the path. As we got closer to the house, the figure in the door grew clearer—it was a woman, and the bundle in her arms was a baby, both with the same coffee-colored skin. Her dark hair was braided away from her face, but the baby's stuck up in feathery tufts.

"Inside, inside," the woman said in a hushed voice, beckoning us over the threshold with one hand. "Quickly, now. Bless the Light Nico wanted to nurse early this morning—I saw your punt arrive through the nursery window. What on earth are you doing here so soon? We didn't expect you for another day at least."

"Trouble in Temper Creek," I said, wearily putting back my hood. I was so tired, I could barely form a coherent sentence. "We were discovered."

"You don't mean to say you came all the way from Temper Creek this very night?"

In the narrow hallway, a man appeared, belting a robe about his waist. "What's going on?"

"It's the queens, Henri," the woman said. "I saw them arrive through Nico's window. Hurry now, go help the Roubideauxs with the punt."

As he rushed out the door, I reached out to the woman. "Lady Benoit, is it?"

"Ysabeau, please, Lady Queen."

"Ysabeau, Rou was hurt last night. Struck in the forehead—he had to have stitches." I wavered slightly on the spot, my legs hollow from bending and straightening all night. "He should be seen by a healer as soon as possible."

She grasped my arm—whether it was to comfort or steady me, I wasn't sure. "I'll send Henri as soon as you're settled. But, Lady Queen, begging your pardon, you look ready to faint on your feet. Come, come, both of you. I'll show you to your rooms."

She hoisted Nico on her hip and started up the narrow staircase. Gemma followed, head down. I glanced back over my shoulder. Rou was stumbling up the walk between Lyle and Henri, his bandaged head hanging from his shoulders. I turned back and hurried up the stairs after Ysabeau.

The house was old but clearly well-loved, with fresh paint and bright hangings. Ysabeau opened a door for Gemma, dipping her a quick courtesy as she passed quietly over the threshold. Nico hung over his mother's shoulder, fixing me with frank, curious eyes.

"In here, Queen Mona." She gestured to the next door over.

I had never been so pleased to see a bed in all my life. With surprising efficiency for operating with only one hand, Ysabeau closed the drapes against the dawn and turned down the linens. Common courtesy should have dictated that I help her in some way, or at least remain standing until she left the room, but I found I couldn't muster the energy. I sank gratefully onto the bed, completely disregarding the fact that

I was still wearing the dirty and torn purple gown from the night before.

"Shall I bring you something to eat, Lady Queen? Would you like to take a bath?"

"Later," I murmured. "Yes, to both. But later, if you please."

"Of course." She opened the wardrobe against one wall and removed a cotton dressing gown. She placed it on the bed beside me and rested her hand briefly on my shoulder—a motherly gesture, though she could only have been a few years older than myself. "Rest yourself, Lady Queen. You're safe here. We'll see to the others. You rest."

My thanks were barely audible. She dipped a courtesy to me, Nico bobbing on her hip, and then retreated back to the hall, closing the door behind her. Numb, sore, empty, I shed my ruined gown, leaving it unceremoniously on the floor. I pulled the fresh dressing gown over my head, crawled into the sweet-smelling linens—a bed had never felt so good before—and was asleep just seconds after my head touched the pillow.

When I woke, muted light was shining through the drapes. I shifted against the stiffness in my body. My lower back throbbed, and I couldn't turn my head without a sharp pain racing up my neck. My arm and hands stung. But my mind was clear and rested. Carefully, slowly, I pushed myself upright.

Someone had brought my trunk in, as well as a tray bearing toast and jam. On the washstand by the wardrobe was a large pitcher wrapped in towels to keep the heat inside.

I opened the drapes to the afternoon light and filled the washbasin with steaming water. Gingerly, I washed my blistered palms and burned arm, blowing on them occasionally to ease the pain. I laved my face and neck and shorn hair, and then toweled off, amazed at how fast my hair dried. I rummaged for the brush in my trunk and swept it through the short tufts, examining my new appearance with a bit more scrutiny. I looked less like Arlen now, perhaps because he didn't usually look this careworn. My thoughts slid to the feeling of Rou's fingers running through my hair as he cut it the previous night—great Light, had it only been last night? I set the brush down and turned away from the mirror, my stomach in knots.

I was just cinching an overdress—muted, unadorned—over a fresh shift when there was a soft knock at my door. I opened it to find Rou on my threshold.

He was conspicuously polished. His bandage had been changed and his scuffed, bloody clothes replaced with a clean set. His silk ascot was tucked neatly into his vest, and his cuffs were buttoned around his wrists. He looked crisp and refreshed and absolutely miserable.

"Hello," I said.

"Hello," he murmured. "May I have a moment?"

I opened the door a bit wider, and he took the barest few steps into the room.

"How's your head?" I asked, closing the door behind him.

"It's fine."

"No, really. Has someone looked at it? Have you taken something for headache?"

"Lady Benoit had a healer come by around mid-morning. The healer said the stitches are perfectly even, and once the wound begins to heal up, I should see someone to get them taken out."

"That's good," I said.

A moment of silence passed between us. He was standing still save for his right hand, where he was agitating Eloi's firesteel around his little finger.

And then he closed the distance between the two of us and dropped to his knees. He reached for my hand and bent his head over it.

"Lady Queen," he said, "forgive me. My behavior last night was inexcusable. I endangered your life and the mission of the Assembly. I have no excuses. Only regret. I'm sorry."

"It's fine," I said.

"No, it's not fine. You could have been hurt or captured or killed. Everything could have fallen apart. I'm sorry."

"It's fine," I said again, twitching my hand in his. "I wasn't captured. Everything didn't fall apart. It's fine."

"Mona." He looked up at me, still holding my hand. "I'm sorry."

"You've already said that," I said, fighting to keep my voice smooth. This conversation could only have one possible ending, and knowing it was making my chest tighten on each breath.

"No, but . . . what you must think of me now, after everything I told you . . . no one . . . no one knows except Lyle, and he holds it against me . . ."

There it was. My opening. I drew my hand out of his. "My feelings for you haven't changed, Rou. You're what you've always been to me—a good ambassador, a clever diplomat. One night of a little too much drinking hasn't changed that."

It stunned him; I could see it behind his eyes. He leaned forward slightly, his hands braced on his knees. "Mona . . . I thought . . . last night, before everything went wrong . . . I thought perhaps you had come to care for me as much as I care for you."

"Last night is over," I said. "It doesn't matter how irrational I was at any point over the last few days. What matters is what I'm telling you now. We have a political relationship, and nothing else."

"I thought . . ."

"You thought wrong," I said firmly. "I made bad decisions, too, but it's done now."

"I just . . . damn it all, Mona, I'm dangerously close to being in love with you."

"Don't say that again, Rou," I said. "Don't say it again."

He blinked several times, his lips slightly parted.

"You know I haven't been able to work for six days?"

I said, my voice rising. "I can't focus on anything—not your Assembly's treaty, not the future of our countries, not the political opportunity Gemma presents to me. We're at a crossroads in history, when the balance of the East could tip one way or the other— Alcoro could either fall into ruin or conquer every country this side of the sea. And all I can think about is you. That's *not* okay, Rou. I know you think me closed up and cheerless and cold, but folk in three nations are depending on me to fix some of history's wrongs. Don't you understand? I don't have the privilege of fawning over you like Heloise Toussaint. I've told you before—I am Lumen Lake. It's not a boast, or a gloat. It's a fact. It's my reality. When I get close to someone, it affects whole countries. It's happened before, and it's happening again now. And it has to stop."

I took a breath, my fists trembling by my sides. He was staring at me—staring like I was sprouting horns or extra heads or something equally atrocious. It struck me again how different his face was from his brother's—even in Lyle's breakdown last night, he'd been guarded, almost ashamed. Rou's face showed everything, betrayed his every thought. It was unnerving, that openness. Again I wished he could hide it better. I gripped the too-short skirt of my gown.

"You will get me to Siere," I said. "You will address me by my title. You will keep your jokes to yourself. And you will behave like the future of the eastern world depends on your actions, because it does. Is that clear?"

He continued to stare, his fingers clenched on the knees of his trousers.

"Is that clear?" I said again.

"Yes, Lady Queen," he said.

"Thank you." I took a step back and twitched my hand toward the door. "Please."

Slowly, incrementally, he rose to his feet. He paused as he stood, and for a terrifying moment the image of Donnel Burke's wounded gray eyes flashed through my memory, but he backed away without another word. He reached my door, turned the knob, and slipped back into the hall like a sleepwalker. The door clicked in its latch.

Only then did I allow myself to slap both my palms over my face and sink to my knees on the hardwood floor. My breath came in sharp gasps, my eyes tearing behind my hands. I had hoped putting Rou in his place would bring me relief, clarity. But it hadn't. I had never felt more despicable.

What happened? Did you break his heart?

I gasped again. *Leave me alone, Mae.*

Mae didn't understand. For that matter, Rou probably didn't understand, either. They couldn't fathom their frivolous, harmless flirtations affecting more than the few people involved. I knew exactly how this looked to them. To them, I was severe, unfeeling—ice. They never saw, they never understood that I wasn't just *me*. I was thousands of other people, and because of that, everything I did rippled outward, like a stone dropped into the lake, creating consequences both foreseen and unforeseen. It had always been this way—and it always would be.

You are a country.

I dropped my hands from my face and wrapped them across my chest, my head bowed forward. It had always been this way . . . but it had never hurt quite this much before. Great Light, how I wished I was the frozen block of stone everyone thought I was. How much kinder, how much easier this would be if I couldn't feel any of it at all.

A floorboard creaked somewhere out in the hall. With no knock or call, my door eased open. I had no time to stand up or wipe my eyes. I looked up through blurred vision, but it wasn't Rou on my threshold.

"No one locked my door," Gemma said softly.

I couldn't answer, realizing that of course she must have heard everything through the single wall separating our rooms. Quietly, slowly, she stepped inside and closed the door behind her. She crossed the little room and sank down to her knees in front of me.

I had no strength, emotional or physical, to order her out and see her door locked behind her. I returned her gold-flecked gaze, unable to think of a single thing to say. She reached into the pocket of her brown overdress and pulled out a handkerchief, folded into a neat square. She pressed it into my hands.

"Did you know," she said softly, "when I agreed to marry Celeno, the price of cornmeal in Alcoro jumped almost three hundred percent?"

I blinked through my tears, fighting against the sluggish weight of shame in my head to determine what this had to do with anything.

"We have these little cakes we bake on special occasions—maybe you've heard of them," she continued. "Corn cakes, soaked in honey and topped with papaya jam. When my folk heard the Seventh King was engaged, they rushed out to replenish their cornmeal to bake corn cakes. But this was in late spring—stores of corn were already running low. The sudden demand wiped out what was left. Prices soared. Poor folk who relied on cornmeal as a staple suddenly couldn't afford it. Theft increased. That summer, fields were ransacked before the corn had fully ripened. Wagons carrying corn were waylaid and robbed." She held out her left hand. "All because I got engaged."

I looked at her ring, a many-faceted white gem, too big for her finger. I looked back at her, my thick, clouded emotions finally yielding to realization.

Rou didn't understand.

Mae didn't understand.

Nobody else had ever understood.

But Gemma . . . Gemma did.

I looked down at the handkerchief in my hands. It must have come from her trunk—embroidered around the edges with the colors of the Cypri banner, purple and gold.

"I almost started a civil war," I said.

She didn't question or press me. She folded her hands over her knees, silent. I closed my eyes.

"I suppose falling in love for the first time is disorienting for anyone," I said. "But after years and years of formality and diplomacy, it was downright earthshaking. I never knew how it felt to be emotionally loved. My father was the only person I can recall who showed me affection, and he died when I was eight. After that, my mother knew her time was running short. She put everything she had into training me for the throne—she ignored my brother Colm, left him to his books. Left Arlen to his nurse. Everything was about my throne. And after she died, everything continued to be about my throne, starting with my immediate coronation.

"And then, when I was fifteen, I met Donnel, the nephew of one of my councilors. He was charming, and handsome, and said things to me nobody had ever said before. I was pretty, I was sweet, I was his own. I couldn't think of a single thing my mother had taught me that was more important than how he made me feel."

I ran my thumbs over the embroidery on the handkerchief. "He proposed only a few months after we met. He asked me in front of my whole court at midsummer. I panicked and said yes. His family was delighted—elevated to the monarchy of Lumen Lake. News raced out to all the islands before the night was even over. But the next day I went to Donnel in private and told him I wasn't ready, that I needed much, much more time. He didn't take it well."

"Did he . . . hurt you?" Gemma asked.

"Not physically. He just said . . . a great many things I haven't ever been able to forget. All those pretty names he had called me—he turned them all around. He laughed at my shock and hurt, mocked me for ever thinking the other things were true."

You skinny, silly little girl. You bought it all, didn't you? You'd be nobody without that thing on your head.

I crumpled the corner of the handkerchief. "But that was only the beginning. He followed me around Blackshell. He memorized my attendants' routines so he knew when he could find me alone. He found a way to place himself in my line of sight wherever I went—he sat in the garden outside my drafting room, he sat in a boat in the water a few yards from my terrace. It frightened me. I couldn't work, I couldn't focus on anything. I was afraid to leave my room or open my drapes."

Sorry, Rou said. *But he sounds like a real sop.*

I put my hand to my eyes. My stomach was turning on familiar waves of dread. It was a relief, in a way, to tell these things to someone who could understand. But I couldn't tell her everything, not the things even Colm didn't know. How Donnel's kisses and touches had gone from thrilling to uncomfortable to frightening. How he *had* hurt me physically without actually resorting to violence, and how I had cried until I made myself sick after he stroked skin no one else ever had while I stood frozen, not knowing how to make him stop. How he had drawn my fingers to his mouth and leisurely sucked them even as I tearfully stumbled through the reasons I wasn't ready to marry him. How Ama had spent more than one night bundled in bed with me, promising to keep watch on the doors and windows so I could finally fall asleep.

No—I still wasn't ready to share that yet. Not here, not now. I rubbed my eyes, nauseated. "Finally I ordered him out of Blackshell and back to his family, and for good measure I fired his aunt, my councilor. She had never done anything wrong—she'd served under my mother before me without the slightest disloyalty. But I dismissed her from my service only so Donnel hadn't even the slightest connection to Blackshell.

"And *that's* when folk started to talk, everyone from the dockhands up to my councilors. For the first time since I had taken the throne, folk were wondering whether an emotional teenager was fit to lead a country alone. Donnel came from a noble family— they had many friends throughout the islands, and he spread stories about how unstable I was, how childish, how easily I could be influenced. Finally a faction of my folk petitioned my council to appoint a regent to vet my rule until I turned twenty. My council rejected it, though it was a scant majority. So the dissenting group planted themselves in Lakemouth and refused to let trade ships into the lake. They seized a shipment of pearls and sailed the boat into the deep water north of the islands, where they set it on fire and let it sink. And then they organized a militia and marched on Blackshell."

I dabbed the handkerchief at the corners of my eyes. "I won't ever forget that night. I was awake with my council from dusk until dawn, debating, arguing, negotiating. By morning, fully half of them were ready to accept the petition, and a few of them were wavering back and forth. It was only five years, they reasoned, and it was only a regent. At that moment, I knew I had failed my mother. Everything she had done—every second of her lessons was to be sure I was capable to rule for myself, not act as a figurehead. All her work, all *my* work, was being undone, all because I fell thoughtlessly in love."

"What did you do?" Gemma asked.

I was silent a moment. "I'll tell you what I *wanted* to do. I wanted to throw every single one of them in prison. I wanted to ruin their families and allies and exile Donnel to Samna."

"But you didn't."

"No. They were all right, of course. I hadn't acted in my country's interests. But I couldn't give in to the idea of a regent, either—that also wasn't in my folks' interest, especially if it was a regent appointed by Donnel and his allies. Instead I gathered a few personal guards and went out to the palace wall. I let the people shout at me. When they quieted enough to let me speak, I told them nothing could be fixed if we couldn't hold a dialogue. I had them select three representatives. I met with them one by one. I had them lay out their grievances. We discussed how I might better meet their demands."

"I imagine that was much harder," she said.

"It was the hardest thing I'd ever done." I looked out the window, gleaming in the late-afternoon light. "They ended up replacing many of my councilors—folk who had been advising Lumen Lake for years. In a way, I sacrificed them for my own good. That's always weighed on me. But I learned, of course, the lesson I'd been taught but had clearly never taken to heart: that I am not just a singular person. That I'm a country, and my actions have consequences far beyond myself. After that, I promised myself that I'd never act so foolishly or so selfishly again."

I envy a monarch's surety, Senator Ancelet had said offhandedly in Puddlewelle. Surety. I had never felt less sure of myself, or my role, than in those weeks. Never—except perhaps in the past day.

I smoothed the edges of the handkerchief. Gemma studied me.

"I have a question," she said. "When you deal with criminal cases, do you fault the criminal or the victim?"

"It wasn't that simple," I said. "Maybe a commoner

can operate that way, but you know you and I can't. We're forced to take responsibility for our actions, even if they're driven by someone else. That's what being a monarch means."

"Perhaps politically. But personally, Mona, what happened to you wasn't your fault. It was the fault of the abuser, of the one who saw you as a means to an end. As a prize. Tell me—do you honestly, truly believe Rou would invite the same kind of fallout?"

"He could, Gemma. Maybe not on purpose, but I can't take that chance with such significant matters at hand." And I didn't want to contemplate the impact such a relationship might have on Lyle. I pinched the bridge of my nose. "I just . . . I'm bad at love. I know I am. I can't make myself focus. I don't make the right choices."

"That's not being bad at love," Gemma said gently. "That's just being *in* love. And it doesn't last, Mona. For good or bad, the wildness of infatuation doesn't last. It mellows out, it grows into something more mature."

"I don't have time to wait for that to happen," I said. "I don't have the luxury of setting aside my responsibility to get swept up in frivolity and romance."

"The urge to love and be loved is in our biology," she said. She pressed her fingers to her chest. "It's not a luxury. It's something we all crave in one way or another. And you weren't drawn to Rou for no reason. He's kind, and rather witty. You've been through a lot, more than most folk. Perhaps you've been missing a little kindness and laughter without realizing it."

I looked up from the worn floorboards. She returned my gaze, her hands folded on her knees. A span of silence stretched between us.

It struck me then—her words. She didn't speak like someone living in fear of an abusive husband. My eyes dropped to her long sleeve again.

"Gemma," I said, my mind and body numb. "Has Celeno ever hurt you?"

She smiled a sad, empty smile. "Not in the way you're asking."

"What do you—"

Someone knocked on my door. From the other side filtered the sound of a babbling baby.

"Queen Mona?"

I cleared my throat. "Yes?"

"I'll have supper ready in half an hour. Shall I bring it up to you, or would you like to come down?"

"I'll come down, Ysabeau. Thank you."

As her footsteps retreated, Gemma slowly got to her feet.

"Wait," I said. "What did you mean? How has he hurt you?"

She held her hand out to me. "Does it matter to you?"

"Yes, Gemma, it does. I don't want to send you back to him if he abuses you."

She smiled again, her hand still outstretched. "Queen Mona, I am going back to him whether you send me or not. But he's never struck me, or physically hurt me."

"I don't believe you," I said.

"I'm not surprised," she said.

I stared at her, wrestling with a sudden surge of emotion so surprising I didn't even know what to call it. I had been raised on the throne of my country, the crown placed on my head at age eleven. Gemma was, politically, a far younger, more inexperienced queen than I. But as she stood in front of me with her hand out, I realized that she knew far more than I had given her credit for—beyond just strategy and politics. She understood something I did not—I just didn't even know what that thing was.

"I don't understand you at all," I blurted. It was both a pointless admonishment and a frustrated confession.

"Perhaps that's why, as I've told you, this plan of yours isn't going to work," she said. "Suffice to say, these past few months since you reappeared in the world have been the most trying of my life, both politically and personally. And yes, I have been hurt in ways I didn't think possible. Such is the risk of love, and life in general. But that's why we strive to be strong enough—to be able to take that risk for the person who's worth it."

She stretched her hand out further. Slowly, I took it and stood, my knees aching from kneeling on the floor. She squeezed my hand, and then released it. She turned and headed back to my door.

"I suppose I'll see you tomorrow." She opened the door. "By the way, I like your hair that way. It suits you."

The door drifted closed behind her. "Thank you," I managed just before it clicked shut. I heard her footsteps circle back to the other side of the wall.

I stood for a moment in the center of the room, gazing into space, my mind reeling with her words and what they meant. A breeze slunk through my open window, warm and mingled with the scents of the Benoits' garden below. I went to the window and drew aside the drapes. The sun was low in the sky, throwing a golden cast on the river. And hurrying up the track toward the town of Dismal Green, casting a sharp shadow on the ground, was a figure I recognized. His cloak hood was up, his step just a bit quicker and more tense than usual. I leaned my head on the window frame, watching Rou disappear around the bend, perhaps to seek out the tavern to wash away the bitter taste I left in his mouth. I almost laughed at the melodrama—at the idea that I could have such an effect—but instead I closed my eyes, struggling against the urge to hurry after him.

Twenty minutes later, I found Ysabeau setting the table, while Nico sat on the floor banging a wooden spoon against a pot. A sunny pitcher of garden flowers spilled over amid the dishes. I noticed there were only three place settings.

"The Roubideauxs won't be joining us, apparently," she said as she arranged flatware on napkins. "Lyle says he has too much work to catch up on. He's on their punt, writing. I have no idea where Rou is."

"Bah bah bah bah!" shouted Nico. He scooted on his bottom until he reached my leg and tapped the wooden spoon against my shoe.

"I'm so sorry." Ysabeau swooped down and hoisted him onto her hip. "Things haven't gone as planned, you know. My brother was going to watch him tomorrow evening, when we thought you would be here. I had planned on going to the market and making you a fine dinner. As it is . . . I had to send Henri running to town for fresh bread."

"Please," I said, taking the cups precariously pinched in her free hand. "You've been more than gracious in taking us in. We showed up unexpectedly, and in a great deal of need. Your offering us a safe house alone is more than enough."

"You're doing our folk a great service, Lady Queen," Ysabeau said, hurrying back to the hearth. "We recognize the risk you're taking, both politically and personally. Our generosity is dwarfed by yours."

I was about to protest this remark, as well as offer to handle the pot she was wrestling off the fire, when the kitchen door burst open. On the threshold stood Henri, his dark eyes wide.

"Alcorans," he gasped. "Coming up the track from town. Coming this way."

Ysabeau straightened, clutching the pot handle with a cloth. "This way? What for?"

His gaze flew to me. "They know you're here."

Ysabeau stared at her husband. *"How?"*

"Someone told them. Someone found them in town and told them."

"No one *knows* . . ."

I was flooded suddenly with a surge of shock. I set down the last cup with a sharp slap. "How close?" I demanded.

"Seven, eight minutes perhaps. I took the short-cut across the marsh, but they're mounted."

Nico buzzed a wet bubble and batted Ysabeau's hair with the wooden spoon. She slung the hot pot onto the table and cradled his little head against her shoulder. "The . . . the cellar," she said to me. "Or . . . the stream house, you can hide there . . ."

"They'll search those places," I said forcefully. My stomach was roiling—a surge of dread washed through me. The image of Rou stealing away down the track blazed before my eyes. If I hadn't seen it myself, I would never have believed it. "They'll search your whole house, and when they find me here . . ." I thought of their well-loved house, their cheery garden, their baby busily burying his spoon in his mother's hair. I took a breath. "No, I'll leave. They won't find me here. Don't delay me," I said, overriding Ysabeau's protest. "There's no time for debate."

"Where will you go?" she pressed. "How will you get away?"

"Like I always do," I said, heading for the kitchen door. "I'll swim."

Henri moved out of my way. "What about Queen Gemma?"

"Give me a minute. I'll try to reason with her." With that, I ran from the room to the staircase, taking the steps two at a time. My heart raged inside me, my rising panic momentarily drowning out the sense of crushing betrayal.

I reached Gemma's door and pounded on it. Without waiting for an answer, I flung it open. She jumped at my entrance, a splotch of ink blossoming over her parchment.

"Your folk are coming," I said breathlessly, striding into the room. "Up from the town. They know we're here."

She stared at me. "How did they know . . . ?"

"Rou went to find them. He went to the village and turned us in."

"He would never . . ."

"He did," I said sharply. "I saw him go into town. Lyle's working on the punt. Unless you've been out of the house in the last fifteen minutes, there's no one else it could have been."

Her eyes were wide; her pen was poised over her page. I drew in a deep breath, trying to keep my panic at bay. "Listen. Your folk can't find us here. If they find the Benoits harboring us, they'll burn their house down, or worse. We have to leave, now."

"Leave . . . for where?"

"For Lumen Lake. We can't travel further into Cyprien with no guides, especially not if your folk are on our trail. I'm going to swim down the river until I hit the main channel." I took another breath. "Come with me. Come back with me to Lumen, where we can put right some of the wrongs between our countries."

She gripped her quill with tight fingers. "No . . . no, I couldn't."

"Why not?"

Her eyes were creased and shining. "You want me to come to Lumen, Mona? The queen who enslaved your folk?"

"I offer you sanctuary. I'll protect you."

"No, I couldn't. I can't."

"You can't stay here . . ."

"I'll make my escape to the village. I'll find my folk there. I won't say a word about the Benoits."

I struggled for words. I didn't want her to turn herself in to her folk. I bunched my skirt in my fists. "You don't have to go back to him, Gemma."

"Yes, I do. He's my husband."

"That doesn't make him a good man."

She shook her head. "I know what you think he's done, what you think he is. But you're wrong. Celeno has *never* hurt me—not that way."

"You've got injuries," I blurted. "You've got bruises. I've seen them—I saw them on your arm." Her eyebrows flew skyward. I pressed on. "*Something happened to you, and it happened before you arrived* in Lilou. Why do you cover them, Gemma? Why do you protect him when he's clearly—"

She swung her knees out from under the desk and stood, and as she did, she tugged back her left sleeve, baring her forearm. The skin of her hand was the sandy tan color of the Canyon-folk, but the barest inch above her wrist, it changed dramatically. Splotches of deep red, almost purple, colored her skin, melding together into one dark mark that disappeared under the hem of her sleeve hitched up to her elbow. I stared at them—from this close, they didn't look as much like bruises as the fleeting glimpse I'd caught on the punt, but they didn't look like any other injury I'd ever seen, either.

She read my mind. "It's a mark," she said. "A natural mark I was born with. Folk call it a wine stain. But mine is darker than most, and much larger." She gestured up her arm, over her shoulder and chest. She pulled aside the edge of her collar, so I could see it on her neck. "The whole left side of my torso, from my neck down to my hip. But it's not an injury, Mona. It's just a mark."

"Why do you cover it?" I said with consternation. "If it's just a mark . . ."

She smiled thinly and pulled her sleeve back down. "That would take much more time to explain than I believe either of us have. Before you assume, it wasn't Celeno." Something flickered briefly in her eyes. "I would ask you not to tell anyone, but as I expect we won't be seeing each other again . . ."

I clenched and unclenched my hands, trying to ease my breathing. I was entirely unsatisfied with this new revelation, but she was right—our time had run out. My hand jumped out to grasp her shoulder. "Gemma," I said. "I truly hope the best for you. Please remember that if you want peace, it's in your power to make it happen. If you reach out to me again, I'll respond. I can't say what actions I'll be willing to take, but I *will* respond to you."

She gripped my wrist briefly. "Thank you. Be blessed in the Light."

I had no words to answer that, so I whirled around and ran back to the hallway, tucking my pearl pendant inside my shift. I bypassed my room—there was nothing there I could take with me. I had no money or weaponry, no food or pack. Nothing. But I had been left with nothing before. Nothing except a singular name in my head, blazing at the very center of my anger.

Theophilius Roubideaux. A flirt, a liar, and ultimately a man too entrenched in his own pride to resist retaliation. Were all men like this? Were all men so willing to topple governments to settle a score? Because here I was, again, unraveling the hopes for three countries all because I was too stupid to resist a charming smile and clever words.

I reached the front door and threw it open. The sun had already set across the river, and the long sloping bank was shrouded in shadow. I took off down the garden pathway, squashing the heads of susans and mums where they spilled onto the pathway. I strained my eyes up the track that led around the bend in the river, but I saw no sign of the Alcorans yet. I wondered if Rou was with them, or if he would wait back in the village. Had they paid him right away, or would they wait until I was bound and captive? My stomach surged again, and I fumbled with the latch on the front gate with movements hastened by anger and fear. As I flung open the gate, it occurred to me that nobody had warned Lyle. But there was no time now to seek him out on the punt. With luck, he would be able to make his own quiet escape, away from the danger his twin had brought.

His words from the previous night echoed in my head. *That impulsive, selfish idiot. He ruins everything.* He knew his brother far, far better than I thought I had. If only I had seen it, too. *Please let Lyle get away,* I thought, praying to nothing, to no one. *Please let him escape.*

The dock was away to my right, close to the bend in the track. By this time, I could hear distant hoofbeats thudding up the riverbank. I swerved in the opposite direction, bearing left down the sloping hill. They wouldn't find me. By the time they reached the Benoits' front door, I would be under the water. I'd shoot through Dismal Green without them ever seeing me. I'd swim for the main channel and dive under their boats in the waterways. Perhaps if I found myself in one of the towns we had already passed through, I could beg help from the Toussaints, or the Brasseauxs, or the Doucets. Perhaps they could help me get back to Lilou. And then I just needed to find a boatman willing to sneak me out of the harbor.

I streaked down the hill for the river. But just as I reached the last stretch of open ground, something stirred in the corner of my eye. A dark shape was tearing toward me in the twilight, silent and swift. My body flushed with infuriating fright—he must have guessed I might try to flee to the river. I put my head down and mustered as much speed as I could. But Rou was faster than me on land, and the distance between us closed in mere seconds. He was going to cut off my access to the water. *The river.* If I could just get to the river . . .

And then he was upon me. He didn't shout. He didn't call out. His hand closed on the back of my overdress, checking my pace. I turned to push him away, but he wound his other hand around my wrist. I struggled against him, too out of breath to curse him.

"It's me," he gasped, his sides heaving. "Mona, it's me."

"I know damn well who it is!" I spat. *"Let go of me!"* I lashed out and wound my fingers in his curls. I yanked.

He staggered and clamped one hand over mine, but his other still held fast to my dress. I twisted, trying to slip out of his grip. He grappled with me, and without warning we pitched forward onto the riverbank. I landed on my right side, my burned arm sliding underneath me. Flailing, I let out a scream of pain and rage.

"Torchfire, Mona, *calm down!*"

"You wretch!" I shouted, struggling against his grip on my wrists. He was frighteningly strong. "You pathetic, worthless wretch!" On impulse, I drove the heel of my hand against the wound on his forehead. Instantly, he buckled like a straw man, his hands clamped to his head.

I heaved him off me, scrabbling in the dirt. He was choking out words amid his pain, but I kicked free of him and staggered to my feet. I took one step toward the river, two, three, when another voice cut through the darkness.

"Blind!"

The world exploded white around me. I howled and clapped my hands over my eyes. *"Lyle!"* I shouted. *"I will hang you both!"*

Another pair of hands closed around my arms as I staggered blindly toward the river. I twisted, rubbing my watering eyes with my fists, but I was too disoriented now to make any kind of escape. I shouted, pouring out my rage, until Lyle gave me a sharp thrash.

"Shut up," he said fiercely, "or you'll bring them right down on us! Rou, go get Gemma!"

"Like you didn't just broadcast our position for miles around!" I pulled against him. "Will you make an even split of the reward money, or is your brother getting a higher cut for doing all the dirty work?"

"Rou hasn't done anything," Lyle said in the same urgent voice. "We have to get to the punt."

"I'm not going *anywhere* with you!" I rubbed my eyes again. The world was beginning to blur back into focus. "Let go of me!"

"Mona." Rou was apparently still on the ground, judging from the direction of his cracked whisper. "Please. If we can get to the punt, we can head north up the river, we can get to the cart . . ."

"I *said*, I'm not going anywhere with you!" I stood over him, blinking tears out of my eyes. Lyle still had a grip on my arm. "What made you come barreling after me, if not to keep me from escaping? How did you know the Alcorans were coming, if you didn't just come back from selling us all out?"

"We don't have time for this." Lyle growled. "Rou, go get Gemma, *now*!"

"I was down on the punt," Rou said. "I've been down there all evening. I saw the Alcorans riding up the track from down the bend. I ran from the dock to see you heading down the hill. I thought you were going to jump in the river."

"I was, until you cut me off!"

"I was trying to catch up with you to get you on the punt! I didn't want to shout. Why on earth would you think I would sell you out?"

"I *saw* you going down the track to the village!" I pulled against Lyle again.

"I didn't . . ."

ASHES TO FIRE 389

"I saw you!"

"It was me," Lyle said, giving me another shake. "I went to the village. I've just run back through the marsh. And now we *have to get to the punt.*"

My sight was clear enough for me to make out their blurred faces. Rou, crouching on the ground, his face screwed up in pain and confusion. Lyle, at my elbow, his eyebrows snapped down over his amber eyes.

I fixed him with a cold stare. "Ysabeau said you were on the punt. You told her you had work to do."

"It's my fault the Alcorans are coming," he said, his voice strained. "But I didn't sell you out."

"What is *that* supposed to mean?"

"Look, I swear I will explain everything, but right now—oh, flaming sun . . ."

He released his grip on my arm and streaked away up the hill. My sight was back in full, and in the dim light of dusk, I saw a figure flying from the front porch toward the track. Gemma.

I turned, rigid, back to Rou. My fists were clenched by my sides.

"Why did your brother meet with the Alcorans?" I asked.

"I don't know."

"He's your brother!"

"We're not the same person!" he said forcefully. A thin line of blood was seeping through the bandage on his forehead. I had split his stitches. "Did you have any doubt, Mona? Did you hesitate at all, or did you really believe I would give you away? What did you imagine I would get out of it?"

I took two slow breaths. My hands were still balled into fists.

"I thought you wanted to retaliate," I said. "For what I said to you earlier."

He gazed at me, his face cut with genuine hurt. "Do you really think me that petty? To give up everything we've worked for over a broken heart? I've told you how I feel about you, Mona. But I love my folk and my country, too."

The first touch of shame flickered through me. Up the hill, Gemma shrieked. Lyle had caught up with her, and she was fighting against him. A horse whinnied down the track.

Slowly, gingerly, Rou picked himself off the ground. "I'll help get Gemma," he said quietly. "You should probably get on the punt." He started up the hill, where his brother was dragging Gemma toward the dock.

"Rou," I said.

He looked back over his shoulder. My words stuck in my throat.

"Your head," I finally said.

Without a word, he turned away from me and hurried up the hill. I wiped the last tears from my eyes and pressed my hands to my face. What was wrong with me?

Gemma was struggling against Lyle with surprising vigor, pleading with him to let her go. It was taking all his effort to move her toward the dock, and so he had no free hand to clap over her mouth as her voice rose in the night. She let her knees buckle, dropping to the ground as a dead weight. He hauled at her, hissing furiously. Rou reached the two of them and pulled her up under her arms, but his urgent words were overridden by her rising voice. From around the bend in the river, a shout rang out. Struggling against both brothers, Gemma ceased her pleading and simply let out a scream, high and long. Lyle slapped his hand over her mouth, but the damage was done.

The urgency of our situation suddenly flooded through me, and I broke from my shame and ran for the dock. Lyle gave up trying to drag Gemma and threw her bodily over his shoulder. But it was too late. Four horses burst around the bend while we were still several strides away. Gemma thrashed again.

"Here!" she screamed. "Here!" She threw all her weight to one side, and Lyle staggered, dropping to one knee. She rolled off his shoulder onto the muddy grass. He hauled her back to her feet, but our time had run out. The four riders wheeled to a halt between us and the dock. Three of them levered loaded crossbows, the dock torches glinting off the heads of the quarrels. One rider had a shapeless black bundle draped across her saddle. The fourth bobbed as his horse stamped agitatedly underneath him. He was rigid, his face blazing with rage.

"Don't move," Celeno commanded.

CHAPTER 12

We froze. Lyle was still holding Gemma's arms behind her back. Rou was several steps in front of me. The Alcorans blocked our access to the dock, their horses snorting and twitching in agitation. Celeno glared through the dim light.

In front of me, Rou made a sudden movement, digging his hand into his sash. Celeno flung out a gloved finger.

"I said, don't move, Roubideaux. I've run all through this cursed country of yours, and I am not in the least bit happy about it. Throw that grenade, and my soldiers will shoot before it even lights. I'd prefer to have you all dragged back to Callais alive where you might make up for some of this nightmare, but I'm not above killing any one of you."

Rou held his position, the flash grenade clutched in his hand, his outline rigid in the torchlight.

"Celeno," Gemma said softly.

He turned sharply in his saddle. "Are you all right?"

"I am, Celeno, don't worry. I'm fine." Her voice carried more than just assurance—it almost sounded like a plea.

Or a warning.

"Good," he replied. His gaze jumped past her to Lyle, still shielded by Gemma. "You there, take your hands off my wife . . . great Light, there are two of you." He looked back and forth between Rou and Lyle. His brow creased in the torchlight. "Two of you. Which one of you . . ." He broke off, waved his hand in agitation. "It doesn't matter. You, whichever one you are, let go of my wife."

"Don't," I said.

Celeno rounded on me. His horse tossed its head at his sudden shift. "Queen Mona . . ."

"King Celeno." I overrode him. "We will not release Gemma to you, not until we've talked, and not unless you can agree to a number of things."

I saw Rou turn his head slightly, trying to catch my eye while simultaneously keeping a watch on Celeno's guards. I looked past him, meeting Celeno's enraged stare.

"Negotiate with me," I said to him. "If you can agree to my terms, I will release your wife."

"You're in no position to barter with me," Celeno said, his voice a bit higher than usual. "You'll release her because I demand it of you, or I'll have you shot right here."

"Yes, and invite open war from all your eastern neighbors," I said. "I have an alliance with the Silverwood. The Silverwood has an alliance with Winder, and Winder with Paroa. Unless you want all of us knocking on your door, you'll hold your fire, and think through this rationally."

Perhaps it wasn't entirely true—I doubted the monarchs of Winder or Paroa would threaten war over my death, but I hoped it would be enough to grant me some leverage. Because at the moment, the only thing holding the Alcorans' fire was the single grenade in Rou's hand—not a comforting thought. Celeno ground his teeth, his gloved fists tight on his reins.

"They won't come knocking if they think you died at the hands of the Cypri—and who's to say otherwise? Who's to say you weren't killed by a bunch of ragtag, backwoods—"

"I am, Celeno," Gemma said—and remarkably, shockingly, he stopped mid-word. She wasn't struggling against Lyle any longer. In fact, she was standing firmly in front of him, as if she were his protector rather than his captive. "Speak with Queen Mona. Let us talk straightforwardly. She and I have had a chance to discuss the policies of our countries, and you know she is meant to play a role in seeing the Prophecy fulfilled." She tilted her head up to her husband. "As I've said before—it may simply be a different role than we originally anticipated."

I looked between them, disturbed by their entangling me in their wretched Prophecy . . . but also intrigued by the opportunities this presented me. Leverage. She'd just given me my leverage.

"Yes—yes," I said, trying to reorganize my thoughts. "I *am* willing to ally with Alcoro, and to help you in your cause. Give me a reason to, Celeno—show me you value your allies. Show me you respect diplomacy, and civilized discourse, and the well-being of the eastern world. Put your weapons away, and let us talk about Cyprien."

"You're . . ." He seemed to struggle for words. "You're not in a position to speak for Cyprien."

"You have made it my position," I said, taking two steps forward to come even with Rou. The crossbow quarrels twitched but held steady—Rou still held the flash grenade in his fist. "By usurping the rightful government of yet another country, and by virtue of that government reaching out for my alliance, you have put me in position to negotiate for Cyprien."

"Negotiate for what? For whom? There is no Cypri government. Are you hoping to replace my banner with yours?"

"I am not of the belief that I have the right to do so. Your prism has blinded you again, Celeno—there *is* a government in Cyprien. There has always been, operating right underneath you." I gestured to Rou standing next to me. "The Assembly of Six is alive and fighting, and they are readying their country to stand against yours."

Celeno's tense face twitched, and his gaze jumped to Gemma.

"It's true," she said.

I could see him grappling internally, and I dismissed the idea of using the tactic of silence—I could sense him leaning just barely in my direction, and I didn't want to jeopardize that by letting him think for too long. Steady and sustained—that was the key now. *Press your case*, my mother would say, *and suddenly yours becomes the only viable option.*

"On behalf of the Assembly of Six," I said before any more time could elapse, "you will grant the Cypri folk their independence in full. Recall every Alcoran citizen you have within Cypri borders. Surrender your hold on their government and industry. Withdraw your ships and release their ports. Effective immediately, you shall respect their border as their own. For this, I will consider your proposition on my role in your Prophecy, and what's more, I will open up full trade with you, provided the Cypri folk oversee their own waterways."

Celeno's horse stamped underneath him, responding to his tension. "And tell me, what do your new allies in the Silverwood think of this plan? Will they be so willing to guard the southern slopes if you break the agreement you so recently made?"

"I break no agreement with them," I said. "King Valien and Queen Ellamae Heartwood are prepared to accept trade through the waterways in exchange for peace among our nations."

"*Peace.*" He spat the word. "I tried for peace in Lilou."

"You tried for a shadow of peace," I said. "True peace comes when you retreat back to your own country and stop trying to claim that which isn't yours."

"I tried for . . ." He cut himself off, his jaw jumping. His horse tossed its head again. Celeno cleared his throat, and when he spoke, his voice was different, tighter. "No, Queen Mona, these terms don't suit me. I reject your demands. And now I demand that you join me in traveling back to Alcoro, where I will negotiate *your* release to your country."

"You'll forgive me if I find that absurd," I said, before checking my next harsh words. I had to stay calm. I had to keep control. I hadn't forgotten how things had gone in Lilou. I had to keep my temper—I had to reflect his irrationality back at him. Let him lose his grip on the conversation, here with no counselors or religious advisors to guide him. I still held the leverage here—he needed me. He needed my cooperation.

I stood tall. "Celeno," I said. "If you don't surrender your hold on Cyprien, not only will I withhold all trade from you for the rest of my reign, but I will reject any proposal you may pose to me. Instead, you will face open war from an allied Lumen Lake, Cyprien, and Silverwood."

"Queen Mona—" he began.

"Winder and Paroa will not trade up besieged waterways," I overrode him. *Press your case.* "And they will fight to keep their trade paths free from your influence. You will ruin your country, Celeno—you, who are meant to elevate it."

"I will not—"

"Accept the requests your neighboring countries are extending to you. Let us build prosperity through diplomacy, not war. Let me fulfill the role I am meant to have in your Prophecy."

His face grew, if possible, tenser than before. He stared at me a moment longer. He glanced once at Gemma, but I refused to break my gaze away to see her expression. And then, as if he had made a quick decision, he shifted to one side. Rou jerked his hand clutching the grenade, but Celeno only swung his leg over his saddle and dismounted. His three soldiers kept their quarrels trained on us—one on me, one on Rou, and one directed just to one side of Gemma and Lyle.

I was glad he was on the ground, at my level, though it struck me as odd. A physical place of power conveys an intangible sense of power—it would have been in his interest to remain on the horse. Surely someone in his position should have learned that principle—but it was starting to strike me how different our approaches to sovereignty truly were. I watched as he stalked to the soldier bearing the dark, shapeless bundle over her mount. He hauled at it. It slid heavily from the horse's back and crumpled to the ground with a dull thud. He nudged it with his shiny black boot. It rolled over.

It was Mae.

She was unconscious, her wrists bound behind her back. She was swathed in a heavy black overdress and stiff boots. Her forehead was pressed into the ground next to Celeno's foot. I managed to stop myself from visibly swaying, but the bottom dropped out of my stomach. My hands clenched on my skirt. She was alive . . . she was *alive* . . . but she was here, on the ground—at the feet of this barely rational king.

Celeno reached under the flap of his saddle and withdrew his own crossbow. With a swift, tight movement, he thrust a quarrel into it, cocked it, and pressed the point against Mae's temple.

"I put it to you again, Queen Mona," he said, his voice higher than ever.

"Celeno," Gemma said with force.

He drew in a breath but continued nonetheless, his eyes still on me. "Come with me to Alcoro, where we might further discuss the issues you've brought up. I'm not opposed to some measure of Cypri independence, though you can be sure I will put all my effort into rooting out this backward river government and putting an end to it. Do this, or you'll lose an ally, and not just politically."

As shocked as I was at the sight of Mae lying prone next to his boot, I couldn't help but hear the fright in his voice, couldn't help but see the tremor in his hands. His eyes glinted, wide and uneasy, like a cornered animal. Despite this turn of events, I could still hold him steady—I would just have to do it carefully.

"What do you gain by killing her?" I asked evenly. "Think, Celeno. You're threatening the life of my powerful ally. The Silverwood army is much stronger than mine, and you can be sure King Valien will forget all thoughts of peace if you kill his wife. What do you gain?"

"A great deal of personal satisfaction, Lady Queen," he said, his voice rising. "Lest you forget, this false queen is the reason we're in this predicament in the first place."

"No," I said. "*You* are the reason we're in this predicament. I can assure you that killing Queen Ellamae won't fix a thing. Put that crossbow away. We're not done talking."

He put his boot on Mae's shoulder, rolling her onto her back. Her arms bent awkwardly underneath her, and her head rolled back, exposing her neck. He pressed his quarrel point against her forehead, his wide eyes on me. Like a child, I thought. Like a child threatening to break a toy in a fit of frustration.

Gemma tugged against Lyle's grip. "Celeno, *stop it.*"

He ignored her, still looking at me. "Come to Alcoro," he said forcefully.

"No," I said. "I will not barter with her life under threat, nor will I comply if she is harmed—"

As I spoke, his gaze flashed between Rou and Lyle again, the muscle in his jaw jumping.

"Which one of you is Lyle Roubideaux?" he interrupted me.

Lyle stepped out from behind Gemma. He lifted his arm and pointed at his brother.

"He is," he said.

Celeno jerked his crossbow up and pulled the trigger.

A cry broke from Rou. But it wasn't a cry of pain. He scrambled forward, away from my side, as Lyle arched backward and hit the packed earth, an arrow sprouting from his chest.

In a flash, Celeno reloaded his crossbow. "Stay where you are, Lyle Roubideaux. You're not so important to me that I won't kill you next."

Rou had lunged forward and froze on all fours, his chest heaving, staring at his twin where he lay in the grass. The flash grenade rolled from his grip, stopping uselessly out of his reach. Lyle spasmed, his fingers digging into the ground. He choked once.

"Theo," he said, his voice wet.

I could swear that in the last twenty-four hours, I had experienced the extreme of every emotion humanly possible—love, fear, confusion, shame, and now rage. I burned with hatred for this man, this unhinged, deranged mockery of a king. I dragged my gaze from Lyle dying on the grass to Celeno. I nearly marched forward, ready to snatch his crossbow away and drive the quarrel between his eyes, but at my movement, his hand jumped toward one of his mounted soldiers. The soldier's finger tensed on the trigger, the quarrel pointed not at my heart, but at my knee.

"Don't think I won't," Celeno said.

Lyle might have said something, perhaps trying to say his brother's name again, but his voice was too full of fluid to be sure. He dug several times at the sash around his waist, finally managing to hook his finger under the fabric. A folded piece of parchment slid halfway out before he spasmed again, losing control of his movement. Rou slid one hand forward in the dirt, reaching toward him, but he was entirely too far away.

Celeno pressed his quarrel against Mae's head again. He was glaring at me.

"How many lives will it take, Mona?" he asked angrily. "There is no peace until the Prophecy of the Prism is fulfilled. I'll give you one last chance to acknowledge that truth before I shoot you somewhere noncritical and have you dragged back to Alcoro. Come with me, or I'll . . . what are you doing, Gemma?"

Amid the tension, Gemma was moving. Slowly, she sank to her knees at Lyle's head. She was weeping, softly, her cheeks streaked with tears.

"Stand up, Gemma," Celeno said, his voice almost quizzical.

She drew in a sharp, audible breath and reached for the high collar of her shift. She unbuttoned the top button, reached inside, and drew out a fine prism on a slender chain. She pulled it over her head.

"Be blessed with the Light," she murmured tremulously. She touched the prism to Lyle's forehead. His eyelids fluttered. "The Light shines upon you." She touched it to his lips. "The Light shines through you."

She touched it to his chest, next to the shaft of the quarrel. "The Light shines within you." With shaking fingers, she reached for his hands, one at a time, and rested them on his chest, under the quarrel. She tucked the prism underneath them. He gave another spasm, and she cradled his head in her hands. "Sleep in the peace of the Light."

Rou's arms were shaking where he crouched on the ground. Celeno was staring at his wife. The point of his arrow had drifted off to one side, away from Mae's forehead.

"Get up," he said, his voice high and tense. "Leave him."

Lyle choked once more, his hands shaking on his chest, and then with two shuddering breaths, his movements stilled. Gemma leaned forward, slowly, still weeping. I thought she might be leaning down to kiss his forehead, but she slid her hand through the grass, where the discarded flash grenade rested.

"Gemma," Celeno said.

She lifted her eyes to me, wet and red.

"Blind," she whispered.

I dove forward onto Rou, driving his head down. I clapped my hand over his eyes and pressed my own into his hair. There was a sharp crackle and several shouts. I heard a crossbow fire. When I snapped my gaze back up, the horses were rearing, Celeno was on the ground, and Gemma was sobbing into her hands.

I staggered to my feet—Mae was lying prone under the trampling hooves. I dashed forward just as one of the soldiers toppled from her saddle. Celeno was scrambling in the dirt, one hand to his tearing eyes, the other groping for his crossbow. I kicked it out of his reach and hauled Mae away from him. Her head lolled forward on her chest, her dark curls spilling over her face. I crouched down and pulled her arms over my back, but as I lunged to my feet, Celeno's hand found my ankle. He cursed and closed his grip on me, furiously blinking the tears from his eyes. But before he could do anything more, Rou's boot swung through the air and collided with his head. Celeno sprawled backward onto the ground amid the frightened horses.

Rou stooped and threw Mae over his own shoulder. I scrambled to my feet. And then we ran, darting through the crush of whinnying horses and shouting soldiers.

"Gemma," I gasped.

"We can't," Rou said hoarsely.

And I knew he was right.

Our boots pounded against the wood of the dock. Behind us, one of the guards must have regained enough sight to aim and fire. A quarrel whizzed over my shoulder—I felt the wind against my bare neck. Another lodged into the hull of the bobbing *Swamp Rabbit* even as Rou jumped on board and flung Mae onto the deck. He ripped our tether free just as I joined him, and in an instant we were shooting into the darkness on the swift current.

He took two staggering steps across the deck when we jarred against a rock in the dark. This was all the motivation he needed, it seemed, for his knees to buckle. He fell forward onto his elbows and dropped his forehead to the deck. He gripped his head in his hands. Clutched in one fist was the parchment Lyle had tried to loosen from his sash—he must have snatched it up before he kicked Celeno. It crumpled as he clenched his hands in his hair.

My stomach twisted inside me. I started toward him, but at that moment Mae gave a sharp groan, still bound and unconscious. Reluctantly, I crouched beside her, loosening the knots on her wrists with shaking hands. I laid her on her back.

"Mae." I held my hand to her mouth—her breath was soft but regular. I unbuttoned her tight collar and pressed my fingers to her neck. Her heartbeat was slow but steady. I checked her hands, her wrists, I felt her back. I couldn't find any wounds, no bruises. But it was dark, and there were other forms of torture that left few marks on the body. As I felt along her scalp for swelling, she twitched. She drew in a dry gasp of air. With a heave, she rolled onto her side, clutching her stomach.

"Mae," I said urgently. "What's wrong with you?"

She choked. "*Water.*"

Most of the crates on the punt had been removed at the Benoits' dock, and I had no idea where a canteen might be. I tore through several parcels on the deck with no success, but Mae wasn't content to wait for me. She dragged herself heavily to the low hull of the punt and plunged her hands into the rushing water. She brought her cupped fingers to her face and drank deeply. This gave way to a bout of hoarse coughing, which devolved into retching, and then she vomited violently into the water, her arms trembling where they clutched the hull.

Finally I found a tin cup nestled in a cook set. I filled it on the far side of the punt and brought it to her. She slumped against the hull, gripping her stomach.

I brought the cup to her mouth. "What did he do to you?"

She took it from me and drank, her eyes closed. "Who knows. Nightshade, probably." Her voice was raw. "Maybe some other herbs. The ass." She clutched her stomach again and groaned.

I shifted her to a more comfortable position. As she brought the cup to her mouth again, we struck another rock. Slowly, our bow swung in the current. I got to my feet on the rocking deck.

I looked down at Rou, still kneeling with his hands twisted in his curls. I glanced again at Mae, who was doubled over in pain. The punt continued to turn broadside in the current, and I hurried into the bow. The pole rubbed against my fresh blisters, but I didn't have time to wrap them now. I thrust the pole into the water and straightened our line. Gritting my teeth against the fire in my palms, I pushed us around a series of rocks jutting out of the water.

A dark hand closed on the pole above mine. I turned and locked eyes with Rou, his face lined and ragged. The moon reflected in his eyes, two ghosts gleaming in the night.

"I can do it," I said.

He pulled my hands off the pole. "I know you can."

I watched as he plunged the pole into the water and worked us free of the shoals. His movements were strong, focused. His vest drew tight against the muscles of his back. I put my hand out, rested it on his shoulder blade. Then the other. He stilled. I slid my hands under his arms and crossed them over his chest. I closed the space between us and rested my forehead in his mass of curls.

He didn't move. I could feel his breath rattling inside him, and I clutched him tighter. I wanted to comfort him, communicate to him that I would be here, that I'd help him. But the truth was, I needed the comfort, too. I didn't understand what had just happened on the riverbank. I didn't know what had gone wrong, why Lyle was now dead. But I did know, finally, how I felt about Rou. Perhaps I was too full of anger and grief to leave room for confusion or doubt. The things I'd felt in the past week, the things I'd questioned and fought and denied—they'd been real all along.

He lifted one hand from the pole and brought it to his face, bowing his head forward. This presented me with the back of his neck, but just as I was about to press my lips to his skin, we scraped along another rock. Behind us, Mae retched again. Rou startled forward, out of my grip, and pushed us into the deeper current.

"You should get in the tent," he said hoarsely. "We're going to pass through Dismal Green."

"Let me do it, Rou," I said. "You're still hurt."

"I can get us to the next outlet and into the bayou."

"And then what?" I touched him as he swayed against the current. "Rou, we don't have anywhere to hide anymore. He'll find us. We need to think . . ."

"I am thinking!" he snapped. "I'm doing a lot of thinking! I'm thinking about a lot of things!"

I snatched my hand away as if I had been burned. He didn't turn around, jabbing his pole with ferocity into the water. Up ahead of us, the lights of Dismal Green flickered around the bend.

"Get in the tent," he said again.

With that, my warm assurance was drowned under the understanding of my own hand in Lyle's murder. If I had not been so despicable to Rou, we might have been together when Henri brought us the news of Celeno's approach. If I had not jumped to conclusions in the Benoits' kitchen, we might have slipped away quietly. If I had listened to Rou when he intercepted me at the river, we might have made it to the punt in time. If I had thought through my strategy, been cleverer with my words, I might have stopped Celeno's arrow.

If, if, if.

Mae was vomiting again, her sides heaving, the tin cup empty. Cheeks red with shame, I filled it again and crouched down beside her, trying to push my guilt aside. She groaned.

"Damn deertick, Celeno. My gut's going to be cramping for a week." She wiped her mouth. "Are my pupils dilated?"

"I can't tell." I put my hand on her shoulder. "We need to get inside the tent, Mae. The fewer folk who see us escaping, the better. Celeno will be on our heels in a matter of minutes."

I helped her stand, and she limped through the tent flap ahead of me. I let it close on Rou's shadowy form, the lines of his body lit with the light of the town.

"Who is that?" Mae asked, settling down in the corner I had occupied just the night before. "How did you end up with a bleeding riverman, and why are you letting him talk to you like a peasant?"

"His name is Rou. He's one of the two who attacked our ship in Lilou."

"And abducted Gemma? That's all anyone has questioned me about this past week."

"Yes. We were going to meet with the Cypri Assembly. I'll tell you about it later. First, I want to know what happened to you after we got split up. I saw you under the water in Lilou. What happened? How did you get out of the harbor?"

"I swam."

"I thought you didn't know how to swim."

"Colm taught me."

I stared at her. "When?"

"This summer. The first time I came back to the lake after my collarbone healed up."

"I thought . . . that you thought . . . that he was still angry with you?"

She rubbed her stomach. "Not particularly. We talked for a long time in the days after you drove out Alcoro. Both of us were sorry, both of us forgave the other. We reached an understanding."

"So why didn't he come to your wedding?"

She shrugged. "I imagine he hates weddings now, doesn't he?"

I continued to stare at her. "Did Valien know?"

"That he was teaching me? Of course." She quirked an eyebrow. "Why wouldn't he?"

My lips moved soundlessly for a moment. "It's just . . . you and Colm, swimming together in secret . . ."

"Oh!" She laughed easily. "Right, Mona. It mostly involved him whacking me on the back and telling me to stop actively drowning myself—when he could make himself stop laughing. Hardly scandalous."

I stopped short of telling her that I myself hadn't heard Colm laugh or joke in over four years. But if Valien knew, I supposed it didn't matter. I gave a little shake of my head to clear it. "Where was I when he was teaching you?"

"Probably trying on gowns or brushing your hair." She sipped her water again. "I'm still not very good. But at least I can keep my head up." Her eyes flicked over me in the dark. "On the subject of your hair, if I wasn't already fighting nightshade hallucinations, I'd say it's missing."

"Yes."

"Who cut it? Did they have to hold you down?"

"No." I didn't want to think back to that evening.

"So you can swim. Another secret you kept to yourself."

"I find the less people know about you, the easier it is to look clever."

"How did you end up with Celeno?"

"Everyone was jumping overboard during the attack, I don't know if you realized. Someone cut a bunch of skiffs loose. I didn't realize Celeno was in the closest one until he dragged me out of the water. Probably saved my life, ironically." She stretched out her legs and kicked off her hard-soled boots with a few sharp movements. "The Alcorans had other ships in the harbor. They brought me to one and locked me up."

"And drugged you?"

"Not at first. Only after I picked their lock a second time. They made several failed attempts, the idiots, like I can't recognize valerian when it's handed to me in a cup." She gripped her stomach, grimacing. "But they managed it tonight."

"How?"

"They held me down and tipped it down my throat, of course." She took another sip of water. "I managed to bite one of them before they put me under. Hope she has puncture wounds."

I gazed at her stonily. "Did they torture you?"

She snorted. "I doubt Celeno has the stomach for torture. Very much into pomp and show, I've found out. A lot of bluster."

"He murdered a man outright just a few minutes ago," I said.

She cocked her head in the darkness. "Who?"

I nodded to the tent flap. "Rou's brother Lyle. Shot him through the chest with his crossbow."

"As you were escaping?"

"As we were negotiating." My mouth twisted on the words.

She was silent a moment. "How did you get away?"

"Gemma." I cradled my head in my hands. "Gemma set off a flash grenade. She blinded her husband so we could escape. Great Light, he's going to execute her."

She turned her empty cup in her fingers. "I don't think he will, Mona."

I looked up sharply. "Mae, I have underestimated this madman far too many times. He murdered Lyle in a bout of frustration—as if he were venting his anger by taking a life. I won't think him above anything ever again."

She stared at her cup. "Every move we made over the last few days, every order Celeno gave, it was all to track Gemma down. He was obsessed with finding her."

"Because it was embarrassing, I expect, for him to lose her to a couple of swamp bandits."

"Not to hear him tell it. That first night, after the attack, he was livid. He shouted at his officers, he drilled me for hours until he went hoarse. But the next night was different. He questioned me alone, without all his handlers present. And he was totally different. I thought he might break down and cry. I finally convinced him I had absolutely no idea where Gemma was, and he looked broken, Mona. I just don't get the feeling he would hurt her."

I dropped my head into my hands again. "Stop. Stop. Stop defending him to me, all of you. I thought he couldn't cause worse hurt than he already has, and he did."

I could feel her studying me. I pressed my palms into my eyes, but the tears seeped out anyway.

"I'm sorry," she said quietly.

She thought I was mourning Lyle, not the hole now torn through Rou. Awkward, snappish Lyle, who by all accounts had betrayed us to the Alcorans.

Who gave up his life for his brother.

I drew my knees to my chest and lowered my forehead onto them. "Me, too."

CHAPTER 13

We would have been lost without Fisheye.

I felt the punt scrape against the bank and went out on deck to find Rou trying to maneuver us into a weedy outlet. He was leaning on his pole, throwing all his weight into making the turn, when a dark shape shot down the river so fast we had no time to determine if it was friend or foe. Even as I tensed, Fisheye swept alongside us in his rickety punt, Mirabelle curled around his neck. With a few swift words, he ushered all three of us onto his boat, jabbering about Alcorans up and down the river. As I helped Mae sit down on his deck, he hopped nimbly aboard the *Swamp Rabbit*. He raised a glinting hatchet and brought it down in three decisive swings. Water bubbled over the deck, and he jumped back onto his boat. With no fanfare or farewell, the *Swamp Rabbit* slipped slowly under the current, poles, tent, and all.

"Git under here, quick now—yer gonna have to git friendly with each other." He flattened us down on his deck and threw a heap of canvas and several bundles of animal furs over us. "Don't move."

We huddled together in the dark, airless space. I heard Mae drawing each labored breath as quietly as she could through her gritted teeth. To my right, Rou covered his mouth with his palm. I was sure my heartbeat was louder than anybody's breathing.

Only a few minutes later, we heard the murmuring of voices. They grew louder—and angrier.

"Blockade," we heard Fisheye mutter. "Budge up, now, g'won," he said loudly, presumably to other riverfolk crowding the waterway. "Let a man through."

"You there!" called a voice over the hubbub. "Stop your boat, in the name of the Seventh King."

The punt bobbed to a halt. "What fer, mister?"

"Every boat in this river must be searched, by order of the king—"

"There is no king in Cyprien!" shouted another voice. A few angry hollers rose in alliance.

"Silence!" snapped the Alcoran. "Chitza, take that man away." Our punt bobbed slightly. "Now, riverman, what's this you have here?"

"It's my bread 'n' butter, is what it is, yer canyonship."

"Beaver skins."

"Yessir. Interested? Only ten silvers a pelt, a real steal."

"What's underneath?"

"Well, that's my canvas, innit, fer when it rains."

There was a snarl of voices from somewhere close by, an onslaught of curses being overridden by someone barking orders. I heard the scraping of hulls jostling against each other in the water.

"Shift it," said the Alcoran at our punt. "And do it quickly."

We held our breaths. *It's over*, I thought. We'd be taken to Alcoro. They'd use Mae and me to barter our countries into ruin. Who knew what they'd do to Rou . . .

"Listen to that, Mirabelle. *Shift yer canvas*, he says." Fisheye raised his voice over the building clamor. "Beggin' yer pardon, mister, but I been shiftin' my canvas fer the last four days at every one of yer little river pickins, and durned if I'm not already a day late gittin' to Bellemere."

"I must insist—"

"*Insist*, he says. Mirabelle, what's an honest riverman to do when he cain't even deliver two dozen beaver backs without gittin' hemmed and hawed at every quarter mile? *Git those skins in*, they says, *winter's a-comin' in the canyons and ladies want 'em fer hats. Don't be late, riverman!* But when I go and try to do what they says, they stop me every step of the way. What'choo think all these folk are riled about, I wonder? *Shift that canvas*, he says!"

"Sir." The Alcoran's voice was sharp. "I warn you—"

"*Warn you*, he says, Mirabelle!" The boat rocked slightly, and I distinctly heard the hiss of an agitated opossum. "Does he stop to think what's gonna happen to all them coldheaded ladies roamin' round the canyon rim?"

"Damn the Seventh King!" shouted a voice. Glass smashed.

"Lieutenant!" called a desperate voice.

"Coldheaded ladies is gonna lead to sinus drips, is what it's gonna lead to, yes'm," Fisheye continued as the sounds of violence built behind him. "And from there to pneumonia, sure as a shoofly, and then they're gonna have ladies droppin' right 'n' left, just keelin' right into the canyon."

"Sir . . ." warned the Alcoran at our punt.

"Lieutenant!"

But Fisheye wasn't slowing down. "How's they gonna keep up with their boats and corn and prisms when they got coldheaded ladies just lyin' all over the canyons with the sinus drips, I wonder, Mirabelle?"

"Ugh!" The punt rocked again, as if someone stepped off it. "You're raving, you are. Go on, hurry along. You're wasting my time. You lot! Break it up!"

We shoved off with a lurch amid the sounds of a full-fledged fist fight. Folk shouted, someone cursed, and there was a mighty splash. The Alcoran's commands were overridden by a surge of cheers. We drifted farther down the river, and the commotion began to fade away until we couldn't hear it any longer. There were several long seconds of silence, broken only by the quiet rush of water. We didn't move under the canvas.

After a moment, Fisheye chuckled.

"Wastin' time, he says, Mirabelle."

I released the breath I'd been holding and fought the sudden, giddy urge to laugh outright. I realized I was gripping Rou's and Mae's hands on either side of me. Mae was gripping me back.

Rou wasn't.

The following days were a series of similar events, one right after another, each just as tense as the last. There were no more safe houses, no more open doors, but Fisheye sped us through the bayou with all the quietness and agility of a water snake. I had underestimated just how much he knew, and just how much the Alcorans misjudged him. If someone called for him to stop, he responded in his usual manner, offering a dozen garbled words devoid of any meaning, and they waved him on with a fair measure of disgust. He skirted us under Celeno's very nose, hiding us beneath an assortment of cargo that he acquired from other River-folk with little more than a nod. Netting, sacks of rice, strategically stacked firewood . . . we spent one evening under cleverly designed crates with false bottoms. We lay just inches from discovery as the Alcorans opened the lids on catches of catfish, holding our breaths as rank fish water dripped through the wooden slats onto our faces.

It was in between the first two of these encounters that Rou sat on the deck and pulled out the folded parchment that Lyle had dug out of his sash as he died. He smoothed it on his knee. He read it once, and then again. He was silent for several minutes— during which I used every ounce of restraint to keep from blurting questions. After a long time, without looking at me, he handed me the parchment. Mae read over my shoulder.

Theo—

I meant to give you this later, once we arrived safely in Siere, but it looks as though I won't have that option anymore. I'm sorry I have to leave the rest of the trip to you, but once you meet the cart outside Dismal Green, you won't need me.

I'm going to Alcoro. There's an engineer in Callais, a colleague of my old tutor, who has offered me a position in her lab. It wasn't a quick or simple process—we've been corresponding for almost two years. She was reluctant to take on a foreigner at first and asked that I submit a sample of my work for her consideration. I agreed to compile my research on incendiary devices and meet her colleagues in Bellemere the day after First Fire to give them my work.

This task to bring the queens to Siere arrived at the eleventh hour, and I only just managed to request the Alcorans meet me in Dismal Green rather than Bellemere to accommodate our route. I assumed there would be no reason to associate my name with Gemma's disappearance, and I planned to complete my transaction before continuing on to Siere and fulfilling my duty to the Assembly (and, presumably, before peace had been secured between our countries).

After Temper Creek, I can't take that chance anymore. Once the Alcorans hear our name connected with Queen Mona's, they'll surely question whether I am somehow involved with their queen's abduction, and both my plan and the Assembly's will be jeopardized. If you're reading this, it means they accepted my work and I am accompanying them back to Callais before they have a chance to hear about Temper Creek. I can only hope, given my presence in Dismal Green just a day after Temper Creek, they'll believe it was a different Roubideaux.

You're probably angry. I can't say I particularly care. I'm tired of being a tool. I'm tired of folk only wanting one thing from me. I never wanted to create weaponry. I was on track to revolutionize the steel industry before I had to leave Bellemere, and after that I had to do what the Assembly requested of me. I won't bother expressing my continued loyalty to Cyprien, because you won't believe me. But it's true. I'm only trying to do what I know I'm meant to do, what Mother gave up so much for. This has been my only chance since Eloi died, and I'm taking it.

I do ask that you assure the Assembly that I will not be developing weaponry for the Alcorans. I plan to continue my work on a refractory converter that could very well halve the expense of manufacturing steel, as well as create a safer workplace for millworkers. I trust that, as per my contract with the Alcorans, my work

will be shared openly between our two countries, and
will not be used by either side in conflict.

I wish you luck in life.

Lyle

It was dated the previous day, the one we spent in Dismal Green. He must have written it while I was asleep, probably planning to leave it on the punt for Rou to find. After reading it a second time, I handed it to Fisheye. He set the end of his pole on the deck and skimmed it.

As he read, I stared into space, slowly processing Lyle's words. One by one, events and comments began to trickle back to me—things I had ignored or misinterpreted. All the work he was hurrying to finish. His outburst at the prospect of spending several days in Temper Creek. His vehement opposition to skipping Dismal Green altogether.

Standing out sharply among everything else was the uncomfortable conversation we'd shared after the disaster in Temper Creek. What an idiot I'd been. What a single-minded, self-centered fool. Of course Lyle Roubideaux hadn't been in love with me. He wasn't trying to awkwardly confess his feelings. He hadn't been worried about the success of our mission. He had been worried that with his name now connected to mine, his hopes to defect to Alcoro had been ruined.

And he had blamed his brother for it, for his mess, his failures.

But before my anger could fully build, it started to

seep away. He'd tried to tell me. *Maybe you should look harder.* In his own way, he had been crying out for help. It was a weak attempt, and one I had misinterpreted, but he had tried. Left alone, his only choice had been to go through with his plan and hope the Alcorans hadn't yet heard the news from Temper Creek. And he had paid the price for it—we all had. I bowed my head forward into my hands.

"Hmph," Fisheye said.

I looked up as he folded the letter. "Did you know about this?"

He gave it back to me and lowered his pole back into the water. "Which part, exactly?"

"That Lyle was planning to go to Alcoro."

"Not in so many words, no. But I knew somethin' was amiss after Fogwaller."

"What happened in Fogwallow?"

He moved his pole to the other side of the punt. "Was skulkin' round some Alcoran boats at the docks. They'd been talkin' bout you, lolly—someone had intercepted a message you wrote, so they knew you was alive and headin' further into the bayou."

My letter to my brothers. Lyle had been right—it had been waylaid. I realized that meant no one back home would know if Mae or I were alive or dead. I pushed this concern aside for the moment. "I didn't give away our route, though."

"No'm, they had no idea where you was or where you was goin'. I loitered 'round to try to figure out what they *did* know, when one of them asked if there was still plans to meet in Dismal Green. At first I didn't think anything of it—what's it to me if a few Canyon-folk have business in Dismal Green? But then they said somethin' 'bout a Roubideaux. Someone they was fixin' to meet."

Rou was staring out into the bayou, his arms around his knees. I looked back down at the letter in my hands. "So you wrote us the note telling us to wait in Temper Creek while you went to investigate."

"Yes'm. After pokin' round I found 'em. Didn't take long—they stood out, bunch of shiny academics in that river town. Pulled a few strings with the innkeeper and found out they *was* waitin' fer the same Roubideaux, somethin' 'bout research and engineerin' and whatnot."

He nudged his pole against a fallen log, maneuvering us around a clump of slimy roots. "Hightailed it up the river to meet you in Temper Creek and figure this whole thing out, but I got stopped a few miles upstream by a whole passel of Alcorans makin' a beeline fer Dismal Green. Word had been shootin' down the river all night 'bout seein' you, Lady Queen, in Temper Creek with some feller Roubideaux. Celeno's folk put two and two together and ran to stake the place out."

"*That's* why we left Bellemere so fast," Mae said. "I was wondering. Celeno was questioning me *again*, when a messenger rushed in and whispered in his ear. His guards dragged me back to the hold so fast they forgot to shackle me to the wall. I was halfway through picking the lock again when they came to drug me."

"Yes'm, he hurried up the river from Bellemere," Fisheye said. "Saw his boat pass myself."

"What happened in Dismal Green?" I asked. "What happened when Lyle went to meet with the Alcorans?"

"Once he'd gone into the inn to meet the academics, Celeno's soldiers surrounded the place. Didn't see what happened inside, but they musta figured things out quick, 'cause the windows lit up like the sun."

"He set off a flash grenade," I said.

"Yes'm, and then lit out into the marsh, but what was done was done. They knew which way he was goin'."

"And they had his book," Rou said. "He didn't have it with him when he came back. Even though Celeno killed the wrong one of us, he got his work anyway. There's enough material in there to let the Alcorans try a new incendiary every day for a month."

"I can't believe he trusted the Alcorans with that kind of work," Mae said, shaking her head. "No matter what agreement they made, he couldn't really believe they wouldn't use his weaponry against his own folk?"

I looked at Rou. "I suppose he trusted that peace would, in the end, be achieved. Or at least, he assumed the end result would be worth the risk. He could focus on what was really important to him—improving his folk's industry. Designing safer steel mills."

Rou looked away. Silence settled among us, broken only by Fisheye's pole moving through the water.

"Tell me something," Rou said suddenly. "That reward for Mona's capture—had news of it reached Temper Creek?"

"F'it had, I wouldn't'a sent you that way, would I?" Fisheye replied. "No, news 'bout the reward hadn't made it up that far. Told you so in my note."

"But at First Fire," I said, my brow furrowed. "That man apprehended me, he tried to take me away . . ."

"Lyle," Rou said without turning around. His voice was empty, dead. "He needed to get us out of Temper Creek. He needed to keep his deadline in Dismal Green. He couldn't have us loitering at Gris' and missing his rendezvous. So he made something up. Probably pointed you out to a desperate bystander—Alderic always was an impulsive fellow—so he could come swooping in with his hero fire. Made it so we had to make a hasty getaway."

A thick silence passed between us. Mae, sitting barefoot on the deck, looked between the two of us.

"He didn't mean it, Rou," I said quietly, aware that I had said the same thing to his brother just a day before. "He didn't mean for you to get hurt."

"Wrong." His voice was harsh. "He didn't mean for me to be *recognized*. He didn't care who got hurt."

"I think he did, Rou. He protected you with his

life. He knew exactly what he was doing when he told Celeno you were him." My guilt rose in me again. Lyle had seen what was coming. He had read Celeno better than I had. "I think he cared a lot."

But my words were empty in his grief, and when he wasn't helping Fisheye move us through the bayou, he was hunched in the cramped stern, his head in his hands. When we were forced to hide under masses of netting or cleverly stacked crates, he turned his back to me, curling into himself. Mae took over dressing my burn and blisters with the supplies Fisheye garnered for us, and she plucked out the split stitches from Rou's forehead before sewing him back up. Fisheye offered him a jug of moonshine for the process, but he refused it, sitting with his eyes closed and hands clenched on his knees while Mae worked silently before him.

During our flight, we watched Cyprien collapse in on itself, its sophisticated subversion laid suddenly bare. No one was pretending to be loyal to Alcoro anymore. We saw russet banners floating half-burned in waterways and red-tinted glass shattered along the docks. Fisheye poled us hurriedly past an Alcoran boat consumed by a blazing inferno—we could feel the heat through the canvas as we huddled underneath.

Alcoro responded, of course. For every riverman or woman we saw driving the Canyon-folk out of town, we saw ten more fleeing into the bayou, families in tow, pursued by Alcoran boats, now armed with cross-bows and ballistae. We saw punts in flames and homes thrown open, their occupants running for their lives.

Cyprien was at war.

I ventured to ask Rou what this meant for the election—how would they declare winners, when would the power shift? Who would be First if Senator Ancelet was voted out? But Rou didn't answer me, his head clutched in his hands as we passed the remains of yet another punt, its charred hull poking out of the swamp like rib bones.

I couldn't bring myself to ask him what he was going to do once we reached Lilou. Coming with us was his safest choice, but he'd said nothing about leaving his country, and I had a hard time fathoming him choosing to follow me over sneaking back to serve the Assembly now that open war had broken out. I steeled myself for that inevitable moment, when we would turn north up the river and he would not. I wondered if he'd even say goodbye to me.

I could almost guarantee, for any number of reasons, that I would never see him again.

It came as great surprise, therefore, when four days after we fled the Benoits', Rou followed me onto the creaky deck of the sailboat in Lilou.

"You don't have to come with us," I said to him.

He didn't look at me. "I can't stay here."

Fisheye clasped hands with our new boatman. It was the dead of night, and we were making our hurried transaction on a narrow, half-rotted dock tucked behind a granary. The water had a filmy sheen, and the air reeked of fish oil. But the boat seemed reasonably sound, and the boatman was someone Fisheye trusted, which was good enough for me. As he shifted a few bags of supplies onto our deck, I reached out and touched his arm. Mirabelle hissed at me.

"Fisheye," I said. "Thank you. I won't forget what you've done for us."

"Hate that it went so wrong." He stroked the opossum's wicked little nose. "But don't you worry, lolly. We'll run Alcoro out afore it's all over. Listen, though." He looked between Rou and me. "Somethin's gotta be done, understand? We cain't just sit by no more."

"No. The time for subtle action is passed. I'll do what I can, but if there's any way to get word to me about what happened with the election, who's in charge . . ."

"We'll git word to you—somehow. We're gonna have to. The Assembly's gonna have a right time tryin' to fight back until we can git organized."

"Lumen Lake and the Silverwood are your allies now," I said. "You won't face Alcoro alone."

We sailed north through the Cypri waterways with a white banner flying from our mast. Mae stood at the hull facing the mountains, waiting to hail any of her folk who might be training arrows on us from the lower lookouts. But the slopes were silent. We would later find out that an unseasonably early snowstorm had blanketed the high ridges, hindering swift travel. Because of this, the scouts who spotted our approach from the Rooftops were slow in bringing their news back to Lampyrinae. The Palisades, in turn, had become icy as fall progressed, and it took Valien two days to make the descent. As a result, word of our arrival reached Blackshell barely an hour before we did.

At the mouth of the lake, we bid goodbye to our gruff but efficient boatman and made our way back among my folk. We had an astonished, jubilant welcome. Some folk had tears in their eyes. The lake and the mountains had both been thrown into disarray after the *Halfmoon* raced back to Lumen Lake with news of the attack on the *Spindrift*. It seemed that Alcoro had initially blamed Lumen Lake for the attack, as if we'd lured Celeno and Gemma on board a ship that was rigged to explode—with us still on it. Before anyone could set the story straight, our folk had been forced to flee back to the lake, rather than stay and begin their own search for us. With no word from Mae and me in the last few weeks, we had been feared dead by most. I was too weary to think what effect this might have had on my brothers and Valien, summoning all my strength to return my folk's greetings and inquiries with lackluster poise.

It was Sorcha's mother, Rhona, who elbowed through the crowd and beckoned us to her own little scow. We boarded gratefully, and I promised that news would be given to folk throughout the twelve islands on the developments in Cyprien. Rhona barely waited for me to finish before she cast off and sailed us swiftly up the shoreline. Mae, fed up with boat travel by this point, threw herself onto the deck and buried her head in her arms, but Rou stood silently at the hull.

We had barely spoken since Lilou. Now he watched the islands slide by, his expression unreadable. The bandages on his forehead had been replaced by a smaller pad of gauze and bound by a strip of linen.

I stood by his shoulder.

"What do you think?" I asked quietly.

He was silent as the towering hulk of Fourcolor slipped past us.

"It's colder, of course, than Cyprien," I said quickly.

"It's fine," he said.

But clearly it wasn't.

I didn't speak again until Blackshell came into view. By this point, word of our approach had spread throughout the palace, and the boats were being made ready to sail for the river. We drew alongside the dock just as a long-legged figure broke from the palace, his emerald cloak flying behind him. Two more figures followed in his wake.

Valien met Mae as she wobbled off the scow, crushing her in his arms. Arlen elbowed past them for me, gripping me by the shoulders and talking very fast. In the back stood Colm, his face lined in the weak sunlight. He looked like Father had on his sickbed—tired, hollow, and spent. I placated Arlen with a hug and a promise of the full tale once we were all inside, and I made my way past Mae and Valien's passionate embrace. I stood before Colm. He barely moved, his arms hanging by his sides.

"It wasn't your fault," I said.

"It was indisputably my fault," he whispered.

I wrapped my arms around him. He lowered his forehead to the top of mine.

"Are you all right?" he asked.

"More or less. Are you?"

"They were going to crown me at the winter solstice if we hadn't heard word of you."

I hugged him tighter. "I've always said you'd make a good king."

"Please don't leave again."

I drew back. "We have to talk. Alcoro is tearing Cyprien apart, searching for us and the Assembly of Six. They're going to need all the help we can give them, and Celeno won't leave the lake alone for long."

"The Assembly of Six? They're still . . ."

"Yes. Have someone gather the councilors."

He looked past me, and I glanced over my shoulder to see Rou hovering by the scow. I beckoned him forward, and he joined me with reluctance, standing an arm's length away from me.

"Rou Roubideaux," I said. "An ambassador for Cyprien, and my guide and safeguard."

Rou cut his honey-colored eyes to me in accusation,

but he said nothing. Colm held out his hand to him.

"Then I owe you a great deal of gratitude," he said. "We all do."

Rou went to shake single-handed, but jumped in with his left as Colm clasped him with both hands, Cypri-style. I felt a spark of gratitude toward my culturally-sensitive brother, even if it didn't change how Rou was feeling toward me.

"My brothers," I said. "Colm and Arlen."

"What happened to you?" Arlen asked me, barely looking at Rou. "What happened to your hair?"

"Inside," I said. "Let's go inside, and I'll tell you everything."

"My queen, I am sorry—I am so sorry."

"There's nothing to forgive, Cavan," I said, resting my hand on his shoulder where he kneeled in the middle of the hall. He had hurried out of the shadows and dropped to my feet as the rest of the group filed into the council room. "It wasn't your fault."

"We should have secured the far side of the ship . . ."

"You did nothing wrong," I said firmly. "No one did. I'm relieved to see you safe."

He ran his palms over his face to clear away his tears, and then he reached into the satchel over his shoulder. "As soon as I heard you had arrived, I ran to get it . . ." He pulled out an envelope of soft felt and withdrew my crown, cradling it in his palms.

"The channel wasn't deep," he said in a cracked

voice. "After the ship went down, the deck was only a few feet below the surface. And I could see it, all bright and shiny amid the wreckage. It wasn't hard to get at it."

I glanced in the council room, where everyone was settling into seats around the long table. I stepped out of view of the room, pulled Cavan to his feet, and threw my arms around him.

Recounting the events of the last few weeks and the implications they presented took the better part of the evening. Describing how the attack on the *Spindrift* had occurred necessitated a great deal of explanation and strategic wording on my part. There had been no loss of life on the dock in Lilou, but the destruction of our flagship was a significant blow to Lumen Lake, and I could not avoid disclosing the fact that the perpetrator of that event was sitting at the table with us. I knew this would be a sticking point—ever since many of my loyal councilors had been replaced by Donnel Burke's surrogates all those years ago, my council sessions had become careful dances of justification and semantics. My councilors were not hostile—not anymore. But they were quick to assume the opposing position, if only to examine all angles more thoroughly. This was good, I constantly told myself. This was healthy. But it had eliminated the implied trust once present in my council sessions, turning informal brainstorming by necessity into formal statements and weighted vocabulary. I'd become practiced at adjusting my language, but my councilors had evolved with me—and that was evidenced now as I laid out the events in Lilou. While they processed and picked apart my carefully chosen words, Rou was silent, his eyes on the grain of the tabletop. I regretted him having to see me this way—it was the same voice I'd used to reprimand him in Dismal Green.

"It was a necessity of wartime, driven by the threat of Alcoro," I said for the fifth time as my councilors posed question after question of trustworthiness, propriety, and diplomatic intent. "It was a loss to our fleet, to be sure—but see what it has gained: an alliance with the Cypri government, an alternative to tying Lumen Lake to Alcoran trade, and a chance to finally protect the southern waterways from further attack. I do not condemn Rou Roubideaux or the Cypri for the loss of the *Spindrift*, and neither should you."

"And of our queen's abduction?" my lead councilor said, the barest touch of derision in her voice.

"Your queen is back," I said with finality. "I cannot speak for Ellamae, but I shall be the judge of my own treatment, and I consider the matter closed. Shall we continue?"

We continued.

Rou did not look up.

For simplicity's sake, I said little of Lyle, informing my councilors only that Celeno was now in possession of knowledge on Cypri incendiaries. Rou stayed quiet through this amendment. Mae, who knew the real story, also kept silent. Her head rested on Valien's shoulder while he alternated between taking disjointed notes and caressing her hand on the tabletop.

Once the greater part of the tale was finished, my councilors had a slew of questions for Rou. How long could Cyprien hold off an Alcoran assault? How did the Assembly of Six wield power in the event of war? Were there ways to communicate with them? Did Cyprien have any remaining semblance of an army? Navy? How would war with Alcoro impact Cypri industry and coastal trade?

Rou weathered these well, offering succinct, careful answers. But when they started asking him about the new technology Celeno now possessed in light of this anonymous defector's report, he grew more and more terse, finally answering most questions with a flat "I don't know." I cut the discussion short, citing that we were weary from the journey, and asked an attendant to show Rou to a guest room. He left the council room before anyone else. The attendant scurried after him to show him where to go.

I watched Rou disappear as my councilors dispersed around me, murmuring amongst themselves. Now, finally, I had the chance to talk privately with him after days of travel on cramped boats. But as I moved toward the door, Mae put her hand on my elbow.

"Give him a little time," she said quietly. "Give him time to grieve in private, in whatever way he needs to grieve."

I hovered at the head of the council table. "But . . ."

"Alone," she said.

I looked to the door as the last of my councilors left the room. Arlen had left with them, but Colm was still seated at the table, a picture of deep thought—furrowed brow, tight lips, chin in his hand. He'd watched me as I spoke about Rou to the council, and I'd hoped he'd discerned nothing but diplomatic alliance in the vacuous space between us. I didn't want to jeopardize that now—if he thought something was amiss, he'd try to shoulder the burden himself, and he didn't need the meaningless weight of any more of my failed relationships. I blew out a breath and took a step back from the door. Satisfied, it seemed, that I wasn't going to tear out of the room, Mae let go of my arm. She turned to Valien as he collected his smattering of notes.

"How early do you need us tomorrow?" she asked me over her shoulder.

"Session will start at eight," I said halfheartedly.

"Mm . . . we might not be here that early."

"As early as you can manage it, then," I said a bit sharper than I meant to. "It will be a double session tomorrow."

"Well, then I suppose we should retire, shall we?" She looped her arm through Valien's with a twinkle in her eye. "Turn in early, yes?"

He smiled at her. "Of course . . . though not before you've had a chance to have a bath."

Her silky smile turned into affront. "I don't need a bath."

He took her face in his hand and kissed her deeply. "You do."

She pursed her lips in a scowl but allowed him to escort her from the room. They disappeared down the hall, their heads together.

I stood at the head of the table, clenching and unclenching my fists and ignoring Colm's gaze.

"Mona," he said.

I let out my breath. "What?"

"Are you going to be all right?"

"Of course."

"Did something happen between you and Rou in Cyprien?"

Damn his emotional discernment. "Yes, he abducted me," I said shortly. I didn't want his pity or compassion, couldn't bear him projecting his own deep loss on me. My situation was nothing like his, and I couldn't stand the thought of him offering his condolences for a frivolous infatuation that was never meant to be. I waved my hand. "You go on. I'm going to organize my notes for tomorrow."

"Let me know if . . ,"

"Yes, yes, I will. Goodnight."

Reluctantly, he got up and exited the room, leaving me alone. I looked at the documents scattered on the table, and then I turned and made for the bank of windows along the wall. I drew back the curtains, revealing little except my own reflection in the darkened panes. I cupped my hands around my face and peered through the glass.

The rooms of the guest wing were across the terrace and down the lakeshore, and they were dark save one in the middle. Rou's room, where I trusted my attendants were stoking the hearth and insisting he ask for anything he needed. Where he'd sit, alone, once they left.

What would he do? Would he climb into bed and grasp at sleep? Would he sit by the fire and stare? Would he pace, would he storm? Would he cry? Any tears he'd shed on our flight he'd hidden with a hand over his face, or his forehead on his knees. Would he let them fall freely now?

Give him time to grieve.

With all my effort, I pushed myself away from the window, met again by my ghostly reflection. I left my notes scattered on the council table and walked out of the room. I headed blindly up the dark hallways to my own chamber and turned the handle on my double doors. In the antechamber, the two guards snapped to attention. Their uniforms were pressed and spotless, but their hair was slightly mussed. The one on the left had pillow marks on her cheek. They'd been roused from bed to return to their post in my antechamber. I murmured for them to take their ease and passed back into my parlor.

It had been kept immaculate, with no sign that I'd been gone. The lamps were lit, the furniture dusted, the hearth blazing with a roaring fire. My bedroom was no different. My haphazard notes from the night before the Alcoran ships arrived were stacked neatly

on my desk. A nightdress was laid out on my armchair. The washbowl steamed on my dresser, and the
covers on my bed were turned down.

Distantly, I discarded the scavenged Cypri overdress I'd been wearing since leaving Lilou. I washed.
I brushed my hair. I slid into my silk nightdress. I sat
in front of my mirror, staring unseeing at my wan
reflection. I looked up at my parents' portrait, where
my father looked tired and my mother looked disappointed. And then I climbed into my bed and pro-
ceeded not to sleep the entire night.

I didn't pace or write. I didn't mutter in front of
my mantel. I just lay in bed, staring up at my canopy,
watching the slow creep of moonlight slide over the
fish-scale embroidery. For hours I catalogued, once
again, everything that had gone wrong, and how I
should have acted in retrospect. It was organized and
endless, a complete compendium of my mistakes,
broken by nothing but the snap of wood on the hearth
and my own dogged heartbeat.

At the ringing of the first bell from the village, the
world still colorless and dim outside my window, my
door opened with the barest creak. In crept my maid
with an armful of firewood.

"Oh," she whispered. "You're awake. I wasn't
sure . . . did you want to take a day abed, or shall I
ring for breakfast?"

This was it, then. The return to life as I knew it.
I sat up.

"Breakfast," I said.

The day crept by in a daze. I arrived early to my council room and drew back the curtains. There was no sign of life from Rou's room. Of course, I told myself irritably. Why would he be on his patio? It was early, and freezing outside—and he had no poi to spin. I hurried away from the window just as the first murmuring began in the hall. When my council entered, I was stoically preparing my notes for the day's double session.

The discussions took my mind off Rou but settled it back on the distressing matters at hand. For hours, we went back over the details from the night before and examined every proposed plan of action from all angles. Colm sat by, diligently taking notes, but I was surprised to hear Arlen offering more input in the discussion, particularly once the general joined us. They spoke with the familiarity of working part-ners, and I realized my youngest brother hadn't been as idle as I'd assumed while I was gone. This gave my spirits the tiniest boost, and I thanked him privately in between sessions. He turned red and shrugged.

"Blame Colm," he said. "He had enough to focus on while they were threatening to crown him, so he left the tactical sessions to me."

"Good," I said.

Mae and Valien showed up partway through the second session, both crownless and loose-collared. They spoke as much as they needed to and no more, clearly impatient for the discussion to wrap up. Valien masked it better than Mae, who spent much of the time idly tracing the muscle lines on Valien's bare forearm. They sat across from me, and I felt my irritation rise more and more, my cheeks and collar growing hot. Finally I found myself unable to focus any longer on what was being said around me, and I snapped that the session was over. My councilors and brothers packed up, each heading off to see to the tasks given to them. I sat rigid amid the shuffle, glaring across the table as Mae leaned into her husband's shoulder and pressed a kiss to his jaw. I heard the deep, quiet murmur he answered with—words that were full of secrets and promise and nothing. Mae gave a slow smile in return and turned to rise from her chair—and then she caught my glare.

"What's up?" she asked without any shred of abashment.

"We are at *war*," I said through gritted teeth.

She raised an eyebrow. "I'm aware."

I clenched my fists on the tabletop. "I need your *help*."

"And we're giving it to you, Mona," she said sharply. "We've been talking, too, you know—about how to organize the Guard and where to focus our effort in the next few weeks. Believe me, we're working on it."

"Then *act* like it," I said, my pain and grief and anger at myself all spilling over at her with full force. "Act like you're concerned about the East falling apart, about the threat to our countries, about the lives being lost in Cyprien as we speak. Pull yourselves together—both of you. You're acting as if there's not a thing wrong in the world, like the past few weeks are all ancient history—"

"Five years," she interrupted me. Her face had darkened while I spoke, and now her voice was cold and scathing. She pushed back her chair and stood. Valien pinched her sleeve in his fingers, apprehensive. "For five years, Mona, I scraped and bargained and worked my ass off to buy myself a few days at the edge of the Silverwood. Val lied to everyone around him and risked his father's wrath to sneak away to see me. He was caught, you know that? The one time we missed our rendezvous was because the king sent the Wood Guard out to drag Val back home, where he locked him in his room for *three weeks*. All that risk, just for a few days of lovemaking out in the hills."

Valien had set his chin in his hand, his gaze on the table, but Mae wasn't finished. Eyes glittering, she twitched aside the loose collar of her tunic, baring the scar on her left collarbone. "And then, when I finally came *back*, I was laid up at my parents' house for two months, trying my damndest not to die. I was there through the summer, while Val was at Lampyrinae. I only moved back to the palace the week before our wedding. And *then*, the night of, we get dragged down here to throw ourselves into battle, only for me to run off down the river to Lilou, where I was *shackled*—" she waved her right wrist at me, which still bore pink abrasions "—to the hull of an Alcoran ship and shouted at for a week, before sneaking through smoke and water to get back *here*, to celebrate our *second* full night of married life.

"When do I get to be happy, Mona? When do I get to rest, and believe in the fact that I'm finally married to the man I've been separated from for the majority of the past six years? Tomorrow? Next week? At the rate things are going, I'm not so sure I can count on us being together past today."

Her words rang in the air, each one landing on me like a quarrel from a crossbow. I sat straight, my fists still clenched on the tabletop, my body flushed with anger at her and anger at myself and anger at Valien for just sitting there, and *shame*—great Light, I hated this crushing weight of shame that had become the ugly melody of my life since Dismal Green.

Mae shoved her chair back under the table. "I am *painfully* aware we are at war, Mona. I'm sorry things didn't work out between you and Rou, but don't take it out on us." She gave a short tug on her husband's sleeve, and he rose with her, his face heavy and downcast.

"We'll see you tomorrow," she said shortly, threading her arm through Valien's and pulling him out the door.

I sat in the empty council room, wrapped in silence, trying to tame the waves of emotion rolling around me. Eventually I gave up and just let them rage—it was nothing less than I deserved. I bowed my head forward and pressed my fists to my eyes, struggling against tears. Now I *did* want Colm. I wanted him to come in and listen patiently. I wanted Arlen, to lighten the mood. Perhaps a councilor would come back to distract me, or a messenger would bring me urgent news. But no one did, because I had sent them all away to do my bidding, and of course none of them would reject a command from me.

I pushed my chair back and returned to the window. Rou's patio was empty.

You are a country.

"Go *away*!" I said forcefully, slamming my fists on the windowsill. The panes rattled. Frustrated, I leaned my forehead against them, my crown clinking on the cold glass. My tears slipped down my cheeks, falling to the sill.

Why did being a country have to mean being so alone?

CHAPTER 14

The next day was the same, and the third. The atmosphere in the council room was heavy and tense. Colm was quiet and focused. Arlen was surprisingly diligent. The only difference was that Mae now sat through the sessions with tight-lipped coolness, while Valien reverted back to the levelheaded formality I had come to expect of him in diplomatic meetings.

Nothing else they could have done would have brought me more guilt.

I saw Rou once from the council room windows. He came out onto his patio in the afternoon to stand at the rail. My heart leaped at the sight of him, a sensation that made me feel both guilty and foolish. There was far too much distance between us for me to make out his face. But I gathered that he was cold—he didn't remain outside for very long.

By the third evening, I was at a breaking point. Mae and Valien were preparing to leave the following morning, finalizing a satchel full of missives to bring over the mountains to Winder and Paroa. Mae was still mad at me, but despite this, I didn't look forward to her departure. It felt too much like losing my last hold on sanity. I stayed up pointlessly annotating documents long after everyone else had gone to bed, trying determinedly to avoid spending another sleepless night staring at my canopy. When I ran out of text to edit, I strode around my bedchamber, trying to work myself into a state of exhaustion. But it didn't work—I only wound myself up. I considered a foolhardy late-night swim, but it was now bitterly cold, past the threshold of biting refreshment. Frustrated, fed up, dressed in my nightclothes, I shoved my feet in my slippers and left the room before I had time to think. I passed through my parlor and into the antechamber, sweeping through before my guards even had time to pull themselves to attention.

The halls were quiet and cold. My feet traced the familiar path through the corridors to the council room—my center of operations, my headquarters, the site of my greatest and worst moments of my reign. I bypassed the banked hearth and pulled aside the heavy drapes, and I settled myself down on the windowsill. The lake twinkled with lights across the water, firesides and lanterns of families warm in their homes. Down the lakeshore, two windows were lit in

the guest wing. The curtains were closed on one—
Mae and Valien's. On the other they were pulled
aside, and I wondered if I might see a shadow on the
wall, or a dark figure pass in front of the light.

I rested my head on the glass again, wondering
for the thousandth time in the past three days what
Rou was doing, what he was thinking and feeling. I
imagined him slouched in the armchair by the fire,
his boots splayed out before the hearth, gazing at the
flames, mourning the death of his brother and the
collapse of his country. Would his thoughts turn to
me—would he reflect darkly on all the ways I'd let
him down, made him feel small, failed him and his
country? Or would he strive not to think of me at all,
forcing his thoughts elsewhere if my face swam into
view?

I closed my eyes and thought back once again
to that night in Temper Creek—those few fleeting
hours when I'd glimpsed what things might have
been like between us. I had tried my hardest to keep
my memories from progressing further, determined
to hold them on the sight of his exuberant dance with
his poi, my fingers tingling from his lips and my heart
full of the anticipation of applauding his performance
with a kiss. But tonight, whether from fatigue or self-
deprecation, my thoughts finally slid past, into the
mess things had become. I drifted back through the
fist fight, the shouting match, the stitches, the escape,
the drunken rambling in the tent. Surprisingly, those

memories weren't as awful as I'd recalled. At least then, I hadn't yet ruined the opportunity to comfort him myself.

M'all dark inside, Mona.

I picked my head off the cold glass, his slurred words resonating through me. Other images came flooding back—not Rou spinning with vigor at First Fire, but him stepping barefoot around the path of his poi at sunrise, quiet and focused.

Know why I spin poi all those mornings, Mona?

Before I had time to even comprehend my own thoughts, the door to the council room creaked open. I whipped my head around, hoping—

Colm.

"I thought you might be here," he said, holding a lamp. At first I was disappointed, but I quickly let the irrational belief that somehow it might have been Rou slide away. Instead, I released a small sigh of relief—now we could talk. Now I could tell him everything, and he would listen without judgment like he always did. He'd understand my pain, even if it didn't match his, and he'd know for sure what I should do. But then I noticed his expression. He looked odd, slightly uneasy—almost surprised.

"What is it?" I asked.

"You have a visitor," he said.

"Now? At this hour?"

"He just arrived in Lakemouth an hour ago, and they brought him to Blackshell, thinking he might need to be locked up. He's a tad . . . peculiar, and a bit difficult to understand. But he says he's got news from Cyprien. I thought you'd at least want to know."

I blinked at him, and then swung my feet off the sill. "Does he have a possum?"

Colm tilted his head. "Do you know him?"

I jumped from the window. "Quick, go and tell Grainne to prepare our finest guest suite."

"Mae and Valien—"

"Our second finest, then, third finest. The best one that's not occupied. Have someone send to the kitchen for food. And make sure there's some for the possum!"

Ten minutes later, I perched on the settee by the fireplace in the guest room as Fisheye held a handful of pecans under Mirabelle's chin. His blown-out straw hat rested on the embroidered arm of the chair, and in his free hand he clutched a crystal goblet of wine as if it were a potato to be peeled. The palace attendants moving around the room to prepare it for occupation were silent, though I saw a few bewildered glances traded among them. Grainne had scurried away under my withering glare after she asked me in a whisper if I wanted her to lay down a drop cloth on the armchair.

"Fancy place," Fisheye remarked, watching an attendant light a candelabra made of fused mother-of-pearl.

"I'm so relieved you made it safely, Fisheye," I said. "I wish I'd known you were coming—I'd have arranged a better reception for you."

"S'no matter, lolly," he said, setting his ragged boots on the silk footstool. "I didn' know I'd be hightailin' up so quick after you'd left. Where's that Roubideaux?"

"Down the hall," I said breathlessly. "I can have someone fetch him . . ."

"Nah, no sense in wakin' him at this hour. I'll catch him tomorrow. News is more pressin' fer you, anyhow."

I drew in a breath, not wanting to divulge that Rou was probably awake. I couldn't bear the thought of him sitting across from me, listening to Fisheye while ignoring me. *Selfish*, I chastised myself. Callous, rash, plaintive, and now selfish.

"What news do you have?" I asked. "The Assembly?"

"In hidin'," he said. "All safe, but scattered. Gonna be hard fer them to convene all together. But that's not all." He brushed bits of nuts off his tattered knee. "The election failed."

"What?" I breathed. "The results . . ."

"They couldn't be tallied 'cross all the provinces afore the fightin' broke out," he said. "Some of the records was destroyed, some was lost in the hullabaloo. S'no tellin' who won and who lost."

I let out a breath. Rou would be devastated. "What does that mean? For us, I mean. For you. Does the Assembly stay the same? Is Senator Ancelet still First?"

"She's gonna have to be. S'a crisis if there's ever been one. She and the others'll have to make do as best they can. But there's more." He collected another handful of pecans for Mirabelle. "Two of the provinces have already fallen. Siere, of course—right on Alcoro's doorstep. And the Crescent Coast."

"What about Lilou?" I asked. "The ports . . ."

"They're bein' held fer now. There's a few Alcoran warships berthed there, but only a handful of Canyon-folk to crew 'em. If Celeno wants to send an army up the river, he's gonna have to sail around the coast."

"So we have a few weeks, at least," I said, my hands clenched on my knees.

"A few. Fer now."

"Can you hold them outside Lilou?" I asked. "If they sent a fleet around the coast, could Cyprien keep them from sailing further north?"

"Might've been able to once upon a time," he said. "But folk's fleein' the main cities. Only reason Lilou hain't fallen is 'cause Celeno was too busy combin' the Draws lookin' fer you. Now he's cut off from his ships in the docks, but there's no tellin' how long that'll last. And besides—Alcoro's got all them incendiaries now. We don't got the edge we had afore."

"Any word on Queen Gemma?" I asked.

"Cain't say fer certain. When I lit out, Celeno's folk were of the mind you was still in the country. Think they locked her up, but I'm not sure where."

"I'm afraid for her," I said, staring at the fire. "After

all that fighting to get back to Celeno, she betrayed him for our sakes. What will he do to her?"

"S'nothin' we can do 'bout it now," Fisheye said, scratching Mirabelle under her chin.

"No," I said, pinching the bridge of my nose. "Nothing except fight our own fight. Perhaps we can secure a victory before it's too late for her." I blew out a sigh and looked up. "Thank you for this information, Fisheye. I don't disregard how dangerous it was for you to bring it to me."

He shrugged a wiry shoulder. "Times is dangerous fer everybody, Lady Queen."

"Yes." I stood. "I'll leave you to get some rest, and I'll have a missive written out for the Assembly in the morning. Please ring for anything you need."

"Will do." He squinted at the painting over the mantelpiece—a grand image of the Palisades at sunset, painted a century before by Lumen Lake's most renowned artist. "Hot damn, you know, I think my auntie's got one a'them pictures in her boudoir."

"I don't doubt it in the slightest, Fisheye," I said with a smile. I made for the door. "Have a pleasant evening."

"And you, lolly."

I closed his door behind me and stood in the darkened hallway, pondering his words. That the ports of Lilou were cut off from Alcoran control was a relief, but how long would they stay that way? Would the Assembly of Six be able to unite the country before Celeno reclaimed any more of the provinces? Gemma.

Would they execute her right away, or would she sit through a trial? Where was she now—locked in the hold of a ship? In a prison? Great Light . . . if only we'd managed to bring her with us as we escaped.

Lolly.

Fisheye's last word caught up with me, and I physically shook my head like a dog shaking off a fly.

Lolly.

I looked down the hallway, where a crack of light filtered out from beneath Rou's door. This was the closest I'd been to him since we'd come back. My feet moved of their own accord, bearing me down the hall. I stood outside his door, gripping the silk of my dressing gown with white knuckles. There was no sound inside, no footsteps or whisper of movement. I drew in a breath and held it, the seconds sliding past.

Know why I spin poi, Mona? All those mornings? 'Cause I'm all dark inside.

I could dive the deepest reaches of the Moon Beds with the breath I was holding. And then, abruptly, I blew it all out. I turned on my heel and hurried down the hall, my dressing gown billowing out behind me. There was one other door lit with a crack of firelight, and I stopped in front of it.

I lifted my fist and rapped. "Mae?"

There was a murmuring of voices inside and the shuffling of cloth. I bit my lip, making myself count to twenty before I knocked again. As I reached nineteen, the door handle rattled, and Mae appeared, wild-haired, clutching a sheet around her shoulders.

She looked me up and down. "This had better be really, really important."

It wasn't, not at all. In the dim interior of the room, I saw Valien lean over the footboard of the bed to better see the door, the fire glowing off his bare shoulders and chest. My gaze jumped back to Mae.

"I need your help," I said. "Can you put something on? It shouldn't take long."

"What's wrong?" she asked. "Are you all right?"

I opened and closed my mouth. She cocked her head at me.

"I don't know," I finally said. It came out more desperate than I meant it to.

She pursed her mouth, drew in a breath through her nose, and blew it out in an aggrieved sigh. "Hang on."

I stood outside her door, trying to keep from twisting my hands. She reappeared a moment later. Her interpretation of "put something on" wasn't a dressing gown or robe, but one of her husband's tunics—and nothing else. She didn't even belt it. But I knew better than to admonish her for it, thankful at least that fashionable Silvern tunics hit mid-thigh, and that Valien was a full foot taller than she.

"What's so important?" she asked, pulling the door closed behind her.

I held up my hand, cupping my fingers as if holding a ball. "Are you familiar with a spherical knot? It's got . . . sort of . . . rows of cord all woven side by side."

She squinted at me in the dim light. "What?"

"A knot. It's a sphere," I said, and now I really *did* sound desperate. "It looks . . . sort of like . . ." I laid my fingers crisscrossed over each other.

"A fist knot?"

"Is it a sphere?"

"Yeah, it's a nautical knot. They use it in Paroa."

"Can you tie it?"

"Yes . . . why?"

"I need you to tie two of them."

She peered at me, confused. "Into just any old thing?"

"No. Come with me."

With another sigh, she followed me down the hall and out of the guest wing. We wound through the adjoining corridor and down a flight of steps, bringing us to the entrance hall. We crossed it, moving out of the formal wings of the palace and into the functional side, passing storerooms and pantries. Mae was silent, keeping her questions to herself. I found the room I wanted—the lamp room. I searched among the crocks of paraffin until I found one that had several wicks soaking inside. I drew them out.

"I need you to tie the knots in these," I said. "And they need to have loops on one side."

She took them, holding them out to avoid getting oil on Valien's tunic. "How big?"

I estimated with my fingers. "Two and a half, three inches."

As she worked, I went to a different storeroom and rummaged through crates of chain link until I found several pieces the right weight. I measured them against my arm and struggled with the wire clippers to cut them the same length. I fed straps of leather through the ends, tying them as tightly as I could. Finished, I carried them back to the lamp room to find Mae toweling the oil off her hands. Wordlessly, I bent a clasp around the loops she had left in the spherical knots and hooked them to the ends of the chains.

"I suppose it's no use asking what this is all about?" she said, watching me.

"No. Thank you. That's all I needed."

She looked at me in the dark, her head cocked again, as I slid the rudimentary poi into an oilproof bag.

"Are you okay?" she asked.

"I don't know," I said again. A moment passed between us in the dark. "You can go back."

"I'll walk with you," she said. "I get the feeling we're heading in the same direction."

I colored but didn't respond, following the loose hem of her tunic out the door and back through the dark hallways. We didn't speak—I was grateful for that. Grateful that despite my harshness and heartlessness, she was still willing to stride along at my side without question.

"I'm sorry, Mae," I blurted as we climbed the stairs past the entrance hall.

"Hush it," she said.

"No, I just . . . I don't . . . I don't know what's wrong with me."

"Well, I do." We turned the corner for the guest wing, and she immediately started unbuttoning her tunic. "And it's not weakness, Mona. You've got to stop telling yourself it is. Sometimes strength, you know, is allowing yourself to try again."

I stopped in my tracks, in part because we'd reached her door, and in part from the shock of hearing her say almost the exact same words she'd said in my anxious dream the night I'd first realized how I felt about Rou. I stared at her. She punched my elbow in a gesture that was clearly supposed to be morally supportive.

"We'll talk tomorrow," she said, and before I could reply, she had entered her and Valien's room and firmly closed the door.

My mouth hung open for the briefest second before turning into a smile—a bewildered, exhausted one, but a smile nonetheless. My gratitude for Mae swelled—not just for her words, but for the conviction her actions brought to them. No one could call Mae weak, and she had fought tooth and nail to be with the person she loved—she and Valien both had. And I was truly happy for them—and happy that they didn't bother keeping their happiness hidden. Buoyed, I quickly turned back up the hall. I stopped again in front of Rou's door, and without allowing myself a moment to pause and reconsider, I reached up and knocked.

No response.

I waited and knocked again.

Nothing again.

Swallowing, ignoring every instinct telling me to go away and leave him alone, I put my hand on the knob. It turned.

The room was empty and unnaturally cold despite the fire in the grate. A brisk breeze hit me, and I saw that the far door out to the lakeside patio was ajar. Beyond it I could see Rou standing hunched at the rail, head down. There were no signs of personal effects in the room, no discarded cloak or half-finished book. No mandolin. No poi. He'd come with nothing. The only things that looked touched were a single pillow on the bed and the tray bearing the evening meal. He'd left the fried fish and potatoes, having eaten only the apple bread. *Tomorrow*, I thought. *Tomorrow I'll send out to the islands for the finest pastry chef in Lumen Lake.* My heart twisted in my chest. Summoning my courage, I passed through the room, stopping only to pick up one of the flickering tapers on the mantelpiece.

The glow from the taper preceded me as I slipped through the patio door, and Rou jerked his gaze over his shoulder. The night was cloudy, and the lake was cloaked in darkness, but in the faint candlelight I registered the difference in his clothing. Gone were his silk ascot and embroidered vest, replaced by a long-sleeved tunic, blue, of the kind my brothers would wear. It was open at the collar, blowing in the chill breeze.

I crossed the patio and set the taper on the rail. And then I stood before Rou, holding the oilproof bag.

"Lady Queen," he said, his voice formal and distant.

I swallowed again. "Fisheye's here. He arrived a little while ago."

He lifted his head slightly. "Why?"

"He has news about the election. It . . . it failed," I said shakily. "There wasn't enough time to tally the results across the provinces before Alcoro started fighting back. So . . . so the Assembly is the same. Senator Ancelet is still First." I knew it would bring him no comfort.

His eyebrows knit together, and his gaze jumped back to the lake. "They'll contest it," he said flatly. "Deschamps and all the others who were running. They won't accept a failed vote."

"I think it's going to be a while before that can happen," I said quietly.

A moment of silence a mile long stretched between us, broken only by the faint lapping of ripples on the shore.

"Is that all?" he finally asked.

"Well . . . no. It's not. I mean, there's other news, but it's not . . . it can wait. But . . . I did want to talk to you. And I understand if you don't want to talk to me, but I have things I need to say, and I'm going to say them once, and then I won't say anything to you ever again, if that's what you want."

He looked down at his hands resting on the rail, where his steel ring glinted in the candlelight. My throat tightened.

"Rou," I began. "I'm sorry. I'm sorry for everything that's happened and for my hand in it all. I'm sorry for how I treated you at the Benoits'. It was cold, and wrong of me. And I lied to you. I feel . . . I feel the same way you felt. About me. I do care about you. I think you're good, and strong, and kind, and you've made me laugh more than anyone ever has. It's just . . . I'm terrible at love. I haven't had much practice. I haven't ever *needed* much practice." Hastily, I dashed at my eyes, trying to prevent the tears I could feel forming. "I don't ask you to give me a second chance. I only ask that maybe one day, you can forgive me for being a queen when I should have been something more."

He turned his head to me, but now I was the one looking away, staring out at the invisible expanse of the lake. I took a breath and pressed on, knowing that if I stopped, I wouldn't be able to start again. "And I'm sorry about Lyle. Great Light, Rou, I'm so sorry. He was brilliant, and he wasn't a traitor to us or your folk. He only wanted to better himself and his country, and nobody can fault him for that. If I could do it all over again, if I could have done things differently . . ." I cleared my throat and wiped my eyes again. "Whatever you need, ask it of me, Rou. I know what it means to grieve. I know what it means to be chased from your home, leaving death in your wake. To miss everything there is to miss. I brought . . . I brought something that might help."

I fumbled with the oilproof bag and drew out the makeshift poi. His head inclined toward them in the dim light.

"I don't know if they're right," I said. "They're probably the wrong length, and the wrong weight. They won't swivel the right way. Perhaps you can go to the smiths and have a better pair made—"

In a sharp, swift movement, he took two steps toward me, clasped my face in his hands, and pressed his lips fiercely against mine. The poi spilled from my hands. My slight gasp was lost to his kiss—as was what was left of my sanity. Shocked, buzzing, flooded with emotion, I tensed, and then I leaned into him, gripping the loose collar of his tunic. His palms were warm as they cradled my face, his thumbs tracing the line of my cheekbones. I closed my eyes, tightening my hold on his collar. His hands slid to my hair, and he ran his fingers through the short tufts at the nape of my neck. He broke away, his lips just an inch from mine, his chest rising and falling with quickened breath. I stood immobile, too stunned to comprehend what had just happened.

"I'm sorry," I whispered again. "I read him wrong, I said the wrong things. I pushed him too far . . ."

He drew back further and clasped my face again. "Lady Queen, I have never, not once, blamed you."

"If I had only done things differently . . ."

"Mona," he said. "I don't know what happened in your past to make you think otherwise, but not every terrible thing is your fault." He leaned his forehead against mine. "I have never blamed you, and I'm sorry if you thought I did."

Surprise welled up in me before collapsing into profound relief. The best outcome I had anticipated from this conversation was a stoic acceptance of my apology, with anger or silence the much likelier scenarios. But he'd kissed me, touched me in a way I hadn't ever felt, not even with Donnel—*especially* not with Donnel—and suddenly not only did I understand Mae's words, but now I believed them as well. I had ridden caution too far and too deep, allowing it to drag me down, weighted by fear and haunted memory. Strength didn't mean holding my breath—it meant breaking loose and making back for the surface.

Perhaps I didn't have to stand alone after all.

I wanted to kiss him again, thrilled with the sudden realization that I could. We were almost exactly the same height, so there was no need to stand on tiptoe. I leaned into him, releasing my iron grip on his collar to thread my arms under his shoulders. He wound his own across my back, tilting his head to better cover my lips with his, cupping the nape of my neck in his hand. He broke away and kissed the corner of my mouth, my jaw, behind my ear. I shivered—not from the cold, but from that warm flush that was back, as if drawing the heat from his body and magnifying it tenfold in my own. I could feel his heart beat against mine, the muscles in his shoulders under my palms. I squeezed him tighter, wanting to close any last space between us. This was so different from how I'd felt my entire life. So different from my last encounter with love all those years ago.

I should have known it would be.

He sighed, turning his face into my hair. "I thought you were furious with me. You *should* be furious with me."

"Why?" I asked, my fingers inching appreciatively over his shoulder blades. "What for?"

He shook his head slightly. "This . . . everything. This is all my fault. My country, yours, the Silverwood . . . the Assembly. The election. Lyle." He drew a breath. "I did it all—I ruined everything in Temper Creek."

My eyes flew open. He didn't blame me—he blamed *himself.*

"No, Rou. *No.*" I drew back from him, grasping his face in my hands. "There's more than enough fault to go around. I could have easily said no to you in Temper Creek—I *should* have. But we both thought it was safe. And it may have been, if Lyle hadn't given us away."

"It was a stupid, reckless mistake. I should never have asked—"

"But it was just that, Rou—a *mistake.* I would be lying if I said I didn't regret it." I cupped his chin and brought his gaze to mine. "But only the part that went wrong. Before that . . . before that, it was the finest night of my life."

His face crumpled, and he bowed his head to press his lips to my fingers.

"I'm an idiot," he murmured.

"No. A bit. Me, too," I said quickly, and there it was—the ghost of a smile flickering at the corners of his mouth, hidden by my fingers. I slid my hand up to his cheek. "But we're going to fix it. Celeno isn't a reasonable person, and I still have my doubts that he ever would have agreed to the Assembly's demands. I'm not saying it's better this way, but I am saying we're going to fix it. And we're going to do it *together*."

He turned his head and kissed the tender skin on the underside of my wrist. "Bless the Light for you, Mona," he said, his eyes closed. "But to be perfectly honest, you don't need me. Not for this, not for anything. I'm a mess."

"All dark inside," I agreed.

He groaned softly and rubbed his eyes. "Can we pretend I never said any of that? I was obnoxiously drunk."

"Yes, you were. But I also think you were being honest." I ran my thumb over his cheek. "Rou, I don't believe in the Light. I can't. I won't ever be able to separate it from what Celeno's done to me and the people I love. But I do believe in what you say about a person's inherent worth and sanctity, and I see that in you—like a beacon. You're not dark inside."

His brows knitted together in the dim light, and he folded me in his arms again. I kissed his hair, his tendrils brushing my skin. Even now, days after leaving Cyprien, he smelled of woodsmoke. I'd thought it was just the scent of the bonfires in Temper Creek, but it clung to him—deep, warm, real. I buried my nose in his hair, wanting to memorize that scent, and the heat of his body, and the press of his arms around me. Rivers to the sea, why hadn't I kissed him that night on the Toussaints' balcony, when he asked me to sit and watch fireworks with him?

Oh, yes—I knew why.

I slid my hand up his back and tapped him on the shoulder. "And, Rou."

He lifted his head.

"Don't fool yourself. I'm a mess, too."

He broke into a smile, the first real one I'd seen since First Fire, but I put my fingers over his lips before he could say anything.

"I don't always . . . I can't always say what I think, or what I feel," I said. "And I can't promise I'll get any better, at least not right away. Things are going to be difficult here, trying to aid Cyprien and prepare the lake and the mountains for war. And things will get dangerous, once Celeno sends his ships up the river."

"Too bad we don't have any experience with danger," he said.

I smiled despite my unease. He clasped my hands between our chests.

"I don't expect things to be easy or calm," he said. "And I certainly don't expect you to change—not now, not ever. I fell for you when I watched you dive off the *Swamp Rabbit* with Gemma at the channel. I fell hard,

Mona—because I saw right then who you really were. On top of being outrageously elegant and poised and slightly terrifying—and sometimes you are, I won't lie—on top of *all that*, you're the bravest, most capable person I've ever met. Hotter fire, stronger steel. And you make me want to be the same way—I'd march into Alcoro and pound on Celeno's front door if you asked me to."

"I think I'd prefer you to stay right here with me," I said.

He grinned and bent his head to kiss my fingers again. "Well, then I'll do everything I can to be useful to you while I'm here. You just told me to ask you for what I need, so I'm going to do exactly that. I need the privilege of standing with you, Mona. For my country and yours. For Lyle, and for Gemma. For everything as big as the balance of the eastern world right down to the space between you and me. That's what I need. Just a place by your side."

This man. I cleared my throat. "Granted."

His eyes crinkled as he smiled, amber in the candlelight. I picked up the burning taper from the rail and held it between us. A soft echo of his grin spread across his face. He stepped away from me and picked up the poi from the ground, looping the leather straps around his fingers. He held the wicks out toward me, and I set the flame to the oil-soaked knots. They caught, and the terrace flared with light. He tested them, swinging them slowly by his sides.

I was smiling when he looked up again. He held the chains out to his sides and stepped forward, pressing his lips to mine once again. Then he took several steps back, and with a few sweeping arcs, he lofted the burning wicks into the night. I blew out the taper. The sky, the lake, the palace, everything went dark, except for the two of us wrapped in a globe of firelight.

I was smiling when he looked up again. He held the chains out to his sides and stepped forward, pressing his lips to mine once again. Then he took several steps back, and with a few sweeping arcs he lifted the burning sticks over the lights. I blew out the lapse. The sky, the lake, the gallows, everything went dark, except for the two of us wrapped in a glow of twilight.

ACKNOWLEDGMENTS

I am grateful, as always, to my fantastic agent, Valerie Noble of Donaghy Literary Group, for being my champion, advocate, and friend. Thanks to my editor, David Pomerico, my publicist, Michelle Podberezniak, my copyeditor, Jena Karmali, and all the team at Harper Voyager for all your hard work and dedication.

A special thanks this time around to all the other Harper Voyager/Impulse authors for your support, encouragement, commiseration, and general camaraderie—without you, I certainly would have lost what's left of my sanity by now. I feel fortunate to share an imprint with you and call you my publishing siblings!

A big thank you to everyone who read *Woodwalker*, left reviews, and clamored for more from Mae and Mona. Your support drives and encourages me!

Thanks to both Anne Marie Martin and Caitlin Bellinger for your feedback and for asserting that you would date Rou were he a real person. Caitlin, thanks as always for your love, support, and stream-of-consciousness edits, which I have come to look forward to greatly with each finished manuscript.

Thanks to my parents, Eric and Lisa Benson, for your edits, encouragement, and bulk purchasing of my books. Thanks to my girls, Lucy and Amelia, for playing so well together as to grant me a few extra minutes of writing time each day.

And thanks to my husband, Will, to whom this book is dedicated—because you're my love story, and all that. Sorry we went with *Ashes to Fire* instead of *Swank Blaze*.

And finally, thanks to Precious the Possum at the Hagood Mill State Fiddling Competition—the only intentional resemblance to a character in this book.

ABOUT THE AUTHOR

Park ranger by summer, stay-at-home mom the rest of the year, EMILY B. MARTIN is also a freelance artist and illustrator. An avid hiker and explorer, her experiences as a ranger helped inform the character of Mae and the world of Woodwalker. When not patrolling places like Yellowstone, the Great Smoky Mountains, or Philmont Scout Ranch, she lives in South Carolina with her husband, Will, and two daughters, Lucy and Amelia.

www.emilybmartin.me/
Facebook.com/EmilyBeeMartin/
@EmilyBeeMartin

Discover great authors, exclusive offers, and more at hc.com.